'I was pulled into *The Memory Wood* from the very ~~first~~ ... by the throat and doesn't let you go. It's an intense, atmospheric, and truly original thriller. Put everything else aside when you enter the Memory Wood, including your expectations'
Shari Lapena

'A taut, spooky debut . . . Beautifully told, with two superbly drawn young protagonists. Lloyd is a rare new thriller talent'
Daily Mail

'What makes this book special is the marvellously executed subterranean power game. Superbly creepy, with an unexpected twist, this is a very grim modern fairytale'
Guardian

'What a book! I haven't read anything quite this exciting since *Room*. You think all the stories have been told, then something like this comes along. Wonderful'
Emma Curtis

'A beautifully written, fast-paced thriller with twists and turns as dark as the cell in which Elissa is confined. We devoured it in a matter of hours'
Heat

'A truly chilling story'
Woman & Home

'A chilling, suspense-filled and heart-wrenching read'
Herald

'Forget everything you think you know about thrillers.
The Memory Wood is a compulsive page-turner where visceral horror
meets Grimm fairytale — a story that's guaranteed to burn itself into
your brain . . . Every twist and distortion evokes a physical response
— you'll be breathless with anticipation, tingling with hope, and numb
with dread from beginning to end'
Press Association

'*The Memory Wood* is impossible to put down. It's so wonderfully
written, creepily atmospheric and chilling'
Karen Hamilton

'A darkly chilling and original novel . . . a series of twists keeps readers
captivated until a shocking climax'
Daily Express

'I was captivated by *The Memory Wood* — a beautifully told,
dark and chilling tale'
Renée Knight

'The dreamy nature of the story slowly dissipates as the danger
deepens, leaving this reader with pounding heart and sweating palms'
Observer

THE MEMORY WOOD

Sam Lloyd

CORGI BOOKS

TRANSWORLD PUBLISHERS
Penguin Random House, One Embassy Gardens,
8 Viaduct Gardens, London SW11 7BW
www.penguin.co.uk

Transworld is part of the Penguin Random House group of companies
whose addresses can be found at global.penguinrandomhouse.com

Penguin
Random House
UK

First published in Great Britain in 2020 by Bantam Press
an imprint of Transworld Publishers
Corgi edition published 2020

A CIP catalogue record for this book
is available from the British Library.

ISBN
9780552176583

Typeset in 11.5/14.5pt Dante MT Std by Jouve (UK), Milton Keynes
Printed and bound in Great Britain by Clays Ltd, Elcograf S.p.A.

The authorised representative in the EEA is Penguin Random House Ireland,
Morrison Chambers, 32 Nassau Street, Dublin D02 YH68

Penguin Random House is committed to a sustainable future
for our business, our readers and our planet. This book is made
from Forest Stewardship Council® certified paper.

For Rae and John Carrington.

The kindest, funniest and most disgraceful in-laws
one could possibly hope to acquire.

PART I

ELIJAH

Day 6

I

When they file back into the room, I'm no longer in the chair. Instead, I'm sitting on the table, bare legs swinging. A pink square of sticking plaster gleams on my knee. Weird, really, that I don't remember injuring it.

They raise their eyebrows when they see I've moved, but nobody comments. The table is bolted to the floor so it can't tip over and hurt me. When I was ten, I broke my leg running in the Memory Wood and nearly died, but that was two years ago. I'm much more careful now.

'Seems like we're all done, Elijah,' one of them says. 'Are you looking forward to going home?'

I glance around the room. For the first time I notice it has no windows. Maybe that's because of the sort of people it usually contains – bad people, not like these in here with me now. They're police, even if they don't wear the uniforms. Earlier, the one who brought me a Coca-Cola told me they wear *play* clothes. He could have been joking. For a twelve-year-old I have a pretty high IQ, but I've never really understood teasing.

For a moment I forget they're still watching me, still waiting for an answer. I glance up and nod, swinging my legs harder. Why *wouldn't* I be looking forward to going home?

My face changes. I think I'm smiling.

I I

We're in the car. Papa is driving. Magic Annie, who lives on the far side of the Memory Wood, says that these days most kids call their parents Mum and Dad. I'm pretty sure I used to do that too. I don't really know why I switched to Mama and Papa. I read a lot of old books, mainly because we don't have money to waste on the newer stuff. Maybe that's it.

'Did they question you?' Papa asks.

'About what?'

'Oh, about anything, really.'

He slows the car at a crossroads, even though he has right of way. Always careful like that, is Papa. Always worried that he'll hit a cyclist or a dog-walker, or a slow-crossing hedgehog.

'They asked me about you,' I say.

In the front seat, Mama turns to look at him. Papa's attention remains on the road. He holds the steering wheel delicately, wrists angled higher than his knuckles. It makes him look like a begging dog, and suddenly I think of the Arthur Sarnoff print that hangs on our living-room wall, of a beagle playing pool against a couple of rascally, cigar-chomping hounds. The picture's called *Hey! One Leg on the Floor!* because the beagle is perched on a stepladder, which is cheating. Mama hates it, but I kind of like it. It's the only picture we have.

'What did they ask you?'

'Oh, you know, Papa, just stuff. What kind of job you do, what kind of hobbies you have, that sort of thing.' I decide not to mention their other questions just yet, nor my answers. Not until I've had a bit more time to think. In the last few days a lot's happened, and I need to get it all straight. Sometimes life can be pretty confusing, even for a kid with a high IQ.

'What did you tell them?'

'I said you're a gardener. And that you fix things.' I make a dimple in the pink plaster on my knee and wince. 'I told them about the crow you saved.'

We found the crow outside the back door one morning, flapping a broken wing. Papa nursed it for three days straight, feeding it bread soaked in milk. On the fourth day we came downstairs to find it gone. Crow bones, Papa said, mend much faster than human ones.

III

We're coming to the edge of town. Fewer buildings, fewer people. On the pavement I see two boys wearing uniform: grey trousers, maroon blazers, scuffed black shoes. They look about my age. I wonder what it must be like to have lessons at school instead of at home. There isn't a book in my house I haven't read ten times over, so I'm pretty sure

I'd do well. Magic Annie says I have the vocabulary of someone with far bigger shoes. There was a playwright, once, who knew sixty thousand words. I'd like to beat him if I can.

As we speed past, I press my palm against the window. I imagine the boys turning and waving. But they don't, and then they're gone.

'Did you talk about me?' Mama asks.

Her head is still sideways. I'm struck by how pretty she looks today. When the low sun breaks through the clouds her hair gleams like pirate gold. She looks like an angel, or one of those warrior queens I've read about: Boudicca, perhaps, or Artemisia. I want to climb into the front seat and curl up in her lap. Instead, I roll my eyes in mock-exasperation. 'I'm not a *complete* witling. Just because I got lost this one time.'

Witling is my new favourite word. Last week it was *flibbertigibbet*, which is Middle English for an excessively chatty person. Everyone's life should contain a couple of flibbertigibbets, preferably with a few witlings to keep them company.

Again, I glance out of the window. This time all I see is fields. 'I hope Gretel's OK.'

'Gretel?' Papa asks.

Immediately, I get a funny feeling in my tummy; a greasy slipperiness, like there's a snake inside me, coiling and uncoiling. Gretel, I remember, is a secret. I look up and meet Papa's eyes in the rear-view mirror. His brow is furrowed. My hands begin to shake.

I glance at Mama. A pulse beats in her throat. 'There *is* no Gretel, Elijah,' she says. 'I thought you understood that.'

In my tummy, more of the snake uncurls. 'I . . . I mean

6

Magic Annie,' I stammer, my words rushing out. 'It's my play name for her. A thing I invented. Just a silly thing.'

Papa's eyes float in the mirror. 'I think Magic Annie suits her better than Gretel,' he says. 'Don't you, buddy?'

My mouth tastes sour, like I've bitten down on a beetle or a toad. I run my tongue over my teeth and swallow. 'Yes, Papa.'

IV

Our estate isn't like those I've seen on Magic Annie's TV. There are no high-rise blocks or rows of modern homes – only woods, fields, barns, cowsheds and the mansion called Rufus Hall. Dotted about the land are a few stone-built cottages, including our own. Tied cottages, they're called.

Beyond the Memory Wood lies Knucklebone Lake. That's not the lake's real name – I don't think it has one. It's just that once, in the reeds lining the bank, I found a tiny trio of bones connected by rotting ligament. They looked like they might form the index finger of a small child. I put them in my Collection of Keepsakes and Weird Finds, a grand name for what's really a Tupperware box hidden beneath the loose floorboard in my room.

Not far from the lake is the place I call Wheel Town. It's more of a camp than anything else, a ragtag collection of trucks and caravans that were driven here long ago and are mostly too rusted up to leave. I've never worked out why the Meuniers tolerate the Wheel Town folk on their land, but they do.

The Meuniers live up at Rufus Hall. Just the two of

them, knocking about with all that space. Leon Meunier spends most of his time in London. On the days he's at the estate, I see him zooming about in his black Defender with a face like he's worried the sky's about to fall. The house and its gardens would be an awesome place to explore, but Papa won't ever let me go.

Our car jerks to a stop. I realize we're home. In the front seat, Mama bows her head. I wonder if she's praying. Looking down, I see my hands have stopped trembling. I pop my seatbelt and grab the door handle, but of course I can't get out. My parents still use the child locks, even though I'm twelve years old.

I wait for Papa to open the door. Then I worm out of my seat. He lumbers up the garden path, shoulders braced as if he's carrying all the world's troubles. Mama and I follow.

Our cottage windows are dark, offering no hint of what lies within. The front door is a single slab of oak. There's no letterbox. Papa rarely gets any post, and when he does it's delivered straight to Meunier. Mama gets nothing at all. Our door has no number, because we don't live on a street. If anyone ever wrote to me, they'd have to put this on the envelope: *Elijah North, Gamekeeper's Cottage, C/O THE RT HON. THE LORD MEUNIER OF FAMERHYTHE, Rufus Hall, Meunierfields*. That's quite a lot to write, which explains why Mama isn't the only one the postman ignores.

There's an upside-down horseshoe nailed to the lintel, put there to catch us some luck. Passing beneath it, I go inside.

I'm in my room, standing at the window. We've been home twenty minutes. I'm itching to escape, but I daren't, not yet.

When I hear the back door clatter open, I step closer to the glass. Down in the garden, Papa looms into view. He tugs a packet of Mayfairs from his chest pocket and lights up. Leaning against the coal shed, he breathes a fog of smoke into the sky. I go to the hall, creep down the stairs and out through the front door.

From our cottage, the Memory Wood is a five-minute walk. I make it in half that time, jogging along the track beside Fallow Field. Overhead, the sky presses down like a steel sheet. The day feels heavy, as if it might crumple under its own weight.

I'm halfway there when I hear the screaming. Twisting around, I see a family of crows squabbling in Fallow Field. Something's got their interest – likely the remains of a rabbit or pheasant that a fox has left. The collective noun for crows, I once read, is *murder*.

Pretty gross.

VI

It's chilly inside the Memory Wood, which is strange because there's barely any wind. There's a steady drip of water, left-overs from this morning's rain. Under my trainers the mulch is soft and wet.

With Fallow Field screened by trees, the screaming of the crows is muted. Ahead, I see a flash of movement. All sorts of things it could be, but there's only one that I fear. My parents didn't mention him on the way home, and I made a point of not asking. Sometimes I worry that speaking his name too often will increase his power over me – and with it, his cruelty.

Maybe *cruelty* isn't the best word. Once, on the TV in Magic Annie's caravan, I saw a Great White burst out of the sea and bite a baby seal clean in half. It looked cruel, but it wasn't, not really – it was just nature. The shark was hungry and the baby seal was prey. The other youngsters stayed out of the water when they saw the shark's fin cutting the surface, which shows the importance of good instincts. Good instincts are something I worry about quite a lot.

Now, in the Memory Wood, I slow my pace. I've seen deer among these trees, but their coats match the woodland so perfectly that often I only notice their eyes. The flash of movement I spotted a moment ago was no deer.

I think about running back to Fallow Field, and from there all the way home. But I came here for a reason, one far too important to ignore.

Bad instincts.

Even though my heart's beating faster than it should, I allow myself an eye-roll. Three weeks ago my favourite word was *melodramatic*. Right now, it's pretty apt. I don't *really* know if I have bad instincts. One thing I've learned, growing up by these woods, is to think twice about trusting what I see.

Steeling myself, I take a forward step. No startled fawn or badger crashes out of the undergrowth. No owl or hawk swoops from the overhead canopy. I take a second step, then a third, twisting my head to check that nothing's creeping up on me.

Minutes later I arrive in the clearing, and suddenly my mouth is as dry as the knucklebones in my Collection of Keepsakes and Weird Finds.

VII

It's a mopey-looking spot. Not the best place for a cottage, which is probably why it was left to rot. Papa once told me that the estate's head gardener lived here, back when Meunier's ancestors needed one. What makes it so creepy is that it's an exact replica of our own cottage, right down to the horseshoe nailed upon the lintel. This one is rusty, though. And it certainly hasn't brought the place much luck.

Not a bit of glass is left in the windows. The branches of an ash tree poke out of what would have been the sitting room. Some of the tiles have vanished from the roof, plundered to repair other buildings on the estate. Papa's work, no doubt – he hates to see useful things go to waste. Those that remain are streaked with bird mess and felted with moss, making the cottage look less like it was built by human hands and more as if it was raised from the soil by an evil wizard's spell. There's a toilety smell about the place, mingling with the stench of something even fouler.

I wish I'd worn my coat. It's chilly in the Memory Wood, but where I'm going it'll be filthy, cold and dark. Screwing up my eyes, I check the clearing one last time. I see dripping trees, tangled bracken, a metallic sky hanging like a guillotine's blade.

Near the cottage's front door there's a lighter patch in the mulch, as if the dead leaves have recently been disturbed. Last time I was here, I'm pretty sure I saw a pallet box outside the entrance, filled with old tools. It's not there now, but there's no dink in the ground marking where it lay. Perhaps I don't remember right. Perhaps it didn't leave a trace.

A cry pierces the silence. From a tree across the clearing, a magpie fixes me with a glossy eye. I think of the old rhyme: *One for sorrow*. When I clap my hands, the magpie flaps its wings, but it doesn't fly off. Moments later I hear an answering shriek. I look up at the cottage's sagging roof and see two more birds perched there.

One for sorrow, two for joy, three for a girl.

Claws of ice climb my spine. I've never liked magpies. Once, I saw an adult bird drag three baby blue tits from their nest. It killed them all before I could frighten it off. I buried the chicks near our laurel bush, making a cross from two lolly sticks and a piece of wire. The worst thing wasn't watching the chicks die, or having to pick their bodies from the grass. It was seeing the parents return to an empty nest, hopping around in confusion as they searched for their babies. One of them even flew down and perched on the cross. I cried and I cried, and when Papa came home and wanted to know what was up, I couldn't even look at him.

Some stuff just isn't meant to be shared.

Besides, Papa wouldn't ever understand a thing like that.

Turning my back on the memory, I edge towards the

cottage, avoiding its blank-eyed stare. Soon, I reach the patch of disturbed mulch a few yards from the entrance. The kicked-over leaves glisten like the whitish bellies of slugs. Has someone, I wonder, dug a trap to capture peeping Toms like me? Perhaps, under this shallow carpet of litter, a pegged sackcloth hides a steep-sided pit. Deadfall traps, they're called, in the survival books I've read. Sometimes their floors are fitted with sharpened stakes to skewer anything that falls in. Sometimes they're empty, forcing whatever's inside to wait for the trapper's return before discovering its fate. The worst option, I always think, would be for the trapper never to return at all, leaving the victim to die of hunger or thirst, knowing all the while that safety lay only a short distance away.

Magic Annie told me a horrible story, once, about a Daddy Fox who fell into a deadfall trap while hunting for his family's supper. Mummy Fox tried to rescue him by throwing down a rope, but while she was hauling him up her feet slipped and she tumbled in too. The five children, when they learned what had happened, made a fox-chain to rescue their parents. The oldest son locked his jaws on to a tree trunk while his brothers and sisters lowered themselves into the hole. Mummy Fox began to climb, and she was halfway to the top when Daddy Fox began to follow her. All that weight was too much for the oldest son, and when his jaws loosened on the tree his entire family tumbled into the hole. He waited at the edge for five days, watching his parents and siblings die, and then he died too – not of hunger or thirst but of heartbreak.

I've never found that story in a book, which makes me wonder if Magic Annie made it up. Often, I've tried to imagine what would happen if I fell into a trap like that.

Papa could hold on to the tree, but with only Mama to help him, how would they reach down far enough to rescue me?

It's not something to ponder right now. There's no deadfall trap beneath these leaves. I'm *procrastinating*, which is a word for putting off something you don't want to do but must. Closing my eyes to calm myself, I count to ten, then backwards to one. I empty my lungs and take a long breath. Finally, my eyelids spring open.

Strangely, the cottage seems closer now, as if it slunk a tiny bit nearer while my eyes were shut.

Disgusted, I shake my head. 'Witling,' I mutter. 'Melodramatic witling.'

Up on the roof, one of the magpies caws and shakes its wings.

I creep towards the entrance. The door, swollen in its frame, has stuck halfway open, revealing a narrow rectangle of dark. I mouse around outside for a bit, building my courage. Then I go in.

VIII

In here I use my nose more than my eyes, as if by crossing the threshold I've transformed into some kind of bloodhound. The cottage reveals itself in a jumble of different scents: mildew and rust, damp mortar and wet ashes, mouldered curtains, weeping plaster, rotten wood. Overlaying that are the smells from an earlier time that my imagination fools me into sensing: woodsmoke, hanging bacon, the yeastiness of fresh bread.

This far into the woods, there was never any possibility

of electricity or gas. Water was fetched from the well near Knucklebone Lake. Light was provided by tallow candles and the burning of lamp oil refined from fish or kerosene or mustard. At least, that's what Papa says.

Now, my nose tickled by old ghosts, I step deeper into the ruin. Its layout, identical to my parents' cottage, is unsettling. It feels like I've catapulted myself forwards to some future date, seeing our home as it'll look after a cataclysmic event: an alien invasion, a zombie plague or a worldwide nuclear exchange.

Paper has peeled from the walls like old skin, exposing plaster blotched with black fungi. A dresser of scarred hardwood stands beside the stairs, flanked by a row of rusted petrol cans. Tucked into one of its alcoves is a parcel of sticks that looks vaguely like a broken wicker doll, but is most likely the nest of some departed bird.

On my left looms the sitting room. Inside I see the ash tree, so strange and out of place that it hardly seems real. The uppermost branches press against the ceiling. It's only a matter of time before they punch through.

As I move along the passage towards the kitchen, the thud of my trainers sounds disconnected, as if this is playing out on an old cinema screen and there's a lag between the images and the sound. For a moment I wonder if I'm really here at all, but I'd have to be pretty crazy to dream up a situation like this and place myself at the heart of it.

Are you looking forward to going home, Elijah?

That's what one of the policemen asked me in the interview room, earlier today. But this isn't my home, just a dirty reflection of it. I step into the kitchen and tell myself that again.

This isn't my home.

IX

This isn't my kitchen. There's no hum of a fridge, no tick of a wall clock. Ivy has invaded from outside, creeping across the ceiling like a rash.

Despite the broken windows and freely moving air, I notice a vague scent of something that wasn't here before. It's not unpleasant but it gives me major jitters. When a breeze stirs the ivy leaves and sets them whispering, the scent is flushed away.

To my right is the pantry door. There's no horror-movie squeak when I turn the handle, no squeal of unoiled hinges when I swing it open. The darkness inside is that of a cave.

I take out my torch and switch it on. The beam – weak and yellow, flickering at the slightest movement – illuminates a cracked tile floor and cobwebs that hang like rags. Towards the back, past shelving that holds a few forgotten jars of preserves, lies a square of purest black that swallows my light completely, because it's the entrance to the cellar where I found her, and where I hope she'll still be.

X

This is the point where I *do* need my courage. Police stations and deadfall traps are nothing in comparison. For as long as I can remember I've had a fear of small spaces, a recurring dream of being trapped underground. These walls are solid enough, but the ash tree in the front room has deformed the ceiling above it. If the building collapses while I'm down in the cellar, who knows if I'll survive long enough to be dug out? Papa would come looking, so I'm not worried about dying from hunger or thirst, but how much air would I need? And how would I cope once the batteries in my torch failed?

Shuffling to the cellar entrance, I begin to descend. The steps are stone blocks, slippery with damp. Halfway down they double back and the greyness behind me winks out. That aroma of something not-quite-right grows stronger, a cleaner smell amid all the decay.

Soon I'm at the bottom. The floor here is uneven, partly dirt and partly solid rock. In one corner lies a metal barrel so orange with rust it's started to collapse. Passing it, I come at once to the barrier that separates this half of the cellar from what lies beyond.

XI

It's constructed from the same boarding you see on the windows of abandoned shops – smooth and yellow, flecked with softwood chips. From here, I can't see any of the timber frame to which it's nailed.

Cut into the centre is a door. Two heavy-duty hinges extend in slim triangles across it. The metal glimmers, cold and bright. All around the jamb is a seam of black rubber. Three large deadbolts provide security. The one at chest height is usually secured with a padlock. I have the key in my pocket, but I won't be needing it today. The padlock has disappeared.

In my dismay I fumble the torch, nearly dropping it. For a crazy second, light bounces around me. Shadows flitter from the walls like bats. I want to flee up the steps to the Memory Wood, but I have a responsibility here. I'm part of this. Whatever happened down in this cellar happened because of me.

A sick taste, now, at the back of my throat. I reach for the topmost deadbolt and slide it back. Pausing, I tilt my head. Did I hear something just then? Down here, in the gloom? Or from somewhere up above? I think of the ash tree's branches pressing at the living-room ceiling and throw back the second deadbolt before I can change my mind.

XII

No sense in dawdling. Nothing beyond this door can hurt me physically. Of that I am sure. I worry, instead, that I'll see something so awful I'll never scrub it from my memory.

Putting my hand on the last bolt, I draw it back.

Pause.

Listen.

No sound breaks the silence. No whisper of a breeze.

I grip the handle, turn it clockwise and pull. The rubber squeals as the door releases from its frame. I step back, blinking into the revealed darkness.

The smell that wafts out is the same one I caught upstairs, but far stronger, so sharp it makes my eyes water. I recognize it, too: household bleach. Not the citrusy kind you sometimes get but the regular stuff, the sort that gets in your nose and feels like it's stripping away the hairs.

The chamber didn't smell like this before. I fear that during my time away something monstrous has happened. When I step inside and shine my torch around, I know it has.

XIII

Just like the rest of the cellar, the floor here is covered with nubs of sharp rock. They press through my trainers and hurt my feet. Three walls of rough-cut stone form part of the cottage's foundations. The fourth, now behind me, is made of the same thick fibreboard I saw on the way in.

A great deal of care has been put into its construction. The open doorway reveals that the false wall is a foot thick, the cavity packed with PVC bags filled with soundproofing. Someone, at some point, has tried to damage the door from the inside. Deep scratches mark the wood.

I can hardly breathe, but somehow I manage to speak: 'Gretel?'

The name rebounds off the walls. In here my voice sounds deeper, more throaty, as if the cellar has aged me fifty years.

'Gretel,' I repeat, and now my voice sounds more twisted than ever. The torch blinks furiously. I try to steady it, pointing the beam at the very centre of the chamber.

Through the bedrock, a U-shaped bolt has been sunk, trapping an iron ring. Previously, Gretel's chain was attached to that ring. Now, both the chain and the girl are gone.

The bleach fumes are thick in my throat. My tummy flops and I gag. Aiming my torch around the chamber, I see that the pillow, the wash bucket and the makeshift toilet have also disappeared. The floor looks like it's been scrubbed. I don't want to think about what's been scoured away, or the meaning of that antiseptic smell.

This is my fault. All of it.

It's too much. My torch clatters to the floor and winks out. Blackness floods in. I lose all sense of myself, of what is real and what is not. I hear choked cries and can't believe they're mine, convinced, suddenly, that I share this space with something hostile, something with claws and teeth. I turn, run blindly for the door, misjudge its location and shoulder-slam the jamb, knocking myself to the floor. A sharp edge of rock cuts my knee. The pain is a bolt of electricity that races up my leg and explodes inside my skull. Crab-like, I scuttle from the chamber and keep going until my arms knock against the cellar's bottom step. Blackness becomes grey. Shadow becomes light. I see an ivy-clad ceiling, a fungus-blotched wall. Then I'm on my knees again, outside this time, back in the Memory Wood and panting great lungfuls of air. Trees swarm around me like wolves gathered to a kill. There's a shrieking in my ears. The magpies have returned: three on a nearby branch, four on the sagging cottage roof. I remember the old nursery rhyme and it chills my bones: *Seven for a secret, never to be told*.

I don't know what to think.

I don't know what to do.

Gretel has gone. And it's all because of me.

ELISSA

Day 1

I

It's Saturday, which means it's a chess day, although in reality every day's a chess day because that's all she ever thinks about. Still, this one's particularly special. Exceptional, in fact. Because this is an English Youth Grand Prix event for which she has been practising, it feels, her whole life.

The £100 prize for the overall winner is small, but money has never interested her. She already owns a set of Staunton chess pieces hand-carved in Brazilian rosewood, the only thing her dad ever gave her worth keeping. They're triple-weighted, gliding about on bases of soft leather. Apart from the Stauntons, all she needs is a board, and she has one of those too: a slab of solid hardwood inlaid with maple and anegre. Her mum bought it from an online shop soon after her dad stopped calling, eating tinned beans for a fortnight to afford it. The one thing Elissa wants in the world that she doesn't have is a date with Ethan Bandercroft from her class, and that's *never* going to happen, even if she wins the prize money.

No, she's excited about the Grand Prix – so excited that each breath threatens to lift her from the ground and carry her clean away – because the winner will be invited on to the English national team to compete at either the World Youth Championship or the World Cadets. To land a place would be the culmination of years of hard work.

'Lissy? Lovely? You OK up there? It's time to go!'

'I'm fine, Mum!' she yells. 'Just coming!'

She grabs the green velvet bag that holds her Stauntons. She won't need them today – at the event they'll use tournament boards and pieces – but she wants them, regardless. They go into her rucksack, along with the other items she's packed. There are two chess books, the first by Jeremy Silman and the second – *Chess Bitch: Women in the Ultimate Intellectual Sport* – by Jennifer Shahade. Along with the books is a lunchbox containing a bottle of Evian, a cling-film-wrapped tuna sandwich, two satsumas, a packet of pineapple Yoyo Bears and a Marks and Spencer chocolate brownie. There's also a roll-up chess mat, a notepad to record her moves and three gel-filled pens secured with an elastic band. Nestled on top is a knitted monkey wearing a tiny white T-shirt. He's a freebie from a PG Tips box, along to masquerade as her mascot. At previous tournaments she's seen similar totems: Lego figures, Pokémon toys, rabbits' feet. It all seems a bit pointless, but she has no wish to distance herself from the other kids she might meet on the tour. As a result, Monkey's been pressed into service.

'But if you throw me off,' she whispers, fixing him with what she hopes is a baleful stare, 'if you do anything to bring disgrace on my family's good name, when we get home I will take you outside to the garden, strap you to the barbecue, and then I will burn you.'

She stares into Monkey's glossy black eyes. If he's fazed by her warning, he doesn't show it. Perhaps, like her, he suspects her words are empty threats. Zipping him into the rucksack, she throws one arm through a strap. On her way to the door she catches herself in the mirror and pulls up.

Her mum bought the dress. It's bottle green, the colour of the ocean on a summer day. It's not something Elissa would have chosen but she sort of likes it, despite how girly it makes her look. She could have worn her normal outfit – jeans, T-shirt, sweatshirt – but today she hadn't wanted to be distracted by clothing choices, so she'd asked her mother to intervene.

The dress is sleeveless. Although she's wearing a cotton vest underneath, her arms are still cold. Going to the wardrobe, she stares at the cardigans hanging up. There are various colours. To help her decide, she restricts her choices to black or white.

Immediately, Elissa realizes her mistake. Black and white are the traditional colours of a chessboard, along with the pieces that move upon them. Will her choice of cardigan influence her game? Her heart begins to jump.

Calm down. It doesn't matter.

And yet the decision has paralysed her. She wants to call out to her mum, but suddenly her jaw feels wired shut.

Black or white? Black or white?

Blackorwhite, blackorwhite, blackorwhite?

It feels like an intricate set of cogs has seized up inside her brain. This happens sometimes. A decision, seemingly routine, will render her helpless. Her muscles freeze and she'll remain in the same position, gently swaying, until something knocks her back into motion.

Black or white? White or black?

She blinks. The movement is involuntary, a reaction to dry eyes.

'Lissy?' Her mum's voice, from downstairs.

Odd that in chess, a game all about tough decisions, she never experiences this. Perhaps that's one of the reasons she loves it.

'Lissy!'

And then, just like that, she's back. Her jaw releases. She lurches forwards, almost colliding with the cupboard. 'White,' she gasps, dragging the cardigan from its hanger before paralysis can reclaim her. At the mirror, she allows herself a final glance. Her black hair is neatly brushed, held by a plastic Alice band the same colour as her eyes. She's always wished her eyes were brown and not green. So many people comment on them. She's never felt comfortable with the attention.

Downstairs, her mum is standing in the hall, clutching her car keys. 'OK?'

Elissa nods.

'Sure you've got everything?'

'Yep.'

'Notebook? Pens? Lunchbox?'

'Yep, yep, yep.'

'Monkey?'

She winces.

Her mum laughs, bends down and kisses her. 'You're going to be great. The important thing is to enjoy yourself.'

'The important thing is to *win*.'

Her mum tilts her head, as if she's in an art gallery assessing a particularly peculiar piece. 'I'm so proud of you, Lissy,' she says. 'I love you so much.'

'Love you too,' Elissa mumbles. And it's true. She really does.

Lena Mirzoyan pushes up her coat sleeve and checks her watch. 'We'd better go. Do you need a wee?'

'Mum!'

'OK, sorry. Bad habit. Let's skedaddle.'

II

They're in the car, heading along the dual carriageway. An Adele song is playing: 'Rolling in the Deep'. Elissa doesn't know much about music but she knows Adele because her mum has her CD and plays it all the time.

The tournament is in Bournemouth, an hour's drive. Registration is at ten, but they left the house at seven. The risk of getting snarled in a two-hour jam this early on a Saturday morning is almost zero, but Lena Mirzoyan lives in fear of letting her daughter down. As a result, they reach the outskirts of Bournemouth exactly two hours before the venue opens.

Examining the Fiesta's dashboard clock, Lena winces. 'We're a bit early.'

'A bit?'

'Oh, Lissy, I'm sorry. I just didn't want to take any chances. I—'

'Mum, I'm kidding. It really doesn't matter. Maybe we can get some breakfast.'

Lena nods, relief spreading across her face. 'I could certainly do with something. I didn't eat anything before we left.'

'Why not?'

She shrugs. 'Nerves, I guess.'

Elissa laughs. 'Why are *you* nervous?'

'Because I know how much this means to you. I want you to do well.'

'Don't you think I will?'

'I think you'll knock 'em dead.'

'Then you've no reason to be nervous.'

Now her mum laughs too. They pass a sign: *WIDE BOYS RESTAURANT! OPEN 7 DAYS, EARLY TIL LATE!* 'How about there? Want to try it?'

It's not the sort of place they usually go. Elissa says yes quickly, before Lena can change her mind. As they drift towards the exit lane, she glances out of the side window and spots a silver BMW barrelling up the inside of them. Her mum notices just in time, swinging right to avoid a collision.

Horn blaring, the BMW shoots past. Elissa gets a split-second view of a face distorted by rage. The car cuts in front. Its brake lights flare. Gasping, Lena slams on her own brakes. Elissa's seatbelt bites her chest. The BMW weaves left and right, toying with them. Then it accelerates away. Elissa stares at the shrinking number plate: *SNP 12.*

'Stupid Nasty Prat,' she hisses, through clenched teeth.

Breathing hard, Lena checks her mirror before taking the exit slip for Wide Boys. In the car park, she turns to Elissa. 'You OK?'

'Sure. Just some loser. Don't let him ruin your day.'

'This day?' her mum asks. 'Not a chance.'

III

Inside Wide Boys, another Adele song is playing. When Elissa rolls her eyes, her mum clocks her expression and grins.

The restaurant is decked out like a sixties American diner: chequerboard floor, red vinyl seats, framed prints of Elvis and Marilyn Monroe. It smells of lemon floor cleaner, fresh pastries and frying bacon.

Lena Mirzoyan grabs an empty table. 'What do you—'

'You choose,' Elissa says quickly.

Taking out her glasses, Lena studies the menu.

A middle-aged couple sits down at the next table. Covertly, Elissa begins to observe them. She loves to people-watch, noting all the little choices others have made during their day.

This morning, the woman beside her decided to wear a jade necklace. She decided to put on make-up, too, choosing her violet lipstick from what was likely a collection of different shades. She chose to wear jeans rather than trousers or a skirt, and boots rather than sandals or trainers. The man decided to shave before coming out. Elissa knows that because there's a smudge of foam behind his right ear. He combed his hair, too, presumably with some kind of product; it looks wet, and ever-so-slightly sticky. Dirt is trapped beneath the nails of his blunt-tipped fingers. While he studies the menu he runs a hand up and down his throat, as if checking for patches the razor missed.

'Stop that,' the woman hisses. 'Always touching yourself.'

He lurches upright, hand dropping to his side. Elissa hides her smile by turning away.

At the smaller table to her right sits an older man. He's wearing a turquoise jumper, mustard-yellow corduroys and toffee-apple-red shoes. A signet ring gleams on his pinkie finger. Against his teapot leans a battered paperback: *The History of the Peloponnesian War* by Thucydides. His mouth twitches as he reads, revealing a set of pointed yellow teeth.

A waitress appears then. She's in her fifties, with blonde hair so glamorously styled she must spend hours maintaining it. Pinned to her T-shirt is a name badge: *ANDREA*. She's at least four stone overweight, all boobs and bum, but she wears it so well it's impossible to imagine her differently.

'Look at them fabulous eyes,' Andrea crows, flashing a red-lipped smile. 'Always wanted green ones myself, but you can't have everything.'

'You *have* green eyes,' Elissa says.

'Oh, don't you go believin' everything you see or hear. I got my contacts in, is all.'

Elissa blinks, stealing a quick glance at her mum. 'You can change your eye colour?'

'Chuckie, you can change just about anything you want if you tries hard enough. Through these puppies I can't see shitums, but at least I got my green peepers, even if I might bring you the wrong-flavoured milkshake because of 'em.' Andrea winks conspiratorially. 'You should see me on Hallowe'en. I wear a pair of eyes that're bright orange, slitted just like a cat's. Scares the bejesus out of people.' She makes her hand into a paw and meows. They both laugh.

'Well,' the waitress continues. 'I'm guessing you didn't inherit those gorgeous greens from your mum. Should we be thanking your dad for 'em?'

'Um . . . I guess.'

'Is he joining you lovely ladies today?'

'He doesn't live with . . . I mean, we don't . . .'

Elissa's mum clears her throat. 'I think, actually, we're ready to order.'

'Great.' Andrea tilts her head. Her fake green eyes gleam. 'What can I getcha both?'

'We'll have a couple of Hound Dog breakfasts,' Lena says. 'Coffee for me. Orange juice for my daughter.'

Hearing that, Elissa is a little disappointed. She was sort of looking forward to Andrea bringing her the wrong-flavoured milkshake, but she doesn't correct the order; the thought of choosing *which* milkshake makes her shiver.

'How'd you want your eggs?'

'One set scrambled, one set fried.'

'Coming right up.'

Andrea saunters off, buttocks swinging inside her tight black trousers.

'Thanks,' Elissa says.

Her mum raises an eyebrow. 'For what?'

'Ordering my food. Don't think I could have done it.'

'Too much choice?'

She nods sheepishly. 'We probably would've missed the tournament.'

'Can't have that.'

'Did she really say *shitums*?'

Lena rolls her eyes. 'That's why I don't like bringing you to these places.' Her smile shows she doesn't mean it.

Soon, Andrea is back, plonking down coffee and orange juice. Five minutes later she returns with two huge plates. 'Who's for fried?'

Elissa raises her hand. There's far too much food for a

thirteen-year-old girl: bacon rashers, eggs, sausage, mush-rooms, fried potato, grilled tomato, beans and a square of fried bread sparkling with grease.

'Whoa,' says the woman with the jade necklace. 'Some-body's hungry.'

Elissa stiffens, wondering if it's a criticism, but when she looks over her fellow diner is smiling.

'Growing girl,' says the man with dirty fingernails.

Thankfully, another waitress appears then, ready to take the couple's order. Spared from further attention, Elissa cleans her knife with a napkin. In the car, she hadn't been that hungry, but now she's famished. As she eats, her thoughts return to the tournament. Her mind becomes a landscape of black and white squares, populated by the carved shapes made famous by Nathaniel Cooke. Once she's cleared her plate – everything except one egg, the mushrooms and the fried potato – she pushes it aside.

Her mum digs in her handbag for her purse. 'Just pop-ping to the loo. Will you be OK?'

'Sure.'

Unzipping her rucksack, Elissa grabs the book by Jen-nifer Shahade and begins to read. She's interrupted by a grunt from the next table. Looking up, she sees the man with shaving foam behind his ear examining the title.

'Funny name for a book,' he says. 'What's it about?'

She looks from the man to his partner, who smiles sym-pathetically, as if to say: *Yes, sweetie, I know he's a little slow. Just humour him for me, would you?*

'It's about chess.'

'Huh. Ain't never been my thing. Used to like a bit of poker, before.'

Elissa nods. Her focus returns to the book. It attempts

to settle there, but she can't help herself. 'Before what?' she asks, glancing up.

Using his knife as a pointer, the man indicates his partner. 'Before . . . you know.'

The woman's smile broadens. If there's a message, this one's probably something like: *See the kind of shitums I have to put up with?*

Elissa blushes. The couple continue to stare, as if expecting something in return for their interest, so she says, 'I've got a chess tournament today, in Bournemouth. First of a Grand Prix.'

When they offer her fuzzy smiles and drift back to their conversation, she sags with relief. Turning away, she sees the man in the turquoise jumper watching her. He shakes his head minutely before returning to his book. Whether he was expressing solidarity at the unwanted interruption, or distaste at her poor social skills, Elissa cannot tell.

A minute later her mum comes back from the loo. Then it's her turn to go. They meet back at the service desk and settle their bill. When they pass their table on the way out, the couple who were sitting beside them are still eating, but the man in the turquoise jumper has gone. Steam curls from his abandoned teacup.

IV

The tournament is being held at the Marshall Court Hotel on Bournemouth's East Cliff. Because they're early, they have no problem finding parking.

Elissa's stomach gurgles and pops. She wishes she hadn't eaten the fried breakfast. There's a strange taste in her mouth, as if her teeth have been coated with grease. An image pops into her head. She's taking the opening move of her first game. When her fingers release the chess piece, they leave a sheen of bacon fat.

'Have you got a wet wipe?' she blurts. 'It's really important.'

Her mum nods, scrambling inside her handbag. She pulls out a sealed pouch. Elissa breaks it open and swabs her hands.

They sit in the car for a while, staring at the white-washed building as seagulls circle overhead. Finally, Lena Mirzoyan taps the dashboard clock. 'Ready?'

'Ready.'

'Game face on?'

'What?'

'I'm not really sure – I just heard it on TV.'

'Oh, Mum.'

V

A giant whiteboard stands in the Marshall Court's lobby. On it someone has written *CHESS THIS WAY* and drawn an arrow pointing left. Elissa follows it to a wide corridor carpeted in a busy geometric fabric. Along one wall, a draperied trestle table is piled with chess merchandise: T-shirts, mugs, travel sets, clocks, home-printed manuals and guides. A grey-haired woman in a fuchsia cardigan sits behind it, smiling as they pass. 'Be sure to come by later,' she says. 'Good luck, missy.'

At the end of the corridor, a registration desk is staffed by a birdlike man with a prominent Adam's apple. Dark hair sprouts from his skinny wrists, which emerge in turn from the frayed cuffs of a pink shirt. Behind him is the ballroom, where rows of tables have been set up.

'Name?' he asks.

'Elissa Mirzoyan.'

The man drags an overlong fingernail down his list. 'And who've you brought with you today, Elissa?'

'Just my mum.'

He tuts theatrically. 'I'd have said you deserve a *much* larger fan club. Got your ticket?'

Elissa winces. Turning to Lena, she asks, 'Can I have the keys?'

'You left it in the car?'

She nods, blowing out her cheeks.

'Want me to come with?'

'No. I'll be thirty seconds.'

Taking the keys, Elissa sprints back down the corridor. Outside, a mud-caked white van has squeezed into the space beside their car. Sliding along the gap, she unlocks the Fiesta's passenger door, leans halfway inside and flips open the glove box. There's the ticket, just where she left it. When she climbs out, the white van rocks gently on its springs. Elissa glances through the driver's window but she can't see anyone inside.

A cloud drags across the sun, casting a sudden pall over the car park. A rash of goosebumps breaks out across Elissa's skin. Clutching her ticket, she edges back along the gap.

On the van's rear bumper – metal, not plastic – is a series of tiny indentations, as if it's been the target of a small-calibre rifle. There's a creepy sticker, too, of a trilby-wearing skull smoking a cigarette. A speech bubble in a heavy gothic font reads: *CHILLAX*. Somebody, at one time or another, has burned a hole through the tip of the skull's cigarette, revealing a cherry of orange rust. Elissa frowns, disturbed without knowing why, and rushes back inside the hotel.

'Disaster averted,' says the man with the hairy wrists. His eyes twinkle as he takes her ticket. She wonders for a moment what he means.

VI

Inside the Marshall Court's ballroom, kids stand with their parents, hovering beside tables or studying the posted pairings. Most are wearing weekend clothes. A few public-school pupils are in uniform.

Elissa's first match is against Bhavya Narayan. When they shake hands, Bhavya's palm is clammy. Still, she seems friendly enough. Her parents, a Hindu couple, beam just as brightly at Elissa as at their own daughter.

Bhavya has a mascot with her – a monkey statuette with four arms. 'It's Hanuman,' she explains, placing it down. Elissa unzips her rucksack and takes out Monkey. She hopes the family won't take offence, but everyone's still smiling.

Soon after, the parents file out and the tournament begins. Bhavya chooses a queen pawn opening. Elissa responds in kind. When the Queen's Gambit is offered – a sacrificial pawn to C4 in return for better board position – she accepts by taking it. Over the next twenty minutes, a furious battle ensues for the centre. Elissa's heart thumps throughout, but she's not tense; at no time does she feel truly threatened, and when Bhavya loses concentration during a fork, Elissa coolly captures her queen. It's a game-destroying move, and the girl resigns shortly afterwards. When the parents return, Bhavya's mother hands Elissa a polythene bag filled with home-made banana chips.

'Phew,' says Lena Mirzoyan when they're reunited. 'I was so nervous outside I think I did a little wee.'

'Mum!'

'Sorry.'

But she isn't sorry, that's plain to see. Her chest, rapidly rising and falling, is clear evidence of her pride. Reaching out, Elissa touches her hand. It conveys her gratitude more than any words could.

At eleven o'clock she begins her second match. This time her opponent is a fair-haired girl called Amy Rhodes. Amy's a cool customer. She doesn't smile like Bhavya did. Neither do her parents, who frown faintly as they examine Elissa. Amy's arrived without a totem, and she gives Monkey a look that Elissa regards as impertinent. As a result, Elissa takes great pleasure in beating her – not as quickly as she could but slowly, crushingly, taking each piece until only the king remains, naked and vulnerable, in one corner of the board. Afterwards, Amy rises from the table without a word.

Next, Elissa plays Ivy May, a girl whose glasses are the thickness of Coke bottles and who plonks down a Peppa Pig mascot with no trace of embarrassment. The match is a slog, and nearly ends in a draw when Elissa loses her second knight, but somehow she pulls through.

At lunchtime, she finds her mum and they seek out a place to sit. Elissa munches her tuna sandwich, the Yoyo Bears and a satsuma. Flicking through her notebook, she reviews her three matches. She tries not to rebuke herself too harshly for her mistakes, but it's difficult – lapses in concentration have almost cost her two of the three victories.

Her fourth match begins at two thirty. Beforehand, she borrows her mum's keys and carries her lunchbox to the car. A moment of solitude, away from the ballroom clamour, will help her reset.

Sitting in the passenger seat, Elissa takes Monkey from her rucksack and examines him. She's certain his presence hasn't affected her play, but for the first time something else occurs to her: has he, perhaps, affected the play of the three opponents she's dispatched?

She thinks about Bhavya's statuette and Ivy's Peppa Pig. Those totems didn't affect *her* – after a cursory glance she'd dismissed them. But could that be said of her opponents' encounters with the deadpan knitted mannequin? It's an interesting thought. Still, she doesn't intend to win by virtue of a psychological trick.

Her next opponent attends a public school well represented in this competition; so far, its pupils have posted an unblemished record. Tweaking one of Monkey's ears, Elissa says, 'I don't mind if you put her off a *little*.' Then she slips him into her rucksack with the food she hasn't eaten and scrambles from the car. When she turns towards the Marshall Court Hotel, gathering her stamina for the afternoon session, day abruptly becomes night.

VII

For a moment, it's too confusing to process. Gone is the grey sky over Bournemouth's East Cliff. Likewise, the hotel's whitewashed frontage. There's a pressure, quite horrid, on Elissa's eyes and mouth. Her world tilts and she thinks she's falling, but she doesn't go down, not entirely. Her heels scrape against the tarmac.

Is this a panic attack? Perhaps something stranger – narcolepsy? Cataplexy? Elissa twists her head and feels, against her ear, the unmistakable curve of a bicep. Simultaneously, she realizes that the pressure on her eyes and mouth comes from fingers pressed against them. She thinks of the public-school girls with their unblemished record, and the cruel tricks kids like to play. Suddenly, her shoes are no longer dragging on the tarmac but scrabbling against it. She makes a fist, brings forward her arm and slams back her elbow. Close to her ear she hears a *whuff* of expelled breath. There's an acrid smell in her nose: the bitterness of stale tobacco smoke. The arm around her neck tightens.

Too strong to be any of the girls she's seen today. And none of them, surely, are heavy smokers.

At last, the reality of what's happening floods in.

She's being taken.

Snatched. Spirited away.

Her mind empties and she becomes a wild thing. She twists, kicks, opens her mouth and bites down on her attacker's hand. Immediately there's a taste on her tongue even worse than old cigarettes. It's dark and dirty, an abattoir foulness, and it blasts her panic into the stratosphere.

She can't breathe, can't scream. Can't hear anything but the crazy tide of her blood. Her head fills with silver, as if a firework has detonated inside her skull.

Elissa's feet bicycle in empty air. A different sound, now, or more like the lack of one: a muting of traffic and seagulls; an absence of wind. Her heels make contact with something beneath her. There's a hollow banging. All at once she realizes she's in some kind of container, a metal one – or, possibly, a vehicle.

With a spasming contortion of her spine, she recalls the white van and its creepy sticker: the trilby-wearing skull smoking a cigarette.

CHILLAX.

Elissa gags, tries to control herself. If she pukes, there's nowhere for it to go. She imagines vomit spurting from her nose, and the idea of *that* is so shocking that her muscles slacken and her head sags. She's unconscious for no more than a few seconds, because when she recovers hardly anything has changed. The fingers over her eyes shift position and she sees a slim triangle of sky. There's a squeal and a thunk: the door slamming shut. It ensures some level of privacy for what comes next.

Breathing in her ear again – elevated, but only slightly. '*Easy now,*' rasps a voice. '*Easy now.*'

She wants to sink her teeth into the stranger's fingers, but she can't bear the prospect of his blood rushing into her mouth.

'*I've got plans for you, darl,*' he tells her. '*You won't die today.*'

She shudders at that. Beneath her, the van shudders in sympathy. Through her confusion she realizes it's the shake of the engine turning over, followed by the liquid rattle of an exhaust.

The sound represents a rupture, a cataclysm. Across the car park, through the lobby and along the carpeted corridor to the ballroom, her mum sits on a cushioned conference chair, munching a tuna sandwich. Already, she might as well be an ocean away.

Bucking, thrashing, using all the strength that her muscles can supply, Elissa struggles to throw off the clamping hands and let out a scream. If she doesn't free herself in the next few seconds it'll be too late, and that ocean will become uncrossable. She grinds her heel down the stranger's shin, slams him repeatedly with her elbows. Then, the unexpected happens; the hand covering her mouth is knocked free.

Elissa draws in breath for a scream. As her lungs begin to fill, she feels something wet against her face – a cloth dripping cold liquid. When her chest expands, she inhales the fumes sloughing off it. Too late, she realizes her struggles haven't saved her but damned her.

The chemical rips into her lungs, blossoming like a gaseous flower. She goes loose, slippery. Her chest deflates and she takes another breath. Now, it's no longer a single flower but an entire meadow. Her anguish fades. She feels euphoric. Something important was happening, but already she can hardly remember. Was there somewhere she had to be? The meadow is calling, and its song is so beautiful that she decides to ignore the tiny voice that pleads with her to hold on, *hold on*.

Elissa's muscles relax and she sinks down. The darkness is not to be feared but accepted, so that's exactly what she does.

ELIJAH

Day 6

I

I'm walking again, through the Memory Wood. It's still light, just about, but the autumn colours have seeped away. I feel like I'm travelling through a pencil sketch, or somebody else's dream. Moving steadily between these trees, it's hard to say exactly when I realize I'm not alone. It's more a slow dawning than anything immediate; a change in the feeling of the woods around me. The wildlife has fallen silent – that's my first clue. Suddenly it seems as if the very trees are holding their breath, and when I turn around there he is, standing beside an ivy-covered oak as if he's been waiting here hours, killing time, even though he definitely wasn't there when I passed by moments earlier.

We stare at each other for what feels like an age. Kyle's face is dark with anger, his blood close to the surface. I can *feel* his intensity. It boils off him like smoke, poisoning the surrounding air. Anxious, I take a backward step, immediately wishing I hadn't. Showing weakness in front of Kyle is always a mistake.

My older brother wears a camouflaged jacket that blends perfectly with the surrounding woodland. *So* perfectly, in fact, that he seems almost unreal, a disembodied face floating above the bracken.

Over one shoulder is his rifle. It's a .22, designed for small game, but with a decent head shot it's powerful enough to kill something much larger. Once, I was playing in the Memory Wood when I heard the crack of his gun and saw him, some time later, dragging a dead muntjac through the trees. 'Hey, Eli,' he shouted. 'Come and have a look at this.'

A month earlier I'd told him his rifle couldn't bring down a deer. Now here he was to prove me wrong. Kyle had prepared his evidence in advance – when he lifted the muntjac's head I saw he'd scalped it.

'See here,' he announced, probing a hole in the white-pinkish mess. 'That's where I drilled him. And look what happened after. Energy in my bullet cracked the top of his skull like an egg.' With a dirty finger he traced the splits in the bone. Then, showing no respect for the creature he had killed, he ripped its head around, so savagely that something in its neck popped like a champagne cork.

'Check out that exit wound,' Kyle said.

A large piece of skull flapped open like a trapdoor, offering a view of the pulped-up brain tissue within. Seeing it, I thought I'd feel sick, but I didn't. I just wondered how it must have felt to the deer, that sudden calamity inside its head. I wondered how such a thing would feel inside my own head, and thought of all the experiences Kyle's bullet would flush away.

Calamity is a word far prettier, I think, than its meaning.

Now, I watch my brother stride towards me, his booted

feet making no sound. I'm pretty sure he's learned how to walk like that from one of his survival magazines. Something dark and crusted is streaked across his cheeks. He stinks, too. Not a human smell but something vile he's cooked up to disguise his scent. I cringe to think what it is, or how he made it.

Only a two-year age gap separates us, but Kyle seems more like an adult than a child. His jaw has lengthened. His eyebrows are thick and black – in a few years I reckon they'll meet. Beneath them his gaze is as cold as a comet, sharp and clever yet utterly lacking in compassion.

'What did you do, Eli?' he snarls. 'Where did you go?'

I knew this showdown was coming, but I wasn't expecting to be quite so scared. Out here, in these darkening woods, Kyle *terrifies* me. This close, he smells dreadful, a rotten-mummy stench that gets in my nose and makes my eyes water.

'Gretel,' I say, swaying on my heels. 'What did—'

Before I can finish my question he swings his fist. It smashes against my cheek, sending me reeling. My heel catches a root and I sprawl into a pile of dead leaves. When Kyle's hand moves to his rifle strap I cry out, convinced he's about to shoot me (*That's where I drilled him, energy in my bullet cracked the top of his skull like an egg*), but the gun stays on his shoulder and I realize he's only bracing it. Bending, he grabs a fistful of my clothing below my chin.

My cheek throbs in time with my heart. I'll have one hell of a bruise. Probably a black eye, too.

Kyle twists my clothes like a corkscrew, choking off my breath. I rear back my head, trying to open my airways. But with my throat exposed, I'm gripped by a sudden panic that he'll sink his teeth into it.

With a disgusted snarl, he releases me. My head smacks against a half-buried stone. Strange, but I'm almost grateful for the pain.

'Gretel—' I say again, clamping my mouth shut when Kyle draws back his fist. His knuckles are scuffed, although not from this encounter. The scabs are prickly and black.

'Don't fuckin' *call* her that,' he hisses. 'I'm done with your make-believe shit.'

I cringe at his language. The worst thing is, he's not even trying to shock me; this is just how Kyle thinks and speaks. A wander through his head would reveal nothing but bad words, naked girls and the mounted heads of dead animals.

I've never understood how we could end up so different. We're like Nelson Muntz and Martin Prince Jr – the bully and the wimpy kid from *The Simpsons*, a cartoon I sometimes watch in Magic Annie's caravan. Still, Kyle has a point; right now, it's important to respect the girl by using her real name. 'Elissa,' I say, blinking up at him. 'Elissa's gone.'

'No shit.' He expels the words so violently that a bolus of spittle flies from his mouth and hits my lip. It buzzes there, a warm nimbus of electricity. 'You might as well use the proper words. She's *dead*, Eli. And whose fault is that?'

I gasp, eyes wide. *Am* I responsible? It's what I've been telling myself ever since I stumbled out of the cellar, but hearing it from someone else is infinitely worse.

Kyle seems to spot some element of doubt in my eyes. It drives him to fury. This time, when his hand strays to his rifle, I'm convinced he's going to put a calamity inside my head. I'm so filled with remorse that I don't even flinch, but my brother pulls up short. 'I fuckin' *liked* her, Eli,' he spits.

'I fuckin' liked playin' around with her. When she wanted, she could say some interesting shit.'

'I . . . I'm sorry,' I stammer. 'I didn't want this. I didn't think they'd find out.'

Kyle straightens, his expression loaded with contempt. 'Well, they did. And now, because of you, she's dead.' He drags a scrap of fabric from his pocket and flings it at my face. By the time I snatch it away he's already turned his back. I watch him march off, kicking through the undergrowth like a stag during the rut.

I fuckin' liked playin' around with her.

I feel a brief pang of jealousy; I thought *I* was the only one who played with Gretel. Pointless to feel jealousy about any of this, but I can't forget Kyle's words. What were they talking about, down in that cellar? And how does he know this is my fault?

I'm thinking so hard about that I almost forget what he threw at me. When I check I see it's a girl's vest, streaked with brown stains. I want to hurl it away, but I can't dismiss Gretel so easily. Clutching the garment to my chest, I croak out a word I've used far too often, and with far too little effect: '*Sorry.*'

Around me the light is dying. I don't want to be in these woods at full dark. Five minutes later I'm shuffle-scurrying along the track beside Fallow Field. The feasting crows I saw earlier have vanished. Whatever they were eating appears to have been consumed.

II

Night, and I'm standing at the kitchen sink, preparing supper. Because of the way we live – wilder than other families, more dependent on the land – it's vital that everyone pitches in. I don't go to school but I have my reading and numbers, and when that's done I have my chores.

When I got home, I found a pheasant lying on the drainer. I know it came from Papa because a shotgun brought it down. It could do with a few days' hanging, but none of us are fussy. Personally, I prefer game with as little flavour as possible.

I don't bother plucking the bird because I'm not going to roast it whole. Instead, I cut off the head and trim away its wings and feet. With a knife, I score along the spine, removing the skin in a single, ripping movement. Opening the chest cavity, I scoop out the innards and toss them in the bin. By the time I'm finished my fingers are slick with blood. The thighs go in the fridge for tomorrow's meal. The breasts I wrap in bacon and put in the oven. While they're cooking I boil carrots and potatoes. All the while I face the wide kitchen window. I can't see anything past the glass, and I deliberately avoid my own reflection.

For some reason, I can't shake the feeling I'm being watched. Clearing away the vegetable peelings, I wonder if Kyle is looking in at me. I imagine the sights of his rifle lining up between my eyes and think of the muntjac he shot, and the calamity inside its head, but I refuse to lower the blinds. There are worse things on this estate than my brother and his gun. It's important to stick to my usual routine, to act as if nothing has happened.

A bottle of wine from Rufus Hall's cellar stands beside the kettle, robed in a fine coat of dust. It wasn't there this morning. The Meuniers donate one now and then, usually to reward a favour from Papa. I wonder what's prompted this particular offering. Neither Mama nor Papa are big drinkers. Most of the time, the only wine they have is what I add to our meals.

I look at the label and see that it's French: a Bordeaux from Saint-Émilion, bottled in 1998. Papa says the amount of dust on a bottle is a good guide to quality. By that standard, this is a decent one. Reaching out, I slide my finger across the neck, revealing a slim window of deeply hued glass. In it I see a reflection of myself, grossly distorted. Quickly, I turn away. Dust falls from my fingers like ash.

The kitchen fills with the scent of cooking meat. I get out some plates, wondering if anyone will join me. Right now, I'm not sure if eating alone would be worse than eating in company. It's warm in here, but the other rooms are cold. The cottage has no central heating and I haven't lit a fire.

My thoughts return to my dead friend. She called me Hansel and I called her Gretel. Renaming things was part of our game. The cottage – not this one but its dark twin inside the Memory Wood – became our Gingerbread House. Somehow, it took the edge off our fears; mine, at least – I was never sure whether Gretel was ever truly afraid although, looking back, I suppose she must have been.

To Jesus, I murmur. *If any of her family are sick or old or just fed up with life, please let them die tonight so she's not all alone.*

If I think about Gretel much longer, I won't be able to

eat, so for a while I push her out of my head. I drain the potatoes and mash them. Then I take the meat from the oven, cut one of the pheasant breasts in half and place it on my plate. It's a tiny portion, but I doubt I'll finish it. I add carrots, fill a glass with water and carry my meal to the dining room. Taking my usual seat, I douse the food with salt, but it makes little difference; when I fork some into my mouth it still tastes like clay.

Somehow, despite my poor appetite, I eat everything. Back in the kitchen, I wash the dishes. I no longer feel watched through the window over the sink, which is a relief, until I remember my bad instincts.

Upstairs, the house is even colder. A wind has sprung up, stirring the curtains in my room. I undress, carefully folding my clothes. Apart from the swishing trees and the shriek of a solitary fox out on Fallow Field, the night is silent.

Going to the window, I draw the curtains. Only then do I tiptoe to the loose floorboard in the corner and carefully lift it aside.

III

Here, inside this cobwebby cavity, is where I keep my Collection of Keepsakes and Weird Finds. The container itself is nothing to boast about, just a Tupperware box that I found one day while rummaging through the Meuniers' bins. Still, I've personalized it a bit. Across the lid, in black marker pen, it says: *TOP SECRET. PRIVATE PROPERTY. DO NOT OPEN WITHOUT PERMISSION.* Carrying the box to the bed, I carefully ease off the lid.

Immediately, I'm greeted by the familiar smells of its treasures. Not all of them are nice. Chief culprit, among the nasty ones, is the trio of knucklebones I found beside the lake. I'm pretty sure they aren't *really* knucklebones, nor any other part of a child. Weird, but even though the cartilage has shrivelled and the bones themselves have dried, their stench never fades. These days, I don't touch them if possible, and yet I can never quite bring myself to throw them away. I'm funny like that – the longer I possess something, the harder I find it to let go. When I became keeper of these bones, I elected myself Rememberer-in-Chief of whichever animal once owned them. If I choose to give them up, it'll be as if that creature never lived.

Now, with care, I lift out the other items in my collection. There's a smooth grey stone, cracked in half to reveal a fossilized ammonite; a pair of glasses which once may have fitted me but do so no longer; a Roman coin; a neatly folded handkerchief with a monogrammed B; a bundle of Panini football stickers; a tartan cat collar and tiny metal bell; a plastic phone card; a rosewood chess piece; a vial of perfume; a blunted Stanley knife; and a silver necklace with links so delicate they slip like sand through my fingers.

Then there are the skulls. Most belong to birds, but among them there's a rabbit and a squirrel, and one that's either a fox or a badger – I'm never quite sure. I cleaned them all with bleach, but a few blackish stains remain. At the bottom is a child's diary, the corners scuffed. The name on the cover isn't mine.

From my pocket I retrieve Gretel's vest. Carefully, I lay it over the diary, adding the padlock key from the

Gingerbread House. Then I pile the other items on top. I'm just resealing the lid when I hear the rattle of a latch downstairs.

The front door opens. There's commotion in the hallway, followed by muttered conversation. The kitchen tap runs. Water roars into a kettle. When I hear footsteps on the stairs I slither off the bed and thrust my collection back into its hidey-hole, leaping away just as the bedroom door swings wide.

Mama sweeps into the room. She stops dead, almost as if she's surprised to encounter me. Her eyes flare, moving to the corner where I was standing, but she can't see it clearly – my bed blocks her view. Perching on the mattress, she pats a section of it. Obedient, I join her.

'I'm sorry you had to eat alone,' she says. With a finger, she traces the floral patterns on my duvet. I watch, captivated. Mama's fingers are flawless. Her skin is like marble and her nails, painted a deep maroon, are perfectly manicured. I don't know how it's possible to work the land like she does and retain such immaculate hands.

'Did you read your Bible?'

'Not yet, Mama.'

'Ephesians tonight, I think. Starting at chapter six.'

I nod, knowing that she'll want me to focus on verse ten in particular.

Finally, be strong in the Lord and in His mighty power. Put on the full armour of God, so that you can take your stand against the devil's schemes.

Not many kids can quote Scripture so easily, but me and the Bible go way back. Mama has always loved Jesus, so it's only natural that she wanted me to love him too.

'Elijah? Are you all right?'

I brush my hand across my eyes, dismayed she's seen my tears. 'Kyle,' I say. 'He blames me for—'

'That boy needs a firmer hand. I'll rein him in, Elijah. You just watch.'

Trouble is, I doubt even Mama wields much power over my brother these days. I look at her hands and wish, more than anything, that she would open her arms and allow me to climb into her lap, the way she did when I was younger.

As if she's read my thoughts, she laces her fingers tightly together.

Out in the hall, a floorboard creaks. My bedroom door opens a second time, revealing Papa. He stares at us for a moment before he enters. Taking off his cap, he twists it like he's wringing out water.

'Eli,' he says. His voice is strained and he sounds tired. I wonder what he's been doing since we came home – fixing tools, probably, or running errands up at Rufus Hall. 'We need to talk about what happened.'

For a moment I think he means Gretel, but of course he doesn't – he's referring to how the police picked me up, wandering along a country lane three miles from Meunierfields.

'I'm sorry, Papa. I just got confused.'

'Because if you were trying to run away—'

'You know I wouldn't.'

He *should* know – I was the one who made the police call him so he could fetch me back.

'Out there, Eli, it's a dangerous world. You might think you know it, but you don't. Round here you have a lot of freedom – space to run about, do what you want. But we can't have you wandering off like that again. Everyone was very worried.'

Mama rises from the mattress and stands beside him. An image of Gretel pops into my head and I try to shoo it away, anxious that my parents will read my thoughts. Luckily, they don't stay long, closing the door behind them. It's only when I exhale that I realize how long I've been holding my breath.

On the nightstand lies my Bible. I'm too exhausted to pick it up. I've already recited the lesson that Mama wanted me to read. Seeing the words in print won't make their meaning any clearer.

Put on the full armour of God, so that you can take your stand against the devil's schemes.

A pull-cord hangs from the ceiling, allowing me to climb beneath the covers before I turn out the light. I'm just about to do that when I notice what's on my pillow.

IV

Blood rushes like a river in my arteries. Downstairs, a TV comes on. I imagine my parents sitting in front of it, their faces bathed in pale light. Canned laughter rolls up the stairs.

On my pillow, so lustrous they could have been minted hours earlier, lie two copper coins. They're tiny, smaller even than the pennies in Papa's change bowl. Both feature the same image: an old-fashioned sailing ship with billowing sails. When I move my head the light winks off them, making it seem like they're gliding across a blood-red sea.

Looking closer, I see they're halfpennies. In Ancient Greece, coins were placed on the eyes of the dead to pay for transport across the River Styx. Whoever left these coins is making a very obvious point, designed to frighten me.

It's worked. I can barely think. My heart knocks like a beating drum.

Have the coins been here all along? I didn't spot them when I came in. For a crazy moment I wonder if Mama left them here, but she wouldn't do that. Strange she didn't say anything, even so – perhaps, like me, she failed to notice them. Papa didn't come anywhere near the bed, which counts him out. And besides, he's not the type to play games.

I don't want to touch the halfpennies, but I can't leave them. When I pluck them from the pillow they're cold against my palm. Tugging open my curtains, I raise the sash window. The moon is up, its light made milky by cloud. Beyond our vegetable garden I see the western half of Fallow Field. A breeze rolls in, cold enough to give me goosebumps.

Winding back my arm, I throw the coins into the night. Darkness swallows them up. I remain at the window, taking deep breaths. There's nothing I can do to fix what's happened. There's little about any of this I can control. But one thing I *can* control is my behaviour from this point: how I act, and what I let others see. When I think of the Gingerbread House, and the awful antiseptic smell rising from its cellar, the snake in my tummy flops and rolls. There's a sound, too, but not from me. It takes a moment to figure out, mainly because I'm not expecting to hear an engine this late. A vehicle appears, bouncing along the track beside Fallow Field. I'm too far away to see it clearly, but it looks – and sounds – like a 4x4. Meunier's Defender, perhaps, or one of the beaten-up runabouts from Wheel Town.

Its headlamps are dark. No shred of light leaks from inside. I watch it skirt the Memory Wood's eastern boundary, heading north towards Knucklebone Lake. I'm so focused on its progress that for a moment I forget that my bedroom light is still on, and that by standing at the window I am clearly silhouetted.

MAIRÉAD

Day 1

I

Detective Superintendent Mairéad MacCullagh is bent over a toilet bowl inside Bournemouth Central police station when her phone starts shrilling. She glances at her bag, source of the interruption. Then she vomits a second time, as soundlessly as she can manage. The adjoining cubicles are empty right now, but another officer could stroll in at any moment.

Bile burns her throat. Her head pulses in time with her heart. With one hand, she tears a strip of paper from the hanging roll. With the other, she fumbles for the phone. 'MacCullagh.'

It's Halley, her DS and general gopher, calling from an internal line. 'Where are you?' he demands, breathless. 'I turned round and you were gone.'

Mairéad frowns at his tone. She blots her mouth with paper. 'What is it?'

'Possible child abduction, East Cliff. Eyewitness saw a girl bundled into a van.'

Mairéad throws the toilet paper into the bowl. She climbs to her feet. For a moment the world grows dim. Worried she'll pass out, she braces her arm against the cubicle wall. If ever she needed a quiet day at the office, this is it.

Halley's voice bleeds back in. '—called from Winfrith. Says it looks bad and he wants you there right away. Guessing you'll be SIO, but we need to move.' He pauses. 'Are you—?'

'I'll be right out,' Mairéad says, hanging up. She spits into the toilet, flushes away the vomit and unlocks the door. In the mirror, she examines her face. Beads of sweat prick her brow. A damp helmet of hair hugs tight against her head. A couple of grey strands, which a few years ago she'd have been diligent enough to yank out, lace the black. Her eyes look bloodshot and lost. 'Jesus Christ.'

Water blasts from the cold tap. Mairéad cups her hands beneath it. Washing the sweat from her forehead, she dries herself with two fistfuls of paper towels. Her stomach clenches again, but the worst is over now. The water, like a benediction, has revived her.

Possible child abduction, East Cliff. Eyewitness saw a girl bundled into a van.

Deep breath in, let it out.

Halley's waiting in the corridor. His jaw falls open when he sees the state of her, but he's wise enough not to say anything. Outside, he slides behind the wheel of a pool car. Usually, she'd insist on driving. Not today. As they squeal away from the kerb Mairéad closes her eyes and buckles in. 'What've we got?'

'First call came in ten minutes ago. Guest at the Marshall Court was looking out of his window at the car park when he saw someone drag a girl in a green dress into a van. Uniform arrived within minutes but couldn't find anyone to back up the story. There's a junior chess tournament taking place at the hotel – hundreds of kids and their families – so the scene's pretty chaotic.

'Few minutes ago, while you were . . . while you were busy,' Halley says, throwing her an awkward glance, 'a mother reported her daughter missing to the tournament organizers.'

'Daughter was wearing a green dress?'

'Yeah.'

Mairéad's stomach tightens, this time not from nausea.

II

The Marshall Court Hotel, a grand Victorian edifice of whitewashed stone, stands high up on East Overcliff Drive, where it peers out across the sea. Mairéad recognizes the place. She's been here with Scott at least twice. Not that she can remember what they were celebrating, or with whom.

A crowd has gathered on the pavement, held back by four community support officers in high-vis jackets. Two more guard the hotel's main entrance. Other officers are visible through the glass doors.

Halley parks on double yellows behind a line of patrol vehicles. Mairéad throws open her passenger door and clambers out. A gritty salt wind twines over the cliff, whipping tears from her eyes. She crosses the road and eases through the crowd to the PCSOs, flashing her ID.

Inside, the hotel lobby is abuzz with activity. Quickly, she finds the duty officer, Neil Carr.

'Missing girl is Elissa Mirzoyan,' he says, handing her a

purse-size photograph. 'Thirteen years old, visiting from Salisbury for the chess tournament. We got that from her mum. It's pretty recent.'

The photo shows a serious-looking girl – black hair, pale skin, unusually-vivid green eyes. She looks young for her age, achingly vulnerable. For someone, perhaps, she looked like prey.

Mairéad feels her knees sag. Suddenly, the light inside the lobby seems far too bright, the scratch of police radios far too loud. For one terrible moment, she's convinced she's going to collapse, right here, in this room full of fellow officers.

If Carr notices something's wrong, he doesn't say. 'I've kept anyone connected to the tournament in the ballroom for now,' he tells her. 'Didn't want people leaving until we'd confirmed identities. Meanwhile, I've got a team doing an open-door search of the premises. Doubt they'll find Elissa, but there's a chance our suspect was staying here and left something behind.'

Sweat rolls from Mairéad's armpits. She feels it gathering again on her forehead. 'What do we have on the van?'

'Very little so far. Only witness is Charles Kiser, an American tourist in his seventies. He watched it happen from the third floor. Can't tell us much except Elissa was dragged into a white van that' – Carr pauses to consult his notes – '"looked old and pretty beat-up". Nothing on the make or number plate. No distinguishing marks.'

'CCTV?'

'Lots in the hotel, but the camera outside hasn't been working for months. I've sealed off the car park. Scenes of Crime are on their way to see what they can dig up.'

'No one touches it in the meantime,' Mairéad says. 'When's our last confirmed sighting?'

Carr nods towards a ceiling-mounted camera aimed at the main doors. 'We've got time-stamped video of Elissa going outside at 14.10. Emergency call came in at 14.16.'

'Six minutes later? Why the delay?'

'Kiser didn't know what number to call so he took a lift down to reception and got them to phone it in. Few minutes after that, Elissa's mum approached the tournament organizers about her daughter. Uniform arrived just as everyone was putting two and two together.'

Mairéad grimaces. She rolls her tongue around her teeth, wishing she had a breath mint. 'OK, we're going to need a search adviser down here to assist. Get a call into Winfrith and ask them to locate Karen Day. I want her, if at all possible. While you're at it, make sure everyone knows we're dealing with a Critical Incident and reacts accordingly. And warn the news office that I'll want to launch a Child Rescue Alert straight after I talk to the mum. Get them this photograph and everything we have so far.'

While Carr summons his sergeants, Mairéad glances at her watch. It's 14.36. Elissa disappeared between twenty and twenty-six minutes ago. This first hour – the golden hour, as it's called – is critical. Already they're nearly half-way through it. A CRA will notify print and broadcast media of the girl's disappearance, triggering an immediate public appeal. An army of civilian volunteers will amplify the message through social media. But Mairéad can't launch the CRA straight away. The contact centre needs to prepare for a spike in calls; neighbouring forces will have to be co-opted into handling overflow. Otherwise, vital information could be lost. Winfrith can organize everything pretty quickly. Even so, it's not instantaneous.

Her stomach clutches. She needs to be sharp here and

she knows she's not. If only she can get through the next hour, she knows she's the best person to lead this. Trouble is, Elissa Mirzoyan might not *have* another hour.

Mairéad tastes bile, or the memory of it. To Halley she says, 'We need a list of all the guests who've already checked out. Also, this is a hotel, which means there must be coffee. Find some.'

As he heads towards the reception desk, her phone rings. It's Snyder, the Dorset ACC, confirming her appointment as Senior Investigating Officer. She thanks him and turns back to Carr, who's just finished briefing his sergeants. 'Where's the mum?'

'We're looking after her in the manager's office.'

'Dad?'

'Not together, apparently. We're trying to track him down.'

'Let's get a photo of him, too. Show it to our witness.'

Mairéad glances around the lobby. She wants to go home and crawl under her duvet. Instead, she rotates her wedding band three times. It's a practised movement, almost subconscious, a routine that sometimes clears her head. 'What's the mum's name?'

'Lena Mirzoyan.'

'Take me to her.'

III

The manager's office – high ceiling, tall windows, stiflingly hot – is carpeted in Black Watch tartan. All the wood is mahogany.

Two uniformed PCs stand by a leather-topped writing desk fiddling with their radios. Lena Mirzoyan sits in a club chair beside a cast-iron radiator spewing out heat. She's suffered no mortal injury, but she still looks like she's dying. Blood has retreated from her face, leaving skin as dry as bandages. Her expression suggests agony on a scale unimaginable.

'Lena,' Mairéad says. 'My name's Detective Superintendent Mairéad MacCullagh. I'm the officer in charge of finding Elissa.'

Lena jerks as if she's been slapped. She glances up, eyes wide and white. 'There's still time.'

Mairéad comes a little closer. 'Time?'

'Her next match only started at two thirty. That's less than ten minutes ago. I'm sure the organizers, under the circumstances . . . I mean . . .' Lena gasps for breath. Her whole body shudders. 'She worked so hard.'

'Lena, I need to ask—'

'They're saying someone *took* her. Pulled her into a *van*. That can't be right. Can it?'

Mairéad crouches down, covering the other woman's hands with her own. Despite the heat inside the office, Lena Mirzoyan feels like a slab of chilled meat. 'I know this is hard to hear,' she says, 'but we're operating on that basis for now. It doesn't mean it's our only focus. We have officers searching the hotel, just in case. The surrounding streets, too. And we're checking all the local transpo—'

Lena pulls back her hands. 'Why would anyone *take* her? Today, of all days?'

'If someone *has* taken Elissa, there's a very good chance it's someone she knows, quite possibly someone you both know. Who might that be, Lena? Do you have any ideas?'

The woman's eyes dart around the office, as if she's searching for an exit. 'There's no one.'

'What about her dad? How's their relationship?'

'They don't *have* a relationship, not any more. And Ian wouldn't . . . He's just not . . .'

Mairéad nods, easing back a little. Regardless of what Lena Mirzoyan believes, her ex will remain a priority until something rules him out. 'These last few weeks – have you noticed any changes in Elissa's behaviour? Anything out of the ordinary?'

'Not that I can remember.'

'Anyone new she was communicating with?'

'I don't think so.'

'Does she have a phone?'

Lena opens her bag and takes out a Samsung. 'She asked me to look after it.'

'You know the password?'

'Yes.'

Unfortunate that Elissa doesn't have the phone – they might have traced her location through it – but at least they can harvest the data. 'That's great, Lena. That's really helpful. Does Elissa own any other devices?'

'An iPad and a laptop. They're both at home.'

'We'll need to look at them right away. I'll have someone drive you back to Salisbury so we can collect them. We'll also need to search her bedroom – see if anything there can indicate where she might have gone.'

Lena's eyes widen further. 'But I can't go *home*. I need to be here. I need to be here for when she comes back.'

Mairéad pauses, tries to imagine what the other woman is feeling. 'Look,' she says. 'This is tough. It doesn't get any tougher. But out there, right now, I have scores of highly trained officers doing their very best to find Elissa and bring her back. They're working to a very well-tested plan. I need you to be brave. I need you to put your trust in us. And I need your help to make sure we have every single bit of information that could make a difference, so that we can do the best possible job. Can you do that for me?'

Lena's chest rises and falls. She makes a sound like a wild animal in distress. Drawing out another phone, she turns it towards Mairéad. On the screen is an image of Elissa. This one's not serious, like the other photograph. In it, the girl is grinning inanely, a red feather boa wrapped around her neck. An older couple cluster behind her, holding party balloons. Their eyes sparkle with love. 'This is her,' Lena whispers. 'This is Elissa. My daughter. My life.'

And Mairéad – thirty-eight years old, no child of her own – understands exactly. In an instant, Elissa Mirzoyan becomes something entirely different to what she was.

Again, that inhuman sound of suffering tears loose from Lena's chest. 'I know you'll try. All of you – I know you will. But you've *got* to succeed. You've got to bring her back. Promise me you will. Promise.'

The woman's expression is one of such desperation, such porcelain-fragile hope, that the room feels barren of air. Mairéad glances at the two officers by the desk.

No one can speak.

IV

Ten minutes later, police track down Lena's ex. He's at his office, in Birmingham, which rules him out as a suspect.

The news is a gut-punch. Increasingly, it looks like they're dealing with something monstrous: child abduction by a stranger. Such crimes are incredibly rare – perhaps fifty cases nationally in a year. The vast majority of those are almost instantly thwarted, either by parents or sharp-eyed bystanders. Only a handful ever get through.

In Bournemouth, officers rush to the borough council's CCTV control centre, where they begin to review footage. Others are dispatched to neighbouring hotels on East Overcliff Drive, in the hope of getting a hit. Uniformed PCs flood the train station. Traffic police are diverted to the main routes out of town. But no one yet knows what they're looking for, and everyone now *feels* the clock running down.

Karen Day, the PolSA Mairéad requested from Winfrith, arrives onsite and takes command of search activities, allowing Mairéad to concentrate on the suspect.

The Child Rescue Alert is activated. Local media leads the initial appeal. National media quickly pitches in. It's precisely the kind of incident that captures public attention. The story is catapulted up the news agenda.

Mairéad tracks down Charles Kiser, the American tourist who raised the alarm. Kiser is credible enough, but he can't tell her anything new, and his description of Elissa's abductor is depressingly vague: a heavy-set man in a bulky waxed jacket. When Mairéad goes up to Kiser's room and looks down at the car park she realizes why. Although the SOCOs working the scene are clearly visible, she sees the tops of their heads but no faces.

The last minutes of golden hour ebb away. Shoulders visibly begin to sag. In the lobby, officers wear expressions of growing consternation. On the street outside, rumours and accusations sweep the crowd. The worst of all crimes has visited the town. Right now, there's no clear path through the horror.

No one feels the pressure more than Mairéad. Her restless stomach and pounding head magnify her difficulties tenfold. Adrenalin is her crutch. Caffeine and paracetamol too.

Only once before has she worked on anything like this – a girl called Bryony Taylor, snatched on her way home from school in Yeovil, a town just beyond the Dorset border. Avon and Somerset Police led that investigation, with Mairéad drafted in to offer support. A year later, the case is still active, but every line of enquiry feels like it's been wrung dry of promise. Already, there are disturbing parallels between that disappearance and this one: both girls snatched in broad daylight, by a man driving a beaten-up white van; both incidents occurring within a fifty-mile stretch.

Officers drive Lena Mirzoyan back to Salisbury, where they'll collect Elissa's laptop and tablet and search her room for clues. Mairéad returns to Bournemouth Central, where she can more efficiently direct operations.

Seventy minutes in. Everyone at the station looks sick. And then, at 15.21, Mairéad catches her first break.

ELISSA

Day 2

I

Her eyes are open, but she can't see. Whether that's because she's blind or is somewhere in perfect darkness, she cannot tell. A hot ball of needles is rolling around inside her skull. The slightest movement encourages it to roll faster, so she tries to hold herself still.

Elissa smells vomit and knows it's her own. As she's processing that, her stomach clenches and she's sick again. It sets a fire in her throat that only water will extinguish. As well as stomach acid, she tastes partially digested tuna, which so revolts her that she heaves once more. Vomit spatters on to a floor she can't see but senses is close.

Is she lying down? Yes, there's pressure all along her right side: cold, hard and uneven. Strangely, her head feels supported.

Inside her skull, the ball of needles shows no sign of slowing. Elissa takes a steadying breath. Searching her memories, she tries to work out what has happened. She encounters nothing but a void – no recollection of waking, of eating, of conversations or people. Has she been in an accident? This is certainly no hospital. Her breathing has an echoey quality. Somewhere, she hears the drip of water.

Keeping her movements slow, Elissa walks the fingers of her left hand in front of her, hoping to discover something that will identify her location. The floor is compacted dirt and rock, but it doesn't feel entirely natural. At the very limit of their reach, her fingers touch something familiar: the strap of her rucksack.

Immediately, the recollections flood back. Elissa's head feels like it's going to burst, that ball of needles running amok. Her stomach seizes again, even though there's nothing left to bring up. The contractions are so intense that she fears the blood vessels in her eyes will rupture. Never has she experienced anything like this, so much pain and horror condensed into such a focused knot.

Monkey; the car journey; breakfast at Wide Boys; Adele; the Marshall Court Hotel; Bhavya Narayan; pineapple Yoyo Bears; Amy Rhodes; Ivy May; dropping off her lunchbox and *oh-God-oh-God-oh-God* the white van, the dented bumper, the trilby-wearing skull smoking a cigarette.

CHILLAX.

She wants to scream, but if she does her head will unzip, spilling a loose mess of brains across cold rock. The recollections keep coming: her heels dragging across tarmac; filthy fingers against her mouth; the wet cloth; the notion of flowers unfurling in her head.

She can't move, can't think. For a while, only the distant drip of water reassures her that time hasn't slowed to a stop.

There was a voice, wasn't there? A few words spoken. She's almost too frightened to seek them out.

Easy now. Easy. I've got plans for you, darl. You won't die today.

No clue in that except the obvious: her kidnapper is a man. She remembers no accent, his words delivered in a whisper that betrayed no hint of his age or background. He didn't seem all that tall, but his grip on her was merciless. She recalls the smell of him, like the churning sweetness of spoiled poultry.

Where is her mum? The thought of Lena Mirzoyan's anguish is almost too much. Elissa swears to herself, right then, that she will survive this – whatever *this* is – survive it no matter what she has to endure. No way will she allow her mum to bear the agony of a daughter's loss.

That promise, once made, has a remarkable effect. The pain in her head remains, but suddenly it's a lot more manageable. She feels a surge of strength in her muscles, a renewed pumping of her heart.

Elissa drags the rucksack close. Her fingers move blindly, searching for the main compartment's zip. She can't do this one-handed, so as carefully as possible she lifts her head. The pain of movement is excruciating. She clenches her teeth, feeling her world rotate.

Gradually, the barbed-wire wrecking ball falls still. With a scrape and a clink she sits upright, which is how she discovers the manacle.

II

Even though this latest revelation is the worst yet, Elissa refuses to let it swamp her. She still can't prevent a sob.

When it bursts free, a single uncontrolled release, the sound is so unrecognizable it's like it came from a stranger.

The manacle, made of pitted iron, encloses her right wrist. From it hangs a set of heavy links. Elissa feels along them to their anchor, a smooth metal ring trapped by a U-shaped bolt. She gives the bolt a tug, but it's solid – two inches thick and set into concrete.

Time, right there, to pause and gather her thoughts. So far, she's doing all right, but another shock, coming any time soon, might just finish her. It's hard to accept that someone has left her like this, as if she's an animal to be caged and then forgotten.

Using her left hand, she checks herself for abrasions, bumps; other signs of injury. There's an unpleasant wet-ness to her dress in places, but the culprit is vomit, not blood, which is gross but OK. Opening her legs, she finds she's still wearing her underwear. The discovery elicits another hard sob, but that's OK too. Better than OK, in fact.

Gone is the white cardigan that gave her so much trouble back at home. Did she take it off at the tournament? If so, she can't remember. On her feet, she's wearing the same shoes. She feels deep scuffs on the heel leather and knows they'll never look as good again. The shoes don't matter, but it does matter that her mum bought them, with money earned through hard effort.

Right there is another reason to survive this: revenge.

It's a ludicrous notion, and Elissa laugh-sobs as she con-templates it. Reaching for her rucksack, she unzips the main pocket. The first thing she feels is Monkey. Hauling him out, she presses his tummy to her face and breathes him in. He smells of home, of bed, of all things good. Best of all, his presence means she's no longer alone.

'We're going to get out of this,' she whispers, face still buried in his softness. 'You just see.'

Propping him in her lap, Elissa delves back into the rucksack. This time, her hand closes around her Evian bottle. She drags it out, fingers working at the cap. It pings away into the dark. She gulps down water, choking as it lubricates her throat. Until now, she had no idea how thirsty she was. Elissa nearly drains the bottle before she realizes her mistake. With a lurch, she pulls her mouth away. Precious water spills down her dress. How long might she have to wait before she can drink again? How utterly *idiotic* to consume her supply with no thought to the future. It's her first error, but it's a serious one. Shaking the bottle, gauging its weight, she knows that, at best, she has only a mouthful of water left. She reaches out with her left hand, hunting for the bottle cap. She recalls it bouncing away. Perhaps it rolled beyond her chain.

In chess, when Elissa makes a mistake that results in a loss, she's learned not to punish herself too harshly, nor analyse her shortcomings too deeply. There's a time for that, but it comes much later. Right now, it's essential she maintains confidence in her ability to cope. Perhaps, if she reduces her situation to the abstraction of a chess match, she might just find a way through. So, instead of berating herself for her lack of discipline, she acknowledges the error and casts it aside. Carefully, she places the bottle on a level part of the floor.

With both hands free, Elissa resumes her search of the rucksack. She touches her bag of Stauntons and hauls it out. Beneath it she finds her two books, along with her notebook and gel pens. Right at the bottom, under the bag of home-made banana chips, she finds a satsuma, squashed but still whole. The temptation to eat the fruit is almost irresistible, but she controls the urge and places it back. The rucksack's rear pocket offers a final gift, and it's a good one: the Marks and Spencer brownie, still in its polythene wrapping.

Elissa has food, and she has a means of keeping herself hydrated. Already, her situation is far better than she'd first assumed. Her next priority is a full examination of her surroundings, mapping every square centimetre of the floor. Using the iron ring as her centre point, she begins a fingertip search. Sharp nubs of rock press at her knees. But she has a task, now, a focus.

In her mind, Elissa forms an empty chessboard, each square measuring the distance between her elbow and middle fingertip. She labels them in the traditional manner, placing the iron ring at the centre of the cross formed by D4, E4, D5 and E5. Methodically, beginning at D5, the upper-left square of the central four, she populates them with what she finds: nothing at all in those except dirt and chiselled rock. From there she moves out to the twelve surrounding squares. At F5, she finds a pool of cold vomit. The pillow that supported her head lies in F4. It's miserably thin – the down is compressed into clotted lumps and the slip smells strongly of mildew. Still, it's better than nothing, and she resolves to look after it. The remaining ten squares of the circuit are empty, except for a patch of foul-smelling slime at C4 that Elissa refuses to investigate too closely.

With the second tier of squares searched and their contents itemized, she moves on to the third, starting at B7. Along the top row, comprising six spaces, she finds an area of flat ground that feels like concrete. As a place to lie down, it's a better prospect than where she first woke.

The upper-right flank of this expanded grid, from G7 down to G5, is as empty as the central four squares. At G4, she finds another patch of drying vomit. The row from B2 to G2 offers nothing of use, but at B3 she finds something surprising.

III

The first item is a bucket, made of hard plastic. One part of the rim is gently contoured, forming a spout from which its contents can be poured. The handle is wire, slightly thicker than a coat hanger. A cylindrical sleeve, also plastic, threads it halfway along. The bucket itself is dry and smells new. At the bottom Elissa finds a single roll of toilet paper.

Her stomach clenches. This is the first clear evidence that her jailer intends to keep her a while. Once again, she refuses to be overcome. Soon, the Evian will work its way through her system. Now, at least, she has found somewhere for it to go. She might be caged like an animal, but she won't have to behave like one.

The second item in B3 is an identical bucket. This one's been filled to capacity with a cold liquid, its surface bearded with bubbles. It smells like cleaning solution: something stronger than Fairy Liquid but not as abrasive as bleach. Floor cleaner, perhaps, or a general-purpose disinfectant.

From B3, Elissa works her way up the rest of the column, dragging her chain as she goes, refusing to consider anything except her immediate task. At B7, in the top-left corner of the tier, she pauses once more. This far from the iron ring, she's at the limit of her chain. Stretching out, she uses her feet to explore the furthest spaces of her constructed board.

At A8, her foot touches a wall. Elissa can tell, from the sound her shoe makes, that it's stone. Slithering on her belly, she follows the wall to H8, where it continues past her reach. Working her way down that column, trying not to scuff her knees on slivers of protruding rock, she comes to H7. There, her foot discovers a collection of little objects. With her heel, she hooks them into G7, where she can better examine them.

The first item, constructed of glazed ceramic, is impossible to identify. Its base resembles a steep-sided saucer from which rises a moulding like a honey pot. The top flares outwards, forming a second saucer smaller than the first. In the centre is a raised socket. A curved handle connects the upper and lower sections.

Elissa's hands move blindly across the surface, hunting for further clues. The underside is the only area unglazed. She thinks something's been scratched there – perhaps the potter's initials – but they're too faint to identify by touch.

Placing it down, she investigates the other items removed from H7: a box of matches and a larger box containing dinner candles. Immediately, the glazed pot's purpose becomes clear: it's a holder, the upper dish designed to catch drips of wax.

Lifting a candle to her nose, Elissa inhales. The wax smell triggers memories of Christmas. Last year, they had a box of these at home – dark-green ones they burned in pewter candlesticks at each end of the mantelpiece. On Christmas Day they put them on the table. Elissa recalls the dinner with her Nana and Grandad, the conversation and laughter.

Now, with memories of that day swelling in her mind, she hunches over, arms wrapped around her head. She begins to weep, and all her tears are for her mum, and her grandparents, and what they'll have to endure thanks to the deviant who snatched her. At some point, still curled foetus-like, she slumps on to her side. When her last, weary shudders dissipate, she closes her eyes and sleeps.

IV

An urge to pee awakens her. At first, she doesn't remember what's happened, where she is, or why it's so dark. Far too soon her awareness floods back, along with recollections of her new world: the manacle; the chain; the buckets; the matches and candles. Something has changed in here, while she's been sleeping, but she can't work out what.

Has night fallen? Has her jailer visited? Is there a breeze, now, where earlier, there was none?

With a lurch, Elissa wonders whether she's being observed. The darkness is absolute, so if anyone *is* watching, they must be using special equipment. She slows her breathing, straining to listen. The silence is that of a vault; she cannot even detect the earlier drip of water.

The discomfort in her bladder grows. Soon, it's all she can think about. Calling up her mental chessboard, she crawls to the waste bucket in B3 and rises to a crouch. Warily, she straightens. It's the first time she's tried to stand. She's relieved to find there's enough space.

With her unshackled hand, Elissa reaches under her dress and tugs down her underwear. She scowls into the darkness. If someone *is* watching, let them get an eyeful if they want: she can think of few things more pathetic than a man who gets his kicks from spying on girls peeing into buckets.

For a moment her anger burns white hot. 'You're a dick bag,' she hisses. 'A stupid, worthless *dick* bag.' It's not the worst insult she knows, but she won't demean herself with something fouler.

The bucket might slip if she puts all her weight on it, so after removing the toilet roll, she rolls up her dress and gathers it together. Then, squatting, she holds her breath.

Initially, despite her aching bladder, Elissa is unable to go. Just as she's about to give up, her muscles relax and she hears the urgent rattle of urine against hard plastic. It sounds like she's spraying seeds or pellets, but the smell is eye-watering, unmistakable. Left alone, the air will grow thick with it, so after pulling up her knickers she goes to the second bucket and pours some of the cleaning solution into the first. All this she does blind. The chain tethering her to the floor scrapes and clinks, a constant companion.

Calling up her schematic, she crawls across the floor to G7, avoiding the pool of cold vomit at F5. She'll have to deal with that soon, before its stench grows any stronger. First, though, a little light.

Elissa pauses at F6, one square from her destination. If the candles and matches have gone, it'll mean someone visited while she was asleep. Abruptly, a more frightening thought surfaces: What if, when she reaches out, she touches some part of her abductor? A warm foot, perhaps. Or a hand.

Her skin crawls. She's never had a wild imagination. This is the last place on earth she should cultivate one. Fearing that paralysis will strike if she delays, Elissa lunges forward, arm outstretched. The movement is clumsy, spasmodic. Her knuckles strike the candle holder and it skitters across the floor.

Idiot!

Reining herself in, Elissa reaches out once again. If she's knocked away the candles or matches, she really will lose it. Fortunately, she finds both boxes right where she left them. Shaking out a candle, she lifts it to her nose. If she hadn't acted so rashly, she'd have somewhere to set it down. Instead, she grips it between her knees. Then, holding the matchbox with her shackled hand, she removes a match.

Elissa pauses to catch her breath. The moment she strikes this light, the full gravity of her situation will become clear. There's a good chance she'll discover something horrifying. Already, some strange inkling of intuition tells her she's not the first resident of this hole. Perhaps the light will reveal something of her predecessors' fates. So far, she's managed to maintain a tiny flame of hope. Ironic if the next one she creates extinguishes it.

Still, she has to know. Knowledge is power, and although her power here is almost non-existent, she's duty-bound to try and increase it. Right now, she's panting for breath, which means she might snuff out the match before it can take. To calm herself, she decides to inventory the contents of each box. After half a minute of steady breathing, Elissa's counted ten candles and thirty-seven wooden matches.

She recalls something she learned at Christmas, from the box of dinner candles her mum bought: each stick, with dimensions almost exactly matching these, had an eight-hour burn time. It means she has the potential, here, for eighty hours of continuous light. The candles offer something else, too, should she wish: a means to measure time.

With a rasp and a hiss, her match flares into life. At first, the light's so bright that she's forced to shield her eyes, but she can't afford to waste it. Quickly, she touches it to the wick.

The flame dips so low she thinks it'll go out. It bobs, a watchful blue eye, and then it takes. A yellow light swells. The darkness recedes.

Elissa holds up the candle and looks around.

V

The first thing she ascertains is that she's alone.

No one lurks outside the limits of her chain. Neither does she see any remains of previous residents – earlier, she was so worried by that prospect she could hardly acknowledge it.

Before her stands the stone wall she discovered while lying on her belly. Looking around, she sees the other walls that form her cell. Two are identical to the first. The fourth is constructed from plywood sheeting. A door has been cut into it, but there's no handle on this side, just a few deep scratches that look deliberate. Above her head, the ceiling's pine planking appears newer than the stone walls.

Overall, the cell's dimensions aren't much larger than the virtual chessboard she created to map it – she needs just three extra columns and four extra rows. She can either resize her board to fit the revealed floor space, or adopt the additional columns and rows into an expanded grid.

Elissa chooses the latter. It'll cause a few oddities with her naming conventions. The new column to the right of H will be I, but she designates the columns to the left of A as Y and Z. Likewise, the four new rows beneath 1 become 0, −1, −2 and −3. This results in corner points at Y8, I8, Y−3 and I−3. As a reference system, it's needlessly complicated, but at least it'll give her brain a workout.

While there's no way of proving it, she thinks she's underground. The floor has an excavated look. The walls seem like the foundations of a larger structure above her head.

For the first time, she sees the colours of the objects she found in darkness. The waste bucket at B3 is cherry red. The cleaning bucket is black. The candles are white and the glazed ceramic holder, which rolled into I8, is a dark and musty green.

One thing Elissa would prefer *not* to see is the gunk in C4 – brownish-red, definitely organic. Nothing about it gives her confidence. Deliberately, she turns away, finding the twin pools of vomit at F5. Beside them is the pillow. It's damp-looking and tatty. The faded case features yellow flowers on an orange background. They don't make designs like that these days – the thing must be forty years old.

Elissa's stomach grips with hunger. Standing, she crosses the floor to her rucksack, awkwardly dragging her chain. A dribble of molten wax rolls on to her knuckles. The pain is intense, but she doesn't drop the candle. With her free hand, she empties the pack, stacking her belongings and placing Monkey on top. 'Don't worry,' she tells him. 'I have a plan.'

Casting the empty rucksack like a fishing net, she drags the holder within reach and plugs in her candle. Only then does she pick the hardened wax from her knuckles, tucking the loose flakes into the matchbox. Everything in this room has a currency. She won't waste a thing.

Now, to the brownie. Elissa opens the wrapper slowly, careful not to destroy it. Easing out the snack like toothpaste from a tube, she takes a small bite – no more than an eighth of what's there – and puts the rest away, folding down the cellophane to retain as much moisture as possible.

She chews greedily. The urge to take another bite is almost all-consuming, but she resists, repacking the rucksack with the brownie at the bottom and retreating as far as her chain will allow. There she stands, bending her legs and lifting her feet, exercising her muscles as best she can.

Abruptly, Elissa decides to do something about the vomit, and drags the wash bucket across the cell. She doesn't have a sponge or cloth, so before indecision paralyses her she unzips her dress. The compulsion to clean has filled her head. Everything else recedes.

Struggling so frantically that she almost rips the dress, Elissa peels off her cotton vest. There's no way to free it from the chain connecting her to the iron ring, but she doesn't care about that. Dunking it in the bucket, she slops cleaning solution over the floor. Elissa works with an empty head, sluicing and scrubbing, squeezing and swilling. By the time she's finished, she's used up far more of the solution than she'd intended and the front of her dress is soaked.

Worse, she's shivering. It's colder in here than she first thought. Without her vest, the chill is far more acute. As the fog of her mania lifts, she realizes the extent of her foolishness. How could she have rated a clean cell over basic warmth? There's no way she can wear her vest again until it dries; and in here that might take for ever. Dismayed at just how badly she has hobbled herself, she wrings it out as best she can.

Miserable, Elissa huddles on her knees. Holding out her hands to the candle flame, she focuses on her breathing until her shivers begin to subside. Around her, shadows dance like slinking wolves.

Then she hears something that originates not in this room but beyond it – the sound, unmistakable, of metal bolts being drawn.

VI

For a moment, all thought abandons her. Like a wild animal, she charges away from the door. One foot kicks over the candle holder, plunging the chamber into darkness. Her chain snaps taut. The manacle bites her wrist, yanking her off her feet.

The pain is *brutal*. Convulsing, Elissa curls into a ball. She clenches her eyes shut, telling herself that if he thinks she's asleep she'll be safe, that he won't hurt her.

With a squeal of rubber seals, the door swings open. Through closed eyelids, Elissa sees a pinkish glow and knows a torch beam is swabbing the room. It settles on her face, and even though her breathing is ragged she tries to feign sleep, forcing her shoulders to rise and fall in long, deliberate movements.

Finally, serrating the darkness, comes her jailer's voice: a whisper, still, but no less sharp because of it. 'I know you're awake. There'll never be anything, ever in this life, that you can conceal from me. Take as long as you need to learn that lesson, but for your own comfort I'd advise haste.'

In the ensuing silence, Elissa hears nothing but the rush of her blood. For the first time she notices a smell: not the sickening sweetness of spoiled poultry but the richness of cooked food.

'When one has a visitor it's polite to acknowledge them, or did your mother never teach you that?' her jailer asks. 'Time to open your eyes, Elissa Mirzoyan, and see what is true.'

He won't be fooled, so there's no point maintaining the pretence. And yet she cannot prise her eyes open.

'I brought you something to eat,' he says, after a long silence. 'Something to drink, too.' His tone has changed: there's a scratch of displeasure that wasn't there before. 'By your silence, I assume you don't want it. No matter. It'll be interesting to see how quickly you remember your manners. Perhaps a little fasting will hasten their return.'

Elissa hears the scrape of his heels. Moments later, the soundproofed door thump-whooshes as it closes. The dead-bolts rattle home.

Immediately, her eyes spring open.

It'll be interesting to see how quickly you remember your manners. Perhaps a little fasting will hasten their return.

Does that mean he'll be gone an hour? A day?

A week?

Elissa sits up straight in the darkness. Her right wrist throbs. When she touches it, her shriek of agony bounces off the walls – the pain is extraordinary, as if she's brushed a raw nerve. There's a wetness there, an *openness*, that's terrifying. Just now, when she scrambled away from the door, the manacle's sharp edge bit into her flesh. The damage is far, far worse than she'd thought.

Supporting her metal cuff, she tries to locate the overturned candle holder. Adrenalin has fried her brain. For a while, she's so jittery she can't even call up her mental chessboard. Her muscles twitch, stray pulses of electricity sending them into spasm. Fireflies dance before her eyes. Disoriented, she crawls back to the iron hoop. Even then, she can't calculate her facing. Is the door to her left or her right? The lack of clarity is paralysing. For long minutes she kneels before her sunken anchor, as if it's a totem from which she can receive guidance.

Finally, an idea breaks through the chaos of her thoughts. The four squares that surround the ring might be empty, but if she can find the soaked floor from F5 to G4, she can realign herself. Within moments she does exactly that. Slowly, a little of her composure returns. Holding the manacle clear of her injured wrist, she begins an exhaustive re-examination of the floor.

At B7, overturned but miraculously unbroken, she finds the holder. The candle itself has rolled loose, so she crawls to G7, lights a new one and screws it into the dish.

Once again, the shadows retreat. This time, the bobbing yellow light reveals something ghastly: her right arm, from fingertips to elbow, is entirely sleeved in blood. The manacle has cut her wrist almost to the bone, the flesh parting like a set of red lips. Blood flows freely from the mouth, dripping to the floor in heavy spatters.

In the movies, when someone suffers an injury, they tear a strip from their clothing to bind the wound. But Elissa can't tear her dress. Either the fabric's too strong or she's too weak.

Her vest lies near the iron ring, filthy and wet. She daren't use it as a binding. When she casts around for alternatives, she notices something she'd missed until now: her rucksack, in which she'd stashed the food and the last of her water, has vanished.

Cold, hungry and in pain, she'd thought her situation could grow no bleaker. And now it has; immeasurably so. As well as her food and drink, she's lost her Stauntons, her books, her notepad and pens. Worst of all is the loss of Monkey. However hard she tries to tell herself he was just a knitted sack, she can't dismiss what he represented. Inanimate or not, he was her companion in this. Now that he's gone, she's truly alone.

Huddling close to the candle, Elissa listens to the slow drip of her blood and her stomach's empty gurgle. Really, she should blow out the light and conserve her supply, but who knows how much longer she'll possess it? Earlier, she'd scolded herself for drinking so much water. Now, she's glad she did. She thinks of her mum, and when that becomes too painful she thinks of Monkey; and when *that* becomes too painful she closes her eyes and thinks of nothing at all.

VII

In the end, it's not a week before her jailer returns, perhaps not even a day, but it's a lot longer than a few hours. In his absence, her tongue has become a blister. By the time she hears the clatter of deadbolts, only a finger's width of the candle remains unburned. Its flame wobbles as the door squeals open.

This time, despite her pounding heart, Elissa doesn't rush for the cell's far corner. Instead, she remains beside the guttering candle and lifts her head. Doing so takes every ounce of her will, but she wants her jailer to know she's unbroken. All her life, her mum has taught her to be strong. This deviant might have stolen her freedom. He won't trample her spirit.

Through the open doorway shines the yellow cone of a torch beam. Elissa squints, tries to peer past it, but everything outside its arc is as black as night. Her jailer's feet scuff across the uneven floor. They pause somewhere in Y3, just outside the reach of her chain.

For a moment she wonders: Is he as frightened of her as she is of him? It's a ridiculous thought, and she dismisses it immediately. Currently, only one person holds the power in this relationship.

The beam lingers on her a while longer. Then it roves around the room, pausing on the buckets at B3, the water stains from F5 to G4, the pillow, the lit candle, the matches, the filthy vest.

Moments later, Elissa finds herself spinning in fresh turbulence, because somehow – contrary to all her expectations – the voice she hears next belongs not to her jailer, but to another.

It falters, high-pitched, and for a crazy instant she thinks of Ethan Bandercroft from school, and the romance she knows will never blossom. It *isn't* Ethan, of course: this voice, although mellifluous, is far less self-assured.

There's something about it, too. Something that makes water of her insides.

ELIJAH

Day 6

I

Throwing myself down, I press my tummy to the floor, but it's already far too late. If the 4x4's driver looked up at my window, I'll have been plainly silhouetted. Everyone on the estate knows this is my bedroom. The driver will know what I've seen.

I think of the copper halfpennies on my pillow: two watchful eyes. The message was clear, and already it'll seem like I've ignored it. But I can't turn back the clock – either on my presence at the window or on events beneath the Gingerbread House.

My heart knocks against the floorboards. It's a horrible reminder of my mortality and it triggers fresh thoughts of Gretel, and everything the poor girl endured. Outside, I hear the loose rattle of the 4x4's exhaust as the vehicle bounces along the track. Gradually, the sound fades.

Climbing to my feet, I snatch at the pull-cord above the bed. Darkness rushes over me. Once my eyes adjust, I step back to the window. Now, the land out there is deathly still – no evidence of humanity, or what passes for it.

Was the vehicle I saw Meunier's Land Rover? I can think of no reason for him to visit that part of the estate so late. Other than the Memory Wood, all that lies in that direction is Knucklebone Lake.

If the late-night traveller wasn't Meunier, perhaps it was one of the drifters from Wheel Town. I know some of them practise a little poaching at this time of year – more than once, among the trees, I've found baited traps or snares. How much of that is down to Kyle, I don't know, but it can't all be my brother's work. Last time I visited Magic Annie I saw no 4x4s parked up, but some of the Wheel Town vehicles are kept under tarps, including the van Kyle used as target practice, until he was made to stop. Like most things around here, a lot remains hidden.

Has Gretel been replaced so quickly? The thought sickens me, but almost as sickening is my undeniable prickle of excitement, my grief at her passing – and my sorrow at another taking – offset by the prospect of a new friend. If the worst has happened, at least I'll have a purpose again. It's pointless to dwell on how the last friendship ended in failure, because they always do.

I think of a story Magic Annie once told me, this one not as brutal as the foxes that fell into a pit. It was about Robert the Bruce, who became King of Scots in 1306. After fighting the English six times and losing, he escaped to the island of Rathlin. Holed up in a cave, he watched a spider try repeatedly to weave its web, succeeding on the seventh attempt. Inspired, Bruce returned to his homeland, where he won his next battle.

I'm no Scottish king, but I do what I can for those who

wake beneath the Memory Wood. Right now, despite my fear of what lurks outside, I feel myself compelled.

Put on the full armour of God, so that you can take your stand against the devil's schemes.

As always, it's easier to read the Bible than to obey it. I don't want to return to the Memory Wood tonight, certainly not to the Gingerbread House, but I know that I must.

From my Collection of Keepsakes and Weird Finds, I retrieve the padlock key. I slip it into my pyjama pocket and feel around for my torch. When I can't find it straight away, my heart begins to thump. Has someone discovered my collection and rooted through it? Of all my treasures, I can't imagine that a cheap plastic torch would interest anyone. Then I recall my last visit to the cellar in the woods; the spinning shadows as my torch slipped from my fingers; the darkness and my sudden panic.

I left it there, didn't I? Left it right where I dropped it. For a while, the memory freezes me rigid. How could I have been so *careless*? How could I have ignored all the lessons I've learned to cover my tracks? If I had reason to return to the cottage before, I have twice the reason now, but I can barely bring myself to climb off my bed.

Feeling for my clothes, I dress before I can change my mind.

I I

Out in the hallway, tiptoeing towards the stairs, it's impossible to keep my movements silent. Each floorboard creaks like it's trying to wake the dead.

Passing my parents' room, I hear their snores and peek inside.

I'm amazed at how vulnerable they look. So easy for someone to creep in and slash their throats while they sleep. *That's* a terrible thought, and yet I can't shake it. I want to slip under the covers and worm between them, but there's far too much at stake.

When I step past their door, towards the stairs, I realize with a lurch that somehow I've turned myself around and am heading back to my own room. The discovery unbalances me. Putting a hand to the wall, I wait for my dizziness to fade.

Now, another thought strikes me. How did my parents fall asleep so quickly? Only a handful of minutes have passed since they were in my room, and yet here they are, deep in slumber. How did they manage to wash, change into their nightclothes and climb into bed, all in such a short space of time?

Did *I* fall asleep? Moments after they walked out, I saw the coins on my pillow. I remember scooping them up and flinging them into the garden. Straight after that, I saw the 4x4.

My scalp contracts. It's not the first time I've suffered a lapse like this. Shaking my head, I hurry down the stairs. When I open the front door and emerge, blinking, into bright sunlight, I can hardly catch my breath. Somehow, day has replaced night. Not only that, I'm wearing different clothes – shorts and T-shirt instead of jumper and jeans. The only constant is the key in my pocket – the key that will unlock the door beneath the Gingerbread House and take me right back to my first meeting with Gretel.

MAIRÉAD

Day 1

I

It's not much of a break, but it's something. Police officers sent to the Royal Princess, a smart thirties-built hotel a few hundred yards from the Marshall Court, notice that one of its security cameras has a direct view of East Overcliff Drive.

They quickly review the footage. Between 14.10 and 14.18 – from Elissa's last known sighting until two minutes after the first emergency call – fourteen white vans pass the hotel. Most are shiny new models. Only a handful could be reliably described as 'old and pretty beat-up'. Due to the camera angle, officers can't make out registration numbers, but they snap images of the vans and forward them to colleagues at the Marshall Court. Within a few minutes, Charles Kiser positively IDs one of them.

The vehicle's an old Bedford CF, a British-built panel van manufactured between 1969 and 1988. Mairéad's older colleagues are familiar with it: back in the eighties, CFs were commonly used as prisoner transports and riot vans.

This one, somebody tells her, looks like the updated model introduced in 1980. There can't be more than a few hundred left on the road.

Because the council has no operational cameras on East Overcliff Drive, the officers at Bournemouth's CCTV control room have so far drawn a blank. But now they have a specific vehicle to hunt, and within ten minutes they get their first reward: at 14.15, a camera on St Swithun's Road recorded the van heading north.

Now, they have a number plate too. It's immediately punched into ANPR, the national network of number-plate-recognition cameras. Almost instantly, the system detects the suspect van and shows its route: straight up the A338 to Downton, six miles south of Salisbury, where it disappears. From Bournemouth, the journey takes thirty-seven minutes. The last camera captures the van at 14.52.

In the investigation team, there's a palpable shift of mood. Everybody knows that thirty-seven minutes driving is thirty-seven minutes where Elissa Mirzoyan probably hasn't been assaulted, probably hasn't been killed.

It's now 15.40. They're less than one hour behind again, but that forty-eight-minute lead means the van could be anywhere in a circle covering ten thousand square miles. And with every minute that passes, the circumference of the circle expands.

Neighbouring forces scramble to offer assistance. Traffic police equipped with mobile ANPR flood major roads inside the perimeter. NPAS helicopters are launched from Bournemouth, Almondsbury and Benton. Meanwhile, a check of the DVLA database shows that the Bedford's number plate is linked to a different vehicle altogether: a Vauxhall Corsa registered to a seventy-eight-year-old woman in Waterlooville,

Hampshire. PCSOs visit her bungalow, where they find the bemused woman, and also her car.

Across the country, airports, train stations and ferry ports are placed on high alert. In Salisbury, officers who drove Lena Mirzoyan home locate Elissa's passport.

At 16.00, Mairéad holds her first press conference. Beforehand, she goes to the toilet and vomits. Conscious of her shocking appearance, she dusts her face with powder and pencils out the redness around her eyes.

Journalists pack the briefing room. Cameras beep and flash. Mairéad explains the timeline, shares further pictures of Elissa and blown-up stills of the van. She explains the route it took, its last-known location, and appeals directly to the public for information. Afterwards, she takes questions, answering as many as she can.

Over two hours have now passed since Elissa disappeared. Everyone knows what that means. She sees it in the eyes of the gathered journalists and afterwards in the faces of her own team. That image – of Elissa larking around in a red feather boa – haunts her throughout.

At 18.10, she updates the media again. By now, the story's developed its own inertia. The press conference is broadcast live on Sky News and the BBC. No, they haven't found Elissa. No, they've no further leads on the van. Yes, they're trawling DVLA records, but the database for model-types of long-defunct manufacturers is shot to shit.

An hour passes. Two more. Soon it's 22.00.

A major incident room is established. Everyone looks forsaken. It's Mairéad's responsibility to maintain morale, but it's desperately hard. The earlier momentum has all but drained away. This remains a missing-person investigation. How long before it becomes homicide?

II

At 01.00, Mairéad concedes she needs sleep. After an update with Karen Day, the PolSA she requested from Winfrith, she formally hands over to her OIC and goes outside to her car. Her stomach is cramping; her head thumps with fatigue. Her flesh feels like an army of insects is crawling around under the skin.

She stops at a twenty-four-hour pharmacy, then heads home. Scott is up, pacing about. He shakes his head when she staggers in.

'It had to be me,' she says softly. 'It had to be.'

Her husband stares at her a long time before answering. 'Hon,' he says. 'You can't do this. You can't.' His tone is far more forgiving than she deserves. 'You're in no fit state to take it on.'

A lump forms in her throat. 'She's thirteen, Scott. I met her mum. The woman's going out of her mind.'

His shoulders slump. And now he just looks weary, miserable. 'What about you?' he asks. 'What about—'

'I can handle this.'

'That's not the—'

'I can *handle* it!'

She didn't mean to shout. And now, suddenly, she can't look at him. Throwing down her coat, she hurries up the stairs. In the bathroom, behind a locked door, she perches on the toilet. When she closes her eyes, she sees a girl in a red feather boa. She recalls Lena Mirzoyan's words in the hotel manager's office: *This is Elissa. My daughter. My life.*

Mairéad's mouth fills with saliva. She wheels around, yanking up the toilet seat just in time. Watery bile spatters against porcelain. Her stomach spasms, again and again. Her eyes feel like they'll pop right out of her skull.

Afterwards, unfastening her bag, she takes out her pharmacy purchases: ten Clearblue pregnancy tests.

Mairéad opens the bathroom cabinet. She stacks nine of the boxes inside. The tenth one she opens. Pulling down her underwear, she sits on the toilet. At first, it's difficult to pee. Eventually, her bladder lets go. She places the Clearblue's tip in the flow and counts to five. Then she replaces the cap.

Now, the wait. Three minutes, according to the leaflet.

Mairéad can hardly breathe. She balances the kit on the side of the bath. Standing, she consults the bathroom mirror. A wraith stares back at her. Bloodshot eyes and mushroom skin.

Mairéad's stomach is knotted, but no longer from nausea. This is fear, pure and simple.

Two minutes.

She recalls something else Lena Mirzoyan said: *I know you'll try. All of you – I know you will. But you've got to succeed. You've got to bring her back. Promise me you will. Promise.*

Mairéad knew the dangers, which is why she remained quiet. But the promise, even though it never passed her lips, is implicit.

Outside, a gust of wind shakes the branches of a nearby tree.

Mairéad takes a breath, exhales. She wonders what Lena Mirzoyan is doing right now. A Dorset-based Family Liaison Officer accompanied the woman home and will stay there until the Wiltshire force appoints someone local.

But however many people are with Lena right now, she'll still feel desolate.

One minute.

Mairéad looks at her watch: 01.26. Sunday morning already. Over eleven hours since Elissa was taken. If the investigation team had discovered anything, they would have shared it.

She examines the Clearblue test. On the LCD display, a tiny hourglass is winking. Her chest feels empty, as if everything's been scooped out.

The hourglass disappears. A message appears.

Pregnant   3+ weeks

Mairéad takes a shuddering breath. She reads the message again, up close this time, just to make sure she's got it right. Three-plus weeks is as accurate as the test can go, but she knows she's closer to nine.

In the corner of the bathroom is a foot-pedal bin. Mairéad prods it with her toe. The lid jumps up, revealing a magpie's nest of discarded Clearblue kits. More are stacked along the windowsill.

It's a terrible waste of money and plastic. But in the eight years they've been trying for a baby, Mairéad's miscarried twelve times.

No one's ever been able to tell her why. It's not hormonal. It's not genetic. She suffers no uterine problems or cervical weakness. Once, one of the many highly paid specialists she's consulted told her she's simply been unlucky. But to Mairéad – and, she knows, to Scott – it feels like a lot more than bad luck. It feels like a tragedy.

Of her twelve failed pregnancies, only three progressed

past six weeks. None of them ever went past eight. Which means that *this* life, cupped like a flower petal inside her womb, faces odds as desperate as those of the girl she's trying to find.

Mairéad thinks of Scott and how he must be feeling, knowing the scale of the task she's just taken on. But if she can't save Elissa Mirzoyan, what chance can she offer this tiny bundle of cells? Perhaps, if she can rebuild one family, she'll get to build one of her own.

It's a terrible thought. She tries in vain to dismiss it.

Downstairs, the TV comes on. Sounds of gunfire and screaming echo up the stairs.

Mairéad stares at the Clearblue kit with a terrible, clutching foreboding.

ELIJAH

Day 3

I

The afternoon that I first meet Elissa, I'm walking through the Memory Wood with no idea of how much my life's about to change.

I'm heading nowhere in particular when I stumble across them: four dark furrows that twist between the trees. They're tyre marks, and it's obvious where they lead. Obvious, too, that something out-of-the-ordinary has happened.

There's no vehicle parked outside the ruined cottage when I arrive, but that's where the tracks converge: one set made on arrival, one set on departure. Magpies caw on the cottage roof. Their calls seem like an invitation: *Elijah, come and see, come and see, come and see.*

Studying the trees and what lies between them, I see no sign of anyone else. Kyle could be watching, but I don't feel that weird itch between my shoulder blades that sometimes signals he's close.

As I step into the clearing there's a commotion to my right. A muntjac springs from the undergrowth and zig-zags in front of me, eyes showing white. I brace for the sound of my brother's rifle, but all I hear is scrabbling hooves as the deer disappears into the trees. My heart, now, is galloping out of control. A minute passes before I'm calm enough to approach the cottage's front door.

Can my hunch about those tyre marks be right? Can the cellar really have a new resident?

The building's dead eyes look hostile. Up on the roof, the magpies' cries sound less invitational than before. I know it's my mind playing tricks, the part that wants to investigate fighting the part that does not.

At the threshold, just like it always does, my curiosity wins out. The need to discover what prize fate has plonked into my lap is irresistible. I think of the crow with the broken wing that Papa nursed back to health. Perhaps, down in the cellar, I'll find my own chance for redemption. Just like the time before. And the time before that.

How many months since Bryony left me, the last resident of this place? It's been so long I've lost count.

It's dark in the hall. I pass the living room, where an ash tree has burst through the floor, and sidle past the old dresser. I feel as if I'm gliding above the floor rather than walking upon it. In the kitchen, I barely see the spreading ivy before I'm through the pantry door and drifting down the stone steps into darkness. My last image is of the pickling jars that line the shelves, their murky contents like foetuses in a museum collection.

The steps double-back. Soon I'm at the bottom. I draw out my torch and switch it on. Before me stands the sound-proofed wall with its reinforced door. All three of the deadbolts are in the closed position, the middle one secured by a padlock. I can hear nothing from the other side.

On the floor, pressed into the dirt, is a single footprint. When I hover my shoe over it, the similarity in size is uncanny. A rash of goosebumps tightens my skin. Is this evidence that the cellar has a new guest? I've been visiting every week for the last six months, but this is the first time I've seen any indication.

There's little else I can glean from the print so I step over it. At the door, I lift my hand to the topmost deadbolt and draw it back. I repeat the move with the bottom bolt. There I pause, flashing the torch behind me. If it shines on Kyle's face, I'll drop dead from a stopped heart, but my brother is nowhere in sight.

Convinced, now, that my inkling is correct, I take out my key and slide it into the padlock. One turn, a click. I drop the lock into my pocket and draw back the last bolt.

Here we are, then. On the cusp of another adventure. They always end the same, but at the beginning – like now – there's often some semblance of hope.

I clear my throat, mentally rehearsing my greeting. First impressions count, even down here in the dark. The rubber seal squeals as the door swings open. Holding my breath, I step through.

II

The first thing I notice is not the girl but the candle – its flickering yellow flame. It'll reveal me if I'm not careful, so quickly I raise my torch, aiming its beam at her eyes. It's unkind but unavoidable – until I know more about this newcomer and her nature, it's vital that I protect myself. I still remember the time I was attacked in here, in the days before the iron ring.

The girl flinches from my light. Then she steadies herself and lifts her chin. Her eyes, narrowed against the glare, are as vivid and green as polished emeralds.

She's nothing like I expected.

They never are.

Silent, I play the beam over the rest of her. My skin tingles as I follow the light. This pause before speaking is magical, a spell I'm reluctant to break. Here, at the start, so much of our relationship is unexplored. My knowledge of her – *our* knowledge of *each other* – is limited purely to what we see. And so far, blinded by my torch, *she* sees nothing at all.

Those green eyes draw me in. Considering them, I want to believe that this time will be different, that everything will turn out all right, that I'll be able to save her from the future she's been dealt.

Her black hair is mussed, damp where it touches her skin. She has what Magic Annie would call Celtic features: high forehead, sharp nose and chin. Her skin is pale, but whether that's natural or because of what's happened to her, I can't tell. She's a little older than me: perhaps a year, perhaps two.

When I spot the manacle on her wrist my heart nearly breaks. Blood has dried in a crust around a deep wound just above it. More blood, fresh and glistening, seeps between the clots. I wonder if she was trying to free herself. If so, she won't have any luck – not unless she smashes her hand to a pulp and pulls it, wet and flaccid, through her restraint.

Flaccid is the word for a body part hanging loosely or limply, especially if it looks gross.

Silent a moment longer, I cast around the room. I see the buckets, fresh candles, a matchbox. There's a wet patch on the floor, near the stinky pillow. The air smells bad. Wrinkling my nose, I try to ignore it. To do otherwise would be rude.

'Hi,' I say, returning my torch beam to her face. 'What's your name?'

The girl's green eyes flare. Her jaw drops open and she scrambles up. It's obvious she was expecting a different voice. I can only imagine the thoughts now rushing through her head.

'I'm Elissa,' she croaks. 'Elissa Mirzoyan. Please – get help. Before he finds you here.'

I've discovered, in these first moments, that it's wise to hold a few things back. I'm not deceitful by nature – at least, that's what Mama says – but trust is built gradually or not at all.

'Before who finds me?' I ask, taking a forward step. I'm still in the safe zone. If she rushes towards the light, the chain will pull her up short. I hope she doesn't try it. The damage to her wrist would be terrible. More importantly, I want this – us – to *work*.

Her throat bobs. 'I don't know. I was in Bournemouth. A chess tournament. He pulled me into a van. Drugged me, brought me here, put this thing on my wrist. Please – it's not safe. You've got to go before he gets back, call the police and tell them I'm here. That you found me, Elissa Mirzoyan, that I'm alive, that I was taken by a man driving a white van with a skull sticker on the bumper, a skull with a hat and a cigarette.'

Her shoulders sag. She sucks in a shuddering breath.

CHILLAX, I think, and wince.

'Are you hurt?'

She shakes her head. 'Not yet. But something bad's going to happen. Unless you get me out.'

I adjust the angle of my torch. 'Your wrist—'

'It's nothing. Just a gash.'

'It's more than a gash. All that blood—'

'Seriously, there are worse things. Can you—'

'My name's Elijah,' I say, and flinch. I hadn't meant to tell her so soon. 'How old are you?'

She blinks, those green fires extinguished then relit. I know she wants me gone, running through the Memory Wood with her message, but she isn't panicking. Not yet.

'Thirteen,' she replies. 'I'm thirteen years old, and my name's Elissa Mirzoyan. *M-I-R-Z-O-Y-A-N*. I live at six, Cloisters Way, in Salisbury. My mum's name is Lena. It doesn't matter if you can't remember all that. Please, just go. Call the police and bring them down here. Tell them *Elissa Mirzoyan* – that you found Elissa Mirzoyan and she's alive.'

I nod, even though she can't see past the beam of my torch. 'You might be a year older than me,' I tell her. 'But Magic Annie says I have a pretty high IQ. I promise I won't forget you. Not ever.'

I see from her reaction that it's a misstep. Something in her expression changes. She draws her injured wrist to her chest.

'Where am I?' she asks.

'Underground.'

'I know that. Where?'

'A cellar. In the Memory Wood.'

'The Memory Wood?'

'That's what I call it. I don't think it has a real name. Least not one anybody remembers.'

She frowns at that. Tries to process it. 'How'd you find me?'

'I was playing. Outside. Thought I'd come down here and explore.'

'You live close?'

'Quite close.'

Elissa screws up her face. 'Could you turn off the torch?'

Her question, like so much of this meeting, catches me off guard. If I do as she asks, the candlelight will reveal me, and that's not something I can allow. I want to save her, but I have to protect myself.

'I . . . don't like the dark,' I tell her, my cheeks growing hot. It's true enough, but it isn't the main reason for my reluctance and so is still a fib of sorts. I hate dishonesty, especially down here. And yet sometimes the truth of a thing is best avoided. At least for a little while.

I watch the rise and fall of her chest. Everything about this feels so finely balanced.

'Will you help me, Elijah?' she asks.

'I want to.'

'Will you go, then? Get the police? Bring them back here so they can release me?'

A few weeks ago, my word of the week was *tenacious*. It suits Elissa perfectly. If I'd been blessed with an older sister, I'd want one exactly like this. I'm so overcome with admiration that for a while I have to look away. I focus on the candle as its flame bobs and weaves.

Once I've mastered my emotions, my attention returns to the girl in chains. 'If you've only just arrived,' I ask, 'then why do you want to leave?'

ELISSA

Day 3

I

His question is so bizarre that for a moment she cannot think.

Elissa opens her mouth, searching for words, for anything that might get this conversation back on track.

She's still thinking when Elijah asks, 'Did he explain the rules?'

It takes the space of two breaths for the full implications of his question to hit. Elissa kicks out her feet, scrambling back. She's halfway across the floor when the chain snaps taut and the manacle chews into her wrist. The pain is sickening. Her scream fills the chamber. Collapsing on to her side, she twists and flops like a cat struck by a car. Blood pulses over her hand. In the grip of that white-hot agony, Elijah's words play over and over.

Did he explain the rules?

There's a pressure in her chest like nothing she's

previously experienced. It feels as if her heart's about to burst. Moments ago, it seemed she'd been thrown a lifeline. No longer.

Elissa clenches her teeth, thinks she might dry-heave. Somehow, she manages to gasp: 'What rules?'

Obscured behind his torch, Elijah sits down. Despite vision blurred by pain and tears, Elissa notes – from the position of the light – that he's settled in C6, easily within the boundary of her chain. She wonders if he knows that. Guesses he probably does.

It hardly matters. She's in no state to fight. And what, anyway, would it achieve? Although he's revealed his involvement, he's disclosed nothing of his intent.

'You're the same age as Bryony,' Elijah says. 'But you don't look like her.'

The pain in her wrist comes in waves. At its peak it smothers her senses.

Time passes. Perhaps five minutes, perhaps an hour. Carefully, Elissa pulls herself upright. 'Bryony,' she says. Her voice sounds like she's speaking through a pillow. 'Is that your sister?'

'Uh-uh. Bryony was my friend. For six whole months. She was pretty, just like you. Except when she was crying, which, towards the end, was quite a lot.'

Elissa's eyes wander to the crimson-brownish stain in C4. 'Was Bryony here?'

Elijah's torch flicks to the door's damaged soundproofing. 'She did that. I told her not to. Told her it'd bring trouble. That's when he sank the hoop. Things got bad after. I was so scared I hardly dared visit.' His throat contracts noisily. 'I'm not a coward. But by then, Bryony . . . She'd turned sorta crazy. Wouldn't listen to anyone, not even me. Still, she got her tree. I made sure of that, even if I couldn't make sure of anything else.'

'Her tree?'

'Picked out a tall one, just like she asked.'

Elissa tries to focus her thoughts. She doesn't have a friend here, not yet, but she senses an opportunity, however small, to create one. 'Why did he bring me here?' she asks. 'What's he going to do?'

II

For a minute or so, Elijah is silent. Then he says: 'Nothing bad. Long as you follow the rules.'

Suddenly, it's an effort to hold up her head. 'What're the rules?'

'They change.'

'Can you tell me who he is?'

'No.'

'Will you help me?'

'As much as I can. I cross my heart.'

She smiles. The effort brings tears to her eyes. 'That's really kind. Really brave, too.'

Elijah's lungs fill, a sound like wind over dead leaves. 'He'll test you. Most people fail.'

'What kind of test?'

'I don't know. But you'll have to figure it out. You won't get a second chance.'

Elissa licks her lips. She glances at her wrist, scarlet and glistening. Wishes she hadn't. 'If I do everything right, will I survive this?'

Behind his light, Elijah remains motionless, as if he's listening for something. Abruptly, he scrambles up.

'What is it?'

'Gotta go.'

'Why?'

'Because,' he says. 'Out of time.'

Her stomach clenches. 'Are you coming back?'

'Soon as I can.'

He goes to the candle and kicks it out.

'What're you doing?'

The yellow beam of his torch swings close. Only exhaustion prevents her from cringing away. Then the light winks off, plunging the cell into full darkness.

Elijah's shoes scratch across the compacted dirt floor. She hears something being unfastened – a belt, or perhaps a strap. A metal zipper is tugged open. Fingers touch her hair, cradle the back of her head. Her heart's thumping so violently it threatens to tear loose from her chest. Now there's something hard against her lips. And shallow breathing, close to her ear.

'Here,' Elijah whispers. 'Drink.'

The object is the lip of a bottle, from the feel of it the kind used for fizzy drinks. She thinks of the wet cloth in the van and feels a scream coming. Panicked, she rears away. 'What is it?'

'Just water.'

This time, when Elijah guides it to her lips, the urge to drink is irresistible. The water tastes clean, untainted. She guzzles it down, heedless of the splashes that soak her dress. When he tilts the bottle away, she gasps for more. He presses it back to her mouth. Their blind intimacy is as awkward as it is undeniable.

Sated, Elissa leans away. Elijah gets to his feet. At the cell door, his torch winks back on.

She angles her head from its glare. 'You can't leave the bottle?'

'Sorry.'

He grows motionless again, as if he's zeroing in on something she can't hear.

'What is it?' she asks, but he doesn't answer. 'Elijah?'

Speaking his name seems to cut through whatever fears have overtaken him. When the torch beam whips back to her face, she says, 'Promise me.'

'Promise what?'

'Promise you won't let me die in here.'

'I'll come back,' he says. 'I promise. Follow the rules and I'll see you again.'

With that, the cell door swings shut.

III

Elissa's first instinct is to light another candle to replace the one that was guttering. But of the original ten, only eight remain. Already, her available hours of light have shrunk from eighty to sixty-four. If she burns another stick, that'll reduce to fifty-six. Burn one more and she'll be down to forty-eight. The prospect of confinement beyond that is unbearable, but it's one she must consider.

Burn a candle? Save it? Banish the darkness? Endure it?

Elissa's jaw muscles stiffen. She feels her face darkening as blood rushes to the surface. Her jaw clenches tighter.

There's no reason to make light in here. There's nothing

new to discover. Then again, a candle offers not just light but heat. And yet . . . and yet those eight remaining sticks are a precious resource. She cannot afford to waste them.

So ration them instead.

Just like you rationed the brownie. Then lost it.

Paralysis strikes. Crouching in the dark, Elissa hears her breath rush in and out of her lungs. When a tremor passes through her, the candle she's holding snaps in two. Unable to move, unable to think, darkness is her only option.

At last, by degrees, the congestion begins to ease. The muscles in her jaw relax; the pressure inside her skull abates. When her fingers uncurl, the severed candle falls to the floor.

I'll come back. I promise.

But Elijah hadn't promised to keep her alive, which was what she had asked.

Follow the rules and I'll see you again.

There's no reason to trust him. There are a million reasons to *dis*trust him. He's clearly damaged goods. But she suspects he's far smarter than he seems.

You might be a year older than me. But Magic Annie says I have a pretty high IQ. I promise I won't forget you. Not ever.

She shudders at that, cringes as she recalls the lilt in his voice as he said it. She recalls the other information Elijah revealed: that she's underground, in a place he calls the Memory Wood; that he lives close; that he was playing outside and only came down here to explore.

That last part is certainly a lie, because he also revealed that she reminds him of Bryony, his friend for six whole months, a previous resident of this hole who was pretty except when she was crying, which was quite a lot towards the end.

Still, she got her tree. I made sure of that, even if I couldn't make sure of anything else. Picked out a tall one, just like she asked.

Even though it's empty, Elissa's stomach begins to clutch. Bracing the manacle, she edges across the floor to the waste bucket. She gags, bringing up a thin stream of bile.

An image blooms in her mind. Suddenly, she's back at Wide Boys, smelling the bacon grease and listening to Adele through the restaurant's speakers. She recalls the waitress, Andrea, in all her bleached-blonde, green-eyed glory: *Don't you go believin' everything you see or hear . . . Chuckie, you can change just about anything you want if you tries hard enough.*

Those words feel spookily far-sighted, a coded message for what's happened since. Elissa wonders if the woman could be involved. She remembers Andrea's sly smile, and the pair of fake eyes kept for Hallowe'en: *bright orange, slitted just like a cat's. Scares the bejesus out of people.* Even though the waitress seemed full of fun and harmless mischief, she's part of the same bad and scary world that spawned the jailer, so her involvement cannot be discounted.

In fact, Elissa can't dismiss the involvement of anyone she met that day. It means her recollections of the tournament, and events immediately prior, have a currency, too, one just as vital to hoard as the physical items in her cell. A careful reconstruction could shake something loose. A half-glimpsed face, a scrap of conversation: any such gem, dredged from her subconscious, might explain why she's here, might even offer her a lifeline.

Trouble is, just as the candles and matches are vulnerable to the whims of her jailer, her recollections of Saturday are vulnerable to the fallibilities of memory.

Thankfully, she has a plan for preserving them.

IV

Slowing her breathing, Elissa calls up the chessboard she designed to map this chamber. Thanks to its earlier expansion, it's now an eleven-by-twelve grid. So far, she's viewed the board from above. Now, she tilts it to form a wall.

To each square, Elissa adds a brass handle. As a test, she focuses on B3, the location of the two buckets. When she blinks, the front of the square rolls forwards like a drawer. The movement is oiled and smooth but not altogether silent – there's a tiny sound of friction, either from ball-bearings or wheels running in grooves. She blinks again and the drawer rolls shut, accompanied by a satisfying click. Now she has a device not just for finding her way in the dark but for preserving – and interrogating – her recent memories.

The top-left square of her grid is Y8. Into its drawer, Elissa loads everything she remembers about Andrea from Wide Boys. The more she deposits, the more of the encounter she recalls: the waitress's T-shirt and name badge; the way she raised her hand like a paw and meowed; her sing-song way of speaking: *Through these puppies I can't see shitums, but at least I got my green peepers, even if I might bring you the wrong-flavoured milkshake because of 'em.*

She recalls something else Andrea said: *I'm guessing you didn't inherit those gorgeous greens from your mum. Should we be thanking your dad for 'em?*

Looking back, the waitress's probing feels far more intrusive and sinister. The enquiries hadn't stopped there, either: *Is he joining you lovely ladies today?* At that point, Lena Mirzoyan had shut Andrea down.

Right now, Elissa can't think of anything else about the encounter, but if she does, these other memories will be waiting. She gives the drawer the gentlest of touches and it rolls smoothly shut.

Next, Elissa opens Z8. It's important to load her memories chronologically, so she steps forward in time to the moment her mum drove into the Marshall Court Hotel's car park . . . and then she stops, sits up straight and rewinds all the way back to Wide Boys, because only in the moment of moving on does she realize there are details from the restaurant visit that she'd almost forgotten, and which might turn out to be vital.

MAIRÉAD

Day 2

I

Mairéad wakes at 05.40, four short hours after going to bed. Dressing in the dark, she tries not to wake Scott. Already, her stomach is convulsing, but she doesn't have to be sick. Not yet.

Downstairs, she flicks on the kettle and phones Bournemouth for an update. The news isn't great. ANPR hasn't snapped the white Bedford van since yesterday afternoon.

The Child Rescue Alert, however, has generated a deluge of possible sightings – both of Elissa Mirzoyan and also the suspect vehicle. All are being investigated.

Another priority overnight has been to piece together the Bedford's journey to the Marshall Court prior to the abduction. So far, it's been traced back to Ringwood, eleven miles north of Bournemouth. From there, its most likely origin would have been Salisbury or Southampton. The former option seems most likely. Downton village, where the van disappeared yesterday, lies six miles to the south. Salisbury is also Elissa's home. That might be a coincidence. It might not.

Mairéad relays a few instructions and hangs up. Then she brews a mug of tea and opens the fridge to grab milk. Big mistake. On a shelf sits a bowl of cooked pasta: Scott's leftovers from last night's meal. A whiff of chorizo is all it takes. She can't even make it to the downstairs toilet, puking instead in the sink.

Never, in her twelve previous pregnancies, did she ever have morning sickness this intense. 'You're a little scrapper, aren't you?' she mutters, touching her belly. And dares to wonder if it's a good sign.

Pouring the tea into a travel cup, Mairéad goes outside to her car.

11

At 06.30, she holds the day's first strategy meeting. Priority lines of enquiry are established and reviewed. Appropriate resources are allocated.

Since the abduction, investigators have been reviewing CCTV footage from inside the Marshall Court, looking for anything suspicious. But with so many visitors, progress has been slow. Two officers have been running background checks on hotel staff and chess-tournament organizers. So far, nothing of interest has surfaced.

Because of the similarities to the Bryony Taylor disappearance a year ago, Mairéad speaks to her contacts in the Wiltshire force and arranges a transfer of the case notes. She liaises, too, with the National Crime Agency Specialist Operations Centre. They'll provide comparative case analysis and behavioural investigative advice.

The man who snatched Bryony Taylor is linked to at least five previous abductions. All the victims were dragged into a decrepit-looking white van. All came from single-parent families. In each of those six cases, videos of the victim were posted to YouTube shortly afterwards. When Mairéad recalls the content, she has to fight off more nausea.

So far, no videos of Elissa have emerged online, but that hasn't stopped rampant press speculation. This morning's *Daily Express* headline screams: *HAS SICKO YOUTUBE KILLER STRUCK AGAIN?* The red tops have reacted with similar hysteria.

How will Lena Mirzoyan cope when she sees that? How will Bryony Taylor's mum react?

At 07.30, Mairéad updates her chief constable. An hour later, she receives a call from Avon and Somerset Police. In a lay-by just outside Downton, a delivery driver has discovered the Bedford CF's discarded plates.

It's an anticipated development, but not a good one. ANPR had already lost the van. Now, there's no chance of the network reacquiring it. Fingerprints lifted from the plates match none on the national database.

At 10.00, Mairéad eats four cream crackers and somehow holds them down. Afterwards, she drives straight to Salisbury.

III

A Ford Focus in Wiltshire Police livery is stationed outside Elissa Mirzoyan's home. The rest of the street is so crammed with cars it's difficult to find a parking space. At least eight vehicles, including two outside-broadcast trucks, belong to the attendant press pack. A good-looking guy in a suit stands in the road, chatting to the driver of a Toyota RAV4. He smokes a cigarette as he talks, scrupulously careful with his ash. Mairéad recognizes him from Sky News. Ducking her head, she peers through the passenger window at Elissa's home.

The house is a decaying thirties semi. Beneath cracked guttering and a badly warped roof, the water-stained whitewash is flaking away. The front garden is neatly tended, even so, and the windows facing the street are spotlessly clean. Lena Mirzoyan might lack money, but she doesn't lack pride.

A uniformed PC stands on the pavement, tasked with holding back door-steppers. Mairéad flashes her ID and walks up the path. Judy Pauletto, the assigned FLO, opens the front door. They exchange grim smiles.

In the living room, Lena Mirzoyan stands by the fireplace, arms tightly folded. She's wearing an expression that Mairéad has seen too many times before: stunned incredulity at how savagely life can change.

On the sofa sit Elissa's grandparents. Mairéad recognizes them from the red-feather-boa photo. She introduces herself, then turns to Lena. 'Please – take a seat. I need to ask a few questions. Some of them you'll have been asked before, but I'd still like to hear your answers first-hand. When you're ready, let's start at the beginning. Walk me through everything that happened yesterday, right from the moment you woke up.'

Taking a deep breath, Lena does exactly that. She talks about the tuna sandwiches she made for Elissa's packed lunch, how they left the house ridiculously early and decided to stop for breakfast en route.

'Where was that?'

'A place called Wide Boys.'

Mairéad knows it – an American-style eatery on the A338 approach road. 'Do you remember anything particular about your visit? Anything at all that stands out?'

Lena shakes her head. Then she blinks. 'Actually, the waitress was . . . She was a little odd. I mean, friendly, but . . . now I think about it, she took quite an interest in Elissa. Even asked if she got her green eyes from her dad.'

'What did she look like?'

'Big woman, early fifties, blonde hair. I'd recognize her, definitely. She was wearing contact lenses – at least that's what she told us. Green, the same colour as Elissa's eyes.'

Mairéad notes it down. She'll send officers to Wide Boys to interrogate the waitress and also to review any available CCTV. 'After your breakfast, you drove straight to the hotel?'

'Yes.'

'How long did that take?'

'I don't know. Ten minutes? Fifteen?'

'What did you and Elissa talk about on the way?'

'The tournament, mainly. How she was feeling.'

'Which was?'

'Nervous. Excited.'

'Do you remember anything about the journey?'

'Not really.'

'After you—'

Lena lurches forwards. '*Stupid Nasty Prat!*'

'I'm sorry?'

'Before we pulled off for the restaurant, we nearly hit some guy trying to overtake us on the inside. I can't believe I *forgot*! He cut in front and slammed on his brakes, almost like he wanted us to go into him. *Stupid Nasty Prat*'s what Elissa said. She made it up from the letters on his number plate. SNP 12, maybe, or SNP 16. It was a BMW – I remember that much.'

'This is good, Lena. This is very good.'

Excusing herself, Mairéad contacts the incident room, directing officers to Wide Boys and instructing Halley to trace the BMW. Afterwards, she asks Lena's permission to look upstairs.

IV

Standing in Elissa's bedroom, it's impossible not to feel emotional. The serenity of the space – airy and uncluttered – competes with a terrible silence. There's a bed, a wardrobe, a desk, a narrow bookcase with volumes neatly ordered. On the wall is a butterfly-shaped clock with a glittery minute hand. Above the bed hangs a framed print of Mount Fuji against a cobalt sky; in the foreground, the branches of a Japanese cherry tree heavy with blossom. On Elissa's desk sits an antique walnut jewellery box inlaid with mother-of-pearl. Mairéad lifts the lid. Inside, on a bed of red velvet, lies a sea-shell bracelet and a Cadbury Crunchie.

She goes to the wardrobe and opens it. When she sees the clothes hanging up, she can't help but touch them. The sleeve of a hand-knitted jumper feels warm, as if it's only just been discarded. The heat is illusory but poignant even so. Mairéad can't imagine how Lena Mirzoyan must feel when she comes in here. Always, motherhood has struck her as a voluntary expedition into terror. But Lena, sitting downstairs, is dealing with trauma beyond comprehension.

She sits on the bed. With one hand, she smooths the duvet. She thinks of the journalists outside, smoking their cigarettes. She thinks of her team, back in Dorset; the officers in neighbouring forces; staff from the NCA, from charities and external agencies. She thinks of Scott, his love and his kindness and his extraordinary patience. And finally she dares to consider the tiny scrap of life in her womb.

Mairéad puts her hands on her belly. Her gaze wanders to the wardrobe and Elissa's rack of clothes. Impossible, now, to escape the feeling that these two lives are interwoven. *Hold on*, she thinks, *please hold on*.

In her pocket, her phone starts buzzing.

When Mairéad stands the room sways around her. She tastes bile and fears she'll vomit, but within a few seconds the feeling passes. Hauling out her phone, she strides from Elissa's room.

ELIJAH

Day 3

I

Closing the door on Elissa – our names are so similar! – I draw the deadbolts and secure the padlock. Then I scurry up the cellar steps. In the shadowed hallway I pause, peering past the half-open front door. I don't see anyone outside, but I keep watch for a full five minutes before leaving.

In the twilight beneath the shedding trees, I carefully make my way home. The further I get from the ruined cottage, the harder it is to believe what just happened.

'*Elissa*,' I murmur.

She's an enigma, a puzzle box wrapped up with a bow. I feel like I've unearthed the corner of a Roman mosaic and can see individual tiles but not the overall design. That's a feeling I have often around here, although never so strongly as right now. It's thrilling – like the adventure books I've read – but it's scary too. If I were wise, I'd leave Elissa Mirzoyan well alone.

Could I leave her down there? Or, a better question – could I live with myself if I did? Earlier, as we got to know each other, her bravery and determination astonished me. She said I was brave, too, but I don't think she meant it. She's clever, perhaps cleverer than me, and that means she's dangerous.

Promise me. Promise you won't let me die in here.

I promised her something, but not that, and I saw from her face that she wasn't fooled.

I touched her. I still can't believe it. I brought water because they're always thirsty when I first visit, but usually I just leave the bottle within reach. With Bryony, over time, we got more familiar, but never like this. I rub my hands on my shorts, worried that traces of Elissa remain on my skin – that someone will know, just by seeing my fingers, what I've been doing.

Touching her wasn't my only mistake. So many things I let slip down there – enough to sink me if she talks. I even mentioned Bryony's tree.

Looking up, I realize that the tree must have been on my mind all along, because during my *cerebrations* – a word for having deep thoughts – I've walked to the part of the Memory Wood where it grows.

The yew stands alone, its lower branches outstretched. Papa once told me that Britain's oldest yews sprouted in the tenth century or earlier, which means they were around before Robin Hood, Henry VIII, even William the Conqueror. Bryony wanted splendour and majesty, but most of all she wanted *longevity* – and that's exactly what she got.

The trunk has split, revealing a cavern-like interior. Attached to the upper boughs are my memories – handwritten on folded paper – of my time with Bryony. *She* asked me to save her too. Unlike Elissa, I gave her my word. Thanks to events I couldn't control, I broke it.

When I place my hand against the yew's trunk, the bark feels warmer than it should, as if Bryony's blood pumps beneath the surface instead of sap.

Suddenly, it's all too much. I wheel around and run, kicking through dead bracken. Overhead, the sky's a sodden rag waiting to be wrung. Bursting free of the Memory Wood, I see, up ahead, the ragtag ring of vehicles that makes up Wheel Town. A little way off, lurched over like a drunk, stands the caravan that belongs to my one true friend, Magic Annie.

II

I'm not always welcome in Wheel Town. Annie says I shouldn't be worried – to most of them, I'm an outsider, just like everyone else who doesn't follow their ways.

She's never shared much about her heritage. Once, she spent an entire afternoon telling me about Romani gypsies and their history, but when I asked if she was one of them she went to the door and spat on the grass. Sometimes I wonder if Annie just picks the coolest bits from cultures she admires, adopting them as her own.

Around fifteen dwellings make up the site, although it's not always easy to work out which ones are homes and which are abandoned vehicles. Of the more permanent structures, eight are caravans, four are converted coaches or buses, two are brightly coloured wagons of the type pulled by horses and one's an old lorry. Not all of them are occupied. Wheel Town's community shrinks and swells with the seasons.

Smoke chugs from tin chimneys, and from a fire pit

where someone's been burning rubbish. Two dogs, chained to a metal pole corkscrewed into the earth, start barking as I approach. They belong to Noakes, the stinky old guy who lives in the lorry.

The dogs aren't Noakes's only animals. His lorry is packed with cages housing chickens, ferrets, even a few mink. For a while, he kept pigs in a rickety scratch-built paddock. Meunier, worried they'd escape and breed with the boar he'd introduced to the Memory Wood, told Noakes it had to stop. For weeks afterwards, Wheel Town reeked of bacon fat.

Looking around, I don't see him, but I hear the squawk of his chickens. Near by, a sullen-looking stranger is bending over the engine bay of a beaten-up Volkswagen, watched by a woman I presume is his partner. A roll-up dangles from the man's mouth. A baby dangles from the woman's hip. They're dressed like they've just walked off a music video: him in a white vest and back-to-front baseball cap, her in a pink tracksuit made of the same velvety material you see on old sofas. Across her backside is a word printed in black gothic script: *HUSTLIN'*.

I've never seen the couple before, and I give them a wide berth as I trudge towards Magic Annie's caravan. When the woman mutters something, her partner's head lifts from the engine block. It's difficult to ignore them but I manage it, keeping my gaze fixed firmly ahead.

III

Balanced on two rusted axels, Annie's caravan is a monstrous-looking thing. Haphazard brick towers support it at either end, but the land here is boggy and her home seems hell-bent on sinking into the earth. Bird poo and lichen have felted the roof, but the windows are clean and the aluminium step-ups below the door shine as if they've just been polished.

To the side is her Juice Farm. I don't know why she calls it that – it's no orchard and there's no fruit. Instead, a row of glossy solar panels faces south, all wired up to a huge lithium-ion battery inside. The Juice Farm lets Annie run a fridge, a music player, a laptop computer and the wonder that drags me back here time and again: a twenty-four-inch Samsung flat-screen TV.

Balancing on the step-up, I rap on her door. I can hear the TV blaring, which means she must be home. The caravan rocks gently. Then the door swings wide.

Annie's wearing her favourite Cowichan sweater. The Cowichan, she once told me, are a First Nations people from Vancouver Island in western Canada, famous – among other things – for their knitting. The sweater features bold geometric patterns in black, white and grey. Over each of Annie's pendulous breasts is a silhouetted mountain bear. On her feet are tasselled buffalo-skin moccasins. Around her throat is a necklace of turquoise stones. They complement her eyes, which have always made her seem far younger than her craggy face suggests. Silver bells hang from her ears. Her hair is the colour of a raven's wing, except at the roots, where it's grey, and one turquoise lock that matches the stones at her throat. Despite her sagging skin, it's obvious from the sharp bones beneath that she was beautiful once. Time can be cruel, but Magic Annie suits her looks; I can't imagine her any other way.

When she sees me, her eyes crinkle like crêpe paper.

'*Anoki*,' she cries, more evidence that she's having a Native American day and that this is not the occasion to call her Magic Annie.

'*Kamali*,' I reply, bowing low. She told me once it means *spirit guide*. It fits her perfectly, and I know she likes it. Stepping back from the door, Annie welcomes me in.

'My trainers are wet,' I say. 'My socks, too.'

'Then strip them off and let's get them dry.'

Following her inside, I surrender my footwear. A greyish haze – musty yet sweet – hangs in the air. On the table by the window a cheroot smoulders in an ashtray. On the sill above the sink a stick of incense throws off silken coils.

'I'll open a window,' Annie says, but I shake my head, sliding on to the U-shaped bench seat that surrounds her table. Although the smoke makes my eyes water, I find it relaxing.

The TV stands on the countertop, angled towards me. It's showing that programme with the judge who sorts out people's squabbles. Annie picks up the remote and mutes the sound. 'These daps of yours are falling apart,' she says, carrying them to the wood stove. 'About time your da bought you a new pair.'

'Maybe.'

'Is that a growling tummy I hear?'

Opening a cupboard, she takes out her biscuit barrel and arranges three pecan-nut biscuits on a plate. Then, pouring a glass of milk, she sets the lot down in front of me.

'What *I* want to know,' she adds, huffing the turquoise lock out of her eyes, 'is what you've been doing in those woods without a jacket or jumper, with wet socks and shoes *and* bare legs.'

My hand freezes in the act of reaching out. Has Annie

somehow learned of my discovery in the Memory Wood? It's only when I realize she's concerned solely about my inappropriate clothing that my heart resumes its beat.

I snatch up a biscuit. Nobody makes them like Annie, gooey and crumbly and packed full of niceness. I'm on to my second before she's filled her kettle and taken down her mug.

The show with the bad-tempered judge finishes. I watch an ad for Bold washing powder, followed by another for Petits Filous. I pluck up the third biscuit and am about to tackle it when Elissa Mirzoyan peers out of the TV screen.

IV

She watches me for at least three seconds before I even make the connection. The girl I met in the cellar looks nothing like this image. *My* Elissa might be dirt-streaked and shivery, she might be bloody and frightened, but she's determined, strong. Chained, yes, but still a dragon.

This girl, by contrast, is a pale imitation. The photograph is a formal head-and-shoulders shot. In it, Elissa's wearing school uniform – blue blouse and striped tie. She looks uncomfortable, reluctant to pull a smile but too polite to object. The result is forced and unnatural. Her eyes, even so, are just as arresting.

Promise me. Promise you won't let me die in here.

I didn't. I couldn't.

But that doesn't mean I won't.

Promise me.

I hear Annie put down her mug. From the counter she

can't see the TV, but any closer and she'll have a perfect view. Just before she comes over Elissa's picture disappears and a whitewashed Victorian building fills the screen. Across the front, in big black letters, is its name: *THE MAR-SHALL COURT HOTEL*. Now, the image changes again – a huge room filled with long tables, covered with chequerboards crowded with little statues. Children hunch over them, deep in thought.

The room is replaced with another. This time there's only one table. Three people sit at it. In the centre, a woman with Elissa's mouth and cheekbones is crying. She reads from a piece of paper as an older man rubs her back. The screen flickers white and I wonder if I'm about to faint. Then I realize there are others in the room that I cannot see, people with cameras taking photographs.

Annie reaches for the remote. I think she's going to change the channel. Instead, she cancels the mute. My ears fill with words I don't want to hear.

'—ust want my daughter back,' the crying woman says, followed by something I can't make out. '. . . precious,' she sobs. '. . . so talented and beautiful.' The cameras go crazy. A telephone number appears onscreen.

'There are people on this earth,' Annie says, 'that have no business walking it.'

When Elissa reappears, we stare at her in silence.

'Did you come for the magic?' Annie asks, eyes still on the TV.

I swallow.

On TV, Elissa is replaced by a weather report. Dark swirls race across a barren land. I wonder how long it'll be before the storm hits.

ELISSA

Day 3

I

After putting Andrea from Wide Boys into the drawer at Y8, Elissa is about to interrogate her memories of the Marshall Court Hotel when she stops and backs up. Although the waitress – with her green eyes, big boobs and attitude – made everyone else fade to grey, she wasn't the only person in the restaurant that day. On the next table sat the couple who engaged her in conversation before she took refuge in her book.

Closing her eyes despite the darkness, Elissa transports herself back to Wide Boys. As she settles in her seat, her mum and Andrea begin to materialize, but she purposely keeps their details vague. The restaurant, too, is sketched in the faintest of charcoal shades. She reserves all the colour for the table on her left and the couple sitting around it.

It's hard, this. Andrea stole so much of the light. The pair are like *bodachs* – shadow creatures from a ghost story Elissa once read. Their faces are foggy blurs. One of the *bodachs* lifts a hand to its throat, stroking and fondling.

Abruptly, Elissa remembers the spot of shaving cream and the man's dirty fingernails.

Colour rushes into the scene. She sees slick-combed hair, mud-stained shoes. The woman has a jade necklace and violet lipstick. *Stop that*, she hisses. *Always touching yourself.*

When Elissa's mum went to the loo, the couple spoke a few words, but the details have slipped away. She does remember the woman's apologetic smile. Did they talk about the chess tournament? Possibly.

To her right, Elissa spots another *bodach*. This one sits alone. Its clothes are clear enough – turquoise jumper, mustard corduroys, toffee-apple-red shoes – but its face is a child's black scribble, entirely absent of features. It swivels towards her and she knows, despite the lack of eyes, that it's evaluating her. Minutely, it shakes its head. With a start, she recalls the older man this *bodach* represents. He'd been reading – a history of some ancient Greek war. At the time, she'd wondered if his head-shake indicated disapproval or solidarity. Now, as she tries to tease more detail from that sooty smudge of a face, it splits open to reveal a set of pointed yellow teeth.

Disturbed by the image, Elissa blinks it away. Wide Boys folds into darkness.

The drawer at Y8 glows with Andrea's vibe. Anything else Elissa puts in there will likely be outshone. Instead she opens Z8 and deposits the three *bodachs*. Even as she's loading them, she recalls the man with dirty fingernails gesturing at her book:

'What's it about?'

'It's about chess.'

'Huh. Ain't ever been my thing. Used to like a bit of poker, before.'

'Before what?'

His knife angles towards the woman. 'Before . . . you know.'

Elissa shudders. Slams the drawer shut. She might have to revisit the contents at some point, but right now they feel toxic, dangerous.

Her memories of Wide Boys exhausted, she's about to move on to the Marshall Court Hotel when she hears the muted but now-familiar rattle of deadbolts.

II

Her first visitor inside this cell was a ghoul, her second a creature even more complicated. She fears both, but of the two, the one whose name she doesn't know scares her most, and when the door opens and she sees a torch far more powerful than Elijah's, she knows it's the ghoul who's returned.

That smell accompanies him, of something rotten and sweet. It gets in her nose and won't let go. His light picks out her manacle, her chain. Then it darts around the floor, pausing at each item of note.

Again, the aroma of food slowly permeates. She hears the shuffle-scuff of approaching feet and cringes, holding herself still. Something is placed on the floor near by.

Silence ensues. Elissa counts to thirty before the ghoul breaks it.

'When one has a visitor,' he whispers, 'it's polite to ack—'

'How long have I been here?'

Her voice is firmer than she'd expected. She's terrified that this attempt at bravery, however pathetic, will back-fire; even more terrified that meek acquiescence will ensure a slow walk towards destruction. A cat, she knows, plays longer with a mouse that fights back.

The ghoul draws a breath, slowly lets it out. In that moment she recalls his words from their first meeting: *There'll never be anything, ever in this life, that you can conceal from me. Take as long as you need to learn that lesson, but for your own comfort I'd advise haste.*

The smell of cooked food intensifies. Her stomach growls, her body admitting to weaknesses that her mouth will not.

'Well, I suppose that's an acknowledgement,' the ghoul hisses, 'even if it's little else. I see your manners haven't improved. Perhaps your mother never taught—'

'How *long* have I *been* here?'

This time, as she asks the question, a fit of shaking claims her. Her jaw muscles spasm and she bites her tongue. The pain is excruciating. Even worse is her anticipation of the ghoul's reaction.

His breathing is steady and slow. 'It's Monday.'

In his tone she hears mockery, petulance and some-thing she can't quite unravel. How can it be *Monday*? If he's telling the truth, she's been gone at least thirty-four hours; possibly as long as fifty-eight. She wonders if the police will have sent someone round to console her mum. It's the kind of thing they do when kids go missing.

For a moment, her distress becomes cold rage. How *dare* this freak create such chaos in her family and expect to go unchallenged? She's never been one for violence, but if she had a blade right now she'd plunge it into him, rip it loose and plunge it in again, stabbing and cutting until nothing remained except ragged meat.

'There's food,' the ghoul whispers, 'but it's the last you'll get for free. From now on, you'll work for your meals. Say you understand.'

She thinks back to her conversation with Elijah:

'Why did he bring me here? What's he going to do?'

'Nothing bad. Long as you follow the rules.'

'What're the rules?'

'They change.'

Elissa lifts her head. 'I understand.'

The torch beam slides off her face, settling on her injured wrist. 'Down here, if you don't keep yourself clean, injuries like that can get infected. First thing you'll feel is the skin getting itchy, getting hot. The flesh will swell, start to suppurate, like it's a piece of fruit someone trod on and left out in the sun. You ever seen an apple in an orchard go all brown and wet? Bad *meat* smells worse, I assure you. And it's not too late in the season for flies, maggots, all kinds of other filth, especially down here in the dark. You'll begin to feel dizzy, confused. You won't even be able to trust your own thoughts.' He clears his throat and spits. Elissa hears a bolus of phlegm land somewhere near by and cringes, thinking of the millions of bacteria it harbours. 'I have disinfectant, antibiotics – all kinds of medical supplies. But they don't come for free.'

'What do you want?'

'There's food on the tray. Also a cloth. Right now, you look a mess – hungry, dirty, unattractive. Eat, clean yourself up, make yourself presentable. Afterwards, you and I – we're going to make you famous.'

Hearing that, she can barely breathe. 'Famous?'

'Eat,' whispers the ghoul. 'Make yourself nice.' Before she can respond he slides out of the cell, leaving her in darkness.

III

Elissa cannot dwell on his words. When she woke in this cellar she made herself a promise: whatever happens, she'll survive it. Fear and adrenalin have tightened her muscles to the point of snapping, but that promise is no less important than it was. Right now, there's food, a means of survival. It might not be here long.

Elissa crawls to G7, where she left the matches; her hands are shaking so badly that the first one she strikes slips from her fingers and dies.

She screams. Tries to take out another. Ends up scattering a pile of them. Finally, tears streaming down her face, she scratches a match into life and cups it long enough for it to take hold. Lighting a new candle, she screws it into the holder.

The flame flickers. Immediately, Elissa sees why. This time, the ghoul hasn't closed the soundproofed door behind him. If not for her manacle, she could slip out of the cell to freedom.

In A6 lies a wooden tray. Upon it stands a plastic bowl. A collection of faded Disney characters parade around the rim. Beside it is a plastic spoon and a Thermos flask, the cap unscrewed. Steam coils from the neck.

Despite her hunger, the thought of eating food prepared by the ghoul is almost unbearable. Only by refusing to think – of what she's about to do, or what's about to happen – does it become possible.

Supporting her manacle as best she can, Elissa inches across the floor. Sharp nubs of rock scratch her buttocks. With her good hand she tilts the Thermos. Something red and wet splatters into the bowl. In the bobbing candlelight it looks like the entrails of a slaughtered animal. Elissa recoils, but the smell is stronger now, more recognizable. When she leans close, she sees spaghetti shapes in tomato sauce.

Snatching up the spoon, Elissa shovels food into her mouth. It's hotter than she expected, scalding her tongue, but she swallows it down regardless.

The shapes are Peppa Pig characters: Peppa, George, a rabbit, an elephant. The food's sheer *cheerfulness*, down here in this filthy cellar, feels horribly out of place. When her spoon scrapes the bottom of the bowl she pours out what's left in the Thermos and eats that too. Then she licks the bowl clean. Should she keep the spoon? It's flimsy as hell. Snapped in half, it might provide a sharp point, but unless she plunges it into her jailer's eye it's unlikely to do much damage. And she's pretty sure he'll have considered that.

There'll never be anything, ever in this life, that you can conceal from me.

The candle flame bows and nods, accompanied by sounds of movement. The ghoul is back.

IV

Dropping the spoon, Elissa scoots as far as possible from the door. She ends up in G2, clutching the manacle to her chest.

The ghoul appears in the doorway, accompanied by an ice-white light that lances her eyes like a needle. She screws up her face, realizing that he's donned a head torch. Light bounces off the walls, casting him in silhouette. There's a scratchiness to his movements – a start-stop jerkiness – that makes him seem subhuman, as if she's woven him from the threads of old nightmares.

Worse, his silhouette makes no sense, boasting a plethora of appendages and spiky protrusions. It's a full minute before she realizes it's an illusion caused by a bulky tripod, which he sets up in Z5. When he attaches something to the mount, Elissa sees, in the light of his head torch, that it's a flip-screen camcorder.

If she doesn't speak, doesn't challenge him, she knows she'll make herself complicit in whatever depravity he has planned. Earlier, adrenalin had given her a voice. Now, the prospect of speaking, of engaging him, is too frightening to bear. And yet she cannot shy away. If she survives this, she'll live with the decisions she made down here for many years to come.

Resting the manacle in her lap, Elissa lifts her head. The box of candles is close. A well-aimed shot might knock over the tripod, smashing the camera. But what would that achieve? Likely just a more brutal ordeal than the one she already faces. What she needs to do – what she remembers from a programme about hostages she once watched – is make him see her as a person, a human being and not an object. She recalls his earlier mention of her manners. Perhaps that's a good place to start.

Elissa clears her throat. 'Thank you for the food.'

If the ghoul hears, he gives no indication. Going to the tray, he examines the contents carefully before carrying it from the cell. She's grateful, now, that she didn't try to steal the spoon. A fragment of memory comes to her, something Elijah said just before he left: *He'll test you. Most people fail.*

The ghoul reappears, his silhouette bristling with new appendages. He deposits something in Z4. When he bends over it, his torch illuminates a second tripod, just like the one supporting the camera.

'It's been a few years since I watched *Peppa Pig*,' Elissa says.

Silent, the ghoul fiddles with the mount.

'You get all kinds of spaghetti shapes these days, don't you? Once, my mum bought me Minions spaghetti. Can you believe they make that? She took me to see the movie, too. It was pretty funny, I guess, but not as good as the first one. We didn't see *Despicable Me* at the cinema, but we have it on Blu-Ray. Some people think I won't like movies because I'm a chess geek, but I do. *Toy Story*'s one of my favourite movies ever, even though I should probably prefer stuff like *Twilight*.'

Completing his work on the tripod mount, the ghoul leaves the cell yet again. She hears him clanking around in whatever antechamber lies beyond the door. Within moments he's back, hunched over like a crab. He's carrying something bulky, but she can't see details. Nor has she glimpsed anything of the ghoul himself except the briefest of snatches: black boots, wet from whatever he's tracked in from outside; large hands, slick with engine grease or something similar.

'They made a third Minions movie,' Elissa says. 'I haven't seen it yet, but I want to.'

He grunts, hefting the box on to the tripod mount.

'My mum said we can stream it on Amazon.' She pauses. 'I hope we get to do that.'

The ghoul steps back, examining his work. Finally, Elissa sees what he's been erecting: an expensive-looking lighting rig. He leaves the cell again, returning with a large battery pack.

'We always have popcorn with a movie. Mum likes salty and I like sweet, so we usually get salty and sweet.'

The ghoul turns to face her.

Caught in that unforgiving white glare, Elissa begins to tremble. Now she has his attention, she's not sure she wants it.

'To be honest,' she stammers, 'we watch TV more than movies. Mum doesn't like soaps, but she gets into all those talent shows. Once you know the people, it's pretty hard not to follow them. I think *X Factor*'s a bit cruel, but I like the dancing one.'

The ghoul steps closer. She hears his breathing, slightly elevated.

Elissa swallows. Tries to still her jaw. She's never been one for small talk; she can't believe how many words she's found to paper over the silence. 'Do you ever wonder how many more series they'll make? I mean, you'd think at some point they'd run out of contestants. It's a shame they only ever make talent shows about singing or dancing. I'd be much more interested in—'

Lizard-quick, he strikes her.

At first, Elissa can't work out what has happened. One moment she's sitting up straight, squinting into that fierce halo of light; the next she's prostrate, her wrist a screaming abomination, one side of her face beating like a second heart. She tastes blood in her mouth, hears a ringing in her ears. The room cuts loose from its moorings and begins to spin.

Elissa squirms, convulses, too pain-wracked to control her movements.

'You don't speak until you're told,' the ghoul whispers. 'Say you understand.'

His voice sounds like it's coming from inside a cupboard. When she answers, her own voice is just as distorted: 'I unner'thand.'

'We're going to make a movie. You're going to do exactly as you're told. Say you understand.'

Elissa begins to weep.

Again, that emotionless whisper: 'Say you understand.'

She swallows a mouthful of blood. 'I unner'thand.'

How foolish – how naive – to think she could challenge him. She can barely breathe for the pain in her wrist, can hardly see past her tears.

Where is her mum? Where are the police? She's been here two days. Why hasn't anyone *found* her?

Her vision fragments, a million glass shards. For a moment she thinks it's some kind of seizure, until she realizes that the lighting rig's been switched on.

Blinking away tears, her eyes slowly adjust. Details bleed out of the miasma. In E4, placed over the iron ring, is a chair that wasn't there before. It's rickety as hell – thin wooden legs and a simple curved back.

Invisible, the ghoul retreats behind the camera. A red LED winks on.

'Sit on the chair,' he hisses. 'Say you understand.'

V

She wasn't expecting this. Not the chair, nor the instruction to sit. She doesn't know how to interpret it. 'I unner'thand,' she splutters, blood spilling over her chin.

Abruptly, the light blooms into different colours, a rainbow spectrum of such beauty that she gasps. For a moment, Elissa wonders if it's God, announcing His presence. She's never had much time for religion, but she knows from RE that God can be merciful, even to those who don't believe in Him. It's a nice idea, but a darker one follows it; perhaps this isn't God at all. Perhaps it's just her body shutting down. Perhaps she's simply dying.

That thought is so shocking that she kicks out her feet and tries to right herself. She can't die in this filthy cell. Taking shallow sips of air, she pushes up.

Elissa stagger-crawls to the chair, rainbow colours swirling around her. It feels like she's in a TV ad for Skittles, or some crazy cartoon. She places her chin on the seat, persuades her legs to scissor out. Something is wrong, but she doesn't know what. Her vision jitters, kaleidoscopic. Her skin feels fuzzy – prickly and delicious. Her heart is racing, but no longer from fear.

She clambers on to the chair. It's an effort to keep her head up, and when it nods against her chest for the third time in as many seconds, she bursts out laughing.

Nothing funny about this, so why is she suddenly so carefree? The ghoul, flickery and lizardy, emerges from behind his equipment. 'Say you understand.' His words are rich, melodic, as if his voice is a xylophone crafted from the world's finest wood.

'I UNNER'THAND!' Elissa screams. She belches, tastes spaghetti sauce and, beneath it, something else: something chalky and bitter. He's drugged her, she thinks. Some kind of hallucinogen, mixed into the food.

The ghoul walks to the chair. Leans close.

He's going to kiss me, and if he does I'm going to puke in his mouth.

Elissa howls with laughter. But the ghoul doesn't kiss her. Instead, with one thumb, he lifts her eyelid.

She blinks, or tries to. His face is a black porridge, host to two runny-egg eyes. He smells atrocious, and when her stomach grips she belches again.

The ghoul mutters something she doesn't catch. He raises his left wrist. Ribbons of light bounce off his watch.

'TIME ITH IT?' Elissa hollers. 'TIME ITH IT, YOU FUCKABOO?'

ELIJAH

Day 4

I

I walk through the Memory Wood like I'm floating, as if the Earth's gravity has entirely drained away. Above me, low-hanging clouds still threaten rain, but the air tastes fresh and clean. I don't look at Bryony's yew when I pass it, nor the other Memory Trees. Soon, I find myself following one of the deer trails that criss-crosses these woods. It leads me, as I knew it would, to the ruined cottage.

Because Annie's magic still runs through me, I step into the clearing with none of my customary caution.

Bad instincts.

Kyle is leaning against the building's front wall. Thanks to my carelessness, there's no avoiding him.

My brother displays little of his usual swagger. If anything, he seems weighed down. His face is smeared with whatever gunk he uses to disguise his scent, but beneath the streaks his skin is pale, washed out. For a moment, as I look at him, I wonder if he's here at all. The sun has fled behind a covering of cloud; Kyle casts no shadow upon the ground.

He grips his rifle in front of him, as if he's making a last stand. When our eyes meet, his chest heaves.

Then he raises his weapon and points it at my face.

11

In more ordinary times, I'd throw up my hands in surrender. But what's happening here is nowhere near ordinary. I don't care about the rifle, don't care that with a precise shot my brother could put a calamity inside my head. Right now, I'm a supernova, glowing with positive energy. Inferior satellites – like Kyle – will be sucked into my mass.

I walk forwards smiling, arms outstretched. Perhaps, by embracing him, I can transfer some of my good vibes.

'The fuck, Eli,' he growls, stepping away from the wall.

'I've come to see her,' I say, turning up my palms the way Jesus does. 'I've come to see Elissa.'

'The fuck you have. Stay back.'

As the distance between us shrinks, some of my euphoria begins to evaporate. 'Is she down there?'

Kyle studies the woods at my back. Then he nods.

'Is she alive?'

'I think.'

'Did you hurt her?'

'*Fuck* you, Eli. I'm tellin' you right now – get away from here and don't come back. This one's trouble. You ain't got the nous to take her on.'

'I don't want to take her on,' I say. 'I just want to help.'

'Like you helped Bryony?'

'That wasn't my fault.'

'The fuck it wasn't.'

I halt in front of him. 'The swearing doesn't scare me. Doesn't bother me one bit.'

He spits something brown on to the ground. 'That right?'

Looking him square in the eye, I say, 'Let me through.'

In response, Kyle raises his rifle and sights along it. A handspan separates my face from the muzzle.

'I'll *end* you, little brother,' he hisses, and I know he means it.

But I know, too, that it won't happen today. Reaching out, I wrap my fingers around the gun. Then, careful not to disturb Kyle's trigger finger, I guide the barrel to my mouth.

I don't really know what I'm doing, but I sense it's important. The metal tastes acidic, like I'm sucking the terminals of a nine-volt battery. With the weapon in my mouth, I can't speak, but there's nothing I need to say. This challenge to Kyle's authority requires no words.

His eyes *burn*. He doesn't recognize the little brother confronting him. Perhaps he fears an imposter. Right now, I feel about as different to the boy he knows as it's possible to get. Annie's magic has something to do with that, I'm sure, but mostly it's down to Elissa.

Kyle's trigger finger twitches inside the guard. If he fires at this angle, the bullet won't enter my brain, but it *will* rip a path through the soft tissue behind my tongue. Perhaps it'll nick an artery in my neck or splinter a vital section of vertebrae. Perhaps it'll sever my tongue at the root.

When the gun starts knocking against my teeth, I can't decide which one of us is shaking. An instant later, my brother yanks the weapon from my mouth. 'Fuckin' retard,' he says. 'Fuckin' *psycho*.'

Again, I open my palms, in that age-old gesture of peace.

'She ain't like the others,' he says.

'I know that.'

'You're gunna cover us all in shit.'

When I step forward, Kyle steps back. If he retreats any further, he'll leave the cottage entrance uncontested.

My brother waits another beat. Then, wordless, he shoulders his rifle and marches away. Seconds later, he's lost among the trees. Soon, all I hear is the cracking of twigs and branches.

I wait until the gentler sounds of the Memory Wood swallow him up. Then I step inside the cottage, walk along the hall to the kitchen, open the pantry door and disappear down the stairs.

III

She's sleeping when I enter.

Sometimes they pretend to do that, especially at the start. Still, I've become pretty good at working out when someone's trying to fool me, and Elissa definitely isn't.

Her brow furrows a little when my torch beam touches her face. Her eyes rove behind their lids. I can't help wondering about her dream.

For a while, I consider peeling back one of her eyelids, just to get another glimpse of the emerald fire I saw when we first met, but that would be a *violation*, which is the word for when you do something to someone without their permission.

Shading the torch with my fingers, I creep closer. Elissa's lying on her side, curled around her injured wrist. A bruise on her left cheek is brand new. Blood is crusted in the corner of her mouth. It looks like she's taken a couple of hard punches, or perhaps just one that knocked her head against the floor.

I *told* her to follow the rules. Why didn't she listen?

Squatting down, I place the back of my hand near her mouth. Her breath tickles my skin as she exhales.

She's like an angel, or a fairy robbed of its wings. Injuries and filthy clothes can't hide her beauty. Beneath the grime, her skin is as flawless as Mama's. Unable to stop myself, I lift my fingers to her hair, feeling its softness. I touched it before when I helped her to drink, so it isn't strictly a violation. Beneath my hand, I sense the warm skin of her scalp, the smooth curve of her skull and, beneath that, the complex miracle of her brain. I imagine the thoughts zipping around those grey folds, her hopes and fears and memories all carried by tiny sparks of electricity.

Asleep like this, she's horribly vulnerable. How easy it would be for someone to hurt her; offhand, I can think of a dozen different ways. The ticking pulse in her neck is so fragile that a lump grows in my throat. Gently, I slide my fingers on to her cheek. There, the skin is hot and damp. I bet if I licked it I'd taste salt.

Elissa's mouth falls open. She moans, fighting whatever monsters stalk her sleep. I see her bottom row of teeth, glimmering with saliva. I want to slide my finger along the ridges and feel their sharpness – but that really *would* be a violation.

Instead, I place my hand directly over Elissa's heart. Even through her dress, I feel its reassuring rhythm and imagine how it must sound, a steady *bm-thm*, *bm-thm*, *bm-thm*. As it jumps against my palm, it's hard to accept it'll ever fall silent. But that's what happens to all our hearts. Especially down here, in this cellar beneath the Memory Wood.

'I'm sorry this happened,' I mutter.

Elissa stirs in sleep, shifting position on the floor.

I turn off my torch and sit in darkness.

Bm-thm, bm-thm, bm-thm.

For a while, I feel so at peace I don't even realize I'm crying.

ELISSA

Day 4

I

Cold fingers against her neck. Her pulse jumps against them.

The rhythm of her heart is all wrong. Earlier, it was racing. Now, it feels far too slow, like a shire horse plodding uphill. The bright colours in her cell have turned white. The voice of her jailer – the one she calls the ghoul – smears and elongates.

'You look into the camera,' he whispers. 'You read the words. Say you understand.'

Elissa rolls her head, screws up her eyes.

'You look into the camera,' he insists. 'You read the words. You send a message to the world and your mother learns you're not dead. Say you understand.'

It takes a while to process his instructions. She can't trust him – that's obvious – but if there's one thing likely to sway her, it's the chance to relieve her mum's anguish.

Which words, though? What does he mean? She opens one eye, groaning as the room rotates. Steadily, it settles. He's placed a whiteboard near the camera. Words are printed upon it. They swim in and out of focus.

Elissa clenches her teeth.

'Do you want your mother to know you're not dead?'

She breathes deep. When she nods, her chin thumps against her chest. 'Yeth.' She spits out blood. 'Yes.'

'Look into the camera. Read the words. Say you understand.'

'I unner'thand.'

The ghoul curses.

Suddenly there's something hard against her mouth, the lip of a plastic beaker. She cringes away.

'Drink.'

Twice, now, he's drugged her. But when cool water touches her lips it's impossible to resist. She drinks hurriedly, greedily, until the front of her dress is soaked.

'Read the words. Say you understand.'

'I understand.'

The ghoul retreats before she can focus, and then he's behind the camera again, fiddling with the controls. The red LED reappears. Elissa knows it's her cue. On the whiteboard, those stark black letters shimmer and grow firm.

'My name . . .' She pauses, swallows. 'My name is Elissa Mirzoyan. Today is the twenty-third of October.'

The LED is like the eye of something terrible from a dream. Elissa avoids it, returning her attention to the whiteboard. Despite the water, her throat is already dry. 'I have not been harmed. I do not wish . . . do not wish . . .'

She reads the rest of the sentence without speaking. Her jaw begins to tremble. Her teeth clatter together in her mouth.

'Again,' the ghoul hisses. 'From the start. No pauses this time. Say you understand.'

'I . . .' Elissa begins. She's hardly listening any more. Her eyes are locked on those stark black letters. Their message is so shocking, so utterly distressing, that it wicks the air from her *lungs. The room rotates faster. She swears the ghoul is cavorting behind his camera, a whirlwind of jagged limbs, as if she's the princess in the fairy tale and he's Rumpelstiltskin dancing in the tower.*

Round and round the room goes. Strength drains from Elissa's limbs. She tries to tighten her grip on the manacle, but there's nothing she can do, and even as she's toppling from the chair her eyelids flicker like bat wings and the studio light, the rancid cell and the ghoul's ragged breathing vanish into a bottomless hole and don't come back.

II

Like before, Elissa's bladder wakens her. For a moment, cruelly brief, she thinks she's in her bedroom, but however hard she scours the darkness, she can't see the blue numerals of her alarm clock. All too soon, reality floods back.

The cell; the manacle; the metal chain.

The ghoul; the camcorder; the red light.

She moans, sliding out her legs. A thousand different pains assail her. It's colder, now. Does that mean it's night? Bracing the manacle, she sits up. The movement triggers a bout of coughing that dislodges something thick from deep inside her lungs. Using the chain as a guide, she inches to the iron ring. From there, she orients herself and heads out to B3, location of the waste bucket.

It's difficult to tug down her knickers without overbalancing, but somehow she manages. Soon, she hears the rattle of her urine against plastic. It smells bad, as if the drugs in her system have befouled it. Worse, as she's squatting over the bucket, she gets the urge to poo, and there's nothing she can do to stop herself.

That smells even worse, and it's not something that'll go away any time soon. She finds the toilet roll and wipes herself clean. Afterwards, she swishes her left hand in the cleaning bucket and dries her fingers on her dress. She'd like to pour some of the cleaning solution into the toilet to mask the odour, but the task defeats her.

Instead, she shuffles across the room to G7, location of the candles and matches. It's a moment's work to make light. When the candle flame swells, it reveals her rucksack, lying in F7.

Elissa cries out, so grateful for this small mercy that she nearly snuffs out the light. Dragging the rucksack over, she delves inside.

The first thing she touches is Monkey. Tears prick her eyes. Ridiculous to feel such emotion towards a stuffed toy. Putting her nose to his tummy, she breathes him in. When she stares into his face, his shiny black eyes brim with sympathy. It's another ridiculous notion, but she cannot dispel it. 'Don't you dare leave me again,' she tells him. 'Don't you dare.'

Setting Monkey down, she inventories the rucksack's contents: Stauntons, notepad and gel pens, satsuma, chocolate brownie, banana chips. Her books have been returned, and her water bottle, which has been refilled.

This time, she won't make the same mistake. Unscrewing the cap, she takes a steady drink. Then, legs crossed beneath her, she places Monkey in her lap and leans over the candle flame, soaking up its heat.

It's Monday, or so the ghoul said. Perhaps by now it's

Tuesday. If so, she's been here three full days, with only a bite of chocolate brownie and a bowl of Peppa Pig spaghetti to sustain her. No wonder she feels faint. Whenever she moves her head, the cell takes a moment to catch up.

Before indecision can paralyse her Elissa breaks open the banana chips and scoffs the lot. Afterwards, she digs out the chocolate brownie and takes two huge bites. She's tempted to eat the whole thing before the ghoul can confiscate it again. Instead, she seals what remains inside the wrapper and reaches under her dress, tucking the package into her underwear.

Monday, or possibly Tuesday.

Which means her mum has endured hell for at least forty-eight hours, possibly seventy-two. Will her dad know by now? Doubtless, Lena Mirzoyan will have tried to contact him, not out of any hope of support but out of a deep sense of duty. Hopefully, he'll be tucked away somewhere unreachable, unaware of current events. Because if he does know, he won't waste the opportunity to blame Lena. His motivation won't be concern for Elissa, only for the pain he can cause, the havoc he can wreak.

She tries to imagine what's happening at home. Will her grandparents have driven down from Birmingham? Will they be sitting on the sofa beside their daughter while a police officer updates them on the search?

There are no leads, Ms Mirzoyan. I'm afraid your girl isn't coming back.

She thinks about her normal weekday routine. On Mondays, her mum doesn't finish work until six, so after school Elissa goes across the street to Mrs McCluskey. The Irishwoman doesn't really like kids, but she likes the money she gets for two hours' childcare, which she feeds into an online casino while Elissa plays chess.

On Tuesdays, Elissa visits Lasse Haagensen, the Danish grandmaster who runs the school chess club. Although there's a small fee for the Wednesday club, Lasse doesn't charge anything for Elissa's one-on-one time. She used to think it was because he liked her mum. These days, she's not so sure. Lasse's flat is weird but cool, full of interesting ephemera. He's an obsessive collector – everything from Victorian mustard spoons to vintage Garbage Pail Kids stickers. Mainly, he collects chess sets. Elissa has played with most of them: delicate pieces sculpted from rare woods, marble or bone; chunkier designs forged from bronze or aluminium; themed sets featuring characters from *Star Trek*, *The Lord of the Rings*, *Alice's Adventures in Wonderland*; and her favourite set of all – a reproduction collection of Lewis chessmen carved from walrus ivory.

Most grandmasters eschew anything but the most basic Staunton designs, believing that even a milliwatt of brainpower wasted on piece identification will negatively affect their game. Lasse doesn't share that concern, which makes him much more fun than other GMs Elissa's met. The only set she won't use features the cast from *The Silence of the Lambs*, with Clarice Starling as the white queen and Hannibal Lecter as her opposite number.

Lasse showed her that movie once, mainly to point out a blooper: when Clarice visits a pair of chess-playing entomologists, their board is set up wrong, with a black square in the near right-hand corner instead of a white one. Then again, the scientists were using beetles for chess pieces, so the whole *thing* was pretty left-field.

Before the ghoul drugged her with the Peppa Pig

spaghetti, she'd been archiving her recollections of Wide Boys – one drawer for Andrea and one for the three *bodachs*. Now, it's time to fast-forward to the tournament itself and see if anything there can offer clues. If not, she'll switch direction and journey further back.

Of course, it's likely the ghoul snatched her purely at random, but even then this exercise could prove useful, because it's in the car park of the Marshall Court Hotel that she was abducted. *Those* memories might be the most important of all. A tiny detail, a half-forgotten snippet, might give her vital leverage.

Closing her eyes, she transports herself three days into the past.

III

The man had had hairy wrists that disappeared into frayed cuffs, but his face, just like the *bodachs'* in Wide Boys, remains frustratingly opaque.

'*Got your ticket?*' he'd asked, prompting Elissa to fetch it from the car. And, just before that: '*I'd have said you deserve a* much *larger fan club.*'

The white van had arrived by then. She remembers looking at the bumper and seeing the grinning skull smoking a cigarette, along with that single word in bold gothic script: *CHILLAX*.

When she'd opened the Fiesta's passenger door, the van had rocked on its springs. Horrible to think it must have been the ghoul, shifting position for a better look. On the van's bumper she'd spotted a cluster of tiny impact dents.

It's all she can remember.

Back in the hotel, she'd presented her ticket. The man with skinny wrists had said something, making her wonder at his meaning.

'Disaster averted.'

In hindsight, those words feel like a sarcastic precursor to what followed, but she mustn't impart meaning where none exists. Looking back, *everything* anyone said or did that day – Andrea at Wide Boys, the three *bodach* customers, the man at registration – seems prescient. But her abduction can't have been a mass conspiracy. Not all those people are complicit.

Skipping forward to the tournament, Elissa recalls her competitors. There was Bhavya Narayan, the smiling Hindu girl with the Hanuman statuette. After the match, Bhavya's parents had given Elissa a bag of home-made banana chips. The idea that they kidnapped her is farcical.

Her next opponent was Amy Rhodes. Amy's parents had been as horrible as their daughter, but they patently weren't kidnappers. After Amy had come Ivy May, with Coke-bottle glasses and a Peppa Pig mascot. There had been nothing noteworthy in that encounter, either. With a sigh, Elissa opens two more drawers in her mental chessboard. Into A8 goes the man with the hairy wrists. Into B8 she loads Bhavya Narayan, Amy Rhodes and Ivy May.

Elissa rolls the drawers shut. Then she opens C8. The darkness it reveals is particularly unsettling, because this is where she'll house her memories of the abduction itself. She's just about to start the process when she hears muted sounds of commotion outside the door.

I V

Blowing out the candle, Elissa lies down and closes her eyes. Even though it's futile, the instinct to feign sleep is irresistible. Since the ghoul's last visit, she's avoided thinking about what was printed on his whiteboard. If she speaks those words on camera, the pain she'll cause is unthinkable.

But if she refuses, what then?

She recalls the darkish stain on the floor – what she believes is the last evidence of Bryony, an earlier resident of this cell.

The door squeals open.

Elissa's heart thumps like a drum.

Footsteps now, accompanied by the mad flitting of a torch. It's not the ice-white light carried by the ghoul. This one, yellow and stuttering, looks like it's transmitting desperate lines of Morse code.

Elijah.

Opening her eyes, Elissa breathes out explosively. She knows, from their first meeting, how fragile he is; knows, too, that he's a part of this. That *should* make him the enemy but, even though she can't trust him, she senses an opportunity here, if only she can work out the right strategy. Elijah doesn't respond well to directness. Down here in the dark, she needs to be more oblique.

When his torch moves to the waste bucket, Elissa wrinkles her nose. 'Sorry. I was going to deal with it. But my wrist . . .' She pauses, closes her mouth. Even though she's shackled and wounded, it's against her nature to admit weakness.

The light picks out her injury. Elijah swallows noisily. 'You said it was just a gash. That it wasn't bad.'

'It's worse than I thought. It goes pretty deep, and it won't stop bleeding.'

'In here, all this damp and rot – a wound like that can get serious really quick.'

'That's what *he* said.'

Something tells her that mentioning the ghoul was a mistake. She needs to distract Elijah, and quickly. 'Don't suppose you have a first-aid kit.'

'Afraid not.'

He shuffles closer, his torch beam focused on her wrist. The wound is a gaping black mouth from which blood steadily dribbles. There's pus, too, a glistening stream.

This close, she hears the nasal rasp of Elijah's breathing. There's something odd about it, something thick and loose. She wonders if he has a facial deformity, some kind of a disfigurement. Perhaps that's why he insists on remaining hidden.

'You could make a bandage,' he ventures.

'Out of what?'

'Your dress. Just a strip, from the bottom.'

'I can't tear the fabric.'

'*I* could.'

'You?'

'If you wanted.'

The prospect of physical contact nearly makes her gag, but her wound needs attention. 'You won't hurt me?'

Elijah's gasp is so loud it's almost theatrical. 'I would

never hurt you.' With a scrape of movement, he edges nearer, torch beam blinking. Elissa can't help but shut her eyes. He doesn't revolt her – not like the ghoul – but she still can't bear him close. When she feels him lift the hem of her dress, it takes an enormous feat of willpower to remain still.

Cold air seeps between her knees. Prising open an eye, she sees he's turned off the torch. She hears him working on her dress, but it's not the ripping sound she'd expected, and it makes her heart beat even faster. 'Is that a knife?'

Elijah stills. As the seconds lengthen, Elissa feels the moisture in her mouth evaporating.

'Are you worried I'll cut you?' he asks.

The question is innocent enough, but in this lightless cell it acquires a disturbing nuance. When she swallows, the sound is monstrously loud, a wordless expression of her unease.

Elijah must have noticed, but he doesn't say anything else. His question hangs unanswered between them. After what feels like an eternity, the blade continues its work, whispering as it severs the fabric.

On his footwear, she smells the loamy richness of leaf mulch. During his previous visit, he told her they were beneath a place he calls the Memory Wood. She guesses that's probably true. Damp earth and forest aren't the only things she smells. There's a fustiness to his clothes, as if they've gone far too long without washing. She wonders how long it's been since he last bathed.

'Kneel up,' he says, once the knife's travelled a half-circuit. Silent, she raises her buttocks. A minute later, Elijah grunts in satisfaction. 'All done. Now we have a bandage.'

'Thanks.'

He makes no move to turn on the torch. 'You know we have to clean the wound.'

'I guess.'

'It's going to hurt.'

'Yeah.'

For a while, he's silent. Then he asks, 'Would you like me to help you?'

Hearing that, she feels like screaming: *I want you to get me OUT of here! I want you to call the POLICE, Elijah! BRING THEM DOWN HERE, LIKE I ASKED!* But she doesn't. Instead, closing her eyes, she murmurs her agreement.

Elijah leaves her side. She hears him rustling around near the door: A3, perhaps, or A4. The ease with which he negotiates the darkness is disconcerting. His mental map of the cell clearly rivals her own. When she hears the scrape of hard plastic against stone, she realizes he's sliding one of the buckets towards her. A whiff of cleaning solution reaches her nose. Some of the liquid slops over the side, spattering on to the floor.

'How'd you want to do this?' he asks.

Elissa feels her mind beginning to seize up. Quickly, she whispers, 'You decide.'

Elijah seems pleased to be given the responsibility. He clicks his tongue absently, like a tradesman assessing a job. She wonders if it's all an act.

'If you held out your arm,' he says, 'I could pour some of this stuff over it. But you'd probably get wet, and then you'd get cold. What we *should* do is dunk your whole arm in. Properly submerge it. Wash out the wound and kill all the germs.'

Elissa clenches her teeth. It makes sense, but she can't bear thinking about how much it'll hurt.

'I'll hold your bracelet,' Elijah tells her. 'You have to do this, Elissa. You've no choice.'

She moans when she hears that, and it's such a pathetic sound – so meek and desperate – that fresh tears begin to well.

'It's OK,' Elijah mutters. And of course it's not. She feels his fingers slide around the manacle. Deprived of light, her mind paints a picture of the boy she cannot see: lamp-like eyes peering over a mouth twisted by a cleft palate into a monstrosity of bulging gums and reaching teeth. The image frightens her, even though she knows it can't be true. Elijah suffers no impediment to his speech. If he's burdened with disfigurement, it's something far less obvious than that.

Bracelet, he called it a bracelet. Like it's a harmless piece of jewellery.

'Ready?' he asks.

'Wait.' Elissa shakes her head. 'I can't, not yet. I'm not ready.'

'You have to.'

'What if . . .' she begins, but she doesn't really have a question. Her wrist is open almost to the bone. The pain, when disinfectant meets raw flesh, will be extraordinary.

'Kneel up,' Elijah urges her. 'Like before.' He lifts the manacle a few inches off her lap and she's so worried about it touching her injury that she complies. With her free hand, she touches the bucket. Elijah guides her arm towards the lip. The chain rattles, snaking out. Soon, her hand is in position.

'You want to go fast or slow?' he asks.

'Fast. Once it's in, don't let me pull away.'

'I'll do my best. Try not to knock over the bucket.'

Elissa's teeth are clenched so tightly her reply comes out as a hiss.

'Ready?' Elijah asks, and before she can reply he plunges her wrist into a sea of screams.

V

The world returns slowly, a gradual awareness of time and space. It's a while before Elissa realizes where she is, or what she has become. Her wrist throbs in time with her heart, but it's not the barbed-wire-in-her-veins agony of before.

She's lying on her side. In her nose is the pillow's mildewed stink. When she investigates with her left hand, she discovers that her injured wrist has been bound with the material cut from her dress. Elijah has done a good job.

Sitting up in the darkness, Elissa listens to the silence, trying to work out if she's alone. Her throat is raw, a memento of her scream. She shuffles over to F7, dragging her chain. Finding her rucksack, careful not to dislodge Monkey, she removes the water bottle and takes a long drink. 'Well,' she says, addressing the knitted mannequin, 'I guess we should see what's what.'

The candle holder is beside the rucksack. It already contains a stub, so Elissa locates the matches. She's just about to strike one when a light winks on from a source near the far wall.

Gasping, she drops the match and scoots backwards. Although the light isn't strong, it's bright enough to disorient her. She shields her eyes, realizing with nausea that she's had company all along.

'You were talking,' Elijah says softly. 'After you went unconscious.'

Elissa takes a moment to compose herself. When she speaks, her voice is barely a croak. 'What did I say?'

'Creepy stuff.'

That he stayed in the cell while she was out cold – that he didn't announce himself immediately when she woke – feels like the most grotesque intrusion. But she won't benefit by mentioning it. 'Like what?'

' "Hallowe'en eyes. Hallowe'en eyes watching out, watching out for me." I didn't like it.'

She couldn't give a damn whether he liked it or not, but hearing the dream words makes her shiver. Suddenly, she realizes how cold she is. 'Thanks,' she tells him. 'For doing what you did.'

'That's OK.'

'I mean it, Elijah. You didn't have to help. I know you're taking a risk, coming down here.'

'It can be our secret. A game.'

'Yes,' she replies. Sensing his enthusiasm, she adds, 'Like we're characters in a story.'

'I like *that*,' he says. 'That's good. That's *really* good.' She hears him snatch up something from the floor and begin to fiddle with it. 'Who would we be?'

'Oh, I don't know. But we'd definitely be goodies.'

'Well, I'm not a baddie.'

'I know you're not, not you, Elijah. You helped me, remember?' Her lips widen into what she hopes looks like a genuine smile. 'We'd . . . we'd be brother and sister.'

The object Elijah plucked from the floor whispers in his fingers. 'Huh,' he says. 'I never had a sister.'

'Brother and sister, like . . . like . . .' Then inspiration strikes. 'Like the kids in that fairy tale. Hansel and Gretel.'

Elijah laughs, delighted. 'I'm Hansel and you're Gretel! Which . . . which makes this . . . the *Gingerbread* House!'

His amusement – so at odds with her situation – is chilling, but she feels like she's on to something so she perseveres. 'I keep wondering what this place looks like above ground. Now I won't be able to get the image of gingerbread walls out of my head.'

'It doesn't look anything like *that* up there,' he replies. 'I wish it did. There's a *tree* growing in the front room, for goodness' sake.'

'Gingerbread walls, icing-sugar windows and a roof made of chocolate, fixed in place with gloopy toffee.'

Elijah chuckles. 'The walls are stone, the windows are all broken and Papa's stripped most of the tiles off the roof.'

Elissa knows she should go on talking, but that last bit has frozen her voice. Through her game, she's caught him off guard, and what he's revealed could be key.

Papa's stripped most of the tiles off the roof.

She clears her throat, sparking a coughing fit so severe she fears she'll be sick.

'What's wrong?' Elijah asks. His torch beam stutters, as if attuned to his unease.

'Nothing. Just . . . I don't know. Coming down with something, I guess. These last few days, I've eaten hardly anything.'

'Do you like pecan-nut biscuits?'

'This isn't really the Gingerbread House.'

'I know *that*, silly.'

Out of the darkness sails a parcel of greaseproof paper, landing by her foot. Unwrapping it, Elissa discovers a lop-sided biscuit. She falls on it like a wolf upon a newborn lamb.

Afterwards, a silence ensues that is almost companion-able. 'I went through your bag,' Elijah says, sounding abashed. 'I found a notebook. Full of what looked like secret code.'

'It is code,' she tells him, screwing the greaseproof paper into a ball. 'But it isn't secret.'

'What's the point of a code if not to keep secrets?'

'For brevity.'

'For what?'

'For making things simple, so they're quickly recorded.'

Elijah sniffs. 'I have secrets. Lots of them.'

'Most people do.'

'Probably not as bad as mine.'

She doesn't know what to say to that, so she keeps quiet.

'The worst ones,' he says, 'I can hardly remember.'

'If you can't remember them, how'd you know they exist?'

His feet scrape restlessly. It's clear he doesn't want to talk about it. Instead, he picks up whatever he was examin-ing earlier. 'I found these,' he says. 'A whole bag of them.'

Elissa raises herself on to her side. She can't see any-thing past the yellow beam of his torch, but she hears the clacking of her Stauntons and knows he's found the draw-string bag.

'What are they?' Elijah asks.

'They're mine.'

'I know *that*, silly. But what *are* they?'

'They're chess pieces.'

'They're pretty. More than pretty. They're beautiful.' Elijah takes a deep breath and sighs it out. 'Almost . . . magical.'

'They're made of Brazilian rosewood,' she tells him '*Dalbergia nigra* – that's the Latin name. It's a vulnerable species now, so they don't make stuff from it any more, but it wasn't when they were carved.'

'They feel warm.'

Elissa nods. She's always thought that, too. 'Sniff them.'

'They smell sweet.'

'The scent never fades. They say it's one of the special things about Brazilian rosewood.'

'What do you do with them?'

'I told you. They're chess pieces.' Elissa inclines her head. 'You haven't heard of chess?'

She hears a huff of expelled breath and curses her carelessness. He's so easy to hurt. So easy to offend, too.

''Course I've heard of it,' Elijah mutters. 'I just never saw the actual pieces before. Or had anyone explain the rules.'

It's a golden opening, and she won't waste it. Feeling more confident in her movements now that her wrist is bandaged, she tucks her legs beneath her. 'Well, if you like, I could teach you.'

'You'd do that?'

'What else am I going to do down here?'

Elijah grunts. 'Not much, I suppose.'

He sounds hurt, and she can't work out why. It bothers her, the not-knowing.

'You could try to escape,' he points out.

Elissa licks her lips. There's no safe answer to that, so she ignores it entirely.

'How long would it take? To teach me chess?'

'If you mean the basics, no more than an hour or so. If you're talking about playing well – then probably an entire lifetime.'

'I have a pretty high IQ.'

'That's great. That'll definitely help. What is it?'

He's quiet for a moment. 'What's what?'

'Your IQ.'

Another pause. 'It's how clever you are.'

Elissa blinks. 'Sure, but what's your score?'

'Score?'

'IQ tests,' she says, 'give a score. The higher your score, the better your ability. What was your result?'

'Um . . . ninety-nine.'

She raises her eyebrows. 'Right, well. You'll have no problem with chess, then.'

Elijah exhales in a rush. 'When could we start?'

'No time like the present.'

'You mean . . . like *now*?'

'Why not?'

'I wasn't . . . well, I hadn't . . . well, OK.'

'Are you sure?'

He's still for a moment. Then: 'Yeah. I'm positive. One hundred per cent.'

'You'd better pass me the pieces.'

The bag curves out of the dark and thumps down in front of her. Elissa cringes at the ill treatment of her Stauntons. Releasing the bag's drawstring, she delves inside. 'This,' she announces, drawing out a fragrant rosewood chess piece, 'is the king.'

Elijah sucks in a breath. 'I want to be him.'

'We'll both get a king.'

'You can't have two kings.'

'In chess, you can.'

'There's only ever one king. The most powerful person in the land.'

'Not in this game,' Elissa tells him. She draws out another piece and holds it up to the light. 'In *this* game, the most powerful person is the queen.'

VI

For the next hour, she talks through the game's basic principles. She teaches Elijah about the six individual pieces, explaining how they move and where they're all set up. That last bit is challenging without a board to aid her, but Elijah's a quick learner; she tests him often and he remembers everything. Elissa grows so focused on her task that, for a while, everything else recedes. She is the teacher and he is the student, and that is *all* they are. And then she moves her right hand and the chain clatters across the floor; the fantasy evaporates and the entire sick nightmare floods back.

'How does the knight move?' she asks, blinking through her tears.

'Side-forward-forward, or forward-forward-side.'

'The bishop?'

'Diagonally, any direction, as far as it likes.'

'Pawn?'

'One step forward, except the first time, which can be two steps, unless it's taking a piece, which it does diagonally.'

'Except . . .'

'*En passant.*'

'Top marks.'

She hears from his tone that he's grinning. 'I never heard of anything as cool as this.'

'Welcome to the best game in the world.'

She can't see his eyes, but she bets they're shining. His breathing has accelerated too. All this excitement, and he hasn't even tried the real thing.

Elijah says, 'I can't wait to play a game.'

Hook, line and sinker.

With a rueful smile, she closes the drawstring bag. 'I'm sure, one day, you'll get the chance.'

Elissa *feels* the atmosphere change – something different in the quality of the silence. 'What's wrong?' she asks.

Her voice is a touch too silky. She hopes she still sounds sincere.

'What's the point of teaching me all this if you've no intention of playing with me?' Elijah demands.

'You want a game with *me*?'

'Of *course* I want a game with you! Otherwise . . . who the hell else am I going to play with?'

'I just thought you wanted to know the rules.'

'No! Where's the fun in that? What's the *point* of that? I don't want to just learn about it. I want to *play*. We *have* to play.'

'We?'

'You and me. Brother and sister.'

'Oh.' She pauses. A smile spreads across her face. 'Hansel and Gretel.'

'Yeah, exactly. Hansel and Gretel, playing chess—'

'—inside the Gingerbread House—'

'—inside the Memory Wood.'

Elissa holds the smile a beat longer. Then she loses it. 'Shame it's not possible.'

'What?'

'I mean, considering you know all the rules. We've even got all the pieces.'

'So what's the problem?'

'I'd have thought that was obvious.' Elissa holds her breath. It's risky to rile him like this, but she thinks it's worth it.

'It's not obvious to *me*.' His voice is raised. If he were standing, he'd probably stamp his foot. Perhaps he's not Hansel, after all. Perhaps he's Rumpelstiltskin.

'Elijah.'

'What?'

'We don't have a board.'

His torch beam freezes. Then it skitters around the cell. 'We don't?'

'Not any more. I had one, in my rucksack. It's more of a mat than a board, but it works just as well. When I woke in here, it was gone.' She blinks, staring fully into the light. '*He* took it.'

A pause of two beats. Then, brightening, Elijah says, 'We can play on the floor.'

'These pieces are hand-carved, based with real leather. The floor would ruin them. We need a board.'

He sighs out a breath. 'And we don't have one.'

She tilts her head. 'Could you get me my play mat?'

'You want me to steal it?'

'It's mine. So it wouldn't be stealing.'

'It's not yours any more.'

'OK. But could you get it?'

'No.'

'Do you know where it is?'

'How could I?'

Elissa shrugs.

'We really can't use the floor?'

The hope in his voice is transparent. She takes great pleasure in crushing it. 'No chance in the world.' Taking out a chess piece, she turns it around and around. The wood slips against her fingers: *shlep-shlep-shlep*.

She can sense Elijah's frustration in the tremor of the torch beam. She's filled him with expectation and now he can't handle his disappointment.

Shlep-shlep-shlep.

'There's *one* way we could play,' she says absently, almost as if talking to herself.

The beam falls still. 'There is?'

'One of the best ways, actually – the way I play a lot at home. It lets you compete against anyone in the world, wherever they are, and whenever you like.'

'That's impossible.'

'It's absolutely possible. You could be in a tent in Timbuktu and I could be at a research station in Antarctica, and as long as we had an internet connection, we could play a game.'

'A what connection?'

This is better than she'd expected. 'Doesn't matter. If we're face to face, we don't even need one of those. We can use pass-and-play.'

'Pass and . . . What're you talking about?'

'I'm talking about the *chess.com* app. In fact, any chess app you like. But that one's the best.'

'What's an app?'

'Are you kidding me?'

'That's unkind,' Elijah says. 'You shouldn't be unkind.'

'I'm sorry. I wasn't trying to be. It's just . . . OK, "app" is short for "application". It's a piece of software, like a game or something, that you use on your tablet or your—'

'Tablet?' he says, scoffing. 'You mean like a pill?'

'No, I mean like a computer. Like an iPad. A flat screen you activate with your fingers. Have you seen one of those, Elijah?'

'Nuh . . . Maybe.'

'Doesn't matter if you haven't. Not as many people use them as they once did. And I don't bother with the *chess.com* app on my tablet, anyway. I prefer using it on my phone.'

He snorts. 'You're telling me you can play chess on a *phone*?'

'If you have the app.'

'How'd you get it?'

'It's free. You just download it.'

He doesn't respond.

'A button press, Elijah. Nothing more.'

'It's that easy?'

'It's that easy.'

'On any phone?'

'Well, not the really old ones. But pretty much any smartphone. Which is most of them, these days.'

'I don't have a phone,' Elijah says. Now, more than any time previously, she wishes she could see his expression.

She shrugs.

There's a minute or so of silence. Then he laughs.

It's not the same sound as earlier. This one isn't joyful. It makes her skin prickle. There's something odd about it. Something not-quite-right. 'What's funny?'

'You're trying to trick me,' he says. 'Aren't you? You want me to bring you a phone so you can call someone to come down here and get you.'

'No, I'm—'

'Yes. You are. You're trying to trick me—'

'Elijah—'

'—and if you think you can trick me, you'll think you can trick him, and then you'll fail the test, and then you won't be here any more and I'll be all alone.'

'I just thought you wanted to play chess.'

'You don't understand the danger.'

'I'm not trying to trick you, Elijah.'

'I don't want you to die.'

'Why would I die?'

'Because you're playing with fire. And that's what happens to people who play with fire. They mess up, and then they die.' He swallows. 'Kyle was right. You're dangerous.'

'Kyle? Is that his name? Is that who brought me down here?'

She's going far faster than she intended, but now she's started she can't hold back. 'Do you know what he's planning? Is there anything I can—'

'Stop, just stop.'

'Please, Elijah, all I'm asking is—'

'*NO!*'

His voice boomerangs around the tiny space.

Elissa lurches backwards. The manacle pulls taut against her wrist. She screams long and hard. Even with her makeshift bandage, the pain is grotesque. It feels like a wolf has seized her in its teeth and is chewing through her flesh.

Elijah scrabbles to his feet. She waits for the feel of his

hands on her skin – over her mouth or around her throat. Instead, all she catches is the erratic flickering of his torch as he charges out of the cell. The door swings closed. Three heavy deadbolts shoot home.

Pain and silence fill the void.

Mostly pain.

ELIJAH

Day 4

I

My head ringing with voices, I crash through the Memory Wood, desperate for peace. I cannot believe I shouted at Gretel; cannot believe, either, that she'd be so foolish – so brave and reckless and gosh-damned *admirable* – to try and trick me.

As I stumble between the trees, my trainers ripping through wet bracken, all I can smell is the sweetness of Brazilian rosewood.

In this *game, the most powerful person is the queen.*

I thought Magic Annie was the only sorceress I knew, but Elissa Mirzoyan has put a spell on me more powerful than any I could have imagined.

Among the gaggle of voices, Kyle's words stand out: *You're gunna cover us all in shit.*

Maybe he's right. Maybe I am. Because if there's one thing I've decided, it's this: Elissa Mirzoyan can't die. Not in that hole. Not while my heart still beats.

She ain't like the others.

If Kyle's right about anything, he's right about that.

Still thinking about what just happened, I lift my head and find that I've wandered into the Memory Wood's most sacred grove. A short distance away, in the shade of one of my Memory Trees, stands Mama.

II

With the autumn light dying, the russet shades of our surroundings are losing their vigour. But Mama doesn't fade. Her hair is like liquid gold, so warm and brilliant it makes my tummy go fuzzy. It's not the only thing about her that seems brighter than the day. She glows with energy, as if the sunshine in her heart has leaked through her skin. Watching her, I'm bewitched. After my morning with Annie yesterday, and my afternoon with Elissa today, it feels like I'm overdosing on magic.

I do this, sometimes, to the people I love. There's a word I read once: *deify*. I'm not sure it's exactly right, but it's pretty close; Mama, to me, has a purity beyond the reach of normal human beings.

She's wearing blue jeans with flared bottoms, a North Face gilet over a plaid work shirt and mud-spattered desert boots. There's mascara on her eyelashes and a maroon smear across her mouth. She looks like I want my wife to look, if I ever end up getting married.

Unusual to find her out here. She doesn't venture into the Memory Wood often, and only ever to pick herbs or mushrooms or to forage a bit of firewood.

A stick cracks under my foot and she flinches, wheeling around.

'Elijah,' she says, and I can see from her expression that I've startled her. Over her shoulder is a sun-faded orange rucksack that looks vaguely familiar; there's a hand-sewn patch on the side, like the ones they make for NASA missions. Mama adjusts the straps until it sits more snugly against her spine. 'You know you're not allowed in these woods. What are you doing out here?'

I think of the Gingerbread House, and Gretel, and how she tried to trick me into bringing her a phone. 'Just playing.'

'Have you seen Kyle?'

'Earlier.'

She tilts her head. 'Is he being kinder to you?'

'He's being OK. I think he's frightened.'

'We're all frightened, Elijah, in our own way. Your brother's no different.' She lifts her gaze to something behind me. I stiffen, realizing that she's calculating my path between the trees. 'How long have you been out here?'

'Not long.'

'Did you do your reading?'

'Yes, Mama.'

Her shoulders relax, and I can tell she's finished admonishing me.

Tugging the collar of her gilet a little tighter, she says, 'There's a *heaviness* to the air, don't you think? I thought the storm would break today, but all we've had is this spotty rain.'

'We need a good downpour.'

'We do. It'll blow away all the cobwebs, freshen up the sky. Elijah, I don't want to find you out here again, understand? This place, these woods . . .' She hesitates, her eyes clouding over. 'Promise me.'

'I swear it, Mama.'

It's an easy promise to make. She didn't ask me to stay away, just to make sure she doesn't find me. Trouble is, with Mama, even the slightest of wool-pulling feels sneaky. 'What're *you* doing here?' I ask.

'Thinking.'

'About what?'

'About you, about Kyle. About your father.'

'What about us?'

'Do you like living here, Elijah? Do you want to stay?'

I stare at her, dumbfounded. The estate, the cottage, the Memory Wood: it's all I've ever known. My throat aches with the pressure of pent-up emotion. *No!* I want to shout. *I hate it! I want to live in a house on a street, with pavements and lamp posts and neighbours. I want to go to a proper school, with other kids my own age. I want a mobile phone, with apps. I want my own chessboard, my own chess pieces. I want them to smell like Gretel's, all buttery and sweet, and I want Gretel to live next door so I can see her whenever I want.*

Instead, I say, 'I love it here.'

Mama thrusts her hands into her pockets. 'I'll see you back at the house, Elijah,' she says. 'After today, I don't want you out in these woods again.'

This time, if I acknowledge her words, I'll trap myself, so I keep quiet. Mama watches me a moment longer. Then she turns and picks her way through the trees. It doesn't take long for the Memory Wood to swallow her up.

At last, I'm alone again. It'll be dark in an hour. I feel far colder than I should. Looking down, I see that my trainers are soaked through. As I walk, I think of the secret world beneath my feet: the damp cellar and its precious resident. I hear the whispery slither of rosewood as it rotates in Gretel's fingers.

In this *game, the most powerful person is the queen.*

Gretel isn't a queen, but she does have power. It's only a matter of time before she uses it. When she does, the fallout will affect us all.

Everyone tells me I'm a clever clogs, a bright spark. But I've no clue what to do next. One thing I do know is that I have bad instincts, which means there's a good chance that, whatever happens, I'll choose the wrong path.

I'm still considering that when the report of a high-powered rifle tears the Memory Wood's silence to shreds.

III

Around me, every pheasant, crow, magpie and jay explodes into the sky, a startled symphony of caws, shrieks and beating wings.

I'm still standing, which means I haven't been shot. That wasn't the sound of Kyle's .22 but the crack of a supersonic bullet compressing the air.

Mama.

My heart rises into my throat. What if she's been hit? An image comes to me of her lying prone, brains strewn about like so much grey Bolognese. I feel something inside my head quiver, as if a wall's about to collapse, but no more than a few seconds pass before my pulse begins to slow. If Mama had been hit – if her thoughts and memories had been scattered across the soil – I'd know. I'd feel it like a cavity in my own head, and when I close my eyes and focus I'm sure that she's OK. When I open them, I see someone emerge from the undergrowth that I wasn't expecting: the lord of Rufus Hall and master of this estate – Leon Meunier.

IV

'*You*,' he hisses, crashing through dead leaves to reach me. 'Good Christ, what have I told you, eh?' He grabs me by the arm and turns me around, checking for what I can only imagine are bullet holes. 'I've made it *abundantly* clear that these woods are off limits. How long have you been out here? What on earth have you been doing?'

I'm about to tell him I've just been playing, but then I remember how much that word seems to rile him. To the lord of Famerhythe, there's work and there's blood sport, and little else between.

Under a tweed jacket, his check shirt is paired with an olive tie embroidered with tiny kingfishers. Over the jacket is a hunter's vest, the same shade of orange as Mama's ruck-sack. Perhaps she was wearing it for the same reason: protection through visibility. Meunier's grey hair, falling in slick ripples like those on a Roman bust, is partially hidden by a cloth cap. His nose is fleshy and pore-pitted. His lips are large for a man's: plump fruits full of dark blood. By contrast, his eyes seem almost entirely lacking in colour.

'Are you deaf or dumb or both?' he demands, shoulder-ing his rifle. 'Well? Cough it out.'

'I . . . I wasn't doing any harm. I was just walking, sir.'

'I could've put a bullet through you. Then where would we have been?'

Meunier glares at me a moment longer. Then a change

seems to come over him. His fierce expression loosens. Those full lips push outwards, giving him the appearance of a Napoleon fish. 'You'd better come with me,' he says, releasing my arm. When he strides off through the trees, I know well enough to keep up.

'What were you shooting at?' I ask, after we've walked a few minutes in silence.

At first, Meunier doesn't answer. As we skirt the clearing where the oldest Memory Trees grow, he crouches beside a sharp impression in the mud. 'See that? The way the dew claws are set so far back?'

'A boar. Did you get one?'

'No. Blighter tore off just before I pulled the trigger.'

Meunier introduced boar into these woods years ago. With no natural predators – except for the man himself – their numbers have swelled. They're scary as hell. If I hear one in the undergrowth, I bolt in the opposite direction.

It seems Meunier has read my thoughts, because he says, 'They're vicious shits. You surprise one – especially a mother with young – it's more likely to attack than run away. If it gets its tusks into you, you've had it. Which is why you shouldn't, under any circumstances, be wandering around these woods. Tell me you understand.'

'I do.'

'Say it.'

'I understand.'

'Better.'

Meunier climbs to his feet. He sets off again, and I trip along beside him. Five minutes later we emerge on to the lane that runs past Fallow Field. His Land Rover Defender is parked halfway across it. 'Hop in,' he says. 'I'll run you back home.'

I can't refuse, even though the prospect makes me sick. That pressure inside my head returns, like a wall's about to collapse. I don't know what's behind it, but I'm pretty sure it's not good.

The Defender smells citrusy, as if it's recently been cleaned. I'm almost too afraid to let my filthy trainers touch the floor.

'Don't fuss,' Meunier says, placing his rifle on the back seat. 'It's valeted every week. If you mess it up, at least they'll earn their money.' His lips spread further apart, and I'm struck by just how horrid it would feel to be kissed by him. Poor Mrs Meunier. Perhaps that's one of the reasons we never see her.

He throws the 4x4 into reverse and performs a thumping three-point turn. Between us, the central console holds a bulky set of keys, a folded *Daily Telegraph*, a black mobile phone and a Zeiss night scope. There's also a brown leather wallet falling apart at the seams, stuffed full of cash, bank cards and receipts. Other than that, the vehicle looks like it's just been driven from the showroom.

Meunier accelerates up the track. When the front wheels bounce over a hump, the quartered newspaper falls open, exposing half the front page.

Gretel stares up at me.

It's such a shock that I slam back in my seat. When Meunier turns towards me I peer straight ahead, praying he won't glance down. I need a distraction, and fast. Pointing to Fallow Field, I ask, 'What's the plan for next year?'

Meunier follows the thrust of my finger. 'Personally, I want to try a biofuel,' he says. 'A starch crop we can convert into ethanol. Something along those lines.'

With his attention diverted, I risk another look at the

paper. The headline swims in and out of focus, but two words are unmistakable: *HOPE FADES* . . .

When we pull up outside my parents' cottage Meunier faces me. 'Remember what I said. Don't let me catch you in those woods again.'

'I won't.'

I have every intention of keeping that promise too. Perhaps I'll get Kyle to teach me his silent walk or lend me his stinky camouflage paint. Clambering out of the Land Rover, I slam the door.

HOPE FADES.

Meunier waits a few moments before driving off. I feel his eyes on me as I trudge up the garden path.

MAIRÉAD

Day 5

Nearly one hundred hours, now, since the abduction. The pressure on the investigation team is huge. Elissa's fate is discussed on radio phone-ins, on social media, by parents collecting their kids from school. Her face appears on every news site and front page. Sightings continue to roll in, an unrelenting tide; to the control room at Winfrith; to forces across the UK. The task of logging them, prioritizing them and investigating or discounting them is a major feat of logistics.

Many of the calls come from dog-walkers on Dorset's beaches. Karen Day, the Police Search Adviser, coordinates a huge team of officers, fire crews and civilian volunteers. Together, they search vast swathes of coast. The RNLI and coastguard provide waterborne support.

Meanwhile, hundreds of Bedford CF vans are tracked down, their owners interviewed and eliminated. The BMW driver who brake-checked Lena Mirzoyan is identified as Stuart Nicholas Pearson, an obnoxious financial adviser in his forties with a string of motoring convictions. He's not a suspect – ANPR data shows him fifty miles away during the abduction. Officers drag him into an empty interview room regardless; leaving him there for a few hours to sweat gives everyone an odd sense of catharsis.

During her Wednesday-morning press briefing, Mairéad is fielding questions from the assembled press pack when she feels a sharp twinge of pain in her lower abdomen. For a few seconds, she cannot speak. Around the room, cameras click and flash. Journalists lean forward in their seats, eyes full of mischief. She knows what they're thinking. Is the pressure getting too much? Are the cracks starting to show? Is she too emotional? Too fragile? Can she be *trusted* with this?

And all Mairéad can think, as she stares into a forest of blank lenses and boom mics, is *Hold on, please hold on, stay with me, please don't go.*

She tries to say something, anything, but pain lances her abdomen once again. She wants to bend double, knows that she can't. Mairéad's ears fill with shouted questions. When she turns her back on the room, the journalists howl like wolves denied a kill. Halley, standing to one side, stares at her in open dismay. She pushes past him without breaking stride.

A minute later she's in a cubicle, leaning against the partition wall. Already, the pain has retreated. But chaos rules inside her head. She cannot get her breath, cannot slow her heart.

At last, she lifts up her skirt and tugs down her underwear. There's the evidence: two spots of blood, stark and accusatory and bleak. Her shoulders sag. And then she's sitting, and her mobile's in her hand, and she's phoning Scott.

'I was just watching you on TV,' he says. 'What is it? Are you OK?'

Deep breath. 'I think it's happening,' she says. 'The baby, I mean. I think I might be losing this one too.'

She's pleased – pathetically so – by her matter-of-fact tone. The last thing either of them needs is hysterics.

'OK,' Scott says. 'I'm here. I'm listening. Talk me through it.'

'There's . . . I felt some pain.' She swallows. 'And there's spotting.'

Silence, on the line, for the space of two breaths.

'Hon, listen to me. I know that's scary, I know. And I know it's your body, and you know what you're feeling, and there's no better judge. But . . . but those symptoms, on their own – they don't necessarily mean you're miscarrying. They don't. I can be out of here in five minutes. I'll come and pick you up. We'll call the surgery, get Dr Michaels to refer us. I'll drive you over to EPAU. And if—'

'Scott, no.' She shakes her head. 'You don't need to do that.'

'I think we should get this checked out.'

'I know. I agree. I'll call the surgery right now. But you don't need to come down here and get me. Seriously. I'm a big girl.' Mairéad forces out a laugh she doesn't feel. Truth is, if the worst really has happened, it'll be easier to face without him there.

Perhaps, on some level, Scott understands that, because he doesn't put up much of a fight. 'Are you sure?'

'I'm positive. Look, I'll phone them now, see what they say, let you know how I get on. And Scott . . . I'm sorry.'

Mairéad hangs up before he can respond. And then she searches her contacts for the surgery. Her hands are shaking so much it's difficult to navigate the directory.

Hold on, please hold on, stay with me, please don't go.

She finds the number and is just about to call it when her phone starts ringing. It's Halley.

'Wherever you are, whatever you're doing,' he says, 'stop right now. We've got something.'

ELISSA

Day 5

I

After Elijah leaves, Elissa's so weary that she curls around her rucksack and sleeps. When she wakes, cold and bruised from the rocky floor, she lights a fresh candle and reviews their conversation. She's gained a few insights, particularly via his throwaway comment about the building above her head: *The walls are stone, the windows are all broken and Papa's stripped most of the tiles off the roof.*

Does Elijah's father own the cottage? Is he restoring it? Since she's been down here, she's heard no building work, but the cell's partition wall and ceiling have been carefully designed to stifle sound. If he *is* renovating the place, he surely isn't blind to what's happening in the cellar, which means there's a chance that Papa is the ghoul. If that's true, it explains a lot of her observations about his son; Elijah, quite clearly, is one deeply troubled individual.

She'll consider him more closely later. Right now, she has another task. Clenching her eyes shut, she calls up her mental chessboard and rolls open the drawer at C8.

This one's going to be tough. Acknowledging her fear, Elissa crosses time and space, all the way back to the car park of the Marshall Court Hotel.

II

She's in the passenger seat of her mum's Fiesta. Monkey's in her lap. Shoving him into her rucksack, she scrambles from the car. Then the day goes dark.

Those first few seconds are the worst to relive. At the start, she was confused about what was happening but not scared. Her life had already changed, but the reality hadn't struck. A panic attack, that's what she'd thought. Or something stranger – narcolepsy, or possibly cataplexy. When her shoes travelled backwards across the tarmac, she wondered if the tournament's public-school girls, with their unblemished record, were playing a prank. Then came the rotten-poultry stink of her abductor; the dark and dirty taste of his hand. That's when she knew.

Now she's in the van itself, heels scrabbling over the back bumper. There's the thunk of a closing door. And that voice: *Easy now. Easy. I've got plans for you, darl. You won't die today.*

She fights then, fights with the spit and venom of a cornered wildcat. When her efforts knock his hands loose, she thinks she has a chance, but almost immediately the cloth is over her mouth and she's breathing butterflies and meadows. She sinks down and down. The van shudders beneath her.

CHILLAX.

That whole episode lasted no more than twenty seconds, and yet her memories of it are so scrambled – so tainted by terror and loss – she can't guarantee they're in the right order. Despite her anguish, Elissa replays those last few moments. Then a third time, even slower.

She sits up straight. Sweat breaks out across her forehead. She can't be sure, even now, that she has the exact order correct. But of one thing she's certain: when the engine turned over, its vibrations shaking the floor, the ghoul was still pressing the wet cloth against her mouth. The revelation is as disturbing as it is revealing: Elissa has not one jailer, but two.

III

Bad enough for the world that one such devil walks upon it. How can there be more? Suddenly, everything she thought she understood about this nightmare lies in tatters. In the wreckage, every one of her assumptions will have to be re-examined. And yet the discovery does nothing to reduce her list of suspects. Everyone she's so far considered – the waitress, the three *bodachs*, those she met at the tournament – could have used an accomplice lurking out of sight.

Loading her recollections of the white van into her virtual chessboard, Elissa fast-forwards to the moment her cell door first opened.

IV

If only she hadn't panicked. If only she hadn't scrabbled like a wild animal to the far wall. In her haste to escape the ghoul, she'd forgotten about her shackle. When the chain snapped taut, the manacle bit into her wrist. Moments later, the ghoul's white light skewered her.

I know you're awake. There'll never be anything, ever in this life, that you can conceal from me. Take as long as you need to learn that lesson, but for your own comfort I'd advise haste.

She'd remained silent, so gut-churningly frightened that all she could do was feign sleep.

When one has a visitor it's polite to acknowledge them, or did your mother never teach you that? Time to open your eyes, Elissa Mirzoyan, and see what is true.

In the coldness of her cell – in the now and not the then – she crawls to her rucksack and quickly inventories its contents: Monkey, water bottle, notebook and gel pens, satsuma and books.

I brought you something to eat. Something to drink, too. By your silence, I assume you don't want it. No matter. It'll be interesting to see how quickly you remember your manners. Perhaps a little fasting will hasten their return.

Elissa examines the notebook. She checks the inside covers and the cardboard back. Then she hauls out her books and checks those too.

Time to open your eyes, Elissa Mirzoyan, and see what is true.

The ghoul called her by her full name – and yet it appears on none of her belongings, nor any of her clothing.

Did he know it before he snatched her? If so, what can she glean from that? If he's learned it since, does that mean her abduction's been widely reported? So far, other than her mum's welfare, she's hardly concerned herself with outside events. Now, for the first time, she begins to consider them.

Elissa's stomach growls with hunger. There's no way of telling how many hours have passed since she ate the pecan-nut biscuit, but it feels like a lot. She's delving into her rucksack for the satsuma when she hears, outside, the rattle of deadbolts.

V

It's not Elijah. She knows by the quality of the light. His is jaundiced, erratic. This – white, unflinching and utterly without mercy – comes from the ghoul's head torch. It swabs over her, paying particular attention to her manacle and chain. She holds her breath while it hovers on the make-shift bandage. Then it dances away to the other objects in the cell.

The ghoul starts to whistle. The sound is dreadful, a tuneless escape of air. He begins to carry in the equipment from his last visit: tripods, camera, studio light and chair.

Should she initiate conversation? Last time, he beat her almost unconscious, but that doesn't mean it's the wrong strategy. She's convinced, even now, that too much compli-ance will destroy her chances of survival. Still, considering the likely consequences, it's hard to ignore his earlier instruc-tion: *You don't speak until you're told. Say you understand.*

Elissa watches the equipment take shape. The studio

light comes on, so bright it stings her eyes. The chair is dragged into position.

Then, silence.

As the seconds elongate, Elissa realizes he's waiting for her to sit. It's an opportunity to resist that she decides not to take. If there's a rhythm to insurgency, instinct tells her this is one of the off-beats. Bracing her manacle, she unfolds her legs. Only as she rises does she realize how stiff her muscles have become.

Chain clanking, she shuffles over. The chair is a hundred times more comfortable than the floor. It's another good reason to postpone her rebellion. Perhaps, if she gives the ghoul what he wants, he'll let her keep it.

Footsteps now, scuffing towards her. The white light darkens as a silhouette passes across it. Elissa presses her knees together, clenching her eyes shut. She senses breathing, inches from her face, and then something new, something entirely inexplicable: a woman's fragrance.

VI

It's sweet yet earthy, a hint of apples warmed by cinnamon. It opens Elissa's eyes and fills her lungs to gasping, because a *woman*, down here in this filthy hole, is the last thing she expected; and right now, a woman, undeniably, is leaning close.

Something soft and wet touches Elissa's forehead. She flinches away, but the chair back stops her moving far. When the object touches her again she submits. It's a cloth, nothing more, moistened with warm water. As it begins to clean her face – gentle, circular movements that gradually encompass her nose, her cheeks, her chin – she detects the vaguest scent of cucumber. There's a brief antiseptic sting when it knocks away a scab. Otherwise, the woman washes her with conspicuous tenderness; such tenderness, in fact, that Elissa's eyes fill with tears. When she shudders and lets out a sob the circular movements cease. For a moment, she fears the woman will embrace her. Instead, the gentle cleansing resumes.

Despite her distress, Elissa's mind works feverishly. In the last ten minutes, everything she believed about this place has been overturned. It's imperative she doesn't tune out.

Soft fingers touch her jaw, encouraging her to lift her chin. Carefully, the cloth scours away grime. Afterwards, a brush is tugged through her hair. The woman is as gentle as before, easing off every time she finds a knot, styling it in a way that feels alien.

Belatedly, Elissa realizes it's an attempt to conceal the injuries inflicted by the ghoul when he last visited. Her work complete, the silhouetted woman steps away.

The studio light shines on Elissa's face, drying the last traces of moisture. Leaning against the tripod is the white-board from the ghoul's previous visit. On it she sees the same words.

The red light winks on.

'You look into the camera,' he whispers from the darkness behind the light. 'You read the words. Say you understand.'

VII

In the hours since their last encounter Elissa has tried to forget the message printed on that board. Now, she can't help but confront it. 'I understand.'

She clears her throat, lifts her head. 'My name is Elissa Mirzoyan. Today is the twenty-fourth of October.' Her chin begins to tremble. 'I have not been harmed. I do not wish . . . I do not wish . . .'

The words on the whiteboard swim out of focus.

'Wipe your eyes,' the ghoul whispers. 'Start again.'

Elissa brushes away her tears. 'Why're you doing this?'

'Look into the camera. Read the words.'

She clenches her jaw. 'My name is Elissa Mirzoyan.' This time, in her voice, there's the merest hint of defiance. If she's forced to say these words, she wants the world to see she doesn't believe them. 'Today is the twenty-fourth of October. I do not wish to be found. I do not wish anyone to look for me. Since finding sanctuary, I've come to realize' – now she speaks through gritted teeth – 'that Lena Mirzoyan is not the good mother I thought.'

The red light observes her a moment longer.

Then it dies.

Elissa swallows. No one who sees the tape will believe she meant those words, but that won't diminish their power to cause hurt.

She can't see the ghoul behind the recording equipment, but she knows he's there. Is the woman at his side?

Lena Mirzoyan is not the good mother I thought.

Staring straight ahead despite the studio light's glare,

she says, 'Why? Why're you doing this? What have I done to—?'

'This is not to punish you,' the ghoul whispers.

'Then who—?'

'You said it yourself. Lena Mirzoyan is not the good mother you thought. And who would know better than her daughter? Who would know better than you?'

'You know I don't believe that. Nor will anyone else.'

'People believe what they're told.'

'Not that.'

She has no idea where this shot of bravery comes from, but for the first time she's successfully engaging him. Despite the danger, she knows she mustn't stop. 'This is wrong. You have to let me go.'

'If I returned you to an unfit mother, what would that make me?'

'Why do you think she's unfit?'

'If you follow the rules, you'll suffer no harm.'

'*Why?* That's what I don't understand! What kind of freak—?'

The word slips off her tongue before she can call it back. It floats in the silence, and she knows, just by listening, that she's badly misstepped.

'Whoever one is, and wherever one is,' the ghoul whispers, 'one is always in the wrong if one is rude.' He waits a while, then adds: 'Maurice Baring wrote that. He was an English dramatist, and a great man of letters.'

Unable to trust her mouth, Elissa presses her lips together.

'I want this to work,' the ghoul tells her. 'We all want this to work. Personally, I think you're a little too head-strong, which means your chances aren't great. But perhaps you'll surprise us yet.'

The studio light winks out. Darkness rushes in. There's a rasp of something metal being unscrewed. A rich scent hits Elissa's nose: Peppa Pig spaghetti.

Her stomach churns.

'You follow the rules,' the ghoul whispers, 'you eat. You break the rules, you're no more. *Say you understand.*'

She drags out the seconds as long as she dares. 'I understand.'

'You forget your previous life because *this* is your life. If you cooperate, things will change. Six months from now, if we get that far, you'll understand why this was necessary. Another year, you'll be thanking us.' He removes the camcorder from its mount. 'We're going to do more of this, you and I. Keep cooperating and you'll get all sorts of nice things. In the meantime, I want you to think about all the ways your mother has let you down. Every little spite, every dereliction, every selfish act.'

Elissa opens her mouth, but the ghoul's characterization of Lena Mirzoyan is so baseless she's rendered mute. She breathes cucumber-scented cleanser, Peppa Pig spaghetti, home-crafted apple-and-cinnamon perfume. If there's any logic to this, she can't find it.

Personally, I think you're a little too headstrong, which means your chances aren't great.

He's right about that. She won't be brainwashed; not by him, not by anyone. Which means time, for her, is almost certainly running out.

Vital she doesn't squander what's left.

ELIJAH

Day 5

I

I was going to leave it until tomorrow to show her what I've done, but I'm so excited I can't wait.

All through dinner I sat on my secret. Watching me, Kyle soon suspected something was up. Usually, I'm pretty quiet at the table, but tonight I talked like a flibbertigibbet while Mama and Papa looked on, bemused. Eventually, Papa put down his cutlery and asked if I was OK. That's when I knew I was in trouble, and that if I talked any longer my mouth would run away completely.

I haven't committed a crime. Not exactly. But that doesn't mean what I'm doing is OK.

After dinner, Papa goes outside for a roll-up. Mama sits in the living room with her sewing while I wash the dishes. Standing at the sink, I look through the window at Papa chugging his smoke into the night.

When I open the pantry door to fetch a tea towel, Kyle – appearing from nowhere – bundles me through it.

Inside, there's no light, just unpainted wooden shelves

filled with tinned goods. My brother talks so quietly not even Mama will hear. I could cry out, but his knife is pressed to my belly. His other hand grips my throat, forcing back my head.

'You're up to something, shithead,' he hisses. His breath is awful, like he's been chewing on roadkill. 'You're tryin' to fuck us, and I ain't gunna let it happen.'

My shirt has ridden up. The point of Kyle's blade presses deeper. When I feel a slow spread of warmth, I think he must have punctured me, until I realize that fear has made me squirt out some pee.

I recall our stand-off yesterday, in the Memory Wood – how I bit down on the barrel of his .22. Why am I so much more frightened now?

'You've got it all wrong,' I mutter. 'I'm not up to anything.'

'Liar.'

The blade tip can't press much harder without opening me up. I imagine it slicing through flesh, my guts spattering on to the tiled floor.

The back door rattles open: Papa, coming back inside. Serpent-quick, Kyle withdraws his knife and retreats.

I I

Another hour passes before it's safe enough to slip out. The wind gusts about me as I skirt Fallow Field. Inside the Memory Wood, the trees bend and swish like angry broomsticks; it's a nasty, frantic sound, and I don't like it at all.

At the centre of the clearing the Gingerbread House stands alone, stone walls slick with rain. I creep through the darkened ground floor, and it's only when I reach the cellar entrance that I dare use my torch. I'm half-expecting Kyle to ambush me again, but my journey down the steps to the partition wall is uninterrupted. Releasing the padlock, I draw back the deadbolts and swing the door wide.

III

'Bet you weren't expecting me,' I say, going in.

Gretel is curled around the iron ring, head on the mildewed pillow. Slowly, she struggles up. Her eyes, as she squints at my torch beam, are bloodshot and dim.

'Hello, Elijah.'

Her voice sounds heavy, like she's filled herself up with dark thoughts.

Hearing it, all my excitement drains away. Near the end, Bryony was like this. I'd hoped Gretel was stronger, but you never really know how someone will handle the bad stuff until they face it. 'Has something happened?' I ask. 'Are you sick?'

She laughs, a staccato burst of sound. There's no humour in it, only misery. On the floor near her feet is a plastic bowl. Apart from a few orange smears, it's been licked clean. Gretel's hair has been styled since I was last here. It suits her, I think, this new look, but I'm sensitive enough not to say anything.

I'm disappointed she's being such a mope. It's not the right time to reveal my secret so I sit down opposite.

'It's cold in here,' she murmurs. 'It's freezing, actually.'

'Up there, it's blowing a gale.'

Gretel looks at the ceiling. 'I don't hear anything. I can't even tell if it's day or night.'

'It's night,' I say. 'Just past eleven.'

She nods listlessly.

'How's your wrist?' After half a minute's silence, I add, 'Gretel?'

'What?'

'How's your wrist?'

'Feels . . . hot.'

'Really?'

'Kind of . . . my whole arm feels hot. Tingly.'

'Maybe it's healing.'

'Doesn't feel like it.'

'Did the bandage help?'

She takes a breath, wheezes it out. 'Elijah?'

'What?'

'You sounded different. When you came in.'

'I did?'

'Like you weren't wearing any shoes.'

Caught off guard, I nearly shine the torch at my feet, revealing myself. I'm so annoyed by her trickery that I start to get up and leave. But when I flex my toes and feel cold, uneven rock beneath them, I realize she's right: I'm barefoot. 'I . . . I must've left the house without them,' I say. But how can that be?

'Do you live close?'

My mind has gone into a tailspin. 'Yeah. But still . . .'

'How far?'

'Five minutes, if I run. Our place, it's . . . it's just the same as this.'

'It's a cottage too?'

'Tied cottages, they're called. All the cottages on the estate are tied.'

Gretel licks her lips, leaving a sheen of saliva. 'Tied how?'

'It means they belong to the landowner and he rents them out to his employees. At least, that's what it used to mean.'

'It doesn't now?'

I shrug. 'I'm no expert.'

'What's the estate called?'

Even if I answer Gretel's question, I doubt she'll remember what I said. And it's nothing I didn't share with Bryony, and all the others before her. 'Meunierfields,' I say. 'Leon Meunier owns it. He's a lord, a hereditary peer, which means if he has children they'll inherit his title. He doesn't, though. Not yet. He's got a wife, but . . .' I shrug. I've never really understood why the Meuniers don't have kids. 'Are you hungry?'

No answer. I look at the licked-clean bowl, stumped for what to do next. Finally, from my pocket, I pull out a handkerchief. 'It's not much,' I say, tossing it into her lap. 'We had cauliflower cheese for supper. I couldn't bring you any of that, but there was a bit of cheese left in the grater. Just Cheddar, but still nice.'

Gretel makes no move to unwrap it. 'Can I trust you, Elijah?' she asks, gazing into my light.

'Of course you can.'

'Is the cheese going to make me sick?'

I can hardly believe the question. 'No.'

'Why do you keep coming down here?'

'Because I like you. Because I want to help you.'

'If you wanted to help me, you'd get me out of here. You'd tell someone. Someone who could do something. You'd tell the police.'

'If I did that, I'd lose you.'

'No. You wouldn't.'

'Yes. Because *they'd* find out. And before anyone could come, they'd kill you.'

'They're going to kill me anyway unless you do something.'

'You don't know that.'

'They killed Bryony.'

'That was different.'

'She wasn't the first. Was she?'

I stare at her. 'What do you mean?'

'Exactly that. Don't tell me Bryony was the first one to wake up in this *bastard fucking place!*'

Gretel whips out a hand, sending the empty bowl skipping across the floor. My ears burn with her profanity. If Kyle was down here, he'd probably have the world's biggest erection.

Snot is running from Gretel's nose. I'm too polite to mention it. Just like I'm too polite to mention the stink coming from the red bucket.

It's not the right moment, but I can't wait any longer. 'I made something,' I say, lifting my T-shirt. 'I made something for us.'

IV

From my waistband, I remove a roll of paper. Careful to remain hidden behind my torch beam, I place it beside the iron ring and retreat to the far wall. 'Can you guess what it is?'

Gretel regards my creation with eyes that have never

seemed so dull. For a while, dismayed, I think she's going to ignore it. Finally, she picks it up, unrolling it like a scroll.

The grid took me two hours to make, marking out the lines with a ruler I stole from Papa's toolbox. I used a pencil to shade the darker squares, sharpening it six times before I was finished. Now, in the torchlight, the paper shines with graphite. 'Eight by eight, just like you said,' I tell her proudly. 'What do you think?'

'It's . . . a little smudgy.'

My tummy clenches as if I've been kicked. 'There was so much colouring-in. I couldn't help getting a few finger-prints on it. I tried my best.'

At that, something seems to wake in Gretel's face. 'It's a pretty good effort,' she says. 'A really good effort, actually. Considering you did it all on your own.'

'Well, I didn't have any help. Not from Papa or Mama or anyone.' My torch beam moves around the cell, landing on Gretel's bag of chess pieces. I can almost hear the whisper of rosewood. Licking my lips, I say, 'We have a board now.'

'That's true.'

'So . . . does that mean we can play?'

My question hangs in the silence. Already, Gretel's fin-gers are shiny with powdered graphite. 'Yes, Elijah,' she says. 'It means we can. Thank you. Thank you for doing this.'

My chest swells. I watch her place my makeshift board on the floor. She uses her palms to flatten out the creases, and then . . . and then . . .

For a moment, my horror is so overwhelming I can't breathe. Due to the angle of my torch, I don't notice the puddle of filthy water until it's too late. The paper soaks it up like a sponge. When Gretel tries to whip it away, a sharp nub of rock tears it to pieces.

'Oh,' she says, distraught. 'Oh, Elijah. I'm . . . I'm so sorry.'

Water drips from the ragged mess.

It's not her fault.

It's just a stupid, stupid accident.

'It's OK,' I tell her.

There's a pressure in my head, as if something's bursting to get loose. I want to reassure her further, but my teeth grind together, making an awful squealing sound.

Gretel's green eyes flare. She edges backwards, as if something in my voice has scared her. 'I mean it, Elijah, I'm sorry. After all that work . . . this place . . . I just . . .'

My fingers flex and unflex. I watch her for a long moment. Gradually, the pressure in my head begins to ease. 'I can make another one,' I tell her. 'It's no problem.'

I don't mention the cramp I got in my forearm while colouring in those squares. Or how much it hurt. Or how excited I was, bringing it down here. Or how she could have been a tiny bit more careful.

Gretel wipes her fingers on her dress. 'If you want a board *that* badly, you should write to FIDE. If nothing else, it'll save you the pencil work.'

'FIDE?'

'The Fédération Internationale des Échecs, in France. Basically, the World Chess Federation.'

'I don't have money for stuff like that.'

'You don't need any. FIDE exists to promote chess. They'll send a basic kit to any kid who writes them a suitable letter.'

I roll my eyes, even though she can't see. 'That can't be right.'

'I promise you it is.'

'For *free*?'

'One hundred per cent.'

I think about it for a while. 'What kind of thing do you have to write?'

'Just a reason why you need the set and a bit about your interest in chess. Favourite player, or opening. That sort of thing.'

'I don't have a favourite player.'

'Not yet, you don't.'

'And you haven't *taught* me any openings.'

My nose wrinkles. I sound like a spoiled brat, but I can't help myself. Suddenly, more than anything, I want my own board and pieces, sent all the way from France. 'Are you sure you won't eat?'

Gretel considers my offering. Then she unwraps the handkerchief and stuffs the cheese into her mouth. For a while, the gloopy sound of chewing fills the silence. 'I can help you write the letter,' she says, between swallows. 'You'd just need to post it.'

'How long would the set take to come?'

She shrugs. 'A week. Maybe two.'

'Is the board made of rosewood?'

Gretel laughs. 'Nope. You'll probably get a standard tournament mat. But they're waterproof, at least.'

'What about the pieces?'

'Plastic.'

I'm sad that I won't be getting hand-crafted versions, like Gretel's. Then again, without her help, I'll be getting nothing at all. 'Can we do it, then?'

She tilts her head and peers into the light, and I find myself wondering if she's as sick, or deflated, as I first thought. 'What will *you* do for *me*, Elijah?' she asks.

Silence falls between us. It feels like we're balancing on a tightrope. 'What do you want?'

'I want you to protect me,' she says. 'I want you to tell me how to survive this.'

'I swear to you, Gretel. I'll do everything I can to make sure nothing bad happens.'

Her head is still tilted. Slowly, she straightens. 'I like it when you call me Gretel.'

'I'd like it if you'd call me Hansel.'

'OK . . . Hansel.'

'Will you do it, then? Will you write to FIDE?'

Gretel indicates her rucksack. 'I have a notebook in there. Pens, too. But I don't think I can write. Not with my wrist the way it is.'

'You could dictate.'

'If they find out about this, about what we're doing. Would they . . .'

'They wouldn't be happy,' I tell her. 'But I can keep a secret, if you can.'

Then I switch off the torch. In perfect darkness, I steal across the floor towards Gretel.

'Hansel?'

She sounds scared. I hear the scrape of her chain and know she's backing away. Sad, really – and pretty pointless. If I intended to hurt her – *which I would never do* – she wouldn't be able to escape. Ignoring Gretel's lack of trust, I fetch the rucksack and dig through it. Finding the notepad, I bend back the cover. Then I uncap a pen.

I can write in pitch-darkness, no problem.

'Shoot,' I say, thinking of the deer Kyle drilled, the calamity inside its head, the calamity inside mine, and what my brother would say if he were down here with us right now.

I flex my toes and wonder what happened to my shoes. Sometimes, life is so gosh-damned strange it hardly seems real.

V

It's later. I'm outside the back door. My feet are so cold I can't feel them. I stayed with Gretel far longer than I'd intended. By the time I snuck out, it was beginning to get light. I only came home because she was getting tired.

I'm not. My head's far too busy for sleep. Gretel's words go round and round. I feel that wall inside my mind trembling, as if the whole thing's about to come crashing down.

If you wanted to help me, you'd get me out of here. You'd tell someone. Someone who could do something. You'd tell the police.

I do want to help her. I do. And yet . . .

They're going to kill me anyway unless you do something.

It doesn't have to be like that.

But I know that's how it is.

I want to help her so badly. But I'm terrified of what'll happen if I try.

The wall shivers. I reach out invisible hands to brace it.

Am I losing my mind? Why did I leave the house without shoes? I'm starting to feel like an actor in a play where all the scenes have bled together. Annie calls it *déjà vu*. Knowing the word doesn't make it any less scary.

Opening the back door, I let myself into the darkened kitchen. Our cottage is unheated, but it's warmer than outside. I wipe my frozen feet on the mat and tiptoe to the hall.

The staircase creaks as I climb it. I hear Papa's snores and Mama's soft breathing. Passing Kyle's room, I enter my own and close the door. Only then do I turn on the light. Near the bed, I see my trainers and wet socks. The room smells strange – damp and unpleasant. There are no copper coins on my pillow, but that doesn't mean no one's visited. I can't shift the feeling that something's wrong.

I go to the bed and sit down. Pulling out the paper torn from Gretel's notebook, I read the letter she dictated:

To Whom It May Concern,

I am writing in the hope that you'll please send me a free introductory chess set. Even though I've learned the full rules, I currently have no board or pieces, and therefore no way of actually playing.

Dietmar Pfister is currently my favourite player. Caspian Alexandr is also very good. Often, they manage to turn the tables on what seem like hopeless situations. There's something particularly exciting about Pfister's game. The way he defeated Jacob Nyback in Tbilisi last year was truly astonishing.

Although I'm a late starter, I hope that with a board and pieces of my own I'll develop into a competent player. Grateful if you could send my set to the address at the top of this letter.

Ever your servant,
Kyle North

Gretel told me a bit about Dietmar Pfister, so that bit isn't a lie. Whether there are other lies, I don't know. The words aren't my own, which means I can't trust them.

But I do want that board, so badly I can think of nothing else. At the top of the page are two addresses. The one on the right is Leon Meunier's, my brother's name above it. The one on the left, I don't recognize. It's somewhere in England, which worried me, until Gretel explained that FIDE has member federations in every country. Luckily, I still remember the address she gave me when we first met: *I'm thirteen years old, and my name's Elissa Mirzoyan. M-I-R-Z-O-Y-A-N. I live at six, Cloisters Way.*

The address on the letter isn't that one. I hate to be suspicious, but I have to protect myself. Earlier, Gretel asked if she could trust me. The question I need to ask is whether *I* can trust *her*. She's already tried to fool me once.

Again, I feel that dizzying sense of a wall beginning to topple. I sway on the bed, trying to keep my balance. Once I've recovered, I read the letter again, searching for traps.

All I need now is an envelope and a stamp. There's a postbox a few miles down the road. If all goes well, I could have my new board within a week.

There are no pennies on my pillow, but that doesn't mean I'm safe. The chess set, like everything else, is a fantasy. I have bad instincts, but thankfully not that bad. Going to the corner, I lift the loose floorboard and retrieve my Collection of Keepsakes and Weird Finds. I place the FIDE application letter inside. It can stay there until the morning, when I'll destroy it.

ELISSA

Day 5

I

In the light of her seventh candle, Elissa eats the scrap of chocolate brownie she hid inside her underwear. The six candles already consumed equate to a forty-eight-hour burn time, but she knows she's been here far longer; knows, too, that she's nearing the limit of her endurance. Her injured arm throbs from her elbow to her fingertips. When she dares to examine it, she finds a foul-smelling pus seeping through the makeshift bandage.

Inside the cell, the temperature has dropped further. Her soiled vest is still wet. Otherwise, she'd have put it back on. Earlier, she dried a small section over the candle flame, but it's a task she can only manage in stages.

On her mental chessboard, the drawer to E8 is open. Into it, she plans to store her every interaction with Elijah, along with her every insight into his character.

It won't be easy. Because Elijah, now she's got to know him better, frightens her more than anyone.

For a start, he's a contradiction. He acts like he wants to

help, but despite her pleas he's consistently failed to raise the alarm. Neither has he been entirely honest. Twice during their conversations he's mentioned his high IQ. Yet when pressed for his score, it was clear he'd never taken a test.

'*Ninety-nine*,' he'd told her, as if expecting that number to impress. Elissa could have explained that the *median* adult IQ is one hundred. Hers is one hundred and thirty-eight.

Even if Elijah *were* to take a test, she doubts the results would impress. The time he took to scratch out his FIDE letter was staggering, and although she didn't see his handwriting, she's convinced it'd resemble that of someone far younger. He's clearly unstable; she suspects, too, that he suffers a form of mental impairment; high-functioning autism, perhaps – something she's encountered a few times on the chess circuit. When she pointed out he was barefoot, he seemed genuinely confused. And yet he was smart enough to recognize her ploy with the mobile phone.

Elijah seems shockingly unaware of the modern world. He hasn't heard of the internet; hasn't heard of apps or tablet computers. Is that because he's led a sheltered life? Or because he's spinning her a lie? And why is he so careful to remain hidden? Is he worried she'll betray him? She could do that easily enough without describing his appearance. Once before, she imagined him as a child-sized monstrosity, with lamp-like eyes and a horribly deformed mouth. Now, unbidden, a new image comes to her; of a boy with smooth skin instead of eyes, and lips as plump and moist as tulip petals. She knows this version of him is just as inaccurate as the first – if Elijah was blinded by deformity, what reason would he have for a torch?

He's probably still her best chance of surviving this, but

the effort of treating him like a friend is exhausting. When she thinks of the affectionate way he calls her 'silly', or his delight at their Hansel and Gretel monikers, her stomach grips with nausea. His voice – petulant at times, thoughtful at others – makes her cringe. There's a quality to it that nags at her, advertising something not-quite-right. When he visits, she feels like Clarice Starling in the company of Hannibal Lecter; or Frodo Baggins in the tunnels with Shelob. Even worse, despite her hope that he'll help her, he's already admitted he couldn't save Bryony.

Still, she got her tree. I made sure of that, even if I couldn't make sure of anything else. Picked out a tall one, just like she asked.

Maybe that's why he calls this place the Memory Wood. She imagines, above ground, a landscape of dripping trees, with children's bones buried among the roots. The thought is enough to set her teeth squealing.

Outside the cell door, the deadbolts rattle in their mountings.

II

It's the ghoul.

Elissa knows by the stink of him and the harsh white beam of his head torch. She waits in silence as he sets up his equipment. Finished, he carries out the red waste bucket, returning with a clean one.

I want you to think about all the ways your mother has let you down. Every little spite, every dereliction, every selfish act.

She *has* thought about that. Aside from Elijah's visits,

she's had little else to occupy her. If the ghoul asks her to talk, she won't disappoint. She's wary of being too placid, of losing his respect, but she's just as frightened of another attack.

'What day is it?' she asks, watching the candle flame as it flickers and sways. In response, the ghoul walks over.

She closes her eyes, bracing herself for a blow. Instead, something is set down before her. When she dares to look, she sees a travel bottle of Evian. All at once she realizes how thirsty she is. Snatching up the bottle, she guzzles the contents.

On goes the studio light, burning her eyes with its fire. In comes the chair, placed in its usual position. Elissa struggles up and shuffles over. The movement wakes a litany of complaints from her battered body. For a moment, as she sits, she's so light-headed she fears she'll pass out.

The ghoul approaches. Taking her chin, he tilts her head towards him. The light bleaches out everything; she can't see his face, anything at all. His stink is in her airways, so ripe and unpleasant the water in her stomach sloshes and churns.

'You messed your hair,' he whispers, pressing a brush into her lap. 'Put it back.'

Elissa obeys, covering the injured side of her face.

The ghoul retreats to his equipment. 'Talk,' he hisses. 'About your mother, like I told you before. Say you understand.'

'I understand. But . . . what do you want me to say?'

'An anecdote. An example of her selfishness. She divorced your father, for a start – that's a rich seam of dereliction right there.'

This freak has no knowledge of her family life, or about

how bad things were between her parents before they split. Or does he?

'Say you understand.'

'I understand.'

The red light winks on. '*Speak.*'

III

Following her monologue, the camera records thirty seconds of silence. Then the studio light dies.

Elissa bows her head. If the recording finds its way online, she hopes her mum will understand.

'You cannot, surely, want to return to a mother like that,' the ghoul whispers.

'We all make mistakes.'

'Some crueller than others. No doubt you consider me your jailer. Perhaps, instead, you should consider me your saviour.'

With her good hand, Elissa indicates her manacle. 'You call this being saved?'

'Cooperate, and you'll get all sorts of nice things.'

'Like what?'

Silence, for a moment. Then the door's rubber seal squeals. The candle flame bobs.

As the ghoul re-enters the cell, Elissa strains her eyes. He's carrying something bulky – something she can see only in silhouette. Her heart begins to thump. There's no guarantee their definitions of 'nice things' concur.

He drops what he's holding. It skitters softly when it hits the floor. Bulky it may be, but it's also light. The ghoul turns without a word and the door squeals again. This time, when he returns, he's carrying a tray. As he sets it down the light from his head torch touches what he just delivered: an inflatable mattress, on which he's thrown a grubby tartan blanket.

'Off the chair,' he whispers. 'On to that.'

Is this a reward for her cooperation? Or the prelude to something monstrous?

Shivering, Elissa slides off her seat. The mattress is so soft, so yielding to her aching limbs, that she cannot suppress a sob. When she manages to drag the blanket around her shoulders, the tears fall faster.

In her nose is the smell of hot food. On the tray is a plastic plate piled with crisp bacon, alongside two fried and congealed eggs. Threads of steam rise from a shallow lake of baked beans.

Elissa drags the tray close. Forgoing cutlery, she feeds herself with her fingers. The bacon is burnt, room temperature rather than hot, and the eggs were cooked some time ago. Only the beans are as they should be, likely because they were poured from a flask.

As Elissa fills her stomach she feels a rush of gratitude as powerful as it is misplaced. 'Thank you,' she mutters, around a mouthful of food. 'Thank you.'

Cooperate, and you'll get all sorts of nice things.

If a single story can achieve a bed, a blanket and a cooked meal, what could she earn with a more dramatic tale? Elijah might profess friendship, but all he's ever brought her is a pecan-nut biscuit and a single piece of cheese. In exchange for a simple anecdote, the ghoul has provided all this.

The realization that she's humanizing him chills her

bones. Already, she's losing her sense of right and wrong, of what's real and what's false. If she isn't careful, she'll lose herself entirely.

'Maybe I was mistaken,' the ghoul whispers as he collects her empty plate. 'Maybe this can work.'

Maybe this can, Elissa thinks.

It is, without doubt, her scariest thought yet.

MAIRÉAD

Day 5

I

The street outside Lena Mirzoyan's home is even more jammed with vehicles than during Mairéad's last visit. As soon as she climbs from her car she's jostled by excited journalists. The PCSO by the gate does his best to hold them back.

'How're you feeling?' someone shouts, a reference to her hapless morning press conference. 'Has the investigation stalled?'

Ignoring the questions, she strides up the front path. Judy Pauletto, the FLO, answers the door.

'Do they know?' Mairéad asks.

Grim-faced, Judy shakes her head. 'I've been keeping them away from the TV.'

The kitchen's at the end of the hall. A uniformed officer hovers at the sink, fiddling with a tea caddy as if he's thinking about making a brew. When he looks up at Mairéad, his expression is as doleful as the FLO's. Everyone, it seems, knows the news she's here to impart.

In the living room, Elissa Mirzoyan's grandparents sit at opposite ends of the sofa, a dimple in the fabric between them.

Lena Mirzoyan stands by the window. Her face is a horror show – puffy skin, poached-egg eyes, stress rash across her forehead. 'Have you found her?' she blurts, and immediately covers her mouth, as if by calling back the words she can insulate herself against bad news.

It's hard, this. For Mairéad, it's always been the worst part of the job. She thinks of Bryony Taylor's mother – of the trauma she suffered, is still suffering. 'We haven't,' she says. 'But we've every reason to believe that Elissa's alive. I need to show you something. You might want to sit down.'

Eyes wide and unblinking, Lena Mirzoyan retreats to the sofa.

Mairéad opens her laptop. 'This is going to be tough. Afterwards, you'll probably have a lot of questions.'

Suddenly, it's hard to find the right words, but the worst torture for any mother in this situation is the not-knowing, so she ploughs on, hoping to avoid any ambiguity. 'There's been a communication – a video, uploaded to YouTube a few hours ago. It shows Elissa talking.'

Lena's throat spasms. She reaches out to her parents. They anchor her firmly, as if she's in danger of lifting off from the sofa. 'It's him,' she whispers. 'Oh God. Isn't it? The one the papers are talking about.'

'We believe so.'

This time, her voice is little more than a flutter of breath. 'Show me.'

Mairéad swivels the laptop screen and hits play.

Lena releases her parents and hugs her knees. On the

laptop, from a slow fade, Elissa Mirzoyan materializes, head angled down like that girl from the movie *The Ring*.

II

In the living room, no one breathes.

Lena raises her hands. She starts to cover her eyes, hesitates. Starts to cover her ears, hesitates again.

Onscreen, Elissa lifts her head. Her skin has the pallor of a dead thing. She stares at the camera and clears her throat. When she speaks, she sounds far older than her thirteen years. 'My name is Elissa Mirzoyan. Today is the twenty-fourth of October.'

'*Oh*,' Lena whispers. '*Oh, my child*.'

The girl's attention flickers to something out of shot. With her left hand, she wipes her mouth. When she nudges the hair that's been brushed halfway across her face she exposes – just briefly – the edge of a bloody bruise. After watching this clip twenty times, Mairéad's convinced the move was deliberate.

'I do not wish to be found,' Elissa says, eyes returning to the camera. 'I do not wish anyone to look for me. Since finding sanctuary, I've come to realize . . .' Now she hesitates, continuing with a clenched jaw: '. . . that Lena Mirzoyan is not the good mother I thought.'

Her face fills the frame for another five seconds. Then the screen goes dark.

Instantly, the living room feels like a vacuum chamber.

'We know she spoke under duress,' Mairéad says. 'We know Elissa didn't mean that.'

Lena blinks, eyes still on the laptop. She looks like someone just opened her chest and tore out her heart. 'I let her go,' she whispers. 'That day at the hotel. Elissa asked me for the car keys and I just handed them over. I could have gone outside with her, but I didn't. I just did what she asked. And now, and now . . .'

'This isn't your fault, Lena. It isn't.'

'What else can you tell me?'

There's no good news to share. Elissa's electronic devices have revealed no useful information. Interviews of those closest to her have unearthed nothing new. People on the periphery – such as Andrea Tomlin, the Wide Boys waitress – have been interrogated and discounted. Despite reviewing thousands of hours of CCTV footage, the team hasn't reacquired the white Bedford van. And while the public response has been phenomenal, so far not a single lead or possible sighting has borne fruit.

'Based on previous cases,' she says, 'we're expecting further communications. They won't be easy to watch, but we'll need your help assessing them.'

A heaviness settles across Lena's features. Her head lolls, as if the muscles in her neck have failed. 'He's done this . . . how many times?'

'Six, that we know of.'

'Six children on YouTube?'

'That's right.'

'Going back how far?'

'Around twelve years.'

'How old is YouTube?'

'Two thousand and five,' Mairéad says.

'So there could be more kids.'

'That's true. We don't know it, but it's a possibility.'

Lena closes her eyes, opens them. 'Of the six you mentioned, how many have you found?'

Mairéad thinks of Bryony Taylor, of her mum's beseeching eyes. 'So far, they're all still missing. But that doesn't mean . . . It doesn't mean they're not alive. Just that they're active cases.'

'Active . . . cases.' Lena rolls the phrase around her tongue, as if trying to decipher it. 'Who is he? Why is he doing this?'

'I can't answer that definitively. But looking at what he made the other girls say, it's possible he harbours some kind of grudge against single parents – single mothers, in particular.'

'A *grudge*?'

Elissa's grandfather, a mild-looking man in a green sweater and tie, enfolds his daughter's hands in his own. 'You think this man knows us?'

'It's possible, although it's likely he doesn't know you well. Based on what we know from previous abductions, it seems he takes children from mothers he deems unfit.'

The grandfather flinches as if he's been struck. 'Detective, I assure you my daughter is far from unfit.'

'I know that. We all know it. But we're not dealing with a rational mind. The justification, in this individual's head, could be something as mundane as letting Elissa watch too much TV, or allowing her too many McDonald's. The good news is that irrational people frequently make mistakes. As I said earlier, we have a vast number of police officers working on this, and they're one hundred per cent focused on finding Elissa. *I* am one hundred per cent focused on finding her.'

Lena rocks back and forth. 'Are you good at this?' she asks. 'At your job, I mean?'

Right now, there's only one answer that's merciful. 'I am, yes.'

'Do you . . . Are you a mum? Do you have a child of your own?'

Mairéad's breath freezes in her chest. She thinks of her bathroom, filled with Clearblue kits; the two spots of blood on her underwear; her promise to Scott, two hours ago, that she'd drive straight to the surgery. 'I'm married,' she says softly. 'That's enough for now.'

'Will I see my daughter again?'

'I hope so, Lena.'

'You hope.'

The woman swallows. Her face looks as brittle as glass. The silence lasts nearly a minute before the trill of a mobile phone breaks it. The ringtone is the chorus from 'Let It Go'. Snatching up her handbag, Lena digs through it for her phone and answers. *'Elissa?'*

Mairéad trades glances with Judy Pauletto, trying not to wince.

'Oh,' Lena mutters. 'Lasse. Yeah, sorry. Hi.' She wipes her forehead. 'You haven't heard.' Another pause. 'Just – I'm sorry, Lasse, I . . . Just watch the TV, OK? I've got to go.' She hangs up, shaking her head. 'Elissa's chess teacher, Lasse Haagensen. I forgot to cancel yesterday's lesson.'

'Does he always call if someone doesn't show?'

'I suppose. Elissa's his best student.'

Mairéad climbs to her feet. 'Thank you, Lena. I'll leave you with Judy for now. She'll answer any questions you have, but you can call me any time. One last thing before I go. YouTube have kept that video up at our request, but I strongly suggest you avoid the site. The comments section is open, and we're monitoring it in real time, but you can imagine the kind of human swine this sort of thing attracts. You don't need to see that, and it won't do you any good.'

Lena nods, but her mind is already elsewhere.

'Can you track him that way?' asks Elissa's grandfather. 'Through YouTube?'

'I'm afraid not. Right now, while we wait for further communication, our priority is the location of that white Bedford van. I have every resource I need, so I don't want you to worry about that. Hundreds of officers, not just from Dorset but from all the neighbouring counties. The National Crime Agency too. The public response has been huge – thousands of people up and down the country out searching. I'm joining the deputy chief constable for another media briefing at six. I'll call you straight after.'

Lena stares in dull acknowledgement.

The déjà vu is awful; it's Bryony Taylor, all over again.

Back in the car, Mairéad sits behind the wheel with her hands on her belly. Since this morning's press briefing she's had no further pain, but that doesn't mean her baby is safe. She needs to phone the surgery, get a referral to the early-pregnancy assessment unit. She wants an ultrasound, right now. Wants to hear a heartbeat and a doctor telling her everything's OK. And yet there are a million different things to do first.

Taking out her phone, she contacts Halley, back in Bournemouth. 'What've you got?'

'Lab came back on the number-plate DNA swabs,' he tells her. 'Not a bean.'

'Great.'

'Are you still at the house?'

'Just left.'

'How's Lena doing?'

'Christ, Jake. I don't know. It's not good.'

'Yeah. Feels like a horror story unfolding, doesn't it?'

Mairéad glances out of the side window at the Mirzoyan home. 'I want to look more closely at Lasse Haagensen, the chess teacher. I know it's been done. But this time I want his whole life turned over.'

She throws the phone on to the passenger seat. With Bryony Taylor, there were three communications and then silence. The window for saving Elissa Mirzoyan is narrowing every hour.

ELISSA

Day 6

He comes for her while she's asleep.

When Elissa wakes, she can't immediately work out where she is. For the first time, there's no sharp floor pressing against her skin. Then she remembers the story she narrated for the camera and the prizes she earned for her duplicity: a bed, a blanket, a hot meal. In the outside world, those things are nothing special. Down here, they're everything.

As soon as she opens her eyes she knows the situation has changed. There's something manic about the ghoul's light as it flits around the cell. He's panting, too. Great gouts of condensation billow from his silhouette.

Once he's checked everything, he lays his torch on the floor, angled towards her. Elissa scrunches up her eyes against its glare. The blanket is around her shoulders, so she's not as cold as before, but she's frightened now. This feels serious.

The ghoul hunches over the iron ring. There's a clink, as of something unlocking. A sharp rattle of chain.

'Up,' he whispers.

Earlier, she thought they'd made progress. Now, the

menace rolling off him drains her stomach of blood. 'What's happening?'

The words slip out before she can call them back. *You don't speak until you're told. Say you understand.* Anxious not to provoke him further, she scrabbles up, supporting her manacle with her good hand.

He comes at her then, a monster in the dark. She can't suppress a scream, and when it rings off the cell walls he grabs her by the neck and shoves her in front of him.

'Please,' she moans. 'Oh, please, don't.'

'Enough,' he hisses. 'Do as you're told and move.'

Elissa stumbles forwards. It's only when she passes beyond the perimeter of her chain that she realizes he's unlocked it. She's free, and yet she's not; the loose end doesn't drag on the floor, which means the ghoul must be holding it.

When he scoops up his torch, light bevels around her. Shadows lengthen and swing. Three more steps and she's through the open door.

In her terror, Elissa can hardly breathe. Nor can she make any sense of the half-glimpsed shapes that bow out of the gloom. *He's going to kill me*, she thinks, convinced beyond doubt. *This could be my last living minute.*

Her breath is a whistle in her throat. Her family is so far away.

Stone steps in front, pressure behind. Elissa struggles up.

So much time she'd thought she had before her. So many years unlived.

The ghoul shoves her again, harder this time. In response she climbs faster, hurrying towards her fate.

Keep good thoughts in her head. Thoughts of family, of love and laughter. But her mind is racing so fast she can't fill it. In her panic, she bites her tongue. The pain is glass inside her mouth.

The ghoul's torch illuminates a switchback. Elissa leans around it.

'Up,' he hisses. 'Up, up.'

In an instant she's back in her mum's Fiesta, parked outside Wide Boys. Lena Mirzoyan is saying something – just a throwaway line, but it's soaked in love, steeped in it . . . And then the scene falls away and she's back on the staircase, emerging into a squalid room that might have been a kitchen long ago. That she'll spend her last moments separated from those she cares most about, with no one to hold her hand, is the worst of all fates.

It's light outside, an afternoon grey. After so long imprisoned in darkness, Elissa's senses are overcome. Her muscles burn with the effort of walking. Her feet trip over floorboards warped by damp.

Ahead, a corridor of sloping shadows. Here, the air's even colder. It presses at her shoulders, her face. 'Please,' she whispers. 'I did what you said. I did.'

The ghoul is behind her. She could glance back and look at him, but she's too scared to do that, too scared to consider what it'll mean if he lets her. Even now, she can't abandon hope.

All at once she's outside, her shoes sinking into soft mulch. Around her, dripping trees point towards an overcast sky.

The Memory Wood, she thinks.

It's so beautiful. The whole world is beautiful. Tears prick her eyes.

Then she sees the white van, parked to her left, and its sticker: a trilby-wearing skull smoking a cigarette.

CHILLAX.

The van doors are open. When the ghoul shoves her she bangs her knees against the bumper.

Suicidal to climb in, but what choice does she have? She can't fight. Her muscles are so slack she can't even run. Somehow, she lifts her right knee, swinging it on to the cargo bed. The ghoul grabs her other leg and flips her.

Elissa tumbles over, unable to protect her wrist. The pain is a white-hot scream. Her stomach clenches and she vomits, a liquid gush. Behind her, the ghoul leaps into the van.

Elissa blinks, but her eyes aren't working. She smells something odd, recalls a vague memory of flowers. There's something wet against her lips, and suddenly she's so scared that she just wants this to end, and quickly.

How many more seconds of life?

How many?

'I'm sorry, Mum,' she whispers.

Then the darkness extinguishes her.

ELIJAH

Day 6

I

Night, and I'm sprinting through the Memory Wood, soaked to the skin. Above me, rain pours from a Bible-black sky. The trees rattle like shaken bones. I'm so cold.

As I run, I try to recall everything that's happened since I last saw Gretel, but my mind's so scrambled I can hardly focus. I think of the letter she dictated, the promise of a chess set all of my own. I knew that would bring trouble, so back in my room I vowed to destroy it. Last night, the letter stayed hidden in my Collection of Keepsakes and Weird Finds. This morning I brought it out here with some matches.

But I couldn't burn it.

Down in that cellar, Gretel lifted the curtains on a world I never knew existed. I so desperately wanted a part of it that I convinced myself it was possible. Returning home, I searched through Papa's things until I found an envelope and a stamp. Then I set off for the Memory Wood's western boundary. I remember my scramble through the barbed-wire fence that borders the lane. How long did I walk before I found the post-box? Two miles? Three?

The letter itself doesn't matter. It's what happened after that's the problem. Up until I posted it, I had a reason to be beyond the perimeter, something to distract me from my fears. But once my task was complete, I fell apart.

I remember getting lost. Seeing things that made no sense. The voices of people asking my name. Next thing I knew, I was in a police car, riding to the station. There was the room with no windows, the Coca-Cola the officers brought me. They didn't wear uniforms, like they do on TV.

We wear play clothes.

I thought they were teasing. I'm not good at being teased.

When Papa whisked me out of there I could have cried with relief. Back home, earlier this afternoon, I waited until he went into the garden for a smoke. Then I crept downstairs and escaped to the Memory Wood. Outside the Gingerbread House I found a patch of disturbed mulch – evidence that a vehicle had come and gone. I never saw it, but I knew, immediately, that it had taken my friend away. Down in the cellar, I found a single print that matched my own shoe, in size if not in shape.

I recall the clatter of deadbolts as I unlocked the door, the stench of bleach so powerful that it burned my nose; the empty cell, the iron ring, the knowledge that something awful had happened.

That's when I fled. This evening, up in my room, Mama urged me to read Ephesians: *Finally, be strong in the Lord and in His mighty power. Put on the full armour of God, so that you can take your stand against the devil's schemes.* But the devil has sunk his claws deep, and in my selfishness I've assisted him.

Once Mama had left, I found the coins on my pillow. Standing at my window, flinging them into the night, I saw a 4x4 bouncing along the track beside Fallow Field. Meunier, perhaps? Someone from Wheel Town? There was no reason for anyone to be out here so late.

That's when I remembered what had happened in the empty cellar, my horror at Gretel's loss causing the torch to slip from my fingers. Instead of retrieving it, I turned and fled, leaving it for anyone to find. Not only that, I left the cell door unlocked.

If my prying is to go unnoticed, I *have* to erase the evidence.

Through the trees, I see the rain-soaked cottage, silhouetted. There's no vehicle parked outside, no sign of anyone else. The rain beats against my scalp. Shoulders hunched, I break from cover.

I I

Twice, as I blindly feel my way down the cellar steps, I nearly fall. My trainers, clogged with wet mud, offer no grip. I'm leaving prints, but there's nothing I can do about that.

At the bottom of the steps I shuffle forwards, hands raised before me. When I fled Elissa's cell earlier this afternoon, I didn't pause to slam the door. Now, I'm wary of striking my head against its edge.

My arm swabs left and right, feeling for obstacles. The

229

stench of bleach isn't as potent as before, but it's still enough to make my eyes water. Finally, my hand touches the door.

It's closed.

When I move my fingers across it I discover that the deadbolts have been drawn. The padlock I'd removed is back in place.

It takes me a moment to process the full implications. Around me, the darkness seems to *breathe*.

III

They know.

That's the most obvious thing.

All this time, I've been so careful to cover my tracks. From the very start, I've understood what's at stake for those who break the rules. My parents can't protect me against what's coming. No one can.

Again, in my head, I feel something shift. The wall I've constructed is losing the battle against what's pushing against it. I don't know what will happen if it falls.

Around me, the darkness feels heavy, like I'm trapped beneath the ocean with a mile of black water pressing down. Squashed by all that pressure, I can hardly breathe.

Will they be waiting when I go back upstairs? I imagine the building's outer walls lit by the beams of a dirty white van.

CHILLAX.

Shuddering, I listen for any sound. But it's silent down here, the deathly quiet of a crypt. When I delve into my pocket I feel the hard curves of the padlock key.

Not thirty minutes ago I was standing at my bedroom window, watching a vehicle bounce along the track beside Fallow Field. The driver *must* have been coming here. The cell had already been stripped of Elissa's presence – washed, scrubbed, disinfected. Was the door resealed as a message, or is there another reason?

My hands are shaking so badly it takes me an age to undo the padlock. I draw back the central bolt. Two others follow. Gripping the handle, I pause in the darkness.

I should walk away, find that police station. Tell the truth this time, instead of lies.

Grimacing, I open the door.

IV

Out of the cell, just like before, rolls that hellish stench of bleach. I hesitate on the threshold, letting it wash over me. Then, clenching my fists, I take a forward step, feeling the way with my toe. I don't expect to find my torch, not now, but at least the act of searching will be a distraction from what might be waiting above ground.

Eyes closed despite the darkness, I move across the cell, sweeping the floor with my foot. I need to do this carefully. I can't afford to miss a single millimetre. I'm halfway to the iron ring – or think I am – when I hear something.

Even though I freeze, straining my ears, my breathing's far too loud, my heartbeat far too fierce. 'Hello?' I venture, bracing for the impact of a hammer, or the slash of a blade.

The darkness pulses like a living thing, a black lung. 'Hello, Elijah,' it replies.

MAIRÉAD

Day 6

I

In Salisbury, Mairéad is back in the Mirzoyan living room for her third visit in four days. Lena and her parents sit opposite. Judy Pauletto hovers near by. Yesterday, Lena looked like a corpse. Right now, she looks worse.

Mairéad doesn't feel much better. This morning she managed a full breakfast, but she barely kept it down five minutes before bringing the whole lot back up. Thankfully, she's had no more abdominal pain since yesterday's press conference, and no repeat of the spotting. Last night, she'd been too dog-tired to arrange a referral to the early-pregnancy assessment unit. Thanks to the latest discovery, she hasn't found the time since.

'There's been another communication,' she explains. 'I won't lie. It's going to be upsetting. But I need you to watch it. You might notice something we haven't.'

With a glance at Judy, she opens her laptop and taps the play button. Elissa Mirzoyan emerges, as if from a nightmare.

The girl looks dreadful. Emaciated, scared, ill. When Lena Mirzoyan sees her daughter, she sags forwards as if her strings have been cut.

Onscreen, Elissa takes a few steadying breaths. Then, in a voice that rasps like wet sand, she says, 'There was this time, last summer. Mum promised to take me to London. I'd always wanted to ride on the Underground, take a Tube to all the famous stops – check out Madame Tussauds, Ripley's Believe It Or Not, 221B Baker Street.'

'Did you go?'

Even though she's watched this two-minute clip thirty times, Mairéad still stiffens when she hears that voice. On the sofa, Lena Mirzoyan recoils.

'Yes,' Elissa replies. 'Although not to any of those places I said. We ended up going to the cinema to see a repeat showing of *Léon*, this old movie my mum likes. I hated it, hated every minute.'

'That doesn't sound fun.'

'No. Afterwards, we were meant to go somewhere for cake. Black Forest gateau, just like she promised.'

'You didn't get cake?'

'We went to a pub. Mum drank five vodkas, then we caught the train home.'

'Your mum sounds like a real bitch.'

Elissa Mirzoyan stares at the camera for five long seconds. When the laptop screen goes dark, Mairéad closes the lid. 'I'm sorry. I know that's hard to watch. It's what seems to motivate him – getting girls to disparage their mothers for the camera.'

Lena lurches to her feet. Eyes wild, she races from the room. Judy Pauletto goes to follow, but Mairéad holds up a hand. 'Give her a moment.'

Within a minute, Lena is back. 'Elissa,' she says, breath-less. 'She's sending us a message.'

II

The air inside the living room acquires a static charge.

Mairéad stands up far too fast. The room drains of col-our. She clenches her teeth, waiting for the dizziness to pass. 'Explain.'

'We did go to London on her birthday, but we never used the Tube. Elissa made me promise we wouldn't – she hated the whole idea. We took a train to Waterloo, and from there we hopped on buses everywhere she wanted to go.'

'You said there was a message.'

Vigorously, Lena nods her head. 'That's part of it, don't you see? Why change that bit of the story? The man who's holding her – he wouldn't know. That bit's just for us. We used buses that day, but Elissa says we used the Tube. I think she's telling us she's underground.'

Mairéad opens her mouth. She glances at Judy Pauletto before saying, 'That's quite a leap.'

Lena shakes her head. 'Not if you know my daughter. Besides, I don't think it's the only message. Those places she mentioned – we never went anywhere like that. We spent the morning in the British Museum and all afternoon at the Science Museum.' She holds out a sheaf of tickets. 'See? I still have our stubs.'

Mairéad's heart begins to beat faster. Already, Judy is scribbling furiously. 'This is good, Lena. This is excellent. What else can you tell us?'

'Those other places. They might be part of the message too. Elissa's only changing certain parts of the story. I think the replacements are meant to give us clues. Madame Tussauds, Ripley's Believe It Or Not, Baker Street – I don't know what she's trying to say, but I know she's saying something.'

'221B Baker Street,' Elissa's grandfather says, 'was the fictional home of Sherlock Holmes.'

Mairéad nods. 'And Madame Tussauds is the waxworks. Perhaps she's hinting at a mask, some kind of disguise. Ripley's Believe It Or Not was the place in Piccadilly that closed down. It had a huge collection of oddities: shrunken heads, five-legged lambs, all kinds of freakish stuff.'

Just for a moment, the strength seems to go out of Lena. Then she straightens. 'We did go for cake, but it was carrot cake, not Black Forest gateau.'

'You think she's telling us she's underground . . . in a forest?'

'I'm sure of it.' And then Lena swallows, because the horror of that is almost unbearable. 'The film she said I liked – *Léon*. I've never heard of it.'

'*Léon*'s a Luc Besson film. About a girl who strikes up a friendship with a hitman after her parents are murdered.'

Lena Mirzoyan sits on the sofa and hugs her knees.

'You've got a very smart daughter,' Mairéad says. 'Would you watch the video with me one more time? See if you notice anything else?'

When Lena nods, Judy Pauletto opens her notebook to a fresh page.

Outside, rainclouds drag a curtain across the sky. Has Elissa Mirzoyan really been imprisoned underground, in woodland, far from prying eyes? If so, her chances of survival, already gossamer-thin, are virtually nil.

Hold on, please hold on.

Abruptly, and with a crushing and inescapable sense of loss, Mairéad realizes that her feelings of nausea have entirely disappeared.

ELISSA

Day 6

I

She wakes to a crashing in her head, like a harbour wall pounded by sea. Her face is stuck to something . . . by glue, or vomit, or blood – she cannot tell. Although her stomach is empty, her bladder is full to bursting.

Is this her coffin? Is that why her head feels so confined?

Her lungs grow tight. It's an effort to breathe. When she tries, fractionally, to move her leg, it slides over something rough and cold. The floor beneath her is uneven. It's also familiar. Somehow, she's back in her cell.

What shocks her most is her relief. Relief that she's back in surroundings she knows, relief that her situation has stabilized. Earlier, she'd convinced herself she was about to die. Instead, it seems she's received a reprieve. She has no idea why the ghoul evacuated her to the van. Perhaps it was a test, or a sick form of entertainment.

The pressure in Elissa's bladder grows. When she raises her head, something cold and slimy drips from her face – partly digested eggs and bacon. With her good hand, she wipes it away.

Next, she feels for the manacle, groaning when she finds it back in place. There's a wetness all along her arm that she knows must be blood. She feels no pain from where the wound reopened – just a vague pulsing – but there *is* a smell, like someone threw a dead thing into a laundry basket of soiled clothes.

A rattling cuts through the chaos of her thoughts. Moments later, Elissa hears the squeal of a rubber seal. Cold air washes over her. Then a voice, wavering and uncertain.

I I

'Hello, Elijah,' she says.

If he hears her response, he gives no indication. She doesn't sense him cross the floor, doesn't see his torch's stuttering beam.

There's shallow breathing. Nothing else.

'Hansel?'

The name hangs in the air, but he doesn't claim it. She hears him shuffle closer. Without candlelight, he could be creeping towards her with a knife and she wouldn't know.

Pulling herself into a sitting position, gritting her teeth against a flood of nausea, she edges backwards. The chain clanks along the floor, betraying her retreat.

'Gretel,' Elijah says. So much emotion chokes his voice that she wonders if he's crying. 'I thought . . . I thought . . .'

Elissa swallows. 'I did too.'

'You weren't here. I came and you were gone. Everything else, too. Just that bleach smell. Like . . . like they did before.'

She licks her lips with a dry tongue. 'Like they did to Bryony?'

Elijah makes a hard sound in his throat.

'Where's your torch?'

'I . . . I got panicked and I dropped it, and then I ran away. It's the reason I came back. I thought you were *dead*, Elissa. What happened?'

He's cycling between names: Elissa, then Gretel. She doesn't know what that means, but she doesn't think it's good.

'*He* came,' she tells him. 'The whispery one. The one I call the ghoul. He took me outside, made me get into his van. Then . . . he drugged me – a cloth across the face, just like at the hotel.'

Elissa winces as another spike of pain lances her. It feels like her brain is pogoing around her skull. She hears further sounds of movement: Elijah, shuffling around the cell, dragging his feet like a zombie. 'What're you doing?'

'Looking for my torch.' After a few minutes of searching, he collapses down somewhere close. 'It's not here.'

'He must have it, then.'

Elissa knows how badly her words will have frightened him. Right now, she doesn't care.

Clearing his throat, Elijah says, 'Can I ask you something?'

'Sure.'

'Promise you won't laugh?'

'I promise.'

'It's going to sound stupid. And I . . . I never asked

anyone before, but . . . is all this . . .' He pauses. 'Is all this real?'

Elissa blinks. 'Real?'

'Sometimes . . . sometimes I think . . . it isn't.'

'What do you mean?'

'I'm not Hansel.'

'No,' she says. 'You're not Hansel. You're Elijah.'

'Am I?'

Elissa waits for him to continue, but he remains silent. After a while, she says, 'This is real, Elijah. All of it. You're real, so am I. So is my mum. So is my family. This place is real, too. It's not where I want to be, and I hope I'm not going to die here. I hope, more than anything, that you're going to help me survive this – but it's real, I promise you. It's about as real as a thing can get.'

Elijah sniffs. 'You don't want to be here.'

'No. I want to go home, see my family. Eat my mum's food. Sit on the sofa with her and watch Netflix.'

'You want me to get you out.'

'I want that more than anything.'

She hears a scrape in the darkness. Something innocent, perhaps. Or something not. She tries to dispel her last vision of him; a boy whose tulip-bud mouth is a grotesque counterpoint to a face devoid of eyes.

When Elijah speaks next, he's far closer. 'Are you frightened of death,' he asks, 'or just the actual dying?'

Elissa flinches. It's an odd question. Right now, everything about Elijah's behaviour is alarming. She can hear his breathing, but it's difficult to pinpoint his location. She knows she has to maintain the conversation, so she tells him the truth: what worries her most is her mum being all alone.

'You could haunt her,' he points out.

'Don't say that.'

'You could haunt me.'

His tone turns her skin to gooseflesh. 'Are you haunted already?'

'Sometimes I think I am.'

'By Bryony?'

'Not her. Bryony was my friend.'

'They killed her.'

'Yes. They did.'

'Why, Elijah? Why did they do that? Why are they doing this?'

'Because . . .' he says, in that awful disembodied voice. 'Because it's what's right.'

III

It's not the answer Elissa was expecting. Her gasp triggers a bout of coughing that's almost impossible to stop.

'Are you OK?' Elijah asks. 'You sound sick.'

'Why did they do that? Why are they doing this?'

'Because . . . Because it's what's right.'

Does he believe that, or is he simply repeating what he's been told?

'My wrist,' she says. 'I think it's infected. I think it's really bad.'

Silence, for a while. Then Elijah scrabbles to his feet. 'Oh, this is all my *fault*,' he moans. 'I could have *done* something, and . . . and I—'

'How can this be your fault?'

'I'm so sorry, Gretel. If only I hadn't been so stupid!'

She frowns. 'I don't get it. You're saying this is because of you?'

'I left the estate. Went through the Memory Wood, all the way to the road. Don't know how long I walked – I think I must've got lost. And then . . . next thing I was in a police station, answering questions. I told them how to contact Papa and he came to fetch me.'

Blood drains from Elissa's stomach. 'You were in a *police* station?'

'Yes.'

'You spoke to them?'

'Uh-huh.'

'What did you say?'

'Well . . . I told them about the crow Papa fixed.'

Her mouth falls open. 'Did you tell them about *me*, Elijah? Did you remember my name, like I told you? *Elissa Mirzoyan.* Did you explain where I was? What was happening down here? Did you tell them how to find me?'

'No, I—'

'*No?*'

'You don't understand!' he shouts. 'I told you already – I wasn't thinking straight. I'd never *been* in a police station before. It was *scary*. I wanted to tell them, of course I did, but by that point I was such a mess I thought they wouldn't believe me. I promised myself I'd say something once I calmed down, but by then I was already home.'

His admission is so crushing, so utterly devastating, that it saps Elissa's remaining strength. She slumps on to the floor, ignoring the nubs of rock that dig into her flesh. 'Where were you going?' she whispers. 'Why did you leave the estate?'

'I . . . I don't know. I think I just needed some time. Time to work things out. My head, it's . . .' His feet scrabble across the floor. 'I can fix this,' he tells her. 'I know I can. I'll figure something out and I'll come back.'

Moments later, the cell door squeals in its rubber frame.

Once he's gone, Elissa finds the matches and lights a candle. Elijah, she knows, isn't going to figure anything out. She'd hoped he was her ally, her chance of survival. But he isn't. When she looks down at her wrist and sees the oozy, swollen mess it has become, she knows her time has run out.

ELIJAH

Day 7

I

Friday morning, and I'm stumbling through the Memory Wood, convinced I'm being followed. Last night, when Elissa was returned to the cell, the open door and my dropped torch would have been discovered. Which means they know someone's been down there. And while they might not yet know *who*, they'll know I left the estate yesterday, that I was at the police station. For a while, fearing what I might say or do, they must have relocated her. Last night, at my bedroom window, the vehicle I saw driving past Fallow Field was probably bringing Elissa back. It's a miracle she's not dead.

Up ahead, the trees are thinning out. Through them, I see Wheel Town, and the greyish expanse of Knucklebone Lake. Threads of mist hug the ground. Smoke wafts from the communal fire pit and Magic Annie's tin chimney.

From the east, carving up the silence, comes the sound of a 4x4 being driven too fast. I reach the treeline just in time to see Leon Meunier's mud-spattered Defender bouncing across the grass.

11

Tyres locking, it slides to a halt in front of Noakes's lorry. The driver's door flies open and Meunier leaps out. I've never seen his face such a livid red. He lifts back his head and bellows.

Growling and snapping, Noakes's two dogs scrabble up. Only their chains, attached to a corkscrew hoop sunk into the marshy ground, hold them back. As Meunier strides into the settlement, still yelling, I creep towards his Defender.

Already, others have begun to appear. Noakes is first, bundled up in his old coat, his skin like spoiled sausage meat, his hands bunched into fists.

The two men begin a heated exchange. Then, from their caravan, the new couple emerge. The woman is dressed in knee-high boots and a voluminous fake fur. Her face is heavily made up. Feathery smudges of blue, green and silver give her the appearance of a tropical bird.

I reach the 4x4. Press myself against the passenger door. I can hear Meunier demanding that the newcomers leave the estate.

Because the Defender's windows are tinted, I can keep out of sight while I listen. Despite that, I can't shake the feeling I'm being watched. Several times I glance back at the Memory Wood, but I see no one lurking among the trees. When I peer once again through the Defender's side window, I spot something I'd missed.

In the vehicle's central console, beside Meunier's phone and wallet, lies today's *Daily Telegraph*. Beneath the newspaper's masthead, a huge image of Gretel stares up at me.

They've used a different photograph this time – a better one, too. In her expression I see clear hints of the woman she might one day become.

Did you tell them about me, *Elijah? Did you remember my name, like I told you?* Elissa Mirzoyan. *Did you explain where I was? What was happening down here? Did you tell them how to find me?*

I know she thinks I failed her. I know she's lost faith in my ability to help. If I'm honest, I've started to lose faith too.

I think of my Collection of Keepsakes and Weird Finds and how much I'd like this image of Gretel to be a part of it. If I can't save her, I have a duty, at the very least, to remember her. As gently as I can, I ease open the Land Rover's door.

III

Autumn thunder rumbles across Meunierfields, chasing a flock of geese that erupts from the surface of Knucklebone Lake. The sound, violent and unexpected, fries my nerves. With the argument still raging behind me, I run for the safety of the treeline. There, kneeling in wet bracken, I tear Gretel's picture from the newspaper.

Back on my feet, I'm about to head home when I see Magic Annie's door clatter open. My spirit guide emerges on to the caravan's front step. Gone is the Cowichan sweater and necklace of turquoise stones. Instead, she's wearing a colourful woollen skirt – what she once told me was a Romanian *fotă*. Her hair is bound up in a white cloth *maramă*.

Descending to the grass, fingers laced before her, Annie approaches the group. She's a gentle moonbeam among them. Meunier's in mid-rant when he notices her. When Annie starts to speak he listens, and when he responds she gives him the same respect.

A minute later, Meunier marches back to his Defender. He accelerates away, tyres spitting grass and mud.

The Wheel Town folk watch him go. The woman with the peacock eyes hisses something at Annie, who narrows her eyes in displeasure.

I've been on the end of that look once or twice. It's an uncomfortable feeling, but the younger woman doesn't seem to care. Following her outburst, she stomps off to her caravan, accompanied by the guy in the cap. Annie and Noakes, wearing troubled expressions, talk a while longer before they part.

Watching them, I can't escape the feeling that everything around here, my own life included, is about to self-combust.

IV

I should leave, now, before I'm discovered, but seeing Annie has made me crave her companionship, so I break from cover and sprint towards her caravan.

She answers on the first knock, ushering me inside. I kick off my trainers and she puts them by the wood stove. While I take a seat near the TV, Annie pours a glass of milk and places three pecan-nut biscuits on a plate. She's about to set them on the table when she pulls up short. *'Anoki,'* she says, despite this not being a Native American day. 'Why the tears?'

Unable to stem them, I wipe my nose on my sleeve. 'What's happening, Annie? What's going on?'

Her brow creases. 'What do you mean?'

I can't tell her the real reason I'm crying, so instead I nod towards the window, at the tracks left by Meunier's Defender. 'Is he kicking you out?'

Annie's eyes crinkle. 'Is *that* what's got you all in a fluster? Don't you worry about that old meanie. Come on, wipe your face and drink your milk.'

There's a tightness in my throat I can't swallow. 'But what if he *does* kick you out?'

'You just listen,' she says, sliding on to the bench seat beside me. 'Old Annie knows a thing or two about Leon Meunier, and you can be sure he knows it too. He won't be kicking anyone out – not today, not tomorrow, nor any time soon.'

Fresh tears run down my cheeks. I want to believe her, but I'm so torn up by thoughts of Gretel's infected wrist and my lost torch that it's impossible to feel any comfort. 'If you went, Annie, I don't know what I'd do.'

She touches my face with a gentle finger. 'You're too good for this world, Elijah.'

I close my eyes, resting my head against her shoulder. Annie strokes my hair. From outside, I hear the familiar clatter of a diesel. I sit up straight as Leon Meunier's Defender swings back into view, pulling up sharply beside the fire pit.

'Saints preserve us,' Annie mutters, rising to her feet.

The car door flies open. Meunier leaps out. Earlier, he looked angry. Now, he looks furious. I think of what I stole from his Land Rover and clench my teeth so hard it hurts.

Taking a breath, Annie adjusts her *maramă*. 'Wait here while I get his attention,' she says, going to the door. 'Then slip off home as quietly as you can.'

'Yes, Annie,' I say.

ELISSA

Day 7

I

Lying on the cell floor, shivering from fever, sweating despite the cold, Elissa listens to the bronchial rattle of her breathing. At her side, her right arm feels like it's metamorphosing into something unspeakable, a process of atrophy busily transforming the flesh.

Earlier, she scraped together enough energy to light a candle. Now, watching it, she concedes there's something wrong with her vision. One moment, the flame fills her view; the next, it accelerates away until it's nothing but a distant pinprick.

On the walls of her cell, *bodachs* cavort and chitter. She knows they're not really there, but in their whispered conversations she hears echoes of the ghoul: *Down here, if you don't keep yourself clean, injuries like that can get infected. First thing you'll feel is the skin getting itchy, getting hot. The flesh will swell, start to suppurate, like it's a piece of fruit someone trod on and left out in the sun . . . You'll begin to feel dizzy, confused. You won't even be able to trust your own thoughts.*

Regardless of the motive, his warning was accurate – right now, she can't even trust her own eyes.

The candle flame rushes close. Pumpkin light fills her head. On the wall, one of the *bodachs* transforms into Andrea from Wide Boys: *You should see me on Hallowe'en. I wear a pair of eyes that're bright orange, slitted just like a cat's. Scares the bejesus out of people.*

The flame bobs and swells. It dives and pirouettes. There's something deeply compelling about its dance, almost as if that yellow teardrop of fire, growing from a blue nimbus, is the periphery where the physical world meets the divine. For a moment, watching it, Elissa feels she's within touching distance of a revelation, an epiphany. Then the light falls away, leaving her desolate.

Already, she's past the peak of what her mind and body can endure. The damp, the lack of food and the ghoul's filthy drugs have all exacted a toll. She's too exhausted to load her memories of Elijah into the virtual chessboard, too punch-drunk to search for more answers. Her attempts at coercion have failed, as have her attempts at subterfuge. Worst of all – worse, even, than her infected wound and her ever-loosening grip on reality – is the knowledge that somewhere, out there, her mum is all alone. Lena Mirzoyan doesn't deserve to lose a daughter, and yet that outcome now seems inevitable.

When Elissa hears the deadbolts rattle in their housings, she wonders if her greatest torment is yet to come.

Who are you kidding? You know it is.

11

There's no voice, no torch beam, and the boomeranging candle doesn't illuminate her guest, but she knows, somehow, it's Elijah. That's neither good nor bad; it just is. She hasn't managed to decipher his involvement. She probably never will.

He hesitates at the threshold, as if he's building his courage. When the silence gets too much, she croaks, 'Hansel?'

Feet slither across stone. Something emerges from the gloom. Elissa squints, trying to focus, but it's no use – the candlelight has retreated again, leaving a miasma of smeared greys.

By degrees, the light returns, but now her vision is skittering, like she's watching images through an old movie projector where the film has slipped from its reel. Out of the mess swims a fleshy blob hosting two dark circles.

Elijah takes a forward step. In the *skip-snatch* jerkiness of Elissa's perception, it's impossible to stitch together the frames and form a coherent whole. Elijah shrinks and swells in size, a restless *bodach* whose dimensions are constantly in flux.

One thing she does notice – from the seething shadows that comprise him – is a hand, buried in a jacket pocket. From the angle of his elbow, it appears he's clutching something; whether a knife, or some other weapon, she cannot tell.

Elissa's mouth runs so dry she can barely speak. 'Elijah?'

He sways on his feet. 'Gretel.'

'Has something happened?'

'I . . . I think.'

'Are you OK?'

'Not really. I don't . . . I just can't . . .'

Elissa's pulse is racing, her breathing too, but she tries to keep her voice steady. 'Did you want to talk about it?'

The muscles of Elijah's forearm tense inside his jacket, as if his grip on the hidden object has tightened. His lungs fill. His breath judders out.

The candle flame dips low, its tip flickering like a reptilian tongue. Again, Elissa's world contracts into darkness. When she hears Elijah crouch down opposite, it's all she can do to resist scrabbling away. One thing she knows, beyond doubt: she *must* maintain the pretence of trust. 'Why did you come back?'

'I wanted to see you.'

'But not to talk?'

'No.'

Elissa waits a beat. 'What, then?'

'I wanted to play,' he says. 'With you.'

There's an edge to his tone that she doesn't recognize. It sounds like he's talking about a doll, a toy, an object constructed purely for his gratification.

Something sharp and painful blossoms in her chest. Summoning all her strength, she pushes herself halfway up. 'Elijah,' she begins. 'When this is—'

'I want to play chess.'

It takes a moment for his words to register. Such is Elissa's relief that she closes her eyes. When she opens them, something about the shifting shadows tells her he's moved a fraction closer.

'I want to play chess too,' she tells him. 'I want that more than anything. But I told you before, we don't have a—'

'I brought a phone,' he says, and suddenly everything is different.

III

At first, Elissa thinks it's a trick, a cruel raising of her hopes. But when Elijah takes his hand from his pocket, the cellar is bathed in blue light.

Her chest grows tight. She can't breathe – doesn't *want* to breathe – worries if she breaks this spell of silence between them that Elijah will come to his senses.

She can't make sudden movements, can't appear too keen, can't afford to let a single ounce of hunger or cunning show in her face. The phone offers a chance of salvation, but she hasn't won it yet. And Elijah, in the past, has proved far more immune to deception than she'd hoped.

You're trying to trick me. Aren't you? You want me to bring you a phone so you can call someone to come down here and get you.

Why, then, has he done exactly that?

A thought strikes her, contracting her skin into gooseflesh. Perhaps *this* is the test for which he's been preparing her.

At last, her oxygen runs out and she's forced to breathe. It's vital she steadies herself. If Elijah notices her agitation, he'll likely turn and run. Her fingers have become claws. Her leg muscles, previously too weak to support her weight, quiver with adrenalin. Could she scratch out his eyes, if it saved her life? Probably. She'd never forget the horror of it, but she might see her mum again. That alone would make it worthwhile.

Elijah, still nothing more than a monstrous grey smear, leans away from her. 'What's wrong?'

She wants to snatch at him, grab hold of him, prevent him from leaving the boundary of her chain. But if she touches him now, uninvited, this chance will turn to dust.

With a dry tongue, she licks cracked lips. 'Thirsty.'

The grey shape looms nearer, until it blocks out all the light. Suddenly, the Evian bottle is at her mouth. Elissa tilts back her head, allowing precious water to slide down her throat. The phone's reflection glows in the plastic bottle. It's so close.

'You poor *thing*,' Elijah murmurs as the last of the water trickles out. 'I should have brought you more to drink. I should've thought.'

'It's OK,' she says, wiping her mouth. 'It's not your fault.'

'Yes, it is. You're down here dying of thirst and all I can think about is a stupid game. It's selfish and stupid and *wrong*.'

'I'm not dying, Elijah. Not yet.'

'You're not well. And that's my fault too. I could've done something. And I didn't. It's just . . .'

Elissa waits, but Elijah doesn't complete his thought. She asks, 'You really came down here to play chess?'

'Yes.' Then, as if convinced she's going to renege on their deal, his voice rises in pitch. 'You *promised*! You said if I got hold of a phone, if I brought it down here, that you'd—'

She holds up her good hand. 'Elijah, it's fine. We might need to check a few things first. And we might have to download some software, but as long as you have the password, we can—'

'Password?'

'Yeah, the—'

'What're you talking about?'

'Sometimes people put passwords on their phones, to stop other people from snooping.'

'How do we get the password?'

'You'd have to ask the person who owns the phone.' She pauses. 'Can you do that?'

'No!'

Elissa's guts twist like a dishcloth. 'Well, if it isn't locked, we won't need one. Not everybody bothers.'

'How do we check?'

'Hold it up,' she tells him. 'Show me the screen.'

Elijah does as he's asked. Again, the blue light appears between them, as if the lid's been opened of a box filled with magic. Elissa tries desperately to focus. Her vision jumps and pulls. Finally, from liquid threads of colour, an image begins to solidify.

The phone is an iPhone; one of the older models. The screen's a little scratched, but it's working well enough. Instead of a password request, it's showing a neat grid of apps.

IV

If there was ever a time to develop a poker face, it's now. Trying to appear disinterested, Elissa considers her options.

'So,' Elijah says. 'What do we do?'

'Go to the App Store,' she tells him, then blinks. 'Sorry. I forgot this is new. You're looking for a blue square with a white A. The A stands for "App". It's where we'll find the chess programme.'

Elijah hunches forward. 'I have it.'

'Give it a press.'

The quality of the blue light changes, and she knows he's in. 'Do you see a little magnifying glass?'

'Yes.'

'Beside it, there should be a blank space.'

'Got it.'

'OK, type into it the—'

'How?'

'Just touch the box. That should bring up a keyboard.'

The light changes colour yet again. 'What do I type?'

'Chess. Then press the button that says "search".'

As he concentrates, Elijah's breath whistles in his nose.

'Well?'

'It's come up with a message.'

'What's it say?'

' "No internet connection. Make sure Wi-Fi or cell . . . u . . . lar data is turned on, then try again." '

'Show me.'

He twists around, scooting backwards until he's right beside her. His proximity overloads Elissa's already battered senses. Elijah's so close she can smell him: a mustiness of unwashed clothes and greasy skin. Something is wrong – desperately so – but she cannot comprehend what. Or perhaps she can, and her mind refuses to accept it.

Gingerly, Elissa reaches out her good hand. She doesn't take the phone, but she steadies it. Elijah's finger brushes her thumb. They both flinch.

Her skin burns where it touches him. She hears her mum's voice, crying out a warning.

Elissa's vision jitters, skips. She swallows, grits her teeth, forces clarity from the swirl of colours. Gradually, the screen resolves. She hunts in vain for a reception bar. Her guts churn. 'There's no signal.'

'What's that mean?'

'These walls, this ceiling – they stop the signal getting through.'

Elijah turns to face her. His eyes, reflecting the phone's blue light, are tiny computer screens. 'You mean, like a lead box stops radiation?'

'Exactly like that.'

As Elissa stares at him, he leans a little closer. The rest of his face materializes; and, with it, the reality of her situation – the reality of *Elijah* – finally emerges.

You'll begin to feel dizzy, confused. You won't even be able to trust your own thoughts.

Elissa feels a scream building, a dense knot of horror that can't be contained. She traps it in her chest regardless, because to release it now, so close to this chance of life, would bring an end to all her hopes.

Elijah's breath is warm against her face. It smells bad, like he has bits of old meat stuck between his teeth. 'We can't play chess?'

Impossible, now, to reconcile that pseudo-innocent voice with the person the candlelight has revealed. Because while Elijah speaks with the pitch and cadence of a twelve-year-old boy, he inhabits, undeniably, the body of a man.

MAIRÉAD

Day 6

I

Lena Mirzoyan watches the recording of Elissa a second time, but she's unable to offer further insight. Her distress, by the end, is so acute that no one with any compassion could put her through it again.

Outside, the sky grows darker, more malevolent. There's no warmth in the Mirzoyan living room. Every surface seems touched by cold. Mairéad can't offer Lena any comfort. All she can think about is the feeling of emptiness in her belly, and the conviction that something is deeply, tragically wrong.

Nine weeks she's carried this spark inside her. Nine weeks she's striven to coach it into fire. The nausea, although debilitating, had been comforting in its own way – evidence that *this* pregnancy, over all her previous failures, was deeper rooted, more impervious to misfortune.

And now it's gone.

Before she leaves Lena, she asks to use the upstairs bathroom. There's no blood when she checks her underwear, no sign of spotting, like before. Pulling up her blouse, she gently probes her abdomen. But she's a detective, not a doctor – she has no idea what she's doing.

Mairéad closes her eyes and concentrates. Has the nausea *really* disappeared? Perhaps that two-minute footage of Elissa has temporarily robbed her of feeling. She'd viewed the clip repeatedly before coming here, but Lena's presence magnified the horror a hundredfold.

Hold on, please hold on, stay with me, please don't go.

She uses the toilet and washes her hands. On the sink, she sees two toothbrushes in a holder, one of them clearly Elissa's. Few other traces of the girl exist inside the bathroom – no spew of teenage beauty products, no cluster of budget perfumes. How light her touch on the world has been. How short-lived her legacy, if she's really gone.

II

On the drive back to Dorset she phones her GP, who arranges a same-day referral to the Royal Bournemouth Hospital's early-pregnancy assessment unit.

Mairéad sits in the waiting room, eyes closed, breathing deep. She decides against calling Scott. He'll try to comfort her, wrap her in love, and she can't risk that. Right now, she's an empty vessel, devoid of all emotion. Exactly how she needs to be.

She forces her attention back to the investigation. Five days now, since Elissa disappeared. Mairéad feels her slipping inexorably further away. Already, she's noticed a change in the nature of the news reporting, grim acceptance beginning to replace hope. Next week, by degrees, Elissa will fade from the front pages. In a month, her story will be relegated to occasional Sunday-paper spreads.

Mairéad, her eyes still closed, reaches out with her mind: *Hold on, please hold on, stay with me, please don't go.* And with that she's back in the waiting room, hands on her belly, waiting for the news she dreads to hear.

III

The sonographer, a loose-jowled woman with auburn hair, isn't one she's met before. Mairéad's relieved about that. She knows most of the staff at the unit. Today, she'll willingly trade their smiles and careful kindnesses for anonymity. The loose-jowled woman introduces herself, but Mairéad doesn't hear her name. There's white noise in her ears, now. It drowns everything out.

Lying on the examination table, she unbuttons her trousers and lifts her blouse. If the ultrasound gel is cold, she doesn't feel it.

The sonographer is talking again, fuzzy words that bounce away without registering. In her right hand she holds the probe, which she presses to Mairéad's belly. On the monitor appears a familiar fan-shaped swirl of grey. The image is grainy and distant, like footage received from deep space. It shifts, coalesces, and now, at the heart of it, a cavity appears, a black bolus of emptiness. The white noise in Mairéad's head becomes a buzzing, all-consuming. Her fingers find her wedding ring, rotating it three times.

The sonographer's chest rises and falls. Her eyes move

from the monitor to Mairéad's belly and back, jowls swinging like a mastiff's. Fractionally, her eyebrows dip. The probe tilts, hunting for a better angle, but Mairéad knows the truth without being told. And she can cope with it; she can.

At last, the woman begins to speak. Her platitudes fall like rain. She gestures at the monitor and Mairéad nods along, carefully arranging her expression. She'll wear this face back to the car, back to Bournemouth Central. She'll wear it for Scott, and for the TV cameras, and for Elissa Mirzoyan's mum.

'—with our consultant obstetrician, but it's up to you.'

Gradually, Mairéad tunes back in. She knows the script from this point on. The miscarriage will happen naturally or it won't. Either way, she'll be back here within a week, to check that no trace of the foetus remains.

'The hardest part's always the not-knowing,' the sonographer says. 'At least you can relax now.'

Through eight years of medical practitioners, Mairéad's met almost universal kindness, courtesy, everyday humanity. And then, every now and then, there'll be someone like this.

Her jaw hardens. The top of her scalp grows cold. '*What* did you just say?'

The woman smiles, as if she's sharing a confidence. 'I can't blame you for zoning out. I said I can get one of the consultants to talk to you, if you like. Either way, you did the right thing by coming in.'

Mairéad's hands sharpen into fists. Her breath is stuck in her throat. She glances back at the monitor, trying to displace her rage, and there, suddenly, she sees it, right at the bottom of the image: the shivery oscillation of a fast-beating heart.

ELISSA

Day 7

I

There's no stubble on his cheeks, no hint of a beard, not even the soft, wispy down she's sometimes seen on the faces of adolescent boys. His skin is frog-pale, his features rounded by fat. Beneath them, the folds of his neck are like rings of molten wax around a guttering church candle. Within those folds, there's no sign of the enlarged larynx that usually forms during puberty. A six-inch scar, which appears to have healed without stitches, runs from his left temple to his chin.

Elissa's vision skips, the colours bleeding into themselves. For a moment she wonders if she's hallucinating, if what she's seeing is a composite monster dredged from the depths of her subconscious. But this is no illusion, no trick of the mind.

In the low light, the rest of him resists much examination, but she has the impression of a large body, more feminine than masculine in its curves. Elijah is obese, but not morbidly so. He looks clumsy, sluggish. His eyes, by contrast, have the deadpan intensity of a lizard's.

As she stares at him, muscles locked solid, the terrible repercussions begin to sink in. Throughout her ordeal, Elijah and the ghoul have been easily distinguishable; the naive boy versus the depraved adult; the high-pitched voice of an innocent versus the whispered demands of a beast.

A whisper, Elissa now realizes, can conceal as much truth as the dark.

Since the beginning, she's had her suspicions of something not-quite-right, of a game being played with rules she hasn't grasped. Elijah might never have played chess, but he's proved himself adept at deception. Perhaps he's even deceived himself.

'Is all this real? Sometimes . . . sometimes I think . . . it isn't.'

'What do you mean?'

'I'm not Hansel.'

'No. You're not Hansel. You're Elijah.'

'Am I?'

Obvious, now, why his voice sometimes sounded so disembodied. Throughout, she'd put that down to her exhaustion or disorientation, or perhaps the ghoul's filthy drugs. Belatedly, she realizes she experienced it only when Elijah was standing, magnifying the difference between the height she imagined him to be and the reality. Upright, he must be taller than six foot.

Despite her horror at what the candle flame has revealed, and the starkness of its implications, Elissa considers her earlier plan. Because of what she's just learned, the consequences of a misstep are likely fatal: *There'll never be anything, ever in this life, that you can conceal from me.* And yet inaction carries consequences just as bleak.

'Elijah, I'm sorry,' she says, trying to smooth the tremors in her voice. 'But if we can't get a signal, we can't download the software. Underground, the phone just won't work. No calls, no data, no nothing.'

The thick folds of his neck contract. She hears him swallow, a hard-sounding *glop*. When he blinks, the computer screens floating in his eyes wink out, then reboot.

This is it.

This is the moment.

Suddenly, it feels like Elissa's entire life has been moving inexorably towards this point. So much hangs in the balance. A future, or no future at all.

Wetting her lips, she leans forwards and kisses him.

II

The world goes still. The blood in Elissa's arteries ceases to flow. Raging rivers become dormant canals. Even gravity seems to fade away. She feels no floor beneath her, no bonds of mass holding her down. If not for the chain, she might float out through the open cell door and up into the night.

Elijah's lips, loose and slightly parted, are rougher than she'd expected. He tastes strange: sour, almost fizzy. Closing her eyes, filling her lungs, Elissa opens her mouth. When she pushes her tongue between his lips, the world returns like air rushing into a vacuum. Her ears roar with equalizing pressure.

She's never, ever in her life, kissed someone like this. She didn't expect it to be so intense. Elijah's tongue is hard and hot, a strip of pan-fried stewing steak surrounded by sharp teeth. If he chose, he could bite down and cut her own tongue to pieces.

And then his mouth is gone.

Elijah reels away from her, groaning as if he's been stabbed. He skates backwards across the floor, a clumsy mess of limbs, until the darkness swallows him. 'What was *that*?' he shrieks, his falsetto voice ringing off the walls. '*What did you DO?*'

When he scrambles to his feet, she's convinced he's going to rush forward and attack her. She'd expected a reaction, but not this.

'*WHAT DID YOU DO, ELISSA?*'

The sight of him scurrying from the light, like a soft-bodied sea creature retreating into its burrow, is burnt on to her brain. Two more backward steps and Elijah is through the open door. It squeals in its frame as he slams it. The deadbolts shoot home.

Elissa leans forward, retching. She wants to vomit, wants the taste of him out of her mouth, but with her Evian bottle empty, she can't afford to lose any fluids. Instead, she spits on the cell floor. That kiss – the dark, compulsive horror of it – belongs in the deepest dungeon of her mind, locked up tight with the key hammered flat.

One hand supporting her manacle, she inches across the floor. Elijah was sitting in D6, but when he lurched away from her, the iPhone fell face down into B7. When she turns it over, she sees a crack running right across the screen. Elissa gasps as if she's been kicked, but the apps are all still visible. When she scrolls sideways with her thumb, the phone responds as it should.

How much time does she have? Once Elijah recovers enough to realize his mistake, it'll take him no more than fifteen seconds to unlock the door. Once he's inside, there's no hope of fighting him off.

She has a phone, but no signal. She can't make calls, can't get online. Her brain is too skittish with adrenalin to cut through the chaos. But there's a way to make this work, there has to be.

Think, Elissa.

Think!

Is that a sound outside? She hunches over the screen, trying to concentrate, trying to tune out her panicked keening.

Tapping the SMS icon, she brings up a blank message. Typing with her left thumb is far trickier than she'd expected, but the software auto-corrects her worst errors. Getting the phone numbers right will be vital.

There's that sound again – something new, that she hasn't heard before. Not from the door, or behind it, but above her head.

Completing the message, Elissa taps the address panel. Carefully, trying to steady her shaking fingers, she keys in all the mobile numbers she knows: her mum, her grand-dad, Lasse Haagensen, Mrs McCluskey.

That sound above her is racing now, rattling and ticking. She wonders what it is, what Elijah – in his rage – has done.

If she presses send immediately, the phone will attempt delivery. After a few failed attempts, it'll abandon the task. Instead, Elissa opens the email programme and writes the same message. Adding email addresses is more laborious than phone numbers. Several times, she has to correct her mistakes. All the while, her heart beats so fiercely it feels like a hammer is breaking through her chest.

The rattling sound above her changes in pitch, becomes a popping, a plinking. Elissa raises her shoulders, terrified without knowing why. Completing the email, she hits send and watches it disappear. Exiting the email app, she finds her SMS and sends it. Then she holds down the power button and puts the phone to sleep. Placing it on the floor before her, she sits cross-legged and waits.

If the phone is reactivated down here, its attempts to send her messages will fail. But if it's switched on outside and finds sufficient reception, her cries for help will be delivered.

Something lands on the floor in the far corner of the cell, bouncing away into darkness. Elissa twists round in surprise as another three hit, trying to work out what is happening.

Then, all around her, there's a pattering like falling rain. Something small and hard strikes her on the head. She recoils, touching her hair. Her fingers come away wet. When she looks up, she sees that the wooden roofing has turned dark.

A few feet away, in F6, the candle flame bobs and flickers. Elissa brings her wet fingers to her nose.

Not water. Not rain.

Fuel.

ELIJAH

Day 7

The storm that's been threatening all week – the one Mama warned me about – has finally broken.

And it's a deluge. Raindrops hammer the ground all around me, as if the Earth's gravity has been transformed into Jupiter's. It feels like someone's tattooing my shoulders, my scalp. Within seconds, I'm soaked through. The sky is so dark and strange I fear something cataclysmic is happening; a solar collapse, a meteor strike or some other extinction event. Has the rain been sent by God to wake those who lie beneath the Memory Wood? Perhaps it's been sent to flush His creation away. I think of Noah and his three sons: Shem, Ham and Japheth. I think of Mama, Papa and Kyle. I think of Gretel, and how she tried to tempt me. Then I turn my mind away, and I run.

I follow my usual path through the woods. Everything looks wrong, like a landscape painted by a lunatic. The storm unleashes its full force. Soon, I can't even remember what I'm running from, or where I'm running to. Rain beats down on my head, scrubbing away my memories.

What happened back there? Why was I so afraid? And what, in my fear, did I just do?

Lightning flashes, so sharp and blue that I lose my balance. The ground rushes up, punching the breath from my lungs. I roll on to my back, gasping.

Bryony is standing over me, beautiful Bryony. Blood sheets down her face from a monstrous gash in her forehead. She was crying, towards the end, but she isn't crying now. 'You *promised* me, Eli,' she hisses. 'You *promised* you wouldn't hurt me.'

'I didn't,' I moan, scrabbling backwards. 'I never even touched you.' Raindrops spatter off my chest. The air's so wet I can hardly see. This storm's fury is savage, elemental, and yet it affects Bryony not at all.

I did touch her, but not like that.

Never like that.

I only helped. That's all I ever did.

'*Help?*' she sneers. 'Is that what you call it?'

In death, she's so much fiercer than in life. As she stalks towards me, I realize she's wielding Kyle's rifle. I think of the deer, and the calamity inside its head, and suddenly I'm scared – *terrified* – because my head is already a calamity, and I couldn't handle another. On my elbows, I crab backwards across the soil.

'You *stink*, Elijah North,' Bryony hisses. 'You stink of lies and betrayal, but most of all you just stink.'

She's walking faster than I can crawl. The rifle barrel swings like a pendulum. Bryony's lips have peeled back. Her teeth, inexplicably, have sharpened into points. I imagine them tearing my skin, reducing my face to ropey tatters.

'Please!' I scream. 'I got you a tree! A tall one, just like you asked!'

She snarls. Her lips split further apart. She looks more like a dog, now, than a girl. Rolling on to my tummy, I jump to my feet and flee.

'*Get back here!*' Bryony shrieks, her voice even fiercer than the storm. '*It's not too late to fix this! IT'S NOT TOO LATE!*'

She's wrong about that. We both know it. It's too late for me, for dead Bryony, for soon-to-be-dead Gretel. I tried to save them, but I couldn't. This always ends the same way.

For a while, as I run, the world retreats completely. When my awareness returns I find myself at the Memory Wood's eastern boundary, with no memory of how I got here, or how much time has passed. Bursting free of the trees, I slip-slide along the track towards home. Lightning rents the sky. The clatter-crash of thunder is so violent that I sprawl on my belly and take a mouthful of putrid mud. For a moment I can't find my feet, slithering eel-like through slime and ruin.

Up ahead, I see our cottage. Kyle is standing outside. He's holding the same rifle Bryony was pointing, which is impossible, until I remember that Bryony's dead, and the girl I saw in the Memory Wood wasn't really there.

By the time I reach the front path I can hardly breathe. My clothes, sodden with rain, stick to me like a second skin.

Kyle raises his gun. 'You fuckin' slug,' he says. 'What have you done?'

'She *kissed* me, Kyle.'

Behind him, the cottage door stands open. Rain has soaked the entrance hall. Grabbing the rifle, I tear it from my brother's grip and cast it into the grass. Then I push past him and go inside.

ELISSA

Day 7

From the ceiling, fuel drips and patters and, eventually, pours. Elissa cowers in darkness beside the hastily extinguished candle, petrol fumes thickening in her throat. Already, she's feeling light-headed. How long can she breathe like this before the air begins to poison her?

She imagines Elijah standing upstairs, preparing to toss a lit match down the cellar steps and destroy the evidence of his crimes. Her horror is a scampering lizard inside her skull. Elissa envisions a yellow glow outside the door, a sudden rolling inferno within. She conjures the shrieking agony of burning skin, the savage intensity of underground immolation. Dying down here was always more than a distant possibility, but she never thought it would be like this.

Something cold and wet touches her finger – the edge of a petrol lake, creeping across the floor. A drip of fuel hits her neck and rolls down her spine. 'God, oh God, hear me, please, I pray to you, please don't let this hurt, please God, don't let it hurt.'

She thinks of her mum, listening to a grim-faced police officer explaining that her daughter's bones have been found. She imagines her visiting the Memory Wood, standing by the burnt-out cottage and peering into a blackened pit, and the image is so lonely, so desolate and goddamned *bleak*, that she begins to weep. Lena Mirzoyan didn't deserve this. Neither of them did. She thinks of the chess Grand Prix, her hopes of winning, her years of dedication. All that sacrifice with no chance of reward. All those dreams turned to ash.

If she could go back, there are so many things she'd do differently, so many people she'd like to know better. If only she'd invested as heavily in friendships as in her game. In hindsight, it didn't have to be a choice. At her funeral, there might be four attendees; six, if Lasse and Mrs McCluskey come along. Six people to commemorate a life, and she has no one to blame but herself. She's hardly touched this world. When she's gone, she'll barely leave a mark.

Then, through the sound of cascading fuel, she hears something familiar: the *rattle-snick* of deadbolts. With an abruptness that shocks her, the door swings open, revealing the slashing white beam of a torch. The sight turns her insides to paste.

'Turn it off!' she screams, trying to shield herself from the wall of flame that will roll over her if the bulb's filament ignites the air. 'Turn it *OFF*!'

The light angles up, examining the ceiling. Then it flits around the cell, coming to a rest where she left the iPhone.

Please, she thinks. *Take it. Take it away, punish me. Punish me, but don't burn me. Whatever you do, please don't set me on fire.*

Elissa sways, so disoriented that she nearly collapses. Her vision begins to skip, turning the torch into a strobe. 'Elijah?' she sobs. *'Hansel?'*

273

He lurches forward, lower legs ranging into view. So fast that she has no chance to cry out, he brings down his heel on the phone, shattering the screen.

Elissa moans, retreats into herself, tries to block out her petrol-soaked dress, the incandescent filament.

Again, his heel comes down. Glass skitters across the floor. The iPhone is reduced to twisted metal. Still the violence doesn't stop.

'Please!' Elissa screams. *'Please! Why are you doing this? What have I ever DONE TO YOU?'*

He kicks away the broken pieces and retreats through the open cell door. He's gone less than a minute. When he returns, the torch is clamped in his teeth. She can't see his face, but the light reveals his hands. In them he carries two petrol cans. Working with silent efficiency, he sloshes their contents over the floor.

ELIJAH

Day 7

I

Everything is falling apart. Everything.

I hardly recognize the cottage as I rampage through its rooms. Downstairs, a mishmash of muddy footprints darkens the floor. I wonder who made them. I wonder what they mean.

You know, says a voice I try to ignore. *Of course you do.*

I think of Bryony, in the Memory Wood. Her mortal head wound. I think of the blow that must have caused it and wonder how anyone could be so cruel.

You know, Elijah. You can't run from this. Not any more.

I feel that wall inside my mind beginning to buckle. If it does, all the horrors stacked behind it will be turned loose. In the carnage, I'll be devoured. 'Mama!' I shout, going from room to room. *'Mama!'*

The house breathes its silence like an accusation.

'She's dead, Eli, and you know it. Mama's dead and gone.'

I wheel around to find Kyle standing behind me. He's

lost his trademark sneer. He watches me with eyes full of knowing.

'Liar!' I scream at him. 'That's just a dirty *lie!*'

Pushing past him to the hall, I race up the stairs. My breath comes in ragged bursts. When my vision falls to pieces I realize I'm crying – crying and shouting for people I should know are long dead. I reach Kyle's room, and when I see what's inside I nearly sink to my knees, because it's *empty*, someone has emptied it, has removed all my brother's things.

How can that be? How can *any* of this be?

Outside, the sky flickers and crashes. Devil-spawned shapes come alive in the shadows.

Staggering on, I reach my parents' room, and that's when I *know* everything's lost. There are no sheets on the bed. The cupboard doors hang crooked, revealing an empty interior. On the dressing table, all Mama's trinkets have disappeared, although that's to be expected because, because—

'Because we buried her,' Kyle whispers, behind me. *'We buried her long ago.'*

I moan, putting my hands to my ears, because I know that's not true. Mama's tree stands in the Memory Wood, I'll admit, but no bones lie between its roots. Her tree is an oak, glorious with foliage in summer, laden with acorns in autumn, a bounty for squirrels, deer and wild boar. Its upper branches are strung with my memories and hopes: letters I've written, drawings I've made, wind chimes and paper lanterns and charms. When the rains come, as they so often do, my shrine is washed away. Yet I always renew it, and with it I renew Mama.

But *this* storm – the one raging outside, and likewise in

my head – could wash her away for good. That thought alone is a calamity, one from which I cannot recover.

All things end. All things.

And now, at last, this has to end too.

Abandoning my parents' room, I clatter back down the stairs. Kyle guards the front door, his eyes like spears. This time, it's easy to ignore him. The whirlwind in my head rages ever more fiercely, but now that I've made my decision, I've found sanctuary within the tumult.

My calmness lasts until Bryony swings out of the living room. '*Dead,*' she hisses, flashing those needle teeth. '*Dead because of you.*'

I veer away, slamming against the bannister. Pain races through my shoulder, but it's nothing to the agonies I've caused. When I turn back to the doorway, Bryony fractures into a million black splinters that melt into liquid as they fall.

I back into the kitchen, and for a moment it's not my own kitchen but the one inside the Memory Wood. Ivy spreads across the ceiling, then recedes. Glass falls from the window, then reappears. The pantry calls me in, calls me down, to a damp cellar choking with fumes.

This is real, Elijah. All of it. You're real, so am I. So is my mum. So is my family. This place is real, too. It's not where I want to be, and I hope I'm not going to die here. I hope, more than anything, that you're going to help me survive this – but it's real, I promise you. It's about as real as a thing can get.

Maybe for her. Not for me.

My lips buzz with electricity, an echo of Gretel's mouth on mine.

She kissed *me*. I didn't imagine it. Our mouths were close together, but she put hers on mine.

All things end. All things.

And there's only one way this can.

The back door is unlocked. I charge through it to the garden. Slipping and sliding, I cross the muddy grass. Above, the sky is a fury of thunder, lightning and driving rain. By the time I reach the woodshed I'm shivering, so cold and disoriented I can barely recall my plan. Earlier, I'd reached the eye of the storm. Now, I'm back in the cyclone.

Finally, I spy it, the tool I need to end this nightmare. I cross the shed to the stump block, where Papa's axe is buried. Licking my lips, I taste Gretel, Bryony's blood, a host of things forgotten and foul.

Wrapping two hands around the shaft, I wrench the axe free of its block.

All things end. All things.

I step out of the woodshed and into the vortex.

II

Crashing through the cottage, I wonder if I'm moving forwards or backwards, through time or place or both. I hear Mama's voice, that passage from Ephesians, verse ten of chapter six: *Finally, be strong in the Lord and in His mighty power. Put on the full armour of God, so that you can take your stand against the devil's schemes.*

Far from standing against the devil's schemes, for too long I've accommodated them.

Cold wind rails through the cottage. In the living room, our only picture thumps against the plaster: the Arthur Sarnoff print of a beagle playing pool. Nothing else adorns these walls, no mirrors of any kind. How anyone could bear their own reflection, I cannot begin to imagine. For as long as I can remember, I've carefully avoided my own.

I step outside. In the front garden, pounded by rain and a flattening wind, Kyle faces me, fists upon his hips.

'Get *back*!' I yell.

'Why the axe, Eli? What're you planning now?'

'I'm going to set her free.'

Kyle's teeth glint as he bares them, bright and feral. 'That's not what you're planning,' he hisses. 'That's not what you're planning at all.'

My mouth falls open. I can hardly believe what I'm hearing. 'You think I'm going to kill her?'

'I *know* you, Eli. I know you like no one else.'

I look at the axe, at the keen edge of its blade. Rain hisses and pings off the metal. Water runs down the shaft. I grip it tighter, heartened by its weight, and for a moment – just one – I think about swinging it at Kyle, burying it in his face and ending his stream of bile.

I couldn't kill Gretel.

I couldn't kill anyone.

'Yes, you could,' he whispers. 'You already have.'

Kyle lifts his finger. When I follow where it points, west past Fallow Field, I see the eastern edge of the Memory Wood; and, rising above it, a dense cloud of black smoke.

MAIRÉAD

Day 7

I

Mairéad is in the Mirzoyan living room for her fourth visit when Lena Mirzoyan's phone starts ringing. Grabbing it from the sofa, the woman answers straight away. Hope, briefly stirred to life, fades from her expression. 'Lasse . . . Yeah. Look . . .' She pauses, listening.

Mairéad glances at Judy Pauletto and sees they're thinking the same thing: *Lasse Haagensen, the chess teacher. Single white male, thirty-four years old.*

'You're where? . . . You're . . . Lasse, hold on. I don't understand . . . Yes . . . OK . . . she *what*?'

Lena leaps up, racing to the window. 'Right now . . . Of course I will! Stay where you are. Don't you move.'

Mairéad's already on her feet. 'The chess teacher?'

'He's outside. Says he can't get past your officer on the gate. Says he has urgent information and needs to speak to us.'

II

Lasse Haagensen is dressed more like a rock star than a Danish chess grandmaster: black boots, leather biker's jacket, tight black jeans. He reminds Mairéad of Jeff Goldblum playing Dr Ian Malcolm in *Jurassic Park*.

Haagensen twitches involuntarily as he talks, as if his brain is discharging excess electricity through his limbs. 'Which one of you is in charge?'

'I'm Detective Super—' Mairéad begins, but Haagensen waves away her introduction.

'No time,' he says, brandishing a piece of paper. 'I have her. I have Elissa.'

Lena Mirzoyan's spine snaps straight. She puts her hands to her mouth. 'What do you—'

'Sir, if you—'

'*Listen* to me,' Haagensen says, clutching the paper like it's a weapon. 'I know where she is. I know where to find her.'

Suddenly, the room is full of competing voices. 'You have her, or you know where she is?' Mairéad demands.

'What?' Haagensen shouts. 'Why're we even discussing this? The latter, of course the latter. Why aren't you *listening*?' He thrusts out the paper. 'Read it. Read that and tell me I'm wrong.'

Snatching it off him, Mairéad scans the handwriting.

To Whom It May Concern,

I am writing in the hope that you'll please send me a free introductory chess set. Even though I've learned the full rules, I currently have no board or pieces, and therefore no way of actually playing.

Dietmar Pfister is currently my favourite player. Caspian Alexandr is also very good. Often, they manage to turn the tables on what seem like hopeless situations. There's something particularly exciting about Pfister's game. The way he defeated Jacob Nyback in Tblisi last year was truly astonishing.

Although I'm a late starter, I hope that with a board and pieces of my own I'll develop into a competent player. Grateful if you could send my set to the address at the top of this letter.

Ever your servant,
Kyle North

Frowning, she glances up. 'What exactly do you think this is?'

'It's a message. A coded message, from Elissa.'

'It looks like some kind of application letter.'

'Yes,' Haagensen says. 'To FIDE.'

'Which is?'

He rolls his eyes, frustrated. 'The Fédération Internationale des Échecs. In other words, the World Chess Federation. I'm a member, but not a representative.'

'So?'

'So why address this to me? Even if I did have something to do with FIDE, they don't give out chessboards to kids. They never have – although Elissa and I once had a conversation about exactly that, where she argued quite forcibly that they should.' He taps the address at the top of the letter. 'Go there and you'll find her. Guaranteed.'

When she doesn't immediately react, Haagensen turns to Lena Mirzoyan. 'Fuck it. If *they* won't, I'll drive you myself.'

'Slow down,' Mairéad snaps. 'You're going nowhere. You said there was a code.'

'Get on the phone, summon the cavalry and you might just save her. Elissa, she loves chess, but she also loves codes. It's been a game of ours since I started coaching her – a little puzzle each week, for one of us to deconstruct. Read that message again. Look at the first letter of each sentence. Put them all together and what do you get? *T.I.E.D.C.O.T.T.A.G.E. Tied cottage.* Look at the address at the top of that letter: Meunierfields. I checked it out on Google. It's an estate up in Shropshire, owned by the lord of Famerhythe: some guy called Leon Meunier.'

Mairéad stares at Judy Pauletto. 'Leon.'

Judy nods. 'The Luc Besson film.'

Swearing, Mairéad digs out her phone.

Oh Elissa, you brave and clever girl. You just hold on. We're coming. We're coming right now.

ELIJAH

Day 7

I

Lashed by rain, I stand beside my older brother and watch the Memory Wood burn. The black smoke, gushing into a storm-darkened sky, freezes my blood in my veins. I cannot believe what I'm seeing and yet this, of everything, I know to be true.

At the heart of that inferno stands the Gingerbread House. I imagine the ash tree in its living room haloed by fire, the roof above it collapsing into flames. I think of the cellar, transformed into a witch's oven. I see the iron ring, the loop of chain, the manacle . . . and suddenly I can't see anything at all.

'It wasn't me,' I whisper. '*It wasn't me.*'

As I stare at that calamity raging in the woods, that filthy column of smoke, my brother lifts his arm and points east across Fallow Field, all the way to Rufus Hall. A sycamore-lined avenue connects it to the public road. Along the avenue, emergency lights flashing, races a convoy of police cars.

I don't know how to feel. I don't know what to do. Silent, I watch the vehicles speed towards Meunier's mansion. This is his land. Behind me stands his cottage. Those trees, burning in the Memory Wood, belong to him too. Perhaps the police will think this is his fault.

I hear the crackle-snap of distant flames, the frenzied screams of wild boar. Those cries, of course, could be illusory. I have, as I've so often said, an overactive imagination.

'It's done,' Kyle says, thrusting his hands into his pockets. 'You won't escape what's coming.'

'I haven't *done* anything.'

'You thought this place was bad, but it's nothing to where you're going.'

'I tried to save her!'

'Same old bullshit, Eli. Trouble is, nobody's listening any more 'cept me.'

'I tried to *SAVE her*!'

Kyle hawks up something foul and spits it into the rain.

I turn and run back up the garden path, splashing through puddles and filth. Above me, the sky unleashes its full fury. Thunder rolls across Meunierfields like the hooves of stampeding cattle. Reaching the cottage's front door, I push my way inside.

III

This place. This hated place. In many ways, it's been a prison as claustrophobic as the Gingerbread House.

I'm still clutching the axe. When I drop it, the bit buries itself in the floor. The shaft points towards the front entrance, refusing to let me forget what's out there, refusing to let me forget what I've done.

Except I haven't done anything.

Certainly not what Kyle said. I didn't save Gretel, but I didn't burn her. I wouldn't.

As I stand, frozen, in the hallway, I can't take my eyes off the axe shaft. It could almost be the pointer of a sundial except, like so many things around here – like Mama, like Bryony, like Kyle – it casts no shadow.

I retreat to the living room, calling for my parents, for my dead brother, even though I know they're not there. I see damp walls, mould-stained furniture, the peeling Arthur Sarnoff print of rascally dogs playing pool.

On a side table beside the only armchair lies a transparent plastic case. Inside is a disc that shines all the colours of the rainbow. There's a name on it: *ELISSA*. I recognize the handwriting.

Rain drums against the window. My breath catches in my throat. I stare at the disc and wonder what it is. Perhaps an alien, or a traveller from the far future, deposited it here while I was away.

Liar! someone screams, deep inside my skull.

LIAR!

It's Gretel's voice. I flee from it.

IV

Trailing wet prints, I slip-slide to the hall. I clatter up the stairs and burst into my bedroom.

The carnage that greets me stops me dead. All across the floor, my stuff is strewn about. A wax jacket – filthy and stinking – lies on the bed. In the corner, the loose floorboard has been ripped away. Beneath the window, scattered haphazardly, are the contents of my Collection of Keepsakes and Weird Finds.

I see the trio of knucklebones I can no longer bear to touch, the Roman coin, the child's diary, Gretel's filthy vest. Amid the loot lies a tiny perfume bottle, its lid removed, a dark stain where its contents have leaked out. I can smell the scent from here, and it immediately reminds me of Mama – not that I ever remember Mama wearing perfume.

Did I do this? Or was it Kyle?

By my desk are the cases for Papa's video equipment. Leaning against them is Kyle's .22. Earlier, I tore that from his hands and cast it into the grass. At least, that's what I thought.

Strange colours swarm up the wall. I think I'm going to pass out, until I realize I'm seeing the reflections of flashing emergency lights converging on my home. That convoy wasn't at Rufus Hall long. Perhaps Meunier directed it here.

If the police find me, there's no way I'll be able to explain; and there's no way they'll listen. Already, a police Land Rover is bouncing across the back garden. It looks so out of place I almost laugh. Abandoning my room, I stagger down the stairs.

I can't go out the back, and now there are flashing lights out the front. Stepping around the axe, I re-enter the living room.

Kyle is standing there. His eyes are gone, his face a beetle-picked horror show. 'You're *fucked*,' he hisses.

When I scream, Kyle dissolves into ashes, revealing the side table. On it lies the rainbow disc printed with Gretel's name. I know it's a DVD. Why do I pretend otherwise? I might be a twelve-year-old boy who's grown up in isolation from modern ways, but sometimes I know more than I think.

If the police find this disc – if they find my fingerprints on it – they'll jump to conclusions that will damn me.

Through the window, I see movement. Police officers, coming up the path. My heart climbs into my throat.

Opening the case, I rip out the DVD. Then, falling to my knees, I post it through a gap in the floorboards. I toss the empty case across the room.

There's hammering, now, and not just from the rain. Stumbling to the hall, I notice the axe, still buried in the floor. It's a moment's work to tear it loose. Behind me, the kitchen door bursts open. Opposite, the front door swings wide.

A woman stands on the step, hair plastered to her scalp. I see no hint of compassion in her expression, no empathy for my plight. My fingers tighten around the axe shaft and I ask myself: Why *should* I see empathy? I know what I've done. And she knows it too.

'Put it down,' she barks, lips pulled back from her teeth. Uniformed officers surround her, grim-faced men who want to do me harm. She's police, just like them, even

though she doesn't wear the uniform. Apart from the pro-
tective vest beneath her waterproof jacket, she's dressed
like an office worker: black trousers; cashmere jumper;
smart shoes.

Play clothes, I think, and smile.

The woman repeats her instruction. In her eyes I see
reflected movement. I turn to find a bearded policeman in
the kitchen doorway.

He raises his hands. 'Easy,' he says. 'Easy now.'

The words send a shudder through me.

'I didn't do it,' I say, turning back to the female officer.
In a sea of hostile faces, hers is the one I fear least. 'I didn't
do any of it.'

It's clear from her stare that she doesn't believe me.

'What's your name?' she asks.

I wheel around, checking the bearded policeman hasn't
crept closer. Then I turn back to the woman. My throat
feels like someone's squeezing it. For a moment I wonder if
I'm choking. I begin to say my name, but this fantasy – this
God-awful charade, into which I've retreated far too long –
is over. Dead and buried.

'Kyle,' I say, laying the axe at my feet. 'I'm Kyle North.'

'Where is she, Kyle?'

'She's gone.'

The detective studies me. Some of the light drains from
her eyes. 'Kyle North, I'm arresting you on suspicion of the
abduction and murder of Elissa Mirzoyan.' Still talking, she
steps into the hall. Her words wash over me like a wave. I
glance behind me to see the policeman edging closer.

I don't want to get hurt so I hold out my hands, palms up.

They wouldn't cuff a twelve-year-old boy.

But they have no qualms about cuffing me.

PART II

MAIRÉAD

I

To put out the blaze in the woods, Shropshire Fire and Rescue use all their available resources, sending appliances from Church Stretton and Craven Arms, as well as back-up units from the larger Shrewsbury station, including a command unit, an FIU and operational support. The crews pump water from a nearby freshwater lake to quell the flames, running their lines through the trees to reach the inferno. The rain helps. Without it, the entire wood might have burned.

When the storm moves south, some time after midday, Mairéad finds herself wishing for its return. Now, instead of thunder, the sky clatters with rotor blades. One of the helicopters is from NPAS in Birmingham, routed here to provide air support, but two others are news media, broadcasting live footage. Outside Meunierfields' gates, the public road looks like a crash site, mobile-broadcast trucks and journalists' cars parked nose to tail.

All week, Mairéad has used the press to keep Elissa

Mirzoyan's face on TV screens, newspapers and social media. Search parties, comprising hundreds of police and civilian volunteers, have combed acres of countryside, both in Dorset, where the girl was snatched, and Wiltshire, her home county.

Thousands of hours of CCTV footage and ANPR data have been reviewed and cross-referenced. Hundreds of Bedford vans have been tracked and checked. Now, six days after the abduction, Mairéad stands in this rain-soaked wood and stares down into an abyss.

Of the building at the heart of the blaze, only the outer walls remain. Everything else – the roof and both floors – collapsed into the cellar, where, the Assistant Chief Fire Officer informed her, it burned so fiercely that almost nothing remains.

Black water fills the cellar to a depth of two feet. A couple of enterprising Scenes of Crime Officers are moving about in the filth, rubberized waders pulled over their white suits. Earlier, one of them stubbed his toe on what he thinks is a metal hoop sunk into a bed of concrete. There's no way of confirming that until the water level recedes, but Mairéad suspects it's true.

There was this time, last summer. Mum promised to take me to London. I'd always wanted to ride on the Underground, take a Tube to all the famous stops – check out Madame Tussauds, Ripley's Believe It Or Not, 221B Baker Street.

Elissa had been smart enough to code a message into the YouTube broadcast, had even managed to embed information into the letter sent to Lasse Haagensen. She hadn't deserved this.

All around the site, blackened tree trunks rise like grave markers from the sodden earth. A female SOCO trudges over, boots squelching in sludge. 'Nothing,' she says, raising her mask and casting around in disgust. 'Fire burned most of it, then the fire brigade flooded what was left.'

'Can't blame them.'

'I don't,' the SOCO replies. 'I blame the animal that snatched her.'

Nodding, Mairéad turns away. The crime scene in the woods might be a lost cause, but at least the cottage where they arrested their suspect remains intact. Upstairs, they found a video camera, a lighting rig and a portable power pack. Scattered across the floor was a magpie's nest of plunder, among which they identified a pair of glasses belonging to Bryony Taylor and a rosewood chess piece. In a cupboard downstairs they discovered a laptop and a stack of homemade DVDs. Some of the discs bore the names of missing children long presumed dead.

The twin cottages, one burnt-out and one intact, aren't the only crime scenes on the estate. Inside Rufus Hall, officers found Leon Meunier hanging from a beam. His death can't be a coincidence, but so far they haven't established a connection.

Picking her way through the mud, Mairéad puts that awful scar in the earth behind her and follows a trail of limp firehoses back to DS Halley's car.

Her thoughts turn to Kyle North. Immediately after his arrest, the man retreated into himself, refusing to answer even the most basic of questions. Losing patience, she asked her West Mercia counterparts to transport him by van to Shrewsbury.

It's her next destination.

The station's custody block is a modern facility comprising sixteen cells. Kyle North is housed in number three. Scowling, Mairéad peers through the viewing window. 'What happened to his face?'

Beside her, Halley glances at DS Roebuck from the West Mercia force.

The other officer lifts his chin. 'Bit of a scuffle getting him into the van.'

Mairéad fixes him with a stare.

'Just a black eye,' he adds, his expression flat. 'It'll heal.'

'I'm counting on you to ensure he receives no other injuries.'

She'd like nothing more than to see Kyle North taken outside and beaten with bats and poles, but if she can't return Elissa Mirzoyan to her family, at the very least she needs to secure a conviction. This case has affected all who've worked on it; she won't allow a few hot tempers and quick fists to derail what comes next.

Inside the cell, North sits on his bunk and stares at the wall. He's a slothful-looking giant, but when required he moves with a sly grace. His skin, greasy and yellow, reminds her of pork-belly rind. There's even a score line in the flesh, an ugly scar that connects his left temple to his chin. His sloping breasts push against his paper suit. Two circular sweat marks make it appear that he's lactating. There's no stubble on his cheeks, no curl of hair at his wrists. As Mairéad considers him, she can't help recalling his awful falsetto voice.

'How old, do you reckon?'

'Thirty?' Halley ventures. 'Thirty-five? Difficult call – he could be older or younger by a decade.'

It's an exaggeration, but not by much. 'Let's get him to an interview room,' Mairéad says, and then she bends double, unable to suppress a groan.

'Boss?' Halley asks. 'What's wrong?'

The pain hits again, worse this time. It cleaves a path straight through her abdomen. She pivots and lurches up the corridor. Halley calls out behind her. With a shake of her head, she dismisses him.

Hold on, please hold on, stay with me, please don't go.

But her plea is worthless, and she knows it. Somehow, during this week-long investigation, the destiny of the life she's been carrying has become inextricably entangled with Elissa Mirzoyan's. Mairéad failed one of them, and now she'll fail the other.

She staggers into the toilets, barricading herself in an empty cubicle. Pain lashes her. Air hisses between her teeth.

She tugs down her trousers, her underwear. There's blood everywhere, bright and wet and accusatory. Mairéad kicks off her heels, quickly strips off her clothes. Lifting the toilet seat, she straddles herself across it. Her breath comes in staccato bursts. She should be at home, in the privacy of her own bathroom, surrounded by familiar things. Instead she's two hundred miles away, locked in a cramped police station toilet within spitting distance of a child killer. But the location doesn't matter. Not really. Right now, she could be anywhere on earth and she'd still be alone.

The pain intensifies. For a while, it's all there is. And then, finally, it begins to ebb.

When Mairéad stands, the evidence of her loss is stark and unequivocal.

How dismal, this. How particular the grief.

Her fingers grope for her wedding band. She needs to speak to Scott, tell him what has happened. But she can't, not yet.

Mairéad opens her bag and searches through it. At least she came prepared. Inside there are wipes, sanitary pads, leggings and fresh knickers. Carefully, she begins to clean herself. Her grief is a boulder rolling towards her, so heavy and sluggish it'll take a little time to arrive. Unbidden, a memory surfaces: Lena Mirzoyan, six days ago, sitting in the manager's office of the Marshall Court Hotel: *I know you'll try. All of you – I know you will. But you've got to succeed. You've got to bring her back. Promise me you will. Promise.*

Mairéad flushes the toilet. She leaves the cubicle as fast as she can. In front of the mirror, she tries to make herself look human. Does she serve Elissa best by handing the interrogation to someone else? Crazy to believe that she can walk out of here and straight into an interview room.

Or is it?

Perspective, right now, is impossible.

She knows what a court would think, should she choose to question Kyle North. She knows what her chief constable would think. But a court will never know, and neither will her boss. She's so invested in this, so invested in Elissa.

That boulder of grief is gathering speed, but it's still some way behind. She can outpace it, dance before it, do what needs to be done.

Jesus.

KYLE

I

At first, being locked up isn't as bad as I feared. The cell is clean, and although the bunk is hard, there's a mattress coated in blue plastic and even a matching pillow. I'd prefer dimmer lights, and the bleach smell is unfortunate, but you can't have everything.

On the floor is a tray of food, now cold. I don't deserve to eat, not after what I did. Every time I close my eyes I see choking black smoke, so instead I stare at the wall. I wonder how many of my Memory Trees have burned. I wonder if Bryony's yew is gone, and Mama's oak.

I think of Kyle, and what will become of him. Then I remember that my brother is dead – that I killed him long ago – and that he wasn't Kyle at all but Elijah, the name I took as my own. Strange how, over time, the stories we tell ourselves come true.

It's quiet right now. I should try to savour the peace. I know what they do to people like me. My black eye in the police van was just the start. After this I'll go somewhere filled with Men Who Do Bad Things. Magic Annie told me all about them – about what they do to you, what they *put* in you. My tummy clenches. I feel that wall inside my head tremble, as if an earthquake is shaking the corridors of my mind. Being alone like this is bearable, but the thought of prison empties my lungs. I should probably kill myself before I have to face it, but I can't even work out how. Hugging my legs to my chest, I hear commotion outside the cell. My ordeal's about to begin.

II

The interview room isn't the same one as before, but that was a different police station and they were different officers. This room is far smaller. Even on my own, it feels like a tight squeeze.

My hands are cuffed. Every time I look at them I think of Gretel and that awful injury on her wrist. I'm pretty sure she was dying, even before the fire – her arm had swollen up like a sun-ripened pumpkin. The pain must have been horrendous, but she never complained. Not like Bryony, whose whining became a bit much towards the end.

Two video cameras bolted to the ceiling watch everything I do. Funny, really. In a way, it feels like I've traded places with those I used to visit.

The door opens. First through it is the woman who arrested me. She looks different to how she did at the cottage, but I can't work out what has changed. Following her is a man I don't recognize. The door's about to swing closed when a third person enters – someone I know well and did not expect to see again. Mama.

III

Such is my joy, my sheer relief at her presence, that I'm only half aware of the detectives as they sit down. Mama doesn't join us at the table. Instead, she leans against the far wall. She's wearing her weekend clothes: blue jeans, desert boots, North Face gilet and plaid work shirt. There's mascara on her eyelashes and maroon lipstick on her mouth. She looks exactly like I want my wife to look, if I ever end up getting married. Some people might think that's weird, but it's not. Mama is perfect, and perfection only comes in one size.

On her back is the sun-faded orange rucksack she was wearing when I last saw her. Only now do I recognize it as Elijah's. Odd that I ever forgot.

She looks so sad that my eyes fill with tears. I want to go to her, wrap my arms around her. But Mama wouldn't ever allow that, and nor would these two detectives. She's sad, not for herself, but for me. Somehow, that makes me feel even worse, yet when I open my mouth to say something she puts a finger to her lips and gently shakes her head.

'Hello, Kyle,' the policewoman says.

When I turn to face her I realize how cramped the room has become. With the three of us huddled around this table and Mama leaning against the wall there's hardly enough air to breathe.

Perhaps she understands my discomfort, because she

gestures at my handcuffs and turns to her colleague. 'Let's have those removed.'

The man stands and crabs around the table. He seems wary, as if he thinks it's a bad idea, but he doesn't say anything, unlocking the cuffs and slipping them off my wrists.

The woman introduces herself as Detective Superintendent MacCullagh. After that she asks my name, which is weird because I told her during my arrest. Then I remember the cameras. 'Kyle North,' I say, glancing at Mama.

'What's your date of birth, Kyle?'

'Third of February.'

'Year?'

'Nineteen eighty-seven.'

'Which makes you . . .'

'Twelve years old.'

MacCullagh pauses, her eyes flat. I hope I haven't offended her. Sliding my hands between my thighs, I vow not to interrupt her again. I'm in trouble here, serious trouble. I won't make things better by forgetting my manners.

'Before we begin,' she says, 'I'd like to explain your rights again. Check that you understand them fully.'

'OK.'

MacCullagh's voice changes, becomes wooden, like in a movie I once watched in Annie's caravan – *Invasion of the Body Snatchers*. It scares me, that voice, until I realize she's reciting something learned by rote. Afterwards, she asks if I want a solicitor – which I think is a kind of lawyer – but I can't see why I would.

I look up at Mama, so grateful she hasn't abandoned me. Earlier, watching the smoke rise over Meunierfields, I convinced myself I wouldn't see her again.

'Did it burn?' I ask. 'Is it gone?'

MacCullagh's face is a mask. 'Did what burn?'

'The Memory Wood.'

I want to ask about the Gingerbread House, too, but I'm not sure I can stomach the answer.

'You mean the woodland a few hundred yards from your house?'

I nod.

'There was a fire, yes.'

'Has it all gone?'

'Not entirely. The rain stopped it spreading far.'

'My Memory Trees,' I begin, and abruptly close my mouth.

'Your Memory Trees?' MacCullagh's voice is gentler now, mesmeric.

'Careful,' Mama says, pushing away from the wall. 'Don't lose yourself.'

'I'm sorry,' I say, addressing both women. 'I think I lost myself.'

MacCullagh leans backwards. Her seat releases a brief farting sound. I know well enough not to smile.

'Kyle,' she says, in that same soft voice. 'I'm not here to judge. I'm not here to make accusations, cause trouble, anything like that. I'm just investigating the disappearance of Elissa Mirzoyan, trying to find out what happened. I know you're a smart guy. What can you tell me about that?'

It's been a while since anyone praised my intelligence. The day Gretel taught me chess, I told her about my high IQ and she asked my score. I'd never heard of an IQ score so I made one up – ninety-nine. It's not a lie if it's true, and there's every chance it is. With an IQ like that, Gretel said, I'd have no problem with chess. And she was right. I didn't. The rules, at least. I still haven't played a game.

Behind the detectives, Mama folds her arms. 'You can't trust her, Elijah. She's trying to flatter you, that's all. She doesn't want the truth. She just wants to lock you up.'

'Kyle? Are you OK?' MacCullagh asks. 'Do you need anything? Some water, perhaps?'

'Yes, please. That would be nice.'

She nods at her colleague, who gives me a steady look and rises from his seat. Mama sidesteps to allow him out. He returns with a plastic cup of water, which he puts down in front of me.

MacCullagh waits a while, until she realizes I'm not going to drink. 'Kyle, when we met you at the house, I asked about Elissa's whereabouts and you said, "She's gone." Do you remember saying that?'

'Uh-huh.'

Mama glances up at the ceiling cameras.

I flinch. 'I mean . . . did I?'

'Do you remember saying it?'

MacCullagh's voice is so hypnotic, so measured and calm. How nice it would be to hear her reading stories before bed. I might have the best mama in the world, but she's rarely around at night. I wonder if this detective has kids. Lucky for them if she does.

'Kyle? Do you remember saying it?'

'Not really.'

Her forehead creases a little. 'A moment ago you said you did.'

'I was . . .' I look up at Mama, who nods. 'I was confused.'

MacCullagh glances over her shoulder, then back at me. I find myself wondering: could these two women ever become friends?

'Listen, Kyle,' the detective says. 'I know this must seem overwhelming. It's a unique situation – for you, for everyone involved. But I'd like you to think about something, if you can. Right now, this very minute, there are people out there – people like Elissa's mum, Elissa's grandparents – who are hurting. They're hurting very badly indeed. They've been separated from someone they care deeply about, someone they love very much, and they desperately want to know what's happened to her. I'm hoping you can help them, Kyle. I'm hoping that you and me, working together, can find a way to ease their suffering.'

I think of the deer my brother shot and the calamity inside its head. I wonder what memories and dreams would be lost if the detective's brains, grey and glistening, were plastered across the earth.

'Kyle?' Her mouth relaxes, her lips easing apart.

Good to have this woman as a mother. Even better to have her as a wife. The wedding ring on her finger is evidence of a husband. I wonder how often he kisses those lips. All the time, probably. I would.

'Elijah,' Mama warns. 'Remember what—'

'I want to help them,' I say. 'I want to help you too. But I'm scared. This is . . . frightening for me.'

MacCullagh nods. She rubs her left arm, as if beneath her blouse her skin has puckered into goosebumps. 'I understand why you'd feel like that. This is a serious situation. A frightening situation. Like I said earlier, I'm not here to judge. I just want to find out the truth and resolve this in the best way possible.' She pauses a beat. 'Do you know where Elissa is?'

'You mean her body?' I ask. 'Or her spirit?'

The detective blinks twice in quick succession. Her

tongue flickers out, just the tip. Seeing it reminds me of the serpent from Genesis. God punished the serpent for its trickery, making it crawl on its belly all its days. I wonder if MacCullagh has studied her Bible recently. I wonder if she's studied it at all.

'Kyle,' she says carefully. 'Is Elissa Mirzoyan dead?'

The answer to that is pretty obvious and *I'm* not even a detective. Still, Mama warned me to go carefully here. The brief glimpse of MacCullagh's tongue has reinforced the danger. 'I couldn't say.'

'You couldn't?'

I shake my head.

'Do you know what happened to her?'

'No.'

A pulse ticks in MacCullagh's throat. She's a cool customer, all right, but she can't control her heartbeat. 'Do you really want to help us, Kyle?' she asks. 'Do you really want to help Elissa's family?'

'Of course.'

'OK. That's good. Then I'd like you to think, very hard, of anything you can tell me about what happened to Elissa, or where she is now.'

Unlike the detective's, Mama's lips are a thin line.

'I'm sorry,' I say. 'I really don't know. I don't know anyone called Elissa.'

It's a while before I manage to meet MacCullagh's eyes. When I do, I see they've moved elsewhere. She opens a folder and searches through it. 'The cottage where we found you, on the Meunierfields estate. Is that your home?'

'Yes.'

Her tone has changed, brisk and businesslike. 'How long have you lived there?'

'Long as I can remember.'

'Alone?'

'No.'

'Who else lives there?'

I glance up at Mama.

'Who else lives there, Kyle?'

'Just me.'

'You rent the property from the Meuniers?'

'Uh-huh.'

'You know them personally?'

Something warns me I'm on dangerous ground again. I think of Leon Meunier, standing in the Memory Wood with his rifle: *I could've put a bullet through you. Then where would we have been?*

Staring at the detective, I realize I've been quiet far too long. I blink, trying to remember her question. At last, I say, 'I don't know them well.'

Nodding, MacCullagh takes a colour photograph from her folder and slides it across the table. 'I'd like to show you something. We'll call this AR1. Is this a photo of your bedroom?'

'Yes.'

Out comes another image. 'We'll call this AR2,' she says. 'It's a closer shot of the floor. Do you recognize what you see?'

'Some of it.'

'There's writing on the box lid shown in the photograph. Please could you read it out?'

I lean forwards, but I don't need a closer look. ' "Top secret. Private property. Do not open without permission." '

'Is that your collection box, Kyle?'

'I think so.'

'You think so?'

'Yes, I mean. It is.'

'The items scattered beneath the window look to me like they came from that box. Am I right?'

'I think . . . Some of them, yes.'

'The chess piece?'

I freeze. For whatever reason, I hadn't noticed the queen, made of Brazilian rosewood, lying at the foot of my bed.

'Kyle, do you recognize the chess piece?'

She's good, this detective. She gets me to admit things, even with my mouth closed. Silence, in this room, could be my worst enemy. 'Yes,' I say, plucking blindly at answers, hoping that inspiration will strike and offer me a way out.

'Where did you get it?'

'A friend.'

'A friend gave it to you?'

'Yes. No. I don't know.'

'You don't know?'

'I . . . I can't remember.'

'What about the vest? The girl's vest, lying right next to it. Did a friend give you that too?'

'I can't . . . I don't recognize the vest.'

'It was in your bedroom.'

'I don't recognize it.'

She nods. 'What about the child's glasses? Do you recognize them?'

'I don't think so.'

'You see the diary, lying beside the glasses?'

'You mean the book?'

'It's a diary, but I agree it looks a bit like a book. Do you recognize it?'

'No.'

'Here's a close-up of the cover. We'll call this AR3. Can you do me a favour and read out the name on the front cover?'

'Now?'

'Yes, please.'

'Bryony Taylor.'

'Do you know Bryony Taylor?'

'No.'

'Did you know she went missing?'

'I didn't.'

'Can you tell me why we found Bryony Taylor's diary in your bedroom?'

My mouth is dry. I look at the cup of water. I desperately want to drink. I know that I mustn't.

'Kyle, you remember when you first arrived at the police station? An officer took your fingerprints and swabbed your mouth for DNA. All these items I just showed you have been sent to our lab. They're being tested right now. We'll know, without any shred of doubt, which ones you've touched. I know you want to help us, so it's important you think hard about the questions I'm asking, and answer them as accurately as you can.'

She slides another photograph across the desk. 'We'll call this AR4. It's a shot of the desk in your bedroom. Do you recognize the boxes beneath it?'

'Yes.'

'What do they contain?'

I swallow. 'The boxes?'

'What's in them?'

There's a lizard-like flickering behind my eyes, as if a tiny creature is burrowing into my brain.

'Kyle?'

'Video . . . video equipment.'

'Yours?'

'No.'

'Whose, then?'

'I . . .'

My vision blurs. I look at Mama, but she's disappeared inside my tears.

'I see you're upset,' MacCullagh says. 'I know this is upsetting. All we want is the truth.'

'I don't know the truth.'

'Is Elissa Mirzoyan alive?'

'I don't know.'

'Was Elissa being held in the' – she looks at her notes – 'the Memory Wood? Was she inside that building when it burned?'

'Please. I don't know. I really don't.'

'Kyle, did you have anything to do with that fire?'

A sob bursts loose from my throat. I sound like a wild animal caught in one of my brother's traps.

MacCullagh repeats her question. When I don't answer, she says, 'I've already told you about the fingerprints and the DNA, and the tests we're doing on the items we found in your bedroom. Let me explain something else. The reason you're wearing a paper suit is because your clothes are being analysed too. But I can tell you, even without waiting for the report, that they smelled very strongly of petrol. So if there's a way you can explain that, it's best you do it now. Because . . . because if you don't, Kyle, it won't look good, and then I might not be able to help you. Can you tell me why your clothes smelled of petrol?'

I wipe the tears from my face.

Poor Gretel.

Like me, she didn't always tell the truth. But at least she always had good reason.

'I . . . I spilt some,' I say. 'Knocked some over.'

'Where was this?'

'The Gingerbread House.'

'The what?'

It's an effort to speak. My throat's so dry it hurts. 'The Gingerbread House. Inside the Memory Wood.'

'You mean the cottage that burned down?'

'Yes.'

'Kyle, I'm going to ask you again. Was Elissa Mirzoyan inside that building when it burned?'

I feel Mama's eyes on me. I can't meet them.

Right now, this very minute, there are people out there – people like Elissa's mum, Elissa's grandparents – who are hurting. They're hurting very badly indeed. They've been separated from someone they care deeply about, someone they love very much, and they desperately want to know what's happened to her. I'm hoping you can help them, Kyle. I'm hoping that you and me, working together, can find a way to ease their suffering.

'Kyle,' the detective says, more forcefully now. 'Were you holding Elissa Mirzoyan inside that cellar?'

Looking up, meeting her gaze, I decide I don't want this woman as my wife. I bow my head again, but I can't shut her out completely.

'I didn't call her that,' I whisper.

IV

For half a minute, nobody speaks. Finally, MacCullagh asks, 'What did you call her?'

'Gretel. I called her Gretel. And she called me Hansel.'

'Hansel and Gretel, the Gingerbread House. Like the fairy tale.'

'It was her idea. She said we could be brother and sister.'

I rub my nose, dismayed to see a smear of pale snot across my hand. Mama raised me to have good manners. I dread to think what this detective must think of me. 'I never had a sister,' I tell her. 'If I ever did, I'd want one just like her.'

MacCullagh leans forward. 'How did the fairy tale end?'

'Not like the book.'

'Was Gretel in the cellar when the Gingerbread House burned?'

'I don't know.'

'Kyle, I realize this is difficult. But you've taken a big step. You've told us you know Elissa – I mean Gretel – and that helps a lot. What we need now is the rest, and I think you're brave enough to share it. We owe it to her mum – an explanation as to what happened.'

I close my eyes. I can feel that wall inside my head beginning to crumble. Suddenly, it's all I can do to brace myself against it. 'I'm not lying,' I say. 'At the end . . . I really don't know what I did.'

MacCullagh takes a breath, slowly lets it out. 'OK,' she says. 'Let's try something different. Let's go back in time, you and I.'

Opening my eyes, I ask, 'You mean like in a time machine?'

'Exactly like a time machine.'

'H. G. Wells wrote a story called *The Time Machine*, but it was fiction. Real time machines don't exist.'

'This'll be a time machine inside our minds.'

I tilt my head, trying to see if she's teasing, but she looks deadly serious.

'I want you to get into the time machine,' she says, 'and take me back to the first time you met Gretel.'

'The *very* first time?'

MacCullagh nods.

When I look past her, I'm shocked – and dismayed – to see that Mama has left the room.

MAIRÉAD

I

She questions Kyle North for another two hours, but despite hearing a lot about his interactions with Elissa Mirzoyan – or Gretel, as he calls her – she's no closer to a confession. Whenever she asks how Elissa ended up in the cellar, he claims ignorance or talks in undecipherable riddles.

Sometimes, as she watches him, she thinks he's laughing at her, that he's deep in some mind game only he understands. He denies any knowledge of the YouTube recordings, even though the equipment used to make them was found in his bedroom. The laptop will doubtless yield further footage, yet he maintains ignorance of that, too.

He's clearly suffering from some kind of psychosis, which means if she doesn't request a full assessment soon she risks compromising the case. Where there's an immediate risk to life, she can bypass the normal protocols and continue to question him, but she no longer believes there *is* a risk to life – everything points to Elissa having been inside that cellar when the fire was set.

As she spars with Kyle, Mairéad feels the shadow of her grief falling over her. Towards the end of the interview, it's an effort to sit up straight in her chair. But she's committed herself to this. No way she can bow out now.

After updating her senior officers in advance of the next media briefing, Mairéad instructs DS Halley to drive her back to Meunierfields. Under a darkening sky, in which helicopters buzz like angry wasps, the estate crawls with grim-faced SOCOs.

Changing into a pair of borrowed boots, she finds Paul Deacon, the crime-scene manager she spoke to on the phone.

'Christ alive,' Deacon says when he sees her. 'You look like death warmed up.' He leads her through the Memory Wood to a clearing untouched by fire. Three mobile lighting towers illuminate it. At the base of a giant yew, easily five hundred years old, a geodesic tent stands beside a huge mound of earth. White-suited officers move around inside.

From the tree's upper bows hang the sodden shreds of what look like paper lanterns. Had Deacon not pointed them out, Mairéad doubts she'd have spotted them. A SOCO, balanced on the upper rung of an aluminium ladder secured to the trunk, is placing something into an evidence bag. Across the clearing, Mairéad notices a second tent beside a matching pile of excavated earth.

'What've you got?'

'Four different trees,' Deacon says. 'All within a fifty-yard radius of this grove, every one of them strewn with these weird decorations. On each trunk, invisible from the ground, we've found a hand-carved name. All of them belong to missing children. This one says Bryony Taylor.'

'Have you found one for Elissa Mirzoyan?'

'Not yet.'

'His Memory Trees,' Mairéad says. She indicates the officers working inside the tent. 'What've they found?'

'Nothing so far. We're down to a depth of seven feet.'

'Nothing at all?'

'No remains, no items of interest, zilch. These trees might be memorials, but they don't appear to be grave markers.'

Mairéad puffs out her cheeks. 'So what has he done with their bodies?'

'We're bringing in dog teams from neighbouring counties. Earlier, I'd have said they'd turn something up no problem. Now, I'm not so sure.' Deacon screws up his face, watching his team work. 'What's your suspect say?'

'He admits Elissa was in that cellar and that he visited her there. Says he knew the other children, too. But on the question of how they got here, and where they went after, he's as slippery as an eel.'

'Sounds like you've enough for a conviction.'

'Plenty, but what I want is to return those kids to their families.'

'Zero chance you'll find them alive. Not after this long.'

'We can ensure they get a proper funeral, Paul. That's something. And I'm not giving up on Elissa. Not yet.'

She gazes through the trees, in the direction of the burnt-out Gingerbread House. In her pocket is a copy of the letter sent to Lasse Haagensen. All children are special, but Elissa Mirzoyan was so plucky, so damned resourceful, that it's difficult – even now – to accept she might be dead.

'Call me,' she says. 'Soon as you have anything.'

Leaving Deacon to his work, Mairéad retraces her steps to Halley's Renault. When she opens the passenger door he's on his phone, watching a live Sky News feed shot from an overhead helicopter.

'What're they saying?'

'That we have Elissa's killer.'

Mairéad scowls. She hopes Judy Pauletto, the FLO, is keeping the Mirzoyans away from the TV. She'd like to drive down to Salisbury and see Lena, but there's too much to do here.

Easing herself on to the seat, she carefully measures out her breath.

'You OK?' Halley asks.

'Yes.'

'You sure?'

She nods, staring straight ahead.

Bouncing along the track from the main road come two Skoda estates in Battenberg markings, *POLICE DOG UNIT* printed along the sides. The news choppers circle lower, greedy for images of this new development.

I I

As they arrive back at the station the sky releases another deluge. In the time it takes to enter the building, Mairéad is soaked through. She's about to haul Kyle North into the interview room for another round of questions when her phone rings. It's Westfield, her chief constable, and he sounds stressed.

'Why haven't you charged North?'

'We're still gathering evidence. There's a—'

'You've got evidence coming out of your ears: Elissa's

possessions in his bedroom, Bryony Taylor's diary and glasses . . .'

'But we don't have Elissa, sir, alive or dead. And we haven't found Bryony Taylor, nor any of the other victims. If I charge him now, there's a good chance he'll go mute.'

'He probably will. So what?'

Mairéad licks her lips. Her mouth is dry; her tongue too. In the last hour she's developed a thirst that no amount of water can quench. 'If he's killed those girls, we want to repatriate them. I think there's a better chance if we keep him on side. I want another session with him.'

'Leon Meunier,' Westfield says. 'Lots of questions coming my way on that. Was it suicide?'

'Don't know yet.'

'So North could've been involved in his death too.'

'It's possible.'

She hears raised voices in the background, a sudden commotion. 'OK,' Westfield says. 'Do what you have to do. But keep me informed. No nasty surprises. I'm sure you don't need reminding how much we're in the spotlight on this.'

'Understood, sir,' Mairéad says, and hangs up.

'Bad?' Halley asks.

'He's got the world breathing down his neck. Wants us to charge North when we can, but not at the expense of cutting corners.' Mairéad leans against the wall. 'Goddammit, Jake. I really thought we'd bring her home alive. After the messages in those video clips, the code she hid in that letter, it felt like . . . like she'd done enough, you know?'

She closes her eyes, opens them. 'In that interview room. Did you feel like you were sitting opposite a child killer?'

'Yeah,' Halley says, grimacing. 'I did.'

Mairéad rolls her neck.

'By the way,' he adds. 'There's an Arya Chaudhuri trying to get hold of you. Wants to talk DNA results.'

'I'll call her back. Priority right now is to squeeze Kyle North for everything we can before he goes mute.'

KYLE

I

I've never felt this alone. The world has never seemed so bleak.

Whatever mistakes I've made in life – and God knows I've made plenty – Mama has never abandoned me. But in the interview room, just when I needed her most, she upped and walked away. I've done bad things – terrible things – yet Mama has always understood. And although she hasn't always praised my choices, she's never punished me too harshly.

Two male officers lead me back to my cell. When I attempt conversation, the taller one shoves me in the back. Feet tangling together, I fly through the cell doorway. My knees strike the floor with a sound like two gunshots. The pain is stunning. I'm so busy thrashing around that I'm only half aware of the door crashing shut.

They hate me. All of them.

Earlier I tried to help, telling Detective Superintendent MacCullagh all I could, but it made no difference: she looked at me just like the others; just like the one who thumped me in the police van.

I didn't answer all the detective's questions, but there's no way that I could. Often, in that interview room, I felt the wall inside my head threatening to topple. If it does, everything will be lost. I have a duty to Bryony and to Gretel – to keep them alive through my memories. Like the knucklebones from the lake, I've elected myself their Rememberer-in-Chief. If I let the wall fail, if I throw myself away, it'll be as if they never existed. Their families will remember them. But they didn't know them like I did. They weren't there at the end.

'So you admit it, then?' rasps a voice.

My back spasms as I twist about. Across the cell, hanging over the bunk, I see two filthy legs, a pair of scuffed leather shoes and the torn hem of a bottle-green dress.

II

I kick out in panic, propelling myself back towards the door. She can't be in here. She can't. And yet when I angle my head, there she is.

Gretel's face looks like a piece of steak left too long on a barbecue, cracked and burnt and black. Her hair is gone, along with her ears and most of her nose. Clear fluid seeps from the fissures in her flesh.

Only her eyes have been spared. They stare with dreadful intensity, two baleful emeralds that have soaked up all the inferno's heat. 'Look at me, Elijah,' she whispers.

I scrunch up my eyes, turn my face to the floor.

'*Look* at me.'

When I summon the courage, I'm surprised to see that Gretel's burns have somehow faded, leaving her grimy and greasy but mercifully untouched by fire. At first, it's too incredible to behold, until I realize she's not really here, and that most things are possible when you have an over-active imagination.

'Oh, I'm here, Elijah,' she says, lifting her arm and tapping her skull. 'Up here, remember? You have a duty. That's what you believe, isn't it? A duty to keep me alive, in your memories.'

'I . . . I never meant to—'

'You think I'm going to go quietly?' she hisses. 'You think I'm just going to *accept* this?' Gretel narrows her eyes, focusing the full power of her gaze. 'Isn't it about time you started telling the truth?'

I'm shivering now, unable to control myself. 'The truth?'

Hands tightening into fists, Gretel slides off the bunk. Her face twists into a leer. ' "And you will know the truth, and the truth will set you free." '

I hug myself.

'You recognize those words, Elijah?'

'John, chapter eight,' I say. 'Verse thirty-two. But why—'

'Do you believe them?'

'Yes, of course, but—'

'Then stop lying, and tell the truth.'

'I didn't kill you. I didn't.'

'The *truth*, Elijah.'

'I'm *telling* you the truth.'

' "And you will know the truth, and the truth will set you free." '

'I tried to save you. I did everything I could!'

My lips are burning. I touch them, remembering Gretel's mouth on mine. I recall my panicked flight from the cellar, the petrol cans in the hall, and then . . . and then . . .

I hear my brother's voice, disembodied and full of blame: *She kissed you, Eli. But maybe you went back for more.*

'I didn't,' I moan. 'I *never* would've done that.'

'You killed her.'

'No. I *saved* her. I saved her for all eternity.'

I hear something else, now. A snapping, a cracking. It sounds like my brother's .22. I'd almost welcome it, a calamity inside my head, until I remember there's no way Kyle can shoot me, because *I'm* Kyle, and I killed my brother long ago.

'Not just your brother,' Elissa whispers.

'Only him,' I tell her, and wish I could believe my own words.

The cracking isn't a bullet but a key, working inside a lock. Behind me, the cell door swings open and now I don't know what's worse: being imprisoned in here with Gretel or going outside to a world that wants me dead.

III

I'm back in the interview room, opposite MacCullagh and her colleague. On the ceiling, two cameras cast disapproving eyes. Every few seconds my gaze strays to the rear wall, but however often I check, Mama never reappears.

'What's happening, Kyle?' MacCullagh asks. 'The custody officer says you were making a racket.'

'I'm fine.'

'Are you able to answer some more questions?'

'I'll try.'

'That's good. Like I said before, it's important you hold nothing back. If you want to help Elissa – if you want to help her family – you need to tell us everything.'

I stare at MacCullagh, wondering what it must be like to spend days mixed up in other people's misery. She looks exhausted – almost as if she's in pain. It's not easy, this. For any of us.

' "And you will know the truth," ' I tell her, ' "and the truth will set you free." '

'Kyle?'

'It's from John, chapter eight. Don't you read your Bible?'

'Not since school.'

'Well,' I say. 'I feel bad for you.'

'I can still appreciate the sentiment. Are you ready to tell the truth? Is that what you're getting at?'

I open my mouth. *Is* that what I was getting at? I spoke without thinking too much about my meaning. Those words were from Scripture, certainly not my own.

Suddenly, in the bleakness of this interview room, everything seems so simple. Mama always loved Ephesians, and I know which verse she would quote: *Each of you must put off falsehood and speak truthfully to your neighbour, for we are all members of one body.*

Sometimes, I've spoken untruthfully. Whatever my reason, I see now it was a sin. There's a verse in the Book of Proverbs that says an honest answer is like a kiss on the lips. To MacCullagh, I say, ' "An honest witness tells the truth, but a false witness tells lies." '

Another line from Proverbs.

She glances briefly at her colleague. 'You're losing me a little here, Kyle. Shall we take a couple of steps back? I just got back from Meunierfields. I took a walk through the Memory Wood.'

I hadn't expected her to say that. 'You did?'

'It's different to how you left it. But we found some of your Memory Trees. Bryony Taylor's. A few others.'

'Did you find Mama's?'

MacCullagh blinks. 'There's a tree for your mother?'

'An oak. You couldn't miss it. If it burned, maybe . . . maybe that's why she disappeared.'

A shadow passes across the detective's face, or appears to: right now, my imagination's running pretty wild.

'We haven't found it,' she says. 'But we have plenty of people searching. If it's there, we'll let you know. You said earlier that you were living in that cottage alone. Was that true?'

'Yes.'

'You rented the place from the Meuniers?'

'That's right.'

'Did you deal with Leon Meunier directly?'

I'm about to answer when I remember Ephesians, and the Book of Proverbs, and my vow to speak the truth. 'No,' I reply. 'And actually . . . I didn't live there alone.'

'Who else?'

'Mama,' I say. 'Papa. And my brother.'

I know they won't believe me, but I can't help that.

'Your brother?'

'Kyle,' I tell her. 'Kyle North.'

Under the table, MacCullagh's phone starts ringing. Ignoring it, she stares at me. 'I thought you were Kyle.'

'Oh.' I nod. 'That's true.' The ringing phone is distracting. I wish she would answer it. My head starts to thump. I close my eyes, open them. 'I guess I mean Elijah.'

MacCullagh flinches. Her chair scrapes against the floor. Still watching me, she pulls the phone from her pocket. When she stands, her colleague stands too. 'Interview terminated, seven forty-two p.m.'

Before I can say anything more, both officers leave the room.

MAIRÉAD

'MacCullagh,' she says, limping along the corridor with DS Halley trailing in her wake. Her mind is racing. She cannot believe what she just heard.

On the line is Paul Deacon, the crime-scene manager at Meunierfields. 'We found two more trees,' he tells her. 'Both with inscribed names.'

'Mama,' Mairéad says, through gritted teeth.

'That's one of them.'

'Don't tell me the other.'

'Elijah,' he replies.

'Shit. Shit, *shit*.'

'We've already started digging. But I'll tell you now, I don't expect to find anything.'

'I want hourly updates. Anything you find in the woods. Anything you find in the cellar. Anything you find in North's cottage, the mansion, or that camp down by the lake.'

'Moment I have something.'

'Even if you don't have something. Hourly updates, Paul.'

Deacon rings off. In the incident room Mairéad finds a spare desk and opens her laptop. Fingers shaking, she keys in a search query. For a moment, her exhaustion wins out; instead of one screen in front of her, she sees three.

Her phone rings again. This time, it's Arya Chaudhuri, from the lab they used to process the DNA. 'Got some results for you,' Chaudhuri says. 'You're never going to guess who he is.'

Outside, the night sky shows no hint of moon. Mairéad thinks of Paul Deacon's team digging through the Memory Wood's sodden earth, and the firefighters pumping black sludge from the ruined Gingerbread House. She thinks of Elissa Mirzoyan, locked inside that cellar; of Bryony Taylor; of all the children who came before.

'He isn't Kyle North,' she says, twisting the laptop towards Halley. 'He's Kyle Buchanan. Abducted from Swindon twenty years ago, along with Elijah Buchanan, his younger brother.'

She indicates a photograph of two laughing boys. It makes her heart ache to look at it. 'Twelve years old – that's what he told us. That's how old he was when he was snatched, and I guess that's when the clock stopped for him.'

Halley's eyes scroll left and right. 'Fuck me,' he mutters. 'We don't just have a suspect. We have a *survivor*.'

KYLE

I

Two uniformed officers return me to my cell. The tray of untouched food has disappeared, which is a shame. For the first time in days I actually feel hungry.

When the officers slam the cell door, the sound rings in my ears, but after it fades all I hear is silence: no voices; no accusations; no appeals. Perhaps this path of honesty is the best course. I haven't told the detectives everything, but I've avoided telling more lies.

The peace doesn't last. Soon, I recall the black smoke rising over the Memory Wood. That wall in my mind trembles, loosened by all the nightmares stacked against it. I read a story, once, of a little Dutch boy who plugged a leaking dyke with his finger. Right now my brain feels like that dyke, but try as I might, I can't fix the leak.

Instead, I lie down on the bunk. My eyes feel gritty so I close them. Tears roll down my cheekbones towards my ears. I'm tired, that's all. Emotional.

11

A commotion outside wakes me. The cell door swings wide, revealing Detective Superintendent MacCullagh beside a woman I don't recognize and an officer in uniform.

'Kyle,' the detective says, in a tone I can't fathom. 'This is Rita Ortiz. She's going to be responsible for your welfare from now on.'

I stare at them both, trying to figure out what's changed. Rita has a wide face framed by oversized glasses. Her black hair is held in place with bobby pins like those used by private investigators to pick locks. I don't think she's police.

'Hello, Kyle,' she says. 'I'd like you to come with me.'

'Where to?'

'We haven't quite figured that out. But somewhere nicer than this. Somewhere you don't have to be afraid. Before that, though, we'll get you a hot shower, some clean clothes. A decent meal.'

She steps forward and I fear she's going to strike me. It's all I can do not to cringe away. When Rita puts a hand on my arm and squeezes, that wall inside my head shakes as if an earthquake has hit. I'm crying again. I can't seem to stop.

'It's OK,' she says. 'You're safe now. No one's going to hurt you again.'

Because of my tears I can't see her clearly, but I can hear her tone and I know she's sincere. When I sob once, loud and hard, it feels like a plug has been pulled. My knees sag. All my strength ebbs away.

They try to hold me up, but they can't support my

weight. I fall in slow motion. Light swirls around me. Rita's hand finds mine and I clutch on to her as best I can. From somewhere, I hear raised voices.

Booted feet smack off the epoxy floor. I feel myself being lifted. For a moment I wonder if I've died and am rising straight to heaven. But even though I've shared some of my story, I haven't shared it all. The parts I haven't told will bar me from God's mercy a thousand times over. Still, it's a pleasant enough feeling, this weightlessness.

Rita Ortiz squeezes my fingers. I can't summon the energy to squeeze back.

III

I have no watch but now and then, in the different rooms I visit, I spy a clock, or someone's wristwatch, and marvel at how quickly time races by. Detective Superintendent Mac-Cullagh appears every so often, but she asks hardly any questions, except to find out how I am. I tell her I'm OK, even though I don't understand what's changed. When I ask about my Memory Trees, she says they've found more of them. Mama's oak survived. Bryony's and Elijah's, too.

For a while, I wait in a first-floor office with a partial view of the road. Outside, in the amber glow of the street-lamps, I see vans bristling with aerials and white dishes. I know they're from TV. I think of the *Daily Telegraph* head-line: *HOPE FADES*. If only someone would bring me a newspaper. I could ask Rita, perhaps, but I doubt she'd agree.

I'm wearing jeans, a white T-shirt, a navy top. They're the

nicest clothes I've ever owned – they smell like they've been washed in rose petals. I have a toothbrush, a tube of paste, even something to spray under my arms. Rita says I can have a haircut later, although it might take time to organize.

When I see her next she has a bag over her shoulder. 'We're getting out of here, Kyle. Somewhere you can be yourself for a bit. Read a book, relax.'

'Will there be biscuits?' I ask. Immediately, my cheeks fill with colour. I didn't want to sound foolish, and now I do.

She laughs. 'Biscuits aren't going to be a problem. In fact, biscuits are mandatory.'

Earlier, I tried to imagine MacCullagh as my wife. But in a contest with Rita Ortiz, she wouldn't get a look-in.

'We'll be leaving in a police van,' Rita says. 'That doesn't mean you're in trouble. But this case has attracted a lot of attention. There are quite a few nosy parkers outside.'

'I saw them.'

She beckons me to the door. 'Well, they aren't going to see you.'

IV

The journey from Shrewsbury police station is one I'll never forget.

Five police officers form a scrum around me and hustle me into the van, so fast that I don't even see the gathered journalists. The flash of their cameras is like lightning.

'Is Elissa Mirzoyan dead?' one of them shouts. 'Did you kill her?'

Then the doors close and we're accelerating away. I

wonder if their cameras picked me out. Elissa made the *Telegraph*'s front page. I hope I don't.

'You can relax a bit now, Kyle,' Rita says. 'The worst is over.'

'How far's this place?'

'Oh, thirty minutes or so.' She smiles. 'Do you like Thai food?'

'I've never had it.'

Her eyes widen in mock-horror. 'You mean you've never tasted pad thai?'

'Nope.'

'What about tom yum goong?'

'Definitely not.'

'Gaeng panang? Moo ping?'

The names are so funny that I can't suppress a giggle. Then I remember Gretel, and the fire, and all the other kids who died. I close my mouth, ashamed.

'It's going to be OK, Kyle,' Rita says.

But this woman who isn't a detective doesn't know what I know.

No one does.

MAIRÉAD

I

Sunday morning, thirty-six hours after learning Kyle Buchanan's true identity, Mairéad is in a car heading to Oswestry police station, nineteen miles north-west of Shrewsbury.

She's slept five hours in the last fifty. She hasn't told Scott about the miscarriage. She's so stricken with exhaustion she no longer trusts her own judgement. And yet she cannot stop.

So far, Mairéad's had three phone updates with Dr Rita Ortiz, the NHS forensic psychiatrist tasked with Kyle's immediate care, and one with Dr Patrick Beckett, Ortiz's boss.

It's a complicated situation. Kyle Buchanan is clearly a victim, but that doesn't preclude him from any involvement in Elissa Mirzoyan's killing. His transfer from the police station is no indication of presumed innocence, simply a concession to his mental-health needs. Kyle might feel safe right now, but everyone's waiting for him to slip up. Mairéad can't forget the petrol fumes on his clothes, nor the sight of him, half crazed, hefting a wood axe in the cottage hallway. The equipment used for filming Elissa was found in the room where he slept, along with other items belonging to abducted children.

There's evidence of one other adult living at the cottage – SOC found an additional set of fingerprints in nearly every room. Likewise, DNA extracted from several hairs – confirmed as male, due to the chromosomal mix – are a negative match for both brothers.

Could Kyle have been indoctrinated? Coerced into becoming an accessory? Ortiz and Beckett certainly think that's possible. Whether he'd be criminally responsible for his actions is a decision for someone else. Right now, Mairéad just wants to uncover the truth.

Unfortunately, because of Kyle's fragile mental state, progress has been minimal. It's clear, now, that he's suffering from a psychosis: his grip on reality seems fundamentally damaged. Underlying schizophrenia, triggered by the trauma of his twenty-year ordeal, is possibly the cause. Dr Ortiz believes Kyle's delusions and hallucinations are unusually complex. It means that even when he thinks he's talking truthfully the reality may be something quite different.

It's clear, too – from his high-pitched voice, lack of body hair and sloping breasts – that he's not just damaged mentally. The force medical examiner thinks his physical abnormalities are due either to the huge stress of his ordeal, a sexual injury suffered during his early confinement or a pituitary defect leading to hypogonadism. An endocrinologist is due to examine him in the coming days.

So far, Mairéad's team has concealed Kyle Buchanan's identity from the waiting media, but this is an investigation

335

spanning multiple forces; it's only a question of time before details leak out. When that happens, the story will go stratospheric.

II

Oswestry police station is a wide brick building dominated by a whitewashed front entrance. Moments after introducing herself at the front desk, Mairéad stands at a computer terminal talking to station sergeant Tony Ferrari.

'Member of the public phoned it in,' Ferrari says, handing her a coffee. 'Saw him wandering aimlessly, like he was lost or maybe confused.'

'Where was this?'

'Few miles from Meunierfields. Patrol car picked him up and brought him here. We gave him a Coke while we figured things out. Thought he had a learning difficulty or something, but he knew how to contact his old man via Leon Meunier at Rufus Hall. After we called, the dad – at least, the guy we thought was the dad – drove over to collect him.'

'He came *here*?'

'See for yourself,' Ferrari says, tapping the computer mouse.

A video image fills the screen. Mairéad recognizes Oswestry's front desk. Around ten seconds in, a man approaches it. Early to mid-fifties, leathery skin, dark hair slicked close to his scalp. He wears a mud-spattered waxed jacket. Greeting the desk sergeant with a flick of his chin, he begins to talk.

There's no sound on the recording. Eyes on the stranger, Mairéad says, 'I want to speak to everyone who came in contact with him.'

'Already rounded them up.'

Onscreen, the desk sergeant says something to a colleague out of shot. The man in the waxed jacket watches, running a hand up and down his throat.

'Creepy-looking bastard, isn't he?' Ferrari says.

Easy to make that kind of judgement in hindsight, but Mairéad has to admit there's something deeply unsettling about the man. 'You've got this footage ready to go?'

'It's all yours.'

Another officer enters the shot. Beside him, pale-faced and frightened-looking, walks Kyle Buchanan.

'The car park,' Mairéad says. 'It's covered by CCTV?'

'Give it a sec and you'll see.'

Almost immediately, the scene changes to outside. In shot is a black Land Rover Defender. The man in the waxed jacket approaches it. Kyle trails behind.

The vehicle's hazards flash.

'We checked it out,' Ferrari says. 'Registered to Leon Meunier.'

The man on the recording clearly isn't the late Meunier-fields peer. A shame he didn't bring the white van used for Elissa's abduction. Mairéad would have liked to see its new plates.

'Good work,' she tells Ferrari. 'We'll get this circulated. In the meantime, I want to speak to those officers.'

KYLE

I

The house reminds me of a place I barely remember, a place of love and warmth and a feeling I can't describe; a place where your throat never got tight and your tummy never twisted up.

The first night here, I lie under a clean duvet on a mattress covered by a crisp white sheet. Every piece of fabric, from the towels to the pillow cases, has the same fresh-flowers smell. When I walk barefoot through the carpeted rooms, I feel no dirt beneath my toes. All the windows have three panes of glass. It's like being inside a spaceship.

Shortly after we arrived I sat down with Rita to a huge meal of Thai food, which is now my favourite thing in the world, ever. She didn't even need to cook it – she just phoned some guy who brought it round in his car.

Rita's not the only person looking after me. There's Ben and Ryan, two policemen who don't wear uniforms. Sometimes, there's an older man with a white beard. Beckett's his name – another doctor, I think. We've had a couple of chats. I like him a lot.

I just wish the questions would stop. Rita disguises them pretty well. Always, at first, it seems like we're having a normal conversation, but soon it starts heading towards places I don't want to go. She asks about Mama, and sometimes about my brother. Mostly, she wants to talk about Papa.

I don't want to talk about him. Now that I'm here, I don't even want to think about him. When she mentions his name, it's a cold wave washing over me. I freeze up. My teeth clamp together. That wall inside my head trembles and shifts.

She asks about Gretel, too. I've told her about the letter I posted, the injury to Gretel's arm, the phone I stole from Leon Meunier. I've even told her about how Gretel kissed me, and how in my panic I fled from the cellar, knocking over the petrol cans in the hall. Rita asked me to describe that in great detail, which was difficult because my memory of it isn't great. I had to make some of it up. Luckily, I don't think she noticed.

Already, the people in this house feel like my new family. But I know it can't last. Like most good things, it's just an illusion.

When I'm not answering questions – or trying to avoid them – I read or look out of the window. There are no other houses in sight of this one. Just fields, a country lane and lots of woods. I'm allowed to walk unchaperoned in the huge back garden, which I do as often as I can.

It's there I think about Gretel and everything we shared. The girl cast such a spell over me that I rerun my memories of her time and again. Gretel tricked me – I realize that now – but I wasn't honest with her either. I wish we'd managed to play chess. Looking back, I suspect she deliberately destroyed my makeshift board.

The fourth night here I can't sleep. Every time I close my eyes I hear Rita's questions. A handful of times I almost go downstairs to find Ben, but I don't want him to think I'm weak. Hours later, exhausted and miserable, I finally fall asleep.

And that's when everything unravels.

I I

Above, the sun is a bright penny, its heat like a hot towel pressed to my face. I'm in a garden, not a big one. Everything about it feels familiar: the uneven path along the washing line, the sandpit enclosed by sunken planks. I hear splashing behind me, a joyful scream, and when I turn around there they are, my family, glorious and complete.

Mama's wearing her stripy swimsuit, her shoulders red from the sun. In one hand she holds Elijah's ice cream, which has begun to melt over her fingers. Those fingers are perfect: the skin soft, the nails smooth and bright. 'Smurf,' she says, smiling. 'We've missed you.'

Elijah, standing in the paddling pool, is just as he always was: cheeky, carefree, bursting with life and mischief. The moment Mama's attention is diverted he jumps in the air and lands on his bottom, sending up a huge plume of water. Mama shrieks in mock-outrage.

I want to go to them, but my feet have fused with the grass. Moments later a crack appears in the ground between us. As it deepens and grows wider, Mama and Elijah sail away, floating on an island all of their own. I hold out my hands, begging them to stay, but they aren't looking at me any more, laughing and splashing and playing.

Now, the scene changes. I'm on a car's back seat, travelling at speed. Sun-scorched leather burns my bare legs. Beside me sits Elijah, his face a round moon of fear. Behind the steering wheel, instead of a driver, is a buzzing cloud of flies.

'What's happening?' Elijah moans. 'Where's Mummy?'

I can't answer. If I open my mouth, the flies will swarm down my throat.

'Kyle! Who IS he? Where's he taking us?'

Mouth clenched shut, I grasp my brother's hand.

In the front seat, the cloud of flies solidifies into a man. He holds the steering wheel delicately, wrists angled higher than his knuckles. His eyes float in the rear-view mirror. 'You behave yourselves back there, boys. Say you understand.'

I scream myself awake, and go on screaming long after I've brought everyone running. At first it's just Ben, and a man I don't know. Then Rita arrives with Dr Beckett. There are questions, and this time I answer them. My reward's a plastic syringe filled with something sweet.

That wall inside my mind has crumbled; the dam has finally burst. 'Where's Mama?' I moan. 'Where is she?' The doctors trade grim looks and usher me back to bed.

The next day, I hardly have enough energy to walk. My head feels like a battlefield machine-gunned by enemy soldiers. I can't eat anything for breakfast. When I refuse lunch, Rita asks if I could manage some Thai food. After I say yes, she drives off to find a supermarket.

I'm flooded by memories so intense they pummel me flat. I hear my brother's voice, begging for help. And I hear Gretel's voice too.

If only I could return to the way things were. Back at Meunierfields, I had a purpose: bring comfort to those who wake beneath the Memory Wood; remember them once they've gone. Here, I have no purpose at all. Wandering through the house, I find Ben in the living room and collapse into an armchair.

'OK, sport?' he asks, and I nod, even though it's not true.

He's fiddling with his phone, so I ask if I can play chess. He doesn't have the app Gretel mentioned, but he downloads one that's similar. When I see the board, all set up, the chaos in my head fades. Ben shows me how to control the pieces with my finger.

I hunch forward, all my attention on the screen. After a moment's uncertainty, I take my first move: queen pawn to D4. To my delight, black responds with a pawn to D5. This time, I don't hesitate, answering with a pawn to C4. Gretel didn't teach me many openings, but she taught me this one. It's called the Queen's Gambit. Black can choose to accept the gambit, or decline.

I wait, barely able to breathe.

Then black accepts.

MAIRÉAD

Monday night, news of Kyle Buchanan's identity leaks out. By Tuesday morning, his face – along with his younger brother's – is appearing on every news outlet. The photo is the one circulated in 1999 after their abduction. In it, the boys grin for the camera, grown-up teeth too big for their young mouths.

The media is screaming for an updated picture of Kyle, but they won't get one; nor will they receive any update on the status of Elijah, mainly because nobody – not those at the safe house, nor anyone at the multiple Meunierfields crime scenes – has any information on his fate. Mairéad suspects he's long dead, but she has no evidence.

Distressingly, the news story has completely shifted away from Elissa. All the attention is on Kyle and his twenty-year confinement. Back at Meunierfields, news helicopters have captured footage of the many forensic tents dotted about the Memory Wood. On TV, retired police officers earn decent beer money providing grim commentaries and forecasts. Mairéad can only wonder how Lena Mirzoyan is feeling, her daughter's disappearance relegated to a sideshow in a media circus focused on the sensational and the grotesque.

The feeding frenzy over the brothers has also diminished the impact of the Oswestry CCTV footage released at the last media briefing. Mairéad had hoped that, by now, the stranger who collected Kyle Buchanan from the police station would be leading every newspaper's front page. But although he features in the coverage, he's given far less prominence than the boys.

While Drs Ortiz and Beckett continue to treat Kyle, Mairéad's investigation team – now coordinating with nine different forces across England and Wales – pores over old files. The Buchanan boys were snatched from a Swindon playground in 1999 while their mother, Karen Wolk, was chatting to a group of mums. No communication was ever received from the brothers' abductor. It's one of the reasons their case was never linked to those that followed. At the time, of course, there were no camera phones, no laptop edit suites, no YouTube.

Back in '99, Wiltshire Police's investigation initially focused on Glenn Buchanan, the boys' father, but although detectives took apart his entire life, they found nothing to implicate him. Nor did the man have any obvious motive; he'd split with Karen shortly after Elijah's birth, but there'd been no animosity. The boys retained their father's surname, which was why Mairéad hadn't even made the connection until Kyle mentioned his brother's name – at the time of their abduction, she'd only just applied to become a police officer. No one can explain why, during his long confinement, Kyle Buchanan decided to become Kyle North. According to Drs Beckett and Ortiz, it's likely just one more facet of the complex fantasy he developed in order to survive.

Sometimes, Kyle indicates a passing awareness of his true age, but mostly he remains in a state of regression. At the safe house, he studiously avoids mirrors, anything that might lead him to contemplate his reflection. Mairéad knows he's the key to unlocking this case, but so far she's learned little of use. And on Tuesday morning, after a night plagued by nightmares, Kyle clams up completely.

That afternoon at Hindlip Hall, the West Mercia HQ in Worcester, she summons Dr Beckett, who suspects that a key pillar of his patient's delusion has collapsed. 'He was asking for his mother,' he says.

In 2004, five years after her sons went missing, Karen Wolk took her own life. 'Did you tell him?'

'At this stage, I think it's unwise.'

'There's a chance Kyle already knows,' Mairéad points out. 'Her death was widely reported. His abductor could've told him. Maybe that's what triggered the psychosis.' She winces, realizing she's playing amateur psychiatrist. 'Sorry.'

Beckett waves away her apology. 'I've placed him on a low dose of clozapine. It's an antipsychotic and it should help with his anxiety. But at this stage I must tell you – I'm deeply concerned about his mental health. Until he stabilizes, I can't allow any more questions about the case.'

Mairéad groans. Beckett's only doing his job, but *he* won't be the one facing Lena Mirzoyan, or the chief constable, or a baying press pack. 'Has he said anything?' she asks. 'Anything at all that might lead us to Elissa?'

'Not a jot.'

'Do you think he knows what happened? Do you think he was involved?'

Frustrated, Beckett rolls his neck. 'I want to help, I

really do. But any answer I gave you would be a complete stab in the dark.'

'Right now, I'd take even that.'

The doctor watches her a moment. She endures his gaze, wondering what he sees. Finally, his expression softens. 'If you're asking me if I think Kyle's deliberately holding things back, then I'd say, yes, I think he is. But that's the hunch of someone who's bet on Southampton to win the Premiership every season since 2012.'

Mairéad takes a breath, sighs it out. 'I know you've got his well-being at heart. But Elissa Mirzoyan's a victim too.'

'I understand that. But Kyle Buchanan's capacity to separate fantasy from reality, even once we're through this current crisis, isn't going to improve any time soon. The moment he feels any pressure or expectation, he's highly likely to fabricate something, just to win approval. He might not even realize he's doing it.'

She closes her eyes. Thinks, immediately, of the desolate void at the heart of her. Senses that boulder of grief about to come crashing down.

She still hasn't told Scott. Unforgiveable, really.

'It's none of my business, I know,' Beckett says. 'And I'm asking in a purely personal capacity. But I've noticed . . .' He pauses, tries again. 'Leading an investigation like this – with all the associated scrutiny – it puts a huge amount of pressure on a person.'

Mairéad glances up at him.

'How are you coping?' he asks.

KYLE

I

When Rita returns with Thai food, she confiscates Ben's phone. 'No contact with the outside world,' she tells the policeman when she thinks I'm out of earshot. 'Do you *want* him seeing the news?'

It's probably for the best. After an encouraging start, I lost my first game of chess. I lost the next six games, too.

I don't manage to eat much. Sensing Rita's disappointment, I force down a few prawn crackers, but they're greasier than the ones we had before. They leave me feeling sick.

I switch between periods of calm and high anxiety. One moment my heart's beating sluggishly, the next it's galloping at top speed. The medicine Beckett's giving me is meant to stop that, but since the first dose I've only pretended to take it. I don't want my senses numbed. At some point soon, I'm going to need them.

I recall the reporters' shouted questions as I was bundled into the police van: *Is Elissa Mirzoyan dead? Did you kill her?*

Perhaps I should have answered. Because I know, now. I know the truth of what happened. There are gaps, still. But I don't have to be a genius to fill them in.

Close to sunset, Ben's shift ends and Ryan's begins. Rita goes home too, taking a carton of pad thai for her supper. I wait for Ryan to come in after his cigarette. Then I go out to the garden. It's cold outside, but I hardly feel the chill. Above me, the sky is restless yet beautiful – like I imagine it must have looked in the early days of Creation. Clouds twist and churn, pulled by conflicting currents. To the west, the sun bleeds molten copper over the horizon. Rarely have I seen such drama in the heavens. Never before has an omen seemed so clear.

I turn my head, looking back at the house where I've spent these last four days. The people I've met in there are good and honest, achingly sincere. But they're not my people. After what I've done – and what I've let happen – we'll never have anything in common.

The lawn climbs towards a part of the garden left to grow wild. I pass a rope swing, a tool shed. The sun finally bleeds out. In the lavender light, my skin feels tight against my flesh, like a shoe that's two sizes too small.

As I walk around the tool shed, shielding myself from the house, I see Papa standing beneath an ash tree. For the length of a heartbeat I wonder if my overactive imagination has woven him from the threads of twilight. But he's as real as the tumultuous sky.

Papa smiles broadly when he sees me. 'You sly little fuck,' he laughs, walking up. The last thing I see is his swinging fist.

II

I'm in a van.

I didn't see it from the outside, but I know which one. I sometimes used its bumper for target practice, until Papa warned me off. He gave me the .22 a few years back – I think the idea amused him. Arming me was a risk, but Papa thrives on danger. Of course, he's not my real papa. But that doesn't matter, not any more.

Beneath me, the van bumps and shakes. When it sways on its suspension, I slide across the floor. Every now and then I hear the roar-hiss of a passing vehicle, but it doesn't happen often. Country roads, I think, and wonder how long I've been unconscious.

No light intrudes. Outside, it might still be dusk, or it might be full dark. When I start to get cold, I search the van's interior. In one corner I discover a tarpaulin, all bunched up. It's crackly and rough, caked in dust and grit, but it's better than nothing. I wrap myself up in its folds. Closing my eyes, I find sleep.

III

Something different in the engine sound wakens me. When I sit up I realize we're climbing a slope.

My thoughts return to the safe house. Ryan won't miss me straight away, but it won't be long before the alarm is raised. I know the police will do everything possible to find me. Papa knows it too, which is why the chance to snatch me a second time will have been irresistible.

I hope Ben doesn't get into trouble. He shouldn't have lent me his phone to play chess, but he couldn't have known I'd phone Papa. They thought I didn't know the safe house's location, but I overheard Rita phoning for Thai food. The address wasn't hard to memorize.

Reaching the top of a slope, the van begins to descend. A minute later we're travelling up another rise, this one even steeper. Earlier, the constant motion lulled me to sleep. Now, it's making me feel sick.

We slow to what feels like walking pace. I try to imagine what's outside. Another estate, like Meunierfields? A wood full of dripping trees, like the one I left behind? Perhaps, instead, we're visiting a burial ground.

The engine dies. A door slams. Footsteps come around to the rear. The door swings open, revealing a clear night sky.

IV

Papa stands by the back bumper. Moonlight floats in his eyes. I catch a waft of him – stale tobacco, unwashed clothes – and wrinkle my nose. Usually, the smell wouldn't bother me, but in the last few days I've taken baths and showers, used deodorant and toothpaste, all sorts of nice things.

'You broke the rules,' he says. 'Not just once, but twice. You *estranged* yourself. Say you understand.'

'Papa, I—'

'*Say you understand.*'

'I understand.'

'Out.'

I expected him to be cross, but there's a tonelessness to his speech that alarms me. This isn't at all the reunion I imagined. Sliding towards the rear doors, I jump down on to grass. The wind whips away Papa's stink, replacing it with ocean salt.

Some distance away, I hear the muted crash of waves. We're on a slope, close to a cliff edge. Far below, reaching all the way to the horizon, lies indigo sea. The moon has launched a fleet of white schooners across its surface.

Above me, stars too numerous to count stud the heavens.

'Where are we?'

Ignoring my question, Papa slams the rear doors. When I turn my head I spot a squat stone shack at the top of the slope. Its corrugated-iron roof lifts and groans in the wind. Firelight glows at a window. Woodsmoke flutters from a tin chimney. Along the left wall stands a rickety lean-to shed, its timbers silvered by moonlight. Walking down the grassy slope towards us is Magic Annie.

V

She's dressed, tonight, as Kamali, my spirit guide. Over her Cowichan sweater, with its bold silhouettes of mountain bears, she wears her necklace of turquoise stones. On her feet are her favourite buffalo-skin moccasins.

Her face crinkles like parchment paper when she sees me. I can smell her perfume, mingling with the thin smoke of her cheroot.

'I thought we'd tamed you,' she says, coming close. 'And all along, you were a little streak of cancer, biding your time.'

'Kamali—'

'Uh-uh,' she snaps. 'That name is dead. You burned it up, same as everything else, in that fire you set.'

'It wasn't me, Annie. I never—'

'Yes, it was. Or might as well have been. And now we've got to start all over. Our time of life, that's not something we relish.' Her lips shrink from her nicotine-browned teeth. 'Why'd you come back?'

'Because there's nowhere—'

'Face on every newspaper, on every TV. Whole *world* wants to hear about *you*, doesn't it? What happened? All get too much?'

'I just want things to go back to the way they were.'

The moonlight has bleached away all colour, leaving Annie as haggard as stone. *Ocean Eyes*, I used to call her. Right now, those eyes are blank windows, utterly lacking in humanity.

'Here,' she says, pressing a hessian sack against my chest. 'Put it on.'

'Annie, please. You don't have to—'

Behind me, Papa drives his fist into my kidney. I sink to my knees, mouth opening and closing like I'm a fish hooked from the sea. The pain is crippling.

Somehow, I drag the sack over my head. The wind blows, flapping the fabric against my face. My nose fills with the stink of rotten onions. Annie grabs my wrist and pulls me forwards.

Is this how my life ends? A short walk with my former spirit guide, followed by a long plunge over a cliff edge?

Annie wheezes as she climbs. A minute later we come to a halt. I stand beside her, wondering whether my next step will lead me inside the shack or over a three-hundred-foot drop. Around us, the wind snaps and moans.

Something jangles at my side. I screw up my face. Annie puts her hand in the centre of my back and shoves.

I stumble forwards, expecting my feet to meet empty air, bracing myself for the stomach-clenching horror of a plummet. A scream is in my throat, but I don't get the chance to release it because suddenly I'm on my knees, wooden planking beneath them.

We're not at the cliff edge. That was just my overactive imagination. I'm inside, I think, but this isn't the shack I saw earlier – I can't feel the warmth of a wood stove. Then I remember the lean-to shed.

Annie instructs me to sit. I hear that jangling again and realize it's a set of keys. Something heavy closes around my wrist. Seconds later, a door bangs shut. I don't have to touch the manacle to know I'm wearing it.

For a while I just sit there, concentrating on my breathing. There's a terrible poetry to this. I think of Bryony, and her accusations as she stalked me through my old home. How she'd laugh if she could see me now.

VI

Dawn brings my first visitor. I know the sun has risen because pale light pokes its fingers through the planking.

Mama sits against the shed's far wall. When I look at her directly I see bare wooden slats, so I stare straight ahead.

'That house. Those people,' I tell her, thinking of my time with Rita, Ben, Ryan and Patrick. 'It was no place for someone like me. For a while I thought it could be. But it wasn't.'

Outside, a fresh morning wind is blowing. I hear the shack's corrugated-iron roof lift and creak. If there was ever a time for confession, it's now.

'I killed him, Mama. I killed Elijah. I'm sorry, but I did.'

My voice breaks when I tell her that. Snot runs over my lip. 'Don't say you forgive me, because I know you can't. I killed him because I wanted to live.'

Mama hugs her knees to her chest.

'Those doctors, they kept asking if he was alive, if he was out there somewhere. What was I meant to tell them? The truth?'

The silence between us is awful, the worst it's ever been. Tears roll down my cheeks. Some stuff just can't stay buried. Elijah's death is one of those things. When I think of my younger brother, my throat aches with the effort of breathing. I've never grieved him, not properly. For far too long I tried to make up for his killing by shedding my identity and letting him live on through me. But I made a poor Elijah, and the Kyle that arose in his place grew into something beyond my control, a creature that displayed every cruel or selfish impulse I've ever felt.

There are no more words, so I don't try to find them. When I look up I realize that Mama's already gone. All that's left is the wind. I don't expect to see her again. She's a shard of memory now, nothing more. Outside, I hear the rattle of a latch.

VII

Cold air races into the shed.

Papa doesn't appear right away, and my nose tells me why: he's brought food – by the smell of it, something hot. He must have laid it on the grass, leaving his hands free to unlock the door. My stomach growls – apart from a handful of prawn crackers, in the last twenty-four hours I've hardly eaten.

Lifting my head, I carefully arrange my expression. It's not too late to rescue this. Papa doesn't give second chances, but there's always a first time. We have a lot of history. I just have to remind him how useful I am.

Ultimately, of course, he isn't the one I need to convince. I think of Magic Annie, standing in her caravan the day Gretel's mother appeared on TV: *There are people on this earth that have no business walking it.*

She wasn't talking about Gretel's abductor; she was referring to the girl's mother. I don't know what Lena Mirzoyan did to attract Annie's disapproval – I probably never will – but the possibilities are endless.

Since my bad dream two nights ago, I've remembered a lot of stuff. Back when Papa snatched me and Elijah, Annie told us that some women weren't worthy enough to raise kids and, unfortunately, Mama was one of them. Good mothers didn't bring up their kids alone. Good mothers didn't feed their kids crap. Good mothers didn't keep a filthy home, or drink alcohol, or do a whole host of other things.

I never recognized Mama in those descriptions, and I'll

bet the other kids who woke beneath the Memory Wood felt the same way. I know Bryony loved her mother. I'm pretty sure Gretel did too.

Annie never had kids of her own. Maybe that's one reason she's so fixed on how they should be raised. Then again, over the years, I've discovered she has strong ideas about almost everything you could imagine.

Magic Annie, I called her. That name grew out of the smoke she made in her caravan on Native American days. It calmed my heart and filled my head with dreams. Over the years, I learned that it wasn't the only magical thing about her; Annie has a hold over people that's nothing short of spellbinding.

For one thing, she forced Leon Meunier to let her set up Wheel Town and made him rent Papa the cottage. I know that the women she introduced to him played a part in the agreement – the one I saw a few days ago, with the *HUSTLIN'* tracksuit and peacock eyes, was the latest in a long line. But only Annie could have made it all happen.

She's wrapped *Papa* so tight around her finger that he's pretty much her slave. The things he's done at her suggestion are too monstrous to describe, and yet sometimes I can almost understand why he did them. Annie makes you *believe* things about the world, about the way it should be. Her words are like whispers directly into your brain. The only way to stay safe around her – and, by extension, around Papa – is through total obedience. None of the other kids ever learned that, even though I tried to warn them.

'*That name is dead,*' she told me last night when we stood beneath the moon as it shone its light on the sea. '*You burned it up, same as everything else, in that fire you set.*'

It's not easy to throw off a name. I know that, because

I've tried. But perhaps Annie was never her real name to start with. Perhaps it's just another of her lies.

One thing that I *know* is untrue is what she said I did in the Memory Wood. When I fled the Gingerbread House after Gretel kissed me, I knocked over the petrol cans in the hall. But I never went back to strike a match, and that fuel wouldn't have burned without one.

Earlier that day, when Leon Meunier stormed back into Wheel Town minutes after driving off, I hadn't realized what was wrong. Now, it's all too clear: he must have discovered the theft of his phone.

When Annie learned of it, too, after going out to meet him, she would have known it was time to leave. Of course, she wouldn't have wanted to leave any evidence. Burning down the Gingerbread House fixed that. Whether she started the fire herself I can't say, but the instruction would have come from her lips.

I think of all this, and when I look up with my carefully remorseful expression, I see that my earlier assumption was wrong, because it's not Papa standing in the doorway, but Gretel.

VIII

She looks different – a pencil drawing of her former self. Her head is bowed and I can't see her face. On her wrist, a grubby bandage has replaced my makeshift dressing. Below it, her purpled fingers have swelled to three times their normal size. In her good hand, she precariously balances a tray.

I want to say something: apologize, or beg forgiveness. Then I remember Mama, leaning against the wooden slats with daylight shining through her. Just because Gretel is visiting, it doesn't mean she's really here.

Crouching down, she places the tray on the floor. One-handed, it's a tricky task. The contents – a bowl filled with stew and a tin mug of water – slide across it and tumble off the end. Gretel stares at the mess. Then she stands and raises her head. At last, I see her clearly, and my blood runs to ice. I simply cannot tell if she's real. Her face is dirty and bedraggled, her eyes as dull as river stones. Beneath the grime, her skin has the pallor of a corpse.

'Gretel—'

'Don't call me that,' she whispers. 'That's not my name.'

'Are you here?' I say. 'Are you real?'

Gretel watches me a long time before speaking. 'You asked me that once before.'

I did. And I still remember her answer, in the cellar beneath the Gingerbread House: *This is real, Elijah. All of it. You're real, so am I. So is my mum. So is my family. This place is real, too. It's not where I want to be, and I hope I'm not going to die here. I hope, more than anything, that you're going to help me survive this – but it's real, I promise you. It's about as real as a thing can get.*

I look at the tray and the overturned bowl of food. I lift my head and look outside at the mounds of tufted grass. The wind blowing through the doorway feels real, which means the door must be open. The food smells real, too, which means someone must have brought it.

My heart feels as light as a dandelion clock. If Gretel really *is* here, it means I can scrub one black mark off a conscience filthy with them.

She glances past me. 'I have to go.'

'Wait—'

Her feet make no sound as she crosses the shed. At the threshold, she hesitates. The wind makes snakes of her hair. Then she's gone.

I blink after her, wondering what just happened.

This is real, Elijah. All of it. You're real. So am I.

But that was then, and this is now.

When my gaze wanders to the far wall, I notice that Mama is back, her knees drawn up to her chest. She doesn't look at me, but this time, at least, she speaks. 'Only one way forward from here. You're a survivor, Elijah. So survive.'

I think of my filthy conscience, and the one black mark I'd hoped to avoid. Then I close my eyes and wait.

ELISSA

As Elissa shuffles across the grass, the wind batters her and she nearly falls. Her head is abuzz; her throat is on fire. In the last few days, her arm has grown so painful with infection she'd amputate it if she knew how. If she survives this – unlikely, given what she's just seen in the tool shed – she can't imagine any doctor could save it.

The ghoul is waiting outside the shack, smoking a roll-up cigarette. He follows her inside and shuts the door.

The witch, Annie, is on her knees by the far wall, loading logs into the wood stove. Watching her, Elissa thinks of the old fairy tale: how Gretel shoved her captor into the oven and released Hansel from his cage. The comparison is so absurd she almost laughs, but there's no breath in her lungs for that.

Knees cracking, Annie climbs to her feet. 'This fucking wind,' she mutters. 'This fucking cold.' Finally, her eyes meet Elissa's. 'You see him?'

'Yes.'

Annie gestures to a footstool. When Elissa sits, the old woman grins. 'Round here, you're a lick of fresh air. You do as you're told, and that's good. I think you want to help us, don't you? I think you want to do the right thing.'

Slowly, Elissa nods her head.

'I'm pleased. Because we like you, girl. We want to invest in you.' She leans closer. 'What did he say? When you took him the food?'

'He asked if I was real.'

Annie grunts. From a wall cupboard, she grabs a packet of pills, popping two from the plastic packaging. 'Here,' she says. 'Take these. They'll help with your arm.'

The witch watches her swallow them, before adding, 'He visited you, didn't he? Down in the cellar. Came there on the pretext of befriending you.' She pauses and her face crinkles. 'It's OK, you don't have to say anything. There'll never be anything, ever in this life, that you can conceal from me.'

Elissa stiffens. The last time she heard those words they came from the ghoul. He's watching her from across the room, smoke drifting from his nostrils.

'Elijah didn't want to be your friend,' Annie says, lowering herself into a rickety chair. 'He was just checking out the competition. He ever tell you that's not his real name? Elijah was his little brother. I'm guessing he didn't share what he did to the poor boy.'

Every time the witch speaks Elissa's grasp on the situation feels like it's collapsing. Facts she'd thought irrefutable suddenly seem in doubt.

'We can't stay here long,' Annie says. 'And we can't leave you behind. I'd like to take you with us, but we don't have room for two. It's you or him.'

Hearing that, Elissa thinks of the promise she made when she first woke beneath the Memory Wood: to survive this horror, whatever the cost.

'That boy,' Annie continues. 'He's a survivor. He values his life above all else. He'll do whatever it takes to keep it.'

'So do I,' Elissa whispers. 'So *will* I.'

She means it, too. Right now, she can think of nothing she wouldn't do to see her family again.

'Those times he visited you, down in the cellar,' the witch says. 'He ever tell you about the others?'

'He told me about Bryony.'

'He tell you what happened to her? How she died?'

Elissa's throat closes up. She shakes her head.

That boy. He's a survivor. He values his life above all else. He'll do whatever it takes to keep it.

'Those pills will make you drowsy,' Annie says, getting up. 'If you stretch out on the floor, you might catch a few hours' sleep. Later, I want you to take him another meal.' Returning to the cupboard, she opens a drawer and removes a knife. The blade is six inches of sharp steel.

'If I were you,' she adds, her turquoise eyes glimmering, 'I'd take this along. Because, believe me, if he gets the chance to improve his situation, he won't hesitate.'

Her tongue pops out, probing yellow teeth. 'Like I said, we can only take one.'

KYLE

Later, Papa visits. He stands in the doorway for a bit, smoking his cigarette. When he steps inside and notices the overturned food bowl, his forehead creases.

'It wasn't me,' I tell him. 'I'm not being difficult. She dropped it.'

'Huh,' he replies. 'What a bitch.'

'It wasn't on purpose.'

'You don't think?'

A silence grows between us. 'She was real,' I say. 'I saw the flames and . . . I thought I'd killed her.'

'You didn't,' Papa says. 'Not yet.'

I raise my head fully. 'Not yet?'

'Annie's in there right now, explaining how things are. She's clever, that Elissa. Ruthless, too. Some of the things she's been saying . . .'

He pauses, spits.

'What things?'

'Oh, stuff about you. Annie told her about Eli. About what you did.'

My blood crashes in my ears. 'Papa—'

'Save it.' He drops his cigarette to the floor, grinding it out with his heel. 'I probably shouldn't even be here, warning you like this.' Retrieving the tray and its contents, he steps out and shuts the door.

Back at the safe house, when I called Papa from Ben's phone, I fooled myself into thinking that this would be easy, that Gretel was already dead, that I could slide back into my old life without a price.

She's clever, that Elissa. Ruthless, too. Some of the things she's been saying . . .

Tilting my head, I listen for any hint I might not be alone. Outside, wind saws at the grass. It's impossible to tell if anyone's close, so I'll have to trust my instincts. They're not always as bad as I make out.

I know I'm a liar. Often, to survive, I've had no choice. I realize how fickle Annie can be; returning without a back-up plan would've been stupid. And while my IQ might not be as high as Gretel's, I'm certainly not dumb.

Putting my free hand behind me, I reach under my T-shirt. The carving knife is fixed against my spine with strips of Elastoplast. I stole it from the safe-house kitchen after phoning Papa.

It takes me a few minutes to release it, working the handle back and forth. I examine the steel, careful – as always – to avoid my reflection. Scooping some dirt from the floor, I rub it on to the blade, dulling the shine. It's dark in the tool shed, but I can't take any chances. As I work I think of Gretel, sitting in the warmth while I'm tethered out here like one of Noakes's dogs.

She's clever, that Elissa. Ruthless, too. Some of the things she's been saying . . .

Placing the carving knife within reach, I prepare myself for what's coming.

ELISSA

I

When she wakes, the witch is standing at the stove, stirring something in a pan. The ghoul is in his chair, smoking another roll-up. It's a domestic scene from a horror movie, so surreal it's almost comedic.

With effort, Elissa pulls herself up. Her right arm feels like it's wrapped in barbed wire. Her fingers are so swollen they look like they'll burst at the slightest pressure. Her back throbs. Her legs feel tingly and light.

She can't even see as well as she could. Unless she concentrates, the ghoul and the witch morph into blurry-faced *bodachs*, exuding malevolence like toxic gas.

Her thoughts turn to Elijah, chained inside the shed. He lied to her about so many things; even, it seems, his real name. And when he had the chance to save her, he chose instead to let her rot.

That boy, he's a survivor. He values his life above all else. He'll do whatever it takes to keep it.

But just like she told the witch, she's a survivor, too.

She's reached the point where nothing, however barbaric, is off limits. Her strength might be failing, but her resolve remains strong. She recalls the knife the witch showed her, and the obvious implication. She's only thirteen. She shouldn't have to think about such things. But if she wants to be fourteen, fifteen, eighteen – if she wants to grow up, lead a useful life – then perhaps it's the only way. Killing Elijah would be a cost she'd bear all her days. But here, now, it's not an act from which she'd retreat. She has a duty – to her mum, to her grandparents, to *herself* – to survive this.

At the stove, Annie pours the contents of the saucepan into a bowl, which she places on a tray. Then she fetches the knife from the countertop. 'Decision time,' she says, facing Elissa.

What if I say no?

What if I refuse to go outside?

What if I lie down, close my eyes and pretend this isn't happening?

All those thoughts and more flash through Elissa's head. She opens her mouth to speak. Instead of protesting, she climbs unsteadily to her feet.

II

Outside, the wind is a living thing, beating the grass into submission. A few miles out to sea, an oil tanker carves a white wake, the only other evidence of humanity. Elissa watches it as she walks. If she dropped the tray and raised her good arm, would anybody see? Even if someone did, she's just a girl waving at a distant ship. Impossible to deduce her true plight from that.

As she approaches the tool shed, awkwardly carrying Elijah's meal, she feels curiously absent of emotion. If fearlessness is a side effect of Annie's pills, perhaps she owes the witch some gratitude.

Her breathing is elevated; her heart is crashing in her chest. When she blinks, or turns her head too fast, the landscape stutters like an image inside a zoetrope. In her mouth, her teeth feel sharper than before. Her tongue passes over their ridges, releasing an effervescent rush of sensation.

Elissa halts outside the shed door. Before she can open it, she'll need to put down the tray. Crouching on the grass, she feels a wet sting of pain beneath her dress, halfway along her right thigh. When she straightens, the feeling disappears, leaving nothing but a warm trickle down her leg. Abruptly, she remembers what's hidden there. And with that mystery solved, she opens the door.

III

From darkness and shadow, details emerge. The *bodach* sits in the corner, tethered by her old chain.

It's a shame, Elissa thinks, that not all *bodachs* are kept like this, tied up in the dark where they can't do any harm. Then she remembers that the pale-faced shape watching her isn't a *bodach* at all, but the one she calls Elijah. She remembers something else, too: that he stole that name from the brother he killed.

Her eyes flick around the floor, looking for a safe spot. But nowhere in here lies beyond the perimeter of that chain. Retrieving the tray from the grass, she gingerly crosses the threshold.

Elijah looks tired and dishevelled, but his eyes remain bright. Forget Hansel and Gretel; right now, Elissa feels like Red Riding Hood approaching the wolf. 'I brought you some food,' she says. 'I'll try not to drop it.'

'Thanks,' he croaks. Then, 'Can you bring it closer?'

Elissa hesitates, trying to stabilize her vision.

'What's wrong?' he asks. 'What did they tell you?'

She shrugs, shakes her head.

Elijah glances at his manacle. His attention wanders to something at his side. 'It's funny,' he says. 'All this – everything that's happening. In a way, it's like the world's most intense chess game.'

She knows what he means, but she can't agree. 'This isn't a game, Elijah.'

'I know *that*, silly.'

'Elijah isn't even your real name. Is it?'

'I . . .' His shoulders quake. 'It was a way of remembering him.'

Carefully, Elissa sets down the tray. Again, she feels a tiny pinprick of pain.

That boy, he's a survivor. He values his life above all else. He'll do whatever it takes to keep it.

Sweat rolls into her eyes. She blinks it away. 'You know, I never really figured out if I could trust you.'

'I can't blame you for that,' he says. 'I wouldn't trust me either. But nothing I ever told you was untrue.'

She knows *that's* a lie. It's so obviously a lie she can hardly believe he said it. When he drags over the tray, she sits down a short distance away, spreading out the folds of her dress.

'Are you OK?' he asks as he eats. 'You seem, I don't know. A bit weird.'

'They gave me something. For the pain. It's made me a little . . .' She raises her right arm, flexing and unflexing her swollen fingers. 'Spaced.'

With her left hand, she reaches under her dress.

Elijah blinks, his eyes fixed on her face.

'He's not your papa, is he?' Elissa says. 'I thought he was, but he isn't.'

'I used to pretend he was. I pretended so well I ended up believing it. It's funny how that happens, don't you think? How you can make things come true if you think them hard enough.'

Elissa takes a shuddery breath. It feels like a butterfly is beating its wings inside her chest. Under her dress, her index finger touches the knife.

Elijah finishes eating. He carefully puts down his bowl.

'They took you, didn't they?' she says. 'When you were a boy. Took you and your brother. Just like they took me.'

Again, Elijah glances off to the side, as if he's searching for something. Perhaps he's avoiding a bad memory. 'Yes.'

'You told me something, right when we first met. It's taken me until now to remember. "I'm only twelve years old," you said. At the time, I was so scared by what was happening that I hardly even picked up on it.' She pauses. 'Is that how old you were when it happened?'

He swallows noisily. Then he moans, a sound like nothing Elissa has ever heard. In that moment, her mind clears of confusion and she recognizes Elijah for what he is – a victim, one who has shared her nightmare, but for a period lasting *decades*. Elissa can imagine the horrors through which he's lived, but not the scale. Little wonder he fabricated such a complex fantasy. 'There's something I have to tell you,' she says, lowering her voice. 'Something they tried to make me do.'

Elijah stares at the far wall. He mutters something, too faint to hear. His shoulders begin to tremble.

'I won't do it,' she tells him. 'Not to you. You lied to me, back in the Memory Wood, but I lied to you too. The letter, the phone, destroying your chessboard. I'm sorry, Elijah. I'm sorry I did those things. I just wanted to get away. You understand that. Don't you?'

'I wanted to get away too,' he whispers. 'At least, I thought I did. Now . . . I don't think I can. I don't think I have a choice any more.'

'You always have a choice.'

'Not if I want to live.'

He lifts his head. Tears roll down his cheeks.

An artery pulses in his throat.

'Elijah—'

Behind her, the wind catches the door and slams it, plunging the shed into darkness. Elissa freezes, Elijah's expression burnt on to her retinas.

'*Queen's Gambit*,' he hisses.

When he lunges forward, she doesn't even have time to scream.

MAIRÉAD

She gets the call as journalists are filing out of the latest media briefing.

Beforehand, to emphasize the point that this remains an investigation into Elissa Mirzoyan's disappearance, Mairéad placed a huge photograph of the girl on a pedestal beside the mic table. Even that didn't focus the minds of the attendant press pack. All the questions were about Kyle Buchanan. And now, in what seems a quite extraordinary security lapse, he's missing.

Admittedly, Kyle hadn't been charged with any offence. Despite his vulnerability, the psychiatric team hadn't applied for a Section 4, which could have detained him. Neither of his doctors believed he was a flight risk.

Working fast, Mairéad establishes the following facts: Kyle was definitely inside the house at 17.30 during shift rotation. According to Ryan Havers, the relieving officer, he went out to the garden at around 17.50.

That, in itself, wasn't unusual. Nor was there any reason to chaperone him. If anything, Dr Beckett believed that short periods of solitude might be beneficial. At 18.05,

Ryan checked outside. Finding the garden empty, he raised the alarm.

In the control room, Mairéad fields calls from her chief constable, her DCC and their opposite numbers in the West Mercia force. Already, the media know something's up, even if they don't know exactly what, and they're pulling in every favour to find out. Should Mairéad pre-empt them? Release a statement, along with an updated photograph of Kyle?

Her phone buzzes. It's Rita Ortiz.

'Beckett told me what happened,' the psychiatrist says. 'I take it you haven't found him.'

'Not yet. And unless you've got something specific, I'm afraid I can't talk.'

'I'm sure it's been done,' Ortiz replies, 'but I just wanted to ask: did you check the officer's phone? Kyle was playing on it a couple of hours before he went missing. I was worried he might see a news report, so I confiscated it. But maybe he called someone.'

'Thank you,' Mairéad says, and hangs up.

Two minutes later, Sergeant Ben Hollingsworth is roused from sleep. A check of his phone log confirms a single outbound call, made at 14.21, lasting ninety-six seconds. Mairéad speaks to the officer directly and learns that the call must have been made while Hollingsworth was making a snack. He falls over himself to apologize.

'Don't resign just yet,' she tells him. 'You might have given us our first decent lead.'

She doesn't need a warrant to access phone-tower records – her team files an automated request to the provider. While they wait for the data to arrive, Mairéad slips outside and phones Scott. When her husband answers, she can't say anything, and it turns out she doesn't have to. He knows, without her having to speak.

'It's OK,' he says. 'Love, it's OK.'

Mairéad stays on the line, connected by a lot more than silence.

KYLE

I

Blood on my hands. Blood on the knife.

Gretel lies a short distance away, face down in the dirt. On her shoulders, I see my bloody handprints, but perhaps that's just my imagination: with the door closed, it's pretty dark.

Out of all the poor souls I encountered beneath the Memory Wood, Gretel affected me most deeply. Whatever happens next, I'll carry her with me always.

Breath whistles in and out of my throat. Outside, the wind sings a lament. I'm not alone in here. Along the back wall sits Mama, her head bowed.

It's agony, this. How long must I wait for Papa? How long before I find out my fate? I look at the manacle on my wrist. Maybe he won't come at all.

I think of the story Magic Annie once told me, of a Daddy Fox who fell into a pit. His family tried to rescue him but they tumbled in as well, all except the oldest brother. Unable to anchor the chain, he was doomed to watch them all perish. Then he perished too.

The tool-shed door swings open. The light of an overcast sky falls over me.

II

It's Papa.

He stands at the threshold, but he doesn't come in. 'She dead?' he asks, his attention on Elissa.

I open my mouth to speak. When no words come, I just nod.

Papa's cigarette smoke wafts into the shed. He runs his tongue over his teeth. 'Didn't think you'd do it,' he says. 'Thought the two of you had something going. But you're a vicious little fucker when it comes to it. Aren't you?'

'I did what you asked. You know I always do.'

'I didn't ask you to do anything.'

I blink. 'Yes, you did. You told me to . . . to . . .'

Hesitating, I rerun our earlier conversation. He'd called Elissa ruthless. Accused her of saying stuff about me. He said something else, too: *I probably shouldn't even be here, warning you like this.*

But that's *all* he said.

'I'm going to miss you,' Papa says. 'It's been good having you around. But this thing between you and the girl; it got way out of hand. It led you into trouble. It led us all into trouble. I've lost my *trust* in you, boy.'

'Papa,' I say, but he shakes his head.

'You *liked* her, Eli. And despite that, look what you

did. Who could feel safe around someone who does the things you do? We might be on the road for months. If you think I'm bunking down next to you every night, risking the chance of a cut throat . . . well, I'm afraid you're mistaken.'

Papa steps into the shed. Crouching beside Elissa, he rests a filthy finger against her cheek. 'Annie only ever takes kids whose folks don't meet her standards,' he says. ''Course, after a while, most *kids* don't meet them either. They lie, try to escape. They exhibit bad manners or a lack of respect. You were different, Eli. You always did the right thing.'

I stare at him, aghast. I know I'm a liar, but Papa's a liar, too. What he just said simply isn't the truth. Once, I was disobedient too.

'But that girl changed you, Eli,' he continues. 'She filled your head with her crap and you weren't strong enough to resist.'

I think of the letter I wrote to FIDE, the phone I stole off Leon Meunier. 'Papa, please.'

The knife lies a few feet from Gretel's body. He reaches out, picks it up. Then he stands and stalks towards me.

III

Queen's Gambit, I think. But Papa still approaches. He's wearing a look that steals my breath: eyes wide, teeth exposed, like he's about to tuck into a steak. Around the knife, his knuckles are white.

'We can do the dance if you like,' he says, 'but I'd really

rather we didn't. This isn't a punishment, Eli. You've been in pain a long time.'

He's right about that. But it doesn't mean I want to die. As Papa draws closer he blocks out all the light. I can no longer see his expression, his intent.

I'm taller than him, but he's stronger. And height makes no difference when you're sitting down. Right now, he towers over me. I can't take my eyes off his silhouetted blade.

Queen's Gambit, I think, but it makes no difference.

Will he stab me? Slash my throat? When I raise my hands to protect myself, the chain clanks across the floor.

'Give it up,' Papa whispers. 'You've got no good reason to stick around.'

A moment later he makes his play, swinging the knife in a fast arc towards my throat.

I have no option but to fend him off. The blade cuts a bright path across my palms. Blood splatters across the tool-shed wall.

I cry out. Not from pain, but shock. I drive my heel into Papa's shin. It doesn't drop him, but I gain a half-second to scramble back. His second slash is aimed at my face. I block it with my forearms, the knife opening my clothes and skin as if they were paper. Changing his grip, Papa thrusts in and out.

At first, I don't even realize I've been stabbed. I kick out with both feet, and this time I knock him off balance. Then the pain hits – a shark bite to my gut, a savage spike of heat.

Papa topples on to me, his face inches from my own. 'Your brother fought too,' he hisses. 'Do you remember?'

Hearing that, something breaks loose in my mind. Suddenly, I'm not in the tool shed at all; I'm back in the cellar beneath the Memory Wood, long ago. In my hand, I'm holding a glass shard. Elijah cowers opposite, beside a smoky candle. *'Please, Kyle,'* he whimpers. *'Please don't.'*

Back in the present, I smash my head into Papa's nose. He rears back and I see the knife, its blade slick with my blood. I grab his forearm, but when he wrenches it away my hands are too slippery to hold on. Papa plunges down, and this time I *feel* the knife go in.

I think of the deer I shot, the calamity inside its head, and how I always believed that would be my end. This is worse. It hurts and it isn't quick. 'Please,' I cough, repeating my brother's plea. 'Please don't.'

But Papa isn't listening. He stabs me again, deeper this time.

When the blade pulls loose, it releases a black fountain.

Behind him, through the tool-shed door, I see overcast sky. Too bad there's no sun, but at least I won't die below ground. That was always my worst fear. By the door, Gretel lies on her face, cheeks smeared with blood.

Her name isn't Gretel, I remind myself.

Just like mine isn't Hansel.

Papa's blade flashes down. This time, my arm knocks it aside. He throws a leg over me, straddling my stomach. Thanks to his weight, I can't breathe.

In the corner, like a wight waking inside its barrow, Gretel lifts her head. She's so pale it seems as if every last drop of her blood has drained away, but I know that can't be true, because the blood that stains her cheeks and clothes is my own, from a cut I opened on my arm moments before Papa entered the shed. Earlier, delivering my last meal, Gretel also brought a knife. I knew they'd send her in here to kill me, and I didn't want her to find out whether she'd try. That kind of knowledge can haunt someone a long time.

Papa slashes at me, opening another gouge across my forearm. With my free hand, I slap at his chest.

Gretel sits up straight, revealing my smuggled knife. She blinks, tries to orient herself.

Reaching out, I get a grip on Papa's arm. He tries to shake me off but somehow I hold on. The knife jerks back and forth. Spittle flies from his lips.

Suddenly, I'm in the cellar again, clutching that shard of glass. *We have to do this, Elijah,* I whisper. *Otherwise, we're never going home.*

Two weeks we'd spent down there, my brother slowly weakening. Obedience had gained us nothing – it was time to try something new. Elijah begged me to change my mind, but I'd already made it up.

Gretel picks up the knife. As she stands, I fear she'll block out the light, alerting Papa to what's happening, but all his attention is on me. *Queen's Gambit,* I hiss as we wrestle. I'm losing blood faster now. I feel my strength failing.

In chess, as in life, a gambit sacrifices something of lower worth to gain an advantage. When it comes to me and Gretel, I am the thing of lower worth. Back at the safe house, I told myself she was dead, but I never really believed it. To find the courage to return, I had to invent a lie: that I intended to go back to the way things were before, that I could forget, all over again, the horrors of which I've been a part.

Papa's knife flashes past my face.

Promise me. Promise you won't let me die in here.

Gretel's words, the first time we met. I didn't promise her that, but I did promise I'd come back.

As she takes an uncertain step towards us, it's all I can do not to look at her. *Queen's Gambit*, I think.

Because Gretel, without question, is my queen.

Papa knocks away my arm. I slap repeatedly at his face. Finally, I can't help myself; I glance over his shoulder at the girl I came here to save. Our eyes meet. I see a spark of recognition, a glimmer of emerald fire.

Somehow, Papa senses the danger. He twists around and I cry out, terrified that my gambit will be in vain. But he isn't as quick as he used to be, and Gretel, despite everything she's endured – maybe even because of it – doesn't hesitate. The carving knife is in her left hand, and the force she puts into her thrust is shocking to behold. I don't see the blade go in, but I know from Papa's reaction that it has. His eyes widen. His own weapon clatters to the floor. Gretel steps back, and when I see her empty hand, I know the knife's still inside him. Better to have pulled it out and plunged it in again, but I can't fault her.

As Papa reaches behind his back I buck my hips and unseat him. He crashes on to his side.

In the cellar beneath the Memory Wood, I might have killed my brother with my actions, but I didn't commit the act. During my only escape attempt, I tried to attack Papa with the glass shard. Unlike Gretel, I hesitated. I'd expected to pay for my failure with my life. Instead, Elijah lost his.

Now, beside me, Papa lifts himself to his elbows. Gretel, standing opposite, has turned to stone.

'Go,' I tell her, through clenched teeth. I don't want her to see this. I don't want her to suffer as I have.

Grunting with effort, Papa sits up straight. I see the knife buried in his back. My goodness, how deep she thrust it. Already, his jacket is soaked in blood.

'Stay there, you little bitch,' he hisses. 'Say you understand.'

I can't wait any longer. Pulling myself up, I loop a length of chain over Papa's head. With both hands, I reel him in.

The links bite into his throat, choking off his breath. He tries to get his fingers under them. To counter him, I pull harder. The distance between us shrinks.

'*Go*,' I implore Gretel. '*Now*.'

At last, my words get through. So much we communicate in our final look. Then she turns and limps from the shed.

Papa's legs kick out, begin to shake. His heels drum against the floor.

When I loosen my grip on the chain, his chest heaves and his lungs fill. I yank out the knife. Then I plunge it into his side. His back arches. He squeals like a butchered pig.

'Elijah,' I whisper, mouth close to his ear.

Our blood runs together on the tool-shed floor. My vision is blackening. But I still have work to do.

Out comes the knife. With a wet ripping, it dives deep. 'Bryony,' I say.

Before this is over, I'll make him remember every one of them.

ELISSA

As she staggers from the tool shed, the wind buffets her, rocking her on her feet.

Bending, Elissa vomits into the grass. She could live a thousand years and still remember how it felt to slam that knife into the ghoul's flesh. But if she finds her way back to her mum, it'll have been worth it.

Her only regret is that she didn't act sooner. By the time she'd gathered her courage, the ghoul had already brutalized Elijah. Only through witnessing that extraordinary savagery could she intervene with violence of her own.

Elissa thinks about going back, but she knows Elijah intends to kill the man who abducted him. She knows, too, that he'll succeed – nothing in this world could have put a brake on the determination she glimpsed in his face.

Clutching her swollen arm to her chest, she orients herself. To her left stands the shack, smoke feathering from its chimney. Near by, the white van is parked with its nose pointing downhill. On the back bumper she sees the trilby-wearing skull smoking its cigarette and feels the burn of its gaze.

CHILLAX.

Instead of obeying, Elissa runs. Except it isn't a run, not really. Heading down the slope, she stumble-trips through the long grass, terrified of falling. Even at walking speed, her momentum threatens to overtake her.

At her back, the shack's front door bangs open. From inside, Elissa hears a witch's furious scream.

MAIRÉAD

I

The land rolls beneath her, a patchwork construction of myriad shades and shapes.

Glimpsed from above, the world is so serene, so beautiful, that one could almost dismiss as folklore the manifold monsters that stalk it. But Mairéad can't dismiss them. For as long as she can remember, her task has been to seek them out. Over the years, she's had her share of success, but it'll all be for nothing if she fails to hunt down the monster who snatched Elissa Mirzoyan, Bryony Taylor, so many others.

Early this morning, under her direction, the tech team in Winfrith finally delivered a result. Ping data for the phone Kyle had called showed that it had received its signal from a tower in Hereford. Shortly after the ninety-six-second exchange, the phone started heading north towards the safe house. Since Kyle's disappearance it hasn't pinged at all, and Mairéad doubts it will again; but three hours ago, thanks to an expedited RIPA data request, she received details of every call and text message the phone made in the last twelve months. Another data request followed, this time for a second mobile device called frequently by the first, which had been near the same Hereford mast when Kyle first dialled out. Soon afterwards, the second phone headed west, all the way to the Pembrokeshire coast near Strumble Head, where it's continued to ping ever since.

The revelation is extraordinary; rather than a single suspect, it seems Mairéad is hunting two. And thanks to a hack of the second device's GPS, she has a location accurate to a few feet. Satellite imagery of the coordinates shows a disused coastal lookout on a wild peninsula surrounded by sea.

Now, sitting inside a black-and-yellow-liveried helicopter from the National Police Air Service base in Bournemouth, Mairéad races towards it. Point to point, it's one hundred and forty miles. Already, she's been in the air an hour.

Dyfed–Powys Police, into whose jurisdiction the location falls, have already been alerted. Ground vehicles are en route. All potential escape roads are being sealed off. A Nelson 38 has launched from the marine unit in Milford Haven, coordinating with the local coastguard service to prevent any departure by sea.

'*Two minutes,*' says her pilot. Beneath them, land surrenders to choppy ocean. The Eurocopter leans right and races north.

Watching the waves flash past below, Mairéad dares to wonder if Elissa Mirzoyan is still alive. She thinks of Kyle Buchanan and the horror of his twenty-year confinement. Unimaginable, that he chose to reunite with those who snatched him.

Earlier, Mairéad took a call from Paul Deacon, the

Meunierfields crime-scene manager. At Rufus Hall, his team had located a diary written by Leon Meunier. Many of its entries concern a small transient community living on his land, presumably at the abandoned lakeside camp. The wording is often cryptic, but it seems the community's matriarch – referred to in the diary as *A* – had long been supplying the peer with women. Whether those involved were paid prostitutes or trafficked members of the traveller community isn't clear. While Meunier had started to suspect that something even worse was happening in the camp, he hadn't yet worked up the courage to report it.

'Whoever set that fire in the woods was long gone by the time we arrived,' Mairéad says. 'If Meunier knew their identities, that gives them the perfect motive for silencing him.'

'My thoughts exactly,' Deacon replies. 'Which means you might not be looking at suicide after all.'

A jagged peninsula swings into view. Felted headlands terminate in cliffs of volcanic rock cracked open by wind and sea. Huge waves foam white around shattered stacks.

'*There*,' says the pilot, pointing.

Mairéad sees the Strumble Head lighthouse sitting squat on its island, and the stubby metal bridge connecting it to the peninsula. Further south-east she sees a U-shaped coastal road, blocked at either end by police vehicles.

The pilot isn't directing her attention to the ground support. Instead, he indicates a dilapidated stone shack, some distance to the east. Parked outside is a rust-flecked white van.

'That's it!' she shouts, adrenalin shortening her breath. 'Take us down.'

II

As the Eurocopter plunges from the sky, Mairéad's stomach rises into her throat. She grips the doorframe, her mind whirling with what-ifs.

At a command from DS Halley behind her, four police cars stationed at the eastern end of the coastal road accelerate along it. At its apex, a gravelled track leads up a steep slope towards the lookout perched at the top.

As if reacting to the helicopter's approach, the door to a lean-to shed beside the lookout clatters open. Someone staggers out. Mairéad snatches up her binoculars and trains them on the figure.

It's her. It's Elissa.

KYLE

I

The average human body, I once read, contains around five litres of blood. But if Papa and I are any indication, that figure is a wild underestimate.

We're drenched. Blood sticks my jeans to my legs, my T-shirt to my ribs. It pulses from the holes in Papa's body and creeps out beneath him in an ever-expanding pool.

He lies between my legs, head resting on my shoulder. The chain from my manacle is still looped twice around his neck. Through the links, I see the weak echo of his heartbeat.

I'm done stabbing him. There's a point, I think, where justice descends into barbarism. One thrust for each boy and each girl he snatched, that's all. I didn't count Gretel, because she took her own revenge.

My own wounds are almost as severe. Three times Papa plunged his blade into me. Two of those injuries I can now barely feel, but the pain from the third is stunning. I don't want to die in this shed, with Papa lying between my legs. Before my strength fails completely, I need to go outside.

And before I do that, I have to kill him.

II

The carving knife is still buried in his flesh. When I yank it out, a last tide of Papa's blood gushes over me. He kicks his legs and sighs.

It's so intimate, this. So weirdly emotional.

Because of my injuries, it takes me a while to draw back my knee and wedge it against his spine. Once that's done, I grasp the ends of the double-looped chain and pull. Papa kicks again, but his struggles make no difference. He gargles, his eyes bulge; it's all quite pathetic.

And then, just like that, it's over.

I unloop my chain from his neck and loll forwards. Closing my eyes, I almost drift off. It's such a shock that I jerk back my head, terrified that my life will end here, in a gross pool of his blood.

A helicopter blasts over the tool-shed roof. Coastguard, probably, on a regular patrol of the peninsula.

Working quickly, in case I pass out fully, I root through Papa's clothes until I find the manacle key. Moments later, I'm free. I roll him off my legs and try to pull myself up. My attempt is a joke – if I wasn't dying, and in a nauseating amount of pain, I'd probably find it funny. My feet scissor back and forth, creating ripples in the blood lake. Somehow, I get a knee beneath me. Finally, I manage to stand. Blood drips from my clothing like rain. If I go down, I won't get back up. I'm panting before I've even taken five steps.

Outside, I hear the asthmatic rattle of a diesel. I recognize it immediately – the white van that ferried me here. If Gretel's trying to steal it, she won't have any luck. Only Papa's ever known the trick of firing up that engine from cold. Sometimes even *he* can't do it on the first attempt. It's probably why he didn't worry unduly about leaving the keys in the ignition.

At last I reach the tool-shed door. The wind on my face, so fresh after the horrors at my back, is a blessing straight from Jesus. What I see unfolding down the slope is without doubt the work of the devil.

ELISSA

I

The scream pierces Elissa's skull like a drill.

Looking behind her, she sees Annie emerge from the shack. Such violence in the witch's expression; for a moment, it freezes her rigid. Seconds later, a wasp-like helicopter blasts past in a violent sundering of the sky. The noise is incredible. It shakes Elissa loose of her paralysis. Turning from the shack, she stumbles down the slope.

In the fairy tale, Gretel burned the witch in her oven before freeing her brother from his cage. Elissa, by contrast, has allowed the witch to live and has left Hansel to his fate. It's a failure of duty that might cost her everything.

The helicopter swoops in again. Printed on the door in bold yellow letters is the word she'd given up hope of ever seeing: *POLICE*.

'Help me!' Elissa shrieks, lifting her good hand to the sky.

This part of the slope is treacherously steep. To her left, jagged promontories thrust mossy elbows of rock into the sea. Far below her, a fleet of police cars bumps along the coastal road, emergency lights flashing. They look so far away.

At her back she hears a groan of metal. Glancing behind her, she sees the witch throw open the van door and climb behind the wheel.

II

The grass is slippery with moisture. Slick arrowheads of rock thrust up from the soil. Elissa knows she can't descend any faster. If she falls, slams her injured arm, she'll lie there screaming until Annie runs her down. Instead, she moves at a worm's pace, carefully picking her way, checking each step before she takes it.

The helicopter plunges past on her left, the *thwap* of its rotors vibrating in her chest.

'Help me!' she shrieks. 'Tell me what I should *do*!'

There's a loose rattle behind her – the van's engine turning over. Elissa slips on to her backside, barely preventing her injured arm from smashing into the ground. For the space of two breaths she sits there, stunned, while chaos flows around her.

Again, the van's engine turns over. Again, it clatters out.

'*Good, bitch!*' Elissa screams. '*That's what you get!*'

In response, the witch runs the ignition a third time. The pistons punch and counter. This time they'll surely catch a spark, but they don't, even though Annie keeps them spinning for a good ten seconds.

The police helicopter blasts past yet again, rapidly losing height. Elissa sees, at the base of the slope, the flat patch of ground for which it's aiming. Its nose angles up. The skids hit the ground and bounce once, twice. The pilot throttles down.

Dragging herself upright, Elissa continues her slow-motion descent. To reach the helicopter, she needs to cover another two hundred metres. If the witch pursues on foot, she'll have thirty metres of rough ground to make up. Annie's fat and old, but Elissa's injured, exhausted. She glances around once again, checking the gap between them.

What she sees is horrifying.

III

The witch can't start the engine, but she *can* release the handbrake.

Sluggish at first, the van rolls forwards. Quickly, it gathers speed, bouncing over rocks and tussocks, rattling like a box of sharp tools.

Already, Annie's halved the distance between them. It's clear from the sheer recklessness of her pursuit that she cares about only one thing: putting Elissa under the wheels.

In the distance, the lead police car swerves off the coastal road and bounces on to the gravel track that serves the peninsula, tyres kicking up mud. It may as well be on a different planet.

Abandoning all caution, Elissa slip-slides down the slope. The van bears down on her, unstoppable, a cacophony of screaming metal. There's simply no way of avoiding it. She thinks of her mum, her grandparents, of all the things she wanted to say. She thinks of the agony her death will cause them, and how fiercely she tried to prevent it.

Far below, one of the helicopter doors swings open. A woman jumps from the cockpit. Four police cars slide to a stop near by.

The woman beside the helicopter waves frantically. Uniformed police officers pour from the parked patrol cars. They wave their arms too.

Behind her, Elissa hears the van. It's shaking so violently it sounds like it's breaking apart. Below, the officers start yelling. She can't hear their words. There's nothing they can say to help.

Elissa skids down a hillock, nearly trips over a rock. She can't outrun what's coming. She hopes her death will be quick, that it won't hurt too much.

As the van's shadow overtakes her, she tries to fill her head with something good, a memory of better times. She doesn't want to face her fate, but in the end she can't resist. Twisting around, she sees the van's front grille filling her vision.

'No!' she screams, her legs giving out beneath her. '*NO!*'

Here it comes.

Here it comes.

Oh Jesus please let there be something after please let this not be it please forgive me Lord please be with me right now right now RIGHT—

She stares through the windscreen.

Her eyes flare.

It's been such a crazy life. So startling and bittersweet.

KYLE

I

Wind on my face. Wind in my hair. A quiet intensity in my heart.

Outside the tool shed, with nothing to protect me from the wind rolling in off the sea, my blood-drenched clothes ripple against my skin.

Above me, grey clouds heavy with rain haul themselves east. Further west, I spot a narrow strip of blue. I'd like to die with a clear sky overhead, but we don't choose how we go – I know I won't get my wish, and that's OK.

Further down the slope, I see Elissa, struggling to get away. She looks so lost and afraid. It feels important, suddenly, to use her real name.

Watching her, I think back to the first time we met. Injured, shackled to the iron ring, her spirit nevertheless blazed with fire. In just over a week, it's been cruelly whittled away.

I think of my own family: Mama, my sweet brother. Like most of God's gentler creatures, we lived in joyful denial of the wolves that prowled among us. Because of our innocence, we were smashed. If I have anything in common with Elissa Mirzoyan, perhaps it's that.

The sound of Papa's van brings me back; its engine turning over and over. Looking around, the first thing I see is the trilby-wearing skull smoking a cigarette.

I found that sticker in a custom-car magazine Papa brought home once. When I stuck it on the van's back bumper, nobody seemed to care. It scared me, that skull, so badly I could barely look at it. If it scared me, I reasoned it might scare other kids too. Maybe, when they saw Papa parked up, they'd see that sticker and run. I don't know if my plan ever worked, but I know exactly how many times it failed, because every time the van delivered a new resident to the Memory Wood I'd load up my .22 and put a round through the bumper.

I'm having difficulty breathing – I can only manage short sips of air. At least the pain of my injuries has dulled. Maybe that's a benefit of bleeding out.

I try to find Elissa again. I spot her a little further down the slope.

How much of ourselves we shared, that week beneath the Memory Wood. How much I feel I learned. I know she never really trusted me. Even just now, when I grabbed her in the tool shed before explaining my plan. But I can hardly fault her for that.

The van's starter motor mewls like it's in mourning. Drained of life, the battery doesn't have enough power to crank the pistons, but the starter keeps on winding.

I know it's Annie behind the wheel. From the punishment she's giving the engine, she must be really pissed off. Limping over to the passenger door, I swing it open.

Her head snaps around. When our eyes meet, her jaw drops open like a hatch.

I can't really blame her. As a rule, I stay away from mirrors, but if I caught my reflection right now, I'm pretty sure I'd be appalled.

Baring her teeth, Annie twists the key. 'That bitch was going to kill you,' she hisses. 'Might've lost her nerve, but she was going to try.'

Back when Annie was my spirit guide, I hung on to her every word. Now, I see she's just a fraud. One hand pressed to my tummy, I haul myself on to the seat.

The helicopter plunges past on our left, its downdraft rocking the van on its springs. Far below us, a line of police cars surges up the coast road. A short distance away, I see Gretel picking her way down the slope.

Getting on to the seat really took it out of me. My vision has blackened around the edges again, leaving a narrow tunnel. I lay my head against the rest and concentrate on my breathing.

'He do that?' Annie asks.

'Uh-huh.'

'He really fucked you up.'

I grunt in reply. There's not much else I can add.

The seat rocks like a crib. My head nods on to my chest. It's comforting, this – I feel like I've drunk too much of Meunier's wine. If only someone would sing me a lullaby, I think I could fall asleep. When my head swings towards Annie, the world smears like runny paint. That's when I grasp the reason my seat's become a cradle. Annie's released the handbrake. We're beginning to roll downhill.

Within seconds, the gentle rocking becomes a violent jostling. 'Wha' you doin'?' I slur, listening to my mangled words.

The van hits a tussock, rears up. Suddenly, instead of sloping grass, all I see is sky. When the bonnet swings back down, the front wheels punch the grass so hard that Annie and I are tossed forwards. I put out a hand to the dash, but I have no strength to brace myself. The little air I've hoarded is punched from my lungs. A spray of blood mists the windscreen.

Gross.

Beside me, Annie rocks back in her seat. She must have headbutted the steering column – her face is veiled in blood. Right now, she looks more like a feasting vampire than my old spirit guide. Regaining her grip on the wheel, she maintains our collision course.

In front of us, bracing her injured arm, Elissa slides over a rock. The van bounces towards her, a two-tonne metal wrecking ball. Unable to offer aid, I slump back in my seat and watch. No one who wakes beneath the Memory Wood really leaves it. No one ever escapes.

Here, at the end, I recall something Elissa once told me, back in the Gingerbread cellar: that we were like Hansel and Gretel, the brother and sister from the fairy tale. Even if she didn't mean it, she'll never know how happy it made me feel.

The van bounces up, slams back down. A crack races across the windscreen. The shaking is now so violent it's impossible to catch a breath.

Outside, just like me, Elissa reaches the end of her

strength. Realizing what's about to happen, she twists around to face her fate.

I push myself back in the seat, hoping to delay the moment. Of a lifetime of bad memories, this will easily be the worst.

When she sees the van hurtling towards her, Elissa lifts her chin. Watching my queen, I'm so proud I want to cry out my admiration. In my ears, I hear that old line of Scripture, the one Mama used to make me read: *Finally, be strong in the Lord and in His mighty power. Put on the full armour of God, so that you can take your stand against the devil's schemes.*

Once, when I was younger, I tried to sabotage those schemes. In the attempt, I lost my little brother. Now, as I look through the cracked windscreen at Elissa, and Elissa looks back through the glass at me, I know I must try again.

With no breath in my lungs, no strength in my muscles, I have no ability to intervene. But intervene I do, sliding across the seat and ripping the wheel towards me.

Annie screams. The van heels over on its side. I don't see Elissa flash by on the right, but I feel no impact against the front grille. We hit a mound, launch up. We're airborne for a good few seconds before crashing back down. Again, Annie's face is mashed against the wheel. One of her teeth pings off the dash.

'Let *go!*' she shrieks, spitting blood.

By turning the wheel so sharply, I've altered our course down the slope. Now, we're crossing it at an angle, towards the tall cliffs that face out to sea.

Annie stamps down on the brake. But even with the wheels locked, we slough off barely any speed.

The cliff edge races closer. The van knocks and shakes, so loud in my ears it's as if I've strapped myself to a moon rocket.

'Bastard!' Annie screams. *'Bastard, let GO!'*

She drives her elbow into my face, knocking my head to the side. Beside me, on the seat, I see something amazing.

III

It's my family.

Elijah, his face alive with mischief, is perched on Mama's lap. When our eyes meet, he smiles and mouths my name.

Mama's arms are wrapped around his tummy. I glance up at her and she smiles at me, too, her face shining with so much love I feel my strength renewed.

Beneath us, the van's wheels bump and thump like those of a runaway train. Annie hits me again. This time, I hardly feel the blow. All my attention is on Mama.

I do notice the sudden silence as we punch over the cliff edge into empty air. Despite the cracked windscreen, I can still see that chink of blue sky. There's sudden screaming beside me. It's easy enough to tune out.

As the nose of the van starts to dip I have a glorious view of the sea. Some distance out, I spot a police boat riding the swells.

There's sound, now, all around: the wind, beginning to roar.

Finally, be strong in the Lord and in His mighty power. Put on the full armour of God, so that you can take your stand against the devil's schemes.

'Kyle,' Mama says. 'Kyle, look at me.'

When I turn my gaze from the water rushing up, I see her loving eyes. Elijah's too.

'Come home,' she tells me.

I go to them.

ELISSA

For a while, she can't do anything but lie on her back in the long grass and stare at the sky. Out to sea, the clouds have separated to reveal a narrow strip of blue. Elissa watches it, listening to the wind, and to a gull crying overhead.

Soon, a face is leaning over her. It's the woman from the helicopter. Weirdly, she seems to be crying.

'Elissa,' she says, touching her as if she's made of glass. 'It's over. You're safe now.'

Elissa nods. Not because she believes it, but because it's the polite thing to do. 'How's my mum?'

'Your mum's a fighter, just like you,' the woman says. She wipes her face clean of tears. 'How's that arm?'

Elissa grimaces. 'Hurts like a—'

She stops, colour rising in her cheeks. A week with the ghoul and she's about to swear in front of a stranger.

'A bitch?' the woman asks.

'Don't tell my mum I said that.'

'I won't.'

Elissa turns her head towards the sea. 'Did you see what happened? What he did?'

'We all saw.'

'I asked him to promise me, right at the start, that he wouldn't let me die. He wouldn't say it. But he did promise he'd come back.'

Elissa sees more faces around her now. She feels herself being lifted.

'I'm Mairéad,' says the woman, taking Elissa's good hand and squeezing it. 'I'm going to take you home.'

It's a word she could hear again and again.

ACKNOWLEDGEMENTS

Huge thanks to my editor, Frankie Gray, who took the rough-sawn timbers of this tale and planed them into shape. Thanks also to Tom Hill, Ella Horne and the rest of the team at Transworld: Tash Barsby, Sophie Bruce, Tom Chicken, Deirdre O'Connell, Sarah Day, Phil Evans, Gary Harley, Emily Harvey, Bethan Moore, Imogen Nelson, Natasha Photiou, Vivien Thompson, Jo Thomson and Hannah Welsh.

Special thanks to my agent, Sam Copeland, for invaluable early feedback, and to Stephen Edwards and Tristan Kendrick at RCW, for finding the book a home in many countries around the world.

I'm very grateful to Detective Inspector Dee Fielding of Surrey Police, who advised on the book's procedural aspects. (Any remaining inaccuracies are, of course, my own.)

My love and gratitude to Julie, for letting me get lost in the Memory Wood for long periods without ever once complaining. And to Noah, Alfie and Jonah, without whom Elissa and Elijah would never have come into being.

Most importantly, my heartfelt thanks to you, the reader, for stepping off the path and following me into the trees. I hope I've returned you safely, not too scratched or bruised.

ABOUT THE AUTHOR

Sam Lloyd grew up in Hampshire, making up stories and building secret hideaways in his local woods. These days he lives in Surrey with his wife, three young sons and a dog that likes to howl. *The Memory Wood* is his debut thriller.

READING GROUP GUIDE

The Memory Wood is told through several different voices and perspectives. How did this structure affect your reading of the novel?

Were there any particular moments you found surprising or moving?

Consider how the balance of power between Elissa and Elijah changes over the course of the novel. Can you identify any key moments that disrupt the balance?

Was there a particular character you identified with, or felt more sympathetic towards? How did your perceptions of the characters change as the novel progressed?

Since the beginning, she's had her suspicions of something not-quite-right, of a game being played with rules she hasn't grasped. How is the theme of play and childhood explored throughout the novel, and to what effects?

What does it mean to be a 'victim'? Discuss the ways in which Elissa breaks with the traditional idea of a victim.

Elissa's case seems to become an issue of personal importance to Mairéad, as well as a professional duty. Do you think she handles her work-life balance well? Would you have made the same choices as her, if you were in her position?

Consider the final chapters. Did you have any different ideas for how the novel might end while you were reading? Do you think the characters get the endings they deserve?